**Praise for *New York Times* bestselling author
Allison Brennan**

Stolen

"The evolution of Lucy and Sean's relationship has been a critical piece of what makes these novels so compelling. Brennan is a true master at providing byzantine plotlines that keep readers guessing as the danger amplifies."

—*RT Book Reviews* (4½ stars, Top Pick)

"All the excitement and suspense I have come to expect from Allison Brennan." —*Fresh Fiction*

Stalked

"Once again Brennan weaves a complex tale of murder, vengeance, and treachery filled with knife-edged tension and clever twists. The Lucy Kincaid/Sean Rogan novels just keep getting better!"

—*RT Book Reviews* (4½ stars, Top Pick)

"The novels featuring Lucy Kincaid and her cohorts are marked with deep characterizations and details of the workings of investigations by private eyes, the police, and the FBI . . . Catch the latest in this series as Lucy continues to evolve in strength and wisdom."

—*Romance Reviews Today*

Silenced

"Brennan throws a lot of story lines into the air and juggles them like a master. The mystery proves to be both compelling and complex . . . [A] chilling and twisty romantic suspense gem." —Associated Press

Titles by Allison Brennan

DEAD HEAT

Allison Brennan

St. Martin's Paperbacks

This is a work of fiction. All of the characters, organizations, and events portrayed in this novel are either products of the author's imagination or are used fictitiously.

DEAD HEAT

Copyright © 2014 by Allison Brennan.
Excerpt from *Best Laid Plans* copyright © 2015 by Allison Brennan.

Best Laid Plans cover image:
Cover design by Ervin Serrano
Cover photograph © Stephen Carroll / Trevillion Images

No Good Deed cover image:
Cover design by Ervin Serrano
Cover photographs:
Street © Semmick Photo/Shutterstock;
Woman © Stephen Carroll / Trevillion Images

All rights reserved.

For information address St. Martin's Press, 175 Fifth Avenue, New York, NY 10010.

ISBN: 978-1-250-07079-1

Printed in the United States of America

St. Martin's Paperbacks edition / June 2014

St. Martin's Paperbacks are published by St. Martin's Press, 175 Fifth Avenue, New York, NY 10010.

10 9 8 7 6 5 4 3 2

ACKNOWLEDGMENTS

Many people have helped me with the Lucy Kincaid series, and I greatly appreciate their time and effort in providing information, details, and support.

First and foremost, I couldn't write this series without the support and guidance of my sharp-eyed editor, Kelley Ragland, and the entire St. Martin's Press team. Special thanks to agent Dan Conaway who is my steady advisor.

The Lucy Kincaid series has been greatly enhanced by the continuing input from the good men and women of the Sacramento FBI office, in particular Special Agent Steve Dupre. He doesn't blink, no matter what I ask, and has shown a knack for helping me brainstorm. Steve was the first one to explain how inter-agency warrant sweeps work. He also connected me with SA Michelle Lee in the San Antonio office which helped immensely as my character Lucy transitioned into her new assignment. And a very special thanks to SWAT Team Leader Brian Jones, who always includes me in training scenarios and introduced me to more men with guns than I dreamed possible. If there are any errors or omissions, it's solely my fault.

The writing community is a warm and friendly place, and I want to give a shout-out to my brothers and sisters in the Kiss of Death chapter of RWA. When I put out a message for help with details about San Antonio—commute times, housing information, and the best place to get BBQ and Tex-Mex—I had a deluge of responses. If I didn't pick your favorite place, know that it was because I didn't get to taste-test all the fabulous possibilities.

My family has always supported my writing career, and without their support I wouldn't be able to do what I love. My husband Dan has been a rock, understanding that writing is my true passion and knowing I need to put in the time. My kids have provided me with inspiration and laughs. And my mom has always been my first reader. Love you all!

PROLOGUE

The thin chain rattled against the metal cot when Michael turned from his side to his back. His sleep had been restless, minutes of deep slumber followed by heart-pounding moments of full alert.

He was sure tonight they would kill him.

His fists tightened until his nails dug into his callused palms. He'd never been prone to anger, but this last year had unleashed something inside him that he only subconsciously understood was a survival mechanism. Maybe it was because his father was a violent man, and Michael feared he was becoming the man he hated.

The key turned the lock at the top of the moldy wood staircase. He sat up and the chain rattled again. He froze. It was always better to be compliant. When there was an opportunity to fight or run, he would seize it.

The door opened, a tiny creak the only sound.

No light came from above, which meant it was still night. No stars or moon cast shadows down here. Night was a good time to kill. No one around to witness his last breath. His body could be thrown into a ravine and eaten by coyotes and vultures until there was nothing left but his chewed bones. Like Richie.

I'm so sorry, Richie.

After they tortured and killed him, they'd go back for the others, kill them now or let them die slowly. Maybe they were already dead. All because Michael had taken the box. Because he thought the box could buy their freedom.

"Boys should never play the games of men."

The general's voice teased Michael, made him squeak in fear even though the general was hundreds of miles away. He had the box back, but none of Michael's blood brothers had been released. He'd killed Javier in front of Michael, as punishment. Javier's pleas were forever burned into his memory.

"Save us, Saint Michael."

Javier had prayed to the archangel, but looked at Michael. At that moment, Michael swore he'd rescue all of them even if he died in the process. He didn't want to live, not after Javier and Richie, not after all the things he'd been forced to do. Except if he didn't survive, who would know what had happened? What about the others? The ones still imprisoned and the ones who would be taken in the future?

The only reason he hadn't died with Javier or Richie was that the general had a special job for him, a suicide job, that would, from what the other boys told him, punish the general's enemies and take back territory the general believed belonged only to him.

This wasn't gang warfare as Michael understood it. Michael had grown up on the rough side of San Antonio; he knew about drugs and gangs and how to steer clear of those who would stab you or shoot you just because they didn't like the way you looked. He'd grown up with a father who worked for men like the general, and he'd seen the evil his father had done. He'd seen worse evil after his father went to prison.

The games of men, the general had said.

This game was *war*, and the loser got death. A battle waged beneath the surface of the city. Everyone could see, but they were still blind to the truth. It was a battle even the police didn't want to fight. They would lose because they had rules.

The longer he was alive, the better chance he had of saving his brothers. He had no one to trust, except the people who had once taken him in. If he could go there, they would believe him.

Would they? After a year they probably think I stole their money and ran away. They won't believe the truth.

But if not Hector and Olive, who else?

The footsteps on the stairs were light. His body relaxed with relief. "Bella," he whispered, before she flipped the wall switch that turned on the dim ceiling light. The switch he couldn't reach when he was chained to the bed.

Bella stepped directly under it, her big brown eyes skittish, her light-brown skin pale.

"Michael," she whispered with a Spanish accent, though she'd told him that, like him, she was an American.

Her little body shook, and she kept looking over her shoulder.

Michael's anger returned. It was an anger that was taking over his body and soul. Sometimes, he thought that the anger was living and breathing inside him. He would become someone else if he lost the battle, but if he won the battle against his rage, he would be dead. Was that what people called a catch-22?

"Did someone hurt you?" he asked.

She shook her head rapidly. "Run away."

He frowned. "What?"

She knelt at the foot of his cot and took a small key from her bathrobe pocket. She unlocked the chains that kept him there. They both jumped when the metal clanged, fearing discovery.

"Uncle Jaime is going to send you to the bad place. I don't want something bad to happen to you, Michael."

He almost didn't believe that she was releasing him. Was this a trap? But he couldn't see any scenario where it could be. Bella wasn't supposed to be down here. It was her older sister, the girl who liked to hurt him, who was supposed to feed him and clean his bucket. But the girl was lazy and enjoyed bossing Bella around.

"Come with me," Michael said without thinking. How would he care for a seven-year-old girl? How could he save his brothers if he had her in tow? Where would they sleep? When would they eat?

She moved away from him. "Everyone's sleeping, but I don't know how long. Mama seems to know when I'm not in my bed. Please, Michael. Just run far, far away. Maine is far away, I looked on a map."

He smiled and stood. His muscles were sore, but he'd been exercising as best he could every day he was down here. He kissed the top of her head. "You are my sister, Bella, stronger than blood."

"Michael, you are my brother. We are stronger than blood."

Michael shook the vision of Javier from his memories. Javier was dead. Murdered.

The bastard who put a bullet in his head would pay. He had to. There had to be justice in the world for a boy who had done nothing to anyone.

"I'll pray for you, every single day." She crossed her heart the way little kids did.

Pray for him. Michael was done with praying. It hadn't helped save Javier. It hadn't helped save any of them. God had turned His back, if He was even there at all. Hector and Olive were wrong. They were all wrong.

Bella handed him a backpack. It was a small pink bag, worn, with blue denim patches. She'd filled it with food and water and a few crumpled dollar bills. He bit his lip, knowing what this backpack meant to her. "I can't take this."

"Go, go. Now. Before they wake up. They won't know it was me, if I go right back to bed. Okay?"

He didn't believe her, and he feared for the little girl, but he also feared for himself and for his brothers who were going to die if he didn't cross the border to save them.

He reached for her hair. She flinched but didn't move. He removed her barrette and twisted it. He scraped up the lock that had been around his ankle, then left the barrette on the end of the bed. "There," he said. "Now they'll think I did this on my own." He hoped. "Be careful, Bella. Put the key back exactly where you found it."

Then he left into the black night.

CHAPTER 1

Two months of planning, two days for the execution, Operation Heatwave had commenced.

More than 150 police officers and federal agents from every major law enforcement organization coordinated to serve active warrants on violent criminals in the largest sweep to date in San Antonio, Texas. Newly minted FBI Agent Lucy Kincaid was thrilled to have been chosen to participate in the action, though it wasn't a surprise—half the Violent Crimes Squad had been tagged. The sweep landed on her three-month anniversary as a sworn FBI agent; ever since her arrival in San Antonio ten weeks ago, she'd been working on this operation.

They were starting at five o'clock Saturday morning and would be working for sixteen hours straight, then start again at five a.m. Sunday. A separate processing center had been set up for those arrested in the sweep. The task force had processed over seven thousand active state and federal warrants to narrow and prioritize cases to those where they had verified intelligence on fugitives' whereabouts, focusing on the most dangerous predators.

Lucy had been briefed and trained, but the execution was far bigger and more intense than she imagined. She and her team would serve the warrant, search the property, arrest the fugitives, and then turn them over to a patrol unit for processing while the team moved to the next target.

DEA Supervisory Agent Brad Donnelly headed Lucy's group of ten cops—eight on the ground and two in the tactical van. Quiroz from her unit was the only other FBI agent. The van was manned by two Bexar County Sheriff's deputies.

Working with so many different levels of law enforcement had been overwhelming at first, but she loved that she could jump in with both feet and learn as she worked. She realized quickly that she didn't love being stuck in her cubicle at headquarters. Ryan Quiroz was a great partner to learn from—he'd been a cop in Houston prior to joining the FBI and seemed to know almost everyone they encountered. He reminded Lucy of her brother Connor—a bit hotheaded and arrogant, but as sharp as they came. And there was the added benefit that everyone liked him, so his goodwill rubbed off on her.

The first house they targeted Saturday morning was textbook. The low-level drug dealer gave up without fanfare. At the second house, the suspect wasn't home. They did a routine search, but the girlfriend (ex-girlfriend according to her) told them she'd kicked him to the curb the week before for stealing from her.

At a staging area near the third target house, Team Leader Brad Donnelly gave a brief rundown of the situation, though they'd been given a file the night before on the targets.

"You know who we're looking for—George and Jaime Sanchez. Brothers, twenty-nine and twenty-six, respectively. You have their photos; know them. They are considered armed and dangerous."

The Sanchez brothers had missed their court date on an attempted murder charge. That they'd been out on bail in the first place had been a stunner to the prosecution, who thought they'd had a high enough bail to prevent their release. But the money was there, and now they weren't.

"We have information that they're staying with their sister, Mirabelle Sanchez Borez. She has a rap sheet but no active warrants. She's hostile, but we're hoping she won't cause a fuss—she has two young girls and seems to have kept her nose clean for the last few years. Her crime, if any, is harboring her fugitive brothers. We have a warrant to search her house."

San Antonio Police Officer Crane scowled. "Bastards got Easy Axe. Should never have been let out of a cage."

"Easy Axe?" Lucy asked.

"Judge Eleanor Axelrod," Crane said with a snort. He was about to continue, but Donnelly cut him off.

"This is a gang-related battle, not directly Texas Mexican Mafia, but the Sanchezes may have gone over or have an allegiance agreement. The younger brother has extensive ties to the drug cartels in Mexico, and we believe that he's the one who took the hit on one of the TMM's rivals. It's going to continue to escalate if we don't shut this down."

Donnelly looked at Lucy. "Kincaid, you're with me this time, you and French. If the girls are in the house, and we believe they are, they may only speak Spanish. They'll be more comfortable with a female Spanish-speaking cop."

"Yes, sir."

"Quiroz, you're with Crane and Everston in the back. Rollins and Butcher, back me up. If sister answers the door, I'll be sending her to you to secure. Our intelligence says that there are only those five people inside, three adults and two children. However, the brothers are prone to bringing home women, so there may be others—hostile or a package, I don't know."

That was a new one for Lucy—Donnelly was the only person she'd met who'd called hostages "packages." But she wasn't surprised—every unit seemed to have a different term for suspects and for innocents.

"Questions?" Donnelly asked.

"Age of the minors?" Quiroz asked.

"Seven and eleven."

Crane said, "Let's rock-and-roll."

They were in full protective gear, except for helmets. As soon as they left the tactical truck they fanned out to their assigned posts. Donnelly rapped loudly on the door. "Federal agents, we have a warrant. Open the door."

There was movement inside, and Lucy saw a pair of large, round brown eyes looking at her through the blinds. She motioned to Donnelly, and he nodded that he'd seen the child.

Donnelly repeated the command in Spanish and Lucy winced. His Spanish was rough and threatening. She took the liberty of talking to the girl directly.

"My name is Lucy, and it would help if you could open the door, please," she said in Spanish. "Your mommy isn't in any trouble. But we need to come in."

It was clear Donnelly didn't understand exactly what she said, but the girl did, and she dropped the blinds. She undid the chain before a loud female voice shouted in Spanish, "Bella! Get away from the door!" Then she shouted at Donnelly in English, "Go away, you got nothing on me."

"Ms. Borez, we have a warrant for the arrest of George Sanchez and Jaime Sanchez. We know they're inside."

"They're not here."

"We need to come in and look for ourselves."

"I don't have to let you in. I know my rights."

"We have a search warrant, Ms. Borez. Make this easy on yourself and your kids."

In her earpiece Lucy heard Crane say, "One of the suspects is climbing out the bathroom window."

"Rollins, you and Butch take him," Donnelly said into his mike. He nodded to Lucy and French. "Cover me."

Gun drawn, Donnelly tried the door. It wasn't locked thanks to the little girl, and he pushed it in.

"Down, down, down!" he shouted.

The two girls looked terrified, particularly the younger child. "Get them out, Kincaid!"

Lucy spoke quickly in Spanish, telling the girls to come with her. Fortunately, they did, and Lucy took them immediately to the tactical truck. She had them behind the truck, to protect them from any potential gunfire.

"You're not going to hurt my mommy, are you?" the younger girl asked.

"No." Lucy hoped Mirabelle didn't do anything stupid. "You're Bella, right?"

"Isabella. My mommy calls me Bella. And my friends. My teachers call me Isabella." She wrinkled her nose.

"That's a pretty name. I'm Lucy. It's short for Lucia." Lucy looked at the older girl. "What's your name?"

The eleven-year-old glared at her. She was scared and angry, but mostly distrustful. "I'm not telling you anything." It pained Lucy that so many parents, particularly those on the wrong side of the law, taught their children to hate and doubt law enforcement.

Bella said, "Are you here because of the boy?"

Lucy's radar went up. "What boy?"

"The boy in the basement. Michael."

The older sister hit Bella across the face, and the girl cried out.

Lucy said with thinly restrained anger, "Do not touch her again." Into her mike she added, "I need an officer."

One of the sheriff's deputies in the tactical van came around back. Lucy stepped aside with Deputy Lawrence while keeping her eyes on the girls. "I need to talk to the younger girl away from her sister. Keep a close eye, though. She's not cooperative."

"Got it."

Lucy pulled Bella aside even though her sister was shouting at them.

"You'll be in *big* trouble, Isabella!" the older girl called after them. "Don't say anything to no cop, I swear, I'll make you pay."

"What's your sister's name?" Lucy asked.

Through tears, Bella said, "CeCe. It's short for Priscilla, but she hates that name."

"Who's Michael?"

"I c-c-can't." She shook her head.

"I won't let CeCe or anyone hurt you."

Bella looked at Lucy with big, frightened eyes. "You're lying."

What had happened to this little girl?

Lucy tried, but Bella wasn't talking, her scared eyes on the house. Lucy listened to her team with one ear. They had George Sanchez in custody, but not Jaime. They were still searching the house, but believed Jaime had left before their own arrival. Mirabelle's car was missing, and it had been there the night before during a surveillance check.

Lucy said into her mike, "Donnelly, there may be someone in the basement. A minor." She didn't need to warn him that Jaime could be hiding there as well.

"Roger that."

To Bella, she said, "It's going to be okay." But that felt like a lie. Here were two minor girls, one who had attitude about authority most likely learned from her family. Their mother was in custody for harboring a fugitive and resisting, and their uncle was in custody for attempted murder and jumping bail. The mother might be released, but what did that mean for Bella and CeCe? Either they would be back home and involved in their mother's sketchy lifestyle, or they would be subjected to foster care.

Neither option was ideal. Lucy would much prefer them to be with family, but what kind of life was this for children?

"Do you know when your uncle Jaime left?"

She shrugged. "I was supposed to be sleeping. But they were arguing and woke me up."

"Do you have a clock in your room?"

She shook her head. "It was still dark. But I didn't go back to sleep, and it got light real quick."

Probably between four and six in the morning.

"Do you know what they were talking about?"

She shook her head, keeping her eyes averted. "I put a pillow over my head. But Uncle Jaime was very upset. Mama was worried. Then I heard the car. That's our only car."

In her ear she heard Donnelly say, "Cellar is clear. But someone was living down here. Kincaid, I need you."

"Two minutes, sir," she said. She motioned for the two officers who were standing next to the patrol car. "I need one of you to stay with Bella." She glanced at CeCe. "And keep her and her sister apart."

"Roger that."

One of the officers squatted down so he was eye level with Bella. "My name is Officer Jim Wyatt. Do you want to see the inside of my patrol car?"

"Am I going to jail?" Bella spoke English well enough, Lucy realized. She probably understood even more.

"No. You can sit in the front seat, okay? We have a computer and a bunch of neat stuff. Some stickers, I think. And my wife made me cookies. Chocolate chip. They're really good."

She gave him a tentative smile and took his hand.

Lucy nodded her appreciation to Wyatt and hightailed it back to the Sanchez house. George Sanchez was cuffed and sitting on the ground with one officer covering him. Nicole Rollins had custody of Mirabelle Borez. Mirabelle stared at Lucy. "You can't talk to my kids! I know my rights, you can't talk to them without me! They're just babies, you have no right, *puta*."

"Shut up," Nicole told her. She rolled her eyes at Lucy.

Lucy ignored Mirabelle and caught up with Donnelly, who took her down the long narrow driveway to the detached single-car garage. A door flush with the ground led to a basement under the garage; stairs led down to a dimly lit and musty room.

Donnelly said, "I've called in a team of dogs. They'll be here in less than an hour. I have a feeling, in my gut, there's something here, but instead of ripping the place apart I'll let the dogs sniff it out."

"Bella, the younger girl, thought we were here because of the boy in the basement. She called him Michael."

He motioned to the opened door. "This was locked from the outside. And it's clear someone was living down there. It's not pretty."

Lucy was used to *not pretty*. She went down the stairs.

The smell hit her first, before she was halfway down the rotting staircase. Human waste. A bare lightbulb hung from the ceiling on a wire; it cast the only light in the room, except for Ryan Quinoz's flashlight. There was a plastic bucket in the corner that had been used as a toilet, and it hadn't been recently cleaned. Flies moved freely around it. Four cots on rusting metal frames took up half the room. Three had no blankets; one had a solitary sheet and an old, torn sleeping bag with a broken zipper. A shelf had remnants of food—crackers mostly. A few bottles of water remained; several more were empty and had been tossed under the cots. Restraints were chained to the beds.

"My first thought was a sanctuary for illegals coming

up from the border," Donnelly said. "But the external lock makes it unlikely."

"Unless they were kept down here for involuntary servitude."

Ryan spoke up. "I busted a place like that when I was a cop in Houston. Sweatshop. Much bigger-scale than this. Illegal immigrants were kept in a storage room under the factory. Eight hours sleep, sixteen hours work. Our numbers guys cracked the books. The average illegal worker would have had to work nine years, six months to pay off the so-called debt. This"—he waved his hand—"this doesn't make sense."

Lucy slipped on plastic gloves and searched the small confines. There was a dirty plate under one cot. A shoe box of cookies, homemade. Both hidden in the far corner, where two cots met, hard to see unless you were looking for them. She also found three paperbacks, in English. She frowned, flipping through the pages. The books were stamped SAN ANTONIO PUBLIC LIBRARY. Mirabelle spoke English, and the girls seemed to understand and speak well enough, though they were more comfortable with Spanish. These were action-adventure books, not really the type two young girls would read.

Lucy hadn't seen a room like the basement before, but she knew all too well what this place had been used for. Prison.

"I'd like to bring Bella down here."

"Why?"

"She thought she was in trouble because of the boy in the basement. Her uncle was worried and angry, and the adults were arguing before Jaime left in Mirabelle's car. What if it wasn't because they got wind of Operation Heatwave, but because of this Michael?"

"This is out of bounds of our warrant," he said.

"If Michael is a minor child in danger, we have an obligation to pursue this."

Donnelly didn't seem like he wanted to agree with her, but she held her own and didn't avert her eyes. She didn't apologize for her opinion, a bad habit she'd worked hard to break over the last year. Finally, he said, "Call her in."

Lucy contacted Officer Wyatt and asked him to bring Bella around to the back of the house. She met him outside the garage. "Wait here, please," she said.

Bella was eyeing the cellar door with fear and apprehension. "It's okay, Bella," Lucy said. "You didn't do anything wrong."

"I did."

"What do you think you did?"

"I made everybody mad. But they don't know it was me. Not even CeCe knows," she added in a whisper.

"I'm not mad at you." Lucy squatted. "Bella, I need your help. Michael needs your help. Can you please come down to the basement with me for just a minute?"

She bit her lip. "You're not going to lock me inside, are you?" she whispered.

Lucy's chest tightened. She shook her head. "You can leave as soon as you want to. I need you for one minute. It would be a big help."

Lucy took the child's hand, and together they went down the stairs. Bella didn't flinch at the smell, though she moved closer to Lucy when she saw Donnelly and Quiroz. The two broad-shouldered men filled most of the available standing space.

Lucy pointed to the books on the end of the cot. "Did you get Michael those books?"

Bella hesitated, then nodded. "CeCe was responsible for feeding him and cleaning his toilet, but she hated doing it. Sometimes, she would let him go all day without food, and once—well, she said he touched her so she hit him with a paddle. He was bleeding and I brought him ice. I snuck him my leftovers. I got the books at the library."

"They're in English."

"He spoke English. His Spanish isn't good."

That was odd.

"Was Michael Hispanic?"

She shrugged. "Yeah."

"Why do you think you made your uncle mad?"

She looked around, eyes wide. "I let Michael go. I let him go because Uncle Jaime was going to send him back to the bad place and Michael told me he would die if he ever went back."

"Back where?"

She shook her head. "He called it the bad place. Michael ran errands for Uncle Jaime. But he went to the bad place and got locked up here. He said he broke rules."

"There are four cots," Lucy said, gesturing.

"Sometimes there are other boys, but I never talked to them. They never stayed long. Michael was different."

"How long was Michael here?"

She frowned, her brows furrowed. "Three or four weeks. I guess."

Over the com, one of Donnelly's people said, "The dogs are here."

"I'll be right up." Donnelly seemed preoccupied, but he turned to Lucy. "We need to talk to the mother." He ordered Ryan to work with the dog handlers, then motioned for Lucy to follow him.

Lucy handed Bella off to Officer Wyatt. Donnelly said to the officer, "Contact Child Protective Services and tell them we need someone who can take the girls."

Lucy's stomach twisted. She didn't say anything until Wyatt left with Bella, then turned to Donnelly. "Is that necessary?"

"We're taking the mother into custody; someone has to

watch the kids. The mother refuses to give us the name of a relative, and unless she cooperates we don't have a choice."

"Can I talk to her?"

"To what end?"

"I don't want to see that little girl become part of the system."

"Neither do I, but there comes a time when you realize you can't save them all. You're still green." He said it with marginal disgust, and Lucy almost corrected him. It was clear that Donnelly was thinking about something different than this situation.

Instead, she said, "Bella said there had been boys here before Michael."

"There were four cots. That's a good guess."

"It's not a guess."

"The girl is seven years old."

"She told us the truth."

Donnelly glanced around, made sure that they were alone, and said, "I'm a drug cop. That's what I know. If you think this is something else, spill it."

"I don't know what to think at this point. But in all the briefings we've had over the last two months, I remember an agent talking about how gangs often force young boys to move drugs for them. Threatening their families, threatening them. Or luring them with promises of money."

"Why lock him up?"

"I don't know." Since her time in San Antonio, Lucy had been immersed in the drug business. Being so close to the border, San Antonio and the outlying areas had become a major hub for drug transportation and distribution, in addition to weapons and human trafficking. The Texas Mexican Mafia and other, smaller gangs worked with the cartels south of the border to move their products. It was a highly profitable, extremely dangerous business. The drugs themselves were one thing; Lucy was focused more on the people the drug trade affected. People like Bella. And Michael.

Donnelly sighed and ran a hand over his face. "I wouldn't put it past Jaime Sanchez to use kids in his operation. I've seen it a hundred times. It fits his personality. He's violent and volatile. But why lock up the kid? Most of the time drug runners like Jaime bribe or manipulate the kids, using their friends and family as leverage."

"Michael is young."

"How do you know?"

"It's how she talked about him. A boy, not a teenager. A boy capable of being abused by her older sister, who's eleven."

"We need to pin this down." Donnelly continued, "I need you to help me get Mirabelle Borez to talk."

"She's not going to turn on her brothers." Of that, Lucy was pretty certain.

"We have leverage. We have her girls."

Lucy hesitated. "I don't think we can use them as a threat."

"Are you going soft on me?"

"I mean, she's not going to budge if we tell her we'll remove the girls from her care, or put her in prison and she'll never see them again."

"And how do you know that?"

"The way she looked at them. Confirmed by the fact that she won't give you the name of a relative who will care for them."

Donnelly closed his eyes briefly. "I forgot for a minute that you were a shrink."

"I'm not—" she began.

He interrupted. "Then how do we make her talk?"

"I don't know. Not until I get her in a room. I've read all the files on the Sanchez family, what you gave us in the briefing last night as well as the original files when we narrowed down the target list. One thing stuck out—George is the weak link. He's the oldest in the family, but has the lowest IQ. Every time they've been arrested, it's George who slips up. He's also the least violent of the family, and I include Mirabelle Borez in that."

"You read her files, too?"

Lucy nodded. "She may be clean on the surface, but I suspect she's been helping her brothers for a long time. Her deceased husband was Jaime's best friend."

"You have a plan?"

"I think we can use the girls as leverage against their uncle."

Donnelly was skeptical. "What makes you think that he cares about them more than their own mother?"

"In the original police report, when they were arrested after New Year's, he asked several times if he would be out in time to go to his niece's birthday party. He seemed unusually upset that he might miss it."

Donnelly obviously didn't remember the conversation. "And," she continued, "I watched the videotapes of the interrogations. He's remorseful."

Donnelly snorted.

"Meaning," Lucy continued, "Jaime is the thinking brother. George loves his brother and goes along with anything he wants. But to George, it's about his whole family, not just Jaime. I think I can get him to talk."

"He won't turn against his brother." Donnelly said it as if it were fact.

"No," she concurred. "Not intentionally. Maybe we can play Mirabelle and George off each other, as long as they don't realize they're being manipulated."

Donnelly's face lit up. "I have an idea. You have a thick skin." He said it as a statement, but his eyes showed doubt.

"Yes."

"I'm counting on it. I like your idea, playing George and Mirabelle off each other. If you're right about George, then this might work."

"What might work?"

"I need you to trust me. I'm going to wing it, but this is what I'm thinking—we talk to Mirabelle where George can hear us. If you're right and she won't help, then we play good cop, bad cop. You're the squishy compassionate do-gooder who doesn't want the girls in foster care, and I'm the big bad brute who doesn't give a shit what happens to them." He assessed her. "I may have to dress you down in order for George to buy it."

"I understand." She hoped. She wished they had more time to plan it, but maybe spontaneity had a place.

"Follow my lead. I'm going to brief Nicole, and you talk to Quiroz. Tell him to keep the com up and be ready. We're doing this now."

CHAPTER 2

Lucy didn't know exactly what Donnelly had planned, but she certainly understood the psychological concept behind playing George and Mirabelle off each other. She told Ryan Quiroz to play along with whatever happened. Ryan was skeptical—despite his hotheadedness, of all the people on her FBI Violent Crimes Squad he was the one she trusted most. She started to explain the idea in more detail, but Donnelly signaled her to approach. He was already talking to Mirabelle, who was standing on the broken concrete driveway. Lucy noted that all the living room windows were open. They hadn't been open when they first arrived.

Lucy didn't hear what Donnelly said, but Mirabelle snapped back, "I'm not talking without a lawyer."

Donnelly said, "That's your right."

"Damn straight." Mirabelle would have been very pretty, with dark hair, large dark eyes, and perfectly smooth light-brown skin—if she didn't have a perpetual scowl.

"We need the name and address of a close relative who can care for your girls," Lucy told her.

"Fuck you, *puta*."

"Kincaid," Donnelly said, "that's not our concern. CPS is on their way."

He gave her a slight nod, and Lucy wished they'd had more time to prepare because she wasn't 100 percent positive what he wanted from her, but it seemed like she was on the right track.

"It would be better for the girls if they were at a relative's house. Someone they know and trust."

"We don't know that they'll be safe with anyone in this family," Donnelly countered. "We need to keep an eye on them. Juvenile detention is the safest place."

"At least let me work on getting them into a foster home."

Mirabelle interrupted. "You can't keep them. They can stay with my mother-in-law."

Donnelly turned to her. His face was hard and unyielding. Lucy would hate to be on his bad side, because she didn't think this was all an act. "Your mother-in-law, Eliza Borez? She has had two felony convictions and is still on probation. No court will turn the girls over to her."

"She did her time, she loves my girls."

"We don't know that she's not involved in what your brothers are doing. I have a team over there now with a warrant searching for Jaime."

"You can't take them. You can't take me! You have nothing on me."

"Harboring two fugitives. Resisting arrest. The dogs are sniffing the house and grounds—think they won't find any drugs?"

"Illegal search!" she cried out.

Donnelly rolled his eyes and stepped away from Mirabelle. "Kincaid!" he snapped, more harsh than necessary. "With me."

She followed Donnelly up three concrete steps that once might have been painted terra-cotta. They matched the cracked porch. Mirabelle was still shouting profanities at them from the driveway. Lucy took a quick look through the windows. George sat inside on the couch, an officer guarding him.

Donnelly said to Lucy, louder than necessary, his Texas accent getting thicker as his voice turned angrier, "I don't know what they teach you in the FBI, Kincaid, but I'm in charge, and if I say the kids are going to juvie, that's where they're going."

"Sir—they're very young. They're innocent—"

"I arrested an eight-year-old drug courier who'd been recruited by his older brother. The innocent-looking kid was carrying a .38 special and could have blown my head off. I don't care how young they are, they were living in this house, they know what's going on."

"Let me talk to them, I can convince them to cooperate, then we can find them a decent foster home. They shouldn't be in juvenile jail. You know what happens there, Agent Donnelly."

"The younger one might get placed with a family, but the older one—she's trouble. You said it yourself."

"No," she said emphatically, looking Donnelly in the eye, "*I* said she was distrustful of authority. I can bring her around. You're not thinking about what's in the best interest of the children. Is there something I don't know about?"

They'd drawn the attention of the San Antonio cops, who tried to hide their surprise at the loud, public argument. Donnelly glared at them, then grabbed Kincaid by the arm and pulled her into the house. The action startled Lucy, who hadn't been expecting the move.

Ryan Quiroz stood with the cop guarding George Sanchez. He was just as surprised as Lucy at Donnelly's actions, but the surprise immediately turned to anger. His eyes narrowed and he said, "Donnelly, what the hell—"

Donnelly cut him off with a look. "Where does the FBI

find new agents these days? The DEA rejection pile? Are you her training officer? You have your work cut out for you."

Ryan reddened and stepped forward. Lucy put up her hand. This was getting out of control. If only she'd had more time to explain to Ryan that this was just an act. She couldn't clue him in now, though; she'd seen the worried expression on Sanchez's face. She had to play this out because it was working.

Lucy said, "Sir, I take full responsibility for my opinions, and I will not be shut down just because I'm new. You're wrong about this." Her heart was pounding in her chest and her stomach was queasy; she hated confrontations, even orchestrated ones. She kept her chin up. "Those girls need to be in a *home*. Not in a virtual jail. It's not fair, just because their mother isn't cooperating, to punish them."

"Life isn't fucking fair, Kincaid. You heard the woman. She doesn't care what happens to them. They're not my problem. My problem is stopping the drug supply from increasing in this city. And, frankly, my other big problem is *you*. I'm calling your SSA right now because I want you off this team."

He stormed out of the house and Lucy let out a large, tension-filled sigh that *wasn't* an act. She took a moment to compose herself and looked around the small living area. It was cluttered but very clean. A faint aroma of lemon cleanser underneath the warm smell of fresh bread. She turned to George.

"I'm sorry, Mr. Sanchez, I did everything I could."

Ryan had a million questions on his face, and he looked like he wanted to follow Donnelly out the door and deck him. "What happened to piss him off? You didn't deserve that. Don't worry about Casilla, I'll explain Donnelly lost his fucking marbles."

"We have a fundamental difference of opinion. And unfortunately, he's in charge." She glanced at the door, then looked at Ryan until she caught his eye. Then she shook her head slightly. She hoped he understood.

George said, "I don't understand. My nieces can stay with their grandmother. Why is he sending them to detention? They didn't do anything wrong."

"Their grandmother has a record and DEA is searching her house." Lucy wasn't sure if that was another bluff on Donnelly's part, but it sounded good. "They can't go there," she added. That wasn't necessarily true; the court would have to make the determination as to whether it was safe for their paternal grandmother to be granted temporary custody. George's father was in prison, and his mother had died of cancer two years ago. Mirabelle's mother-in-law had a criminal background, and her father-in-law had died young on the wrong end of a gang battle. It was a cycle with the family. Criminals for generations. If CeCe and Bella didn't get out now, while they were young, they would be trapped as well, marrying into other criminal families. It made Lucy ill to think about it. But she could only focus on helping them today.

"There has to be someplace!" George pleaded. "Let Mirabelle stay. She didn't do anything, she couldn't. All she did was let us stay here. We're family. Everything else, it was all me and Jaime. She's not part of this."

Lucy sat across from him. "She's not helping herself," she told him. "She's refusing to cooperate. The dogs are searching for drugs. You know they'll find something."

He didn't contradict her, so she suspected she was right.

"She might get out on bail, but it'll take time," Lucy continued. "Those juvenile detention centers—they're awful. If the girls are lucky, they'll find themselves in a group home, but even those are filled mostly with troubled kids. And finding a place that can take both of them—almost impossible. It breaks my heart. That's why I was fighting with

Agent Donnelly about pulling some strings to get them placed together in the foster care system. It isn't perfect, but it's better than the alternatives."

Lucy was making it up as she went along. She had some familiarity with the juvenile justice system, and some with foster care, but she had no idea what the process was, especially here in San Antonio. But this was a game, a bluff, and she had to get George to turn.

"Why won't he? Doesn't he care about them? They're just little girls!"

"Honestly? I don't think he cares about anything except finding your brother." That was certainly true. From the beginning of this operation, Donnelly had been focused on Jaime Sanchez. Even before the raid this morning.

"This is not fair, Agent Kincaid. This is not fair."

"I agree. But you heard Agent Donnelly. He wants me off his team. If my boss can't talk him out of it—well, it's out of my hands."

Ryan said, "Lucy, we're not backing down off this. Casilla isn't going to—"

But Lucy had already given Donnelly the cue to reenter, and Ryan shut his mouth when Donnelly walked in with Officer Wyatt and Bella right behind him. Bella was asking, "Can I bring my doll? She'll miss me."

"No," Donnelly said gruffly. "Only a change of clothes. And any medicine you need. No personal belongings in detention."

Lucy's heart broke at the tears that filled Bella's eyes. The girl stared at Donnelly, then looked at her shuffling feet. Did he really have to go this far?

"Brad," Lucy said, intentionally using his first name, "you can't do this."

"I can and I will," he said. "First, I'm writing you up for insubordination and disobeying orders. Casilla won't pull you, but he's going to get an earful from me."

George pleaded with Donnelly. "*Por favor*, don't do this. Don't send Isabella to a bad place."

A bad place. That was the same phrase that Bella had used in relation to Michael, the boy in the basement.

Bella leaned into Officer Wyatt, her little body shaking.

"Her mother has tied my hands," Donnelly said, focusing on George. "I told her if she cooperates, she can stay here with the girls. I offered probation. I had the AUSA on the phone willing to write it all up. She refused. Now I'm stuck. You think I like being an asshole? It comes with the job when women like your sister care more about themselves than their kids."

"I will. I'll—I'll help you. But only if you don't send the girls to a bad place. Please, I beg you."

The room was silent.

George turned to Lucy. "Please, appeal to him. Tell him the girls need to be together, that they need a home. Not a jail."

Lucy looked at Donnelly. "Sir?" she said quietly. "Brad? It's the right thing to do."

"What do you know?" Donnelly asked George.

He shook his head. "I give you nothing until I know that you won't break your promise. I don't trust you."

"I give you my word."

He snorted. "Your word means nothing. You would do this to little girls? Send them to a prison? Make them cry? I want it written. I want it legal."

Donnelly appeared to consider the request. Then he swore under his breath and said, "I need to call the AUSA." He stepped out again.

Bella looked from Wyatt to Lucy. "Lucy?" she said in a whisper. "Am I being locked up? Did I do something bad?"

Lucy knelt in front of her. She spoke quietly in Spanish. "No, Bella, you did nothing wrong. You will not be locked up anywhere. Officer Wyatt is going to take you to your room. Pack a suitcase of everything you think you need. Including your doll. Especially your doll. Then pack a suitcase for CeCe."

"She doesn't like me touching her stuff."

"This one time. You can tell her I made you do it."

Bella bit her lip, then nodded.

Lucy stood. Quietly, in English, she said to Wyatt, "Thank you."

"What was that about?" he asked.

"I'll explain later." She glanced at George, who looked broken and defeated sitting on the sagging couch. "It was necessary."

"She's a sweet kid. She's scared."

"Thanks for watching out for her."

Wyatt and Bella walked down the short hall. Ryan fumed. "I'm gonna smack that guy, Lucy. He wants to write you up? Hell, I know his boss. She would never put up with that shit. I'll write *him* up, see how he likes it."

"It's okay," Lucy said, but Ryan wasn't paying attention to her. He was watching Donnelly through the window. She had some feathers to unruffle when this was all over, but she couldn't do it in front of George.

Wyatt and Bella were done before Donnelly came back. "Where now?" Wyatt asked Lucy.

"Donnelly's working on it."

"It's getting hot outside."

"There's a back patio, take her there."

Bella pulled on Wyatt's hand. "Mr. Wyatt?" she asked. "Can I say good-bye to Uncle George?"

Wyatt looked at Lucy. She took Bella's hand and walked her over to George. Bella handed her uncle a photograph. It had the plain gray background of a school picture. Bella wore pink and her hair was shiny and pulled back with a pink-and-blue headband. "So you don't forget me."

Since he was cuffed, he couldn't take the photo. Lucy took it from Bella and slid it into George's pocket, after she looked at the reverse. Just in case there was something that shouldn't be written on the other side.

BELLA BOREZ AGE 7 written in painstakingly perfect letters.

"Okay?" she said.

Bella nodded, then gave her uncle a tight hug. "I love you, Uncle George. I'm sorry you're in trouble."

Lucy followed Wyatt and Bella to the covered porch. Bella said, "Lucy, Uncle George isn't a bad person. He sometimes does bad things. Is that why he's going to jail?"

"Yes," she said. "And you know what? I don't think he's a bad person, either. Maybe he just needs the chance to do the right thing. Like you did, this morning, when you told me about Michael."

Bella thought on that. Then she crooked her finger until Lucy's ear was close to her mouth. "Uncle Jaime is a real bad person," she whispered. "Sometimes he's nice, but he makes my mama cry."

Donnelly was talking through her earpiece, asking her to come out front. Wyatt was on the same frequency and said, "I'll stay with her."

Lucy walked around to the front of the house and was surprised that there were twice as many police cars and tactical vehicles as when they'd first arrived. Donnelly was talking with the head of the K-9 unit, and Mirabelle was restrained in the back of a police car. She didn't see CeCe.

Lucy said, "You wanted me."

Donnelly motioned to the K-9 leader. "They found a small amount of heroin packaged for sale hidden behind a panel in the room the children shared. We'll get prints off it. There were trace amounts in other parts of the house, but it looks like Jaime cleaned them out when he left this morning."

"You think Mirabelle is part of this?"

"Yes—during the search we found several illegal guns. Coupled with the drugs, we can go either misdemeanor or felony, depending on what she says. But she's not helping her case, and she's protecting her brother. First said she gave him the car, then said he stole it. She definitely knows more. A lawyer will have her out on Monday, my guess, after arraignment, unless the AUSA can get a judge to set a prohibitive bail."

"George?"

"The AUSA wants Jaime bad enough, I can make a deal with him. But he has to give us something solid."

"And the girls?"

"They're being sent to a foster home that has worked with at-risk kids before, far from this neighborhood. They'll be safe."

"I think Bella knows more than she told us," Lucy said. "But I don't think she's intentionally withholding information. She might not know what's important to us and what isn't."

"I'm not stopping you from talking to her."

Lucy considered. "We should let her adjust and talk to her tonight or tomorrow morning. It's overwhelming right now. I don't think I can get anything more until she feels safe."

He gave her shoulder a brief squeeze. "Good job, Kincaid. Casilla was right about you."

"You really called my supervisor?"

He eyed her quizzically. "No—you know that was all an act."

"Yes, but—"

"He's the one who recommended you and Quiroz for the task force. I was skeptical since you're a new agent. Ask anyone around here—I'm not a fan of rookies."

The K-9 officer concurred. "He's not."

"I want you as part of the takedown when we locate Jaime Sanchez. I'm sure Casilla will agree. You earned it."

"Thank you, Agent Donnelly."

"Don't thank me yet. This isn't going to be easy, and it's certainly going to be dangerous. Ready to tackle George Sanchez?"

"Yes."

They walked back into the house. Donnelly said, "My AUSA wants good-faith information. Something that proves to us you're willing to cooperate. If it pans out, the girls go to a nice, safe foster home in a very good neighborhood until this situation is resolved. If it doesn't, they go in the system, just like every other kid with family in jail. Do you understand?"

George glanced at Lucy. "I get this in writing, right?"

"Yes," Donnelly said, not giving Lucy a chance to answer. "Give us one thing we can verify now."

He seemed skeptical and kept looking at Lucy. She said, "George, I won't let anything bad happen to Bella and CeCe."

"What if you can't stop him?" George asked in Spanish. Lucy didn't know if Donnelly had picked up on the comment, but if he did, he didn't react.

Lucy replied in Spanish. "I have friends in high places. I'll keep them safe. I promise you that. They aren't part of this. But you need to be honest with us. Verifiable information. Do you understand?"

George hesitated. He looked into his lap, as if the answers were written on his dirty jeans. Then he said, "We use a place on Thirty-Ninth for storage. Jaime just moved a bunch of guns there. But he has people guarding it, you know."

Lucy thought it interesting that George started with *we* but ended with *he*—Jaime. Confirming that the younger brother was the leader.

"Address," Donnelly said.

George looked at Lucy. He gave them the exact address. "Can I see my nieces? Please?"

"Bella only," Lucy said. "Officer Wyatt will bring her back in. But then she and CeCe are leaving."

"Is CeCe okay?"

"Yes," Lucy said and left it at that.

Outside, Donnelly said, "Why not let him see the other kid?"

"I don't want CeCe to know that he's helping us," she said quietly. "We can't trust her not to spread the word that George is turning snitch. She won't understand that she could put him in danger."

"Eleven," Donnelly muttered.

It hurt, Lucy realized, that she couldn't trust the girl. They now had an obligation to protect not only the girls, but George Sanchez as well.

That little motherfucking brat was going to be gutted and left to die in the streets, like the rat he was.

Where would he go? Jaime already put a man outside Michael's old foster home, but would he be stupid enough to go back there? For a kid, he was a smart little bastard.

But not smart enough. Jaime would find him and kill him for jeopardizing this operation. If the plan didn't go off perfectly, the general would be gunning for Jaime, and no way in hell was Jaime going to die. This had been *his* grand plan, his brilliant strategy to unite three smaller gangs into a cohesive group. Smaller than the Texas Mexican Mafia, but more powerful because they were smarter. They would swear allegiance to the TMM, but the general had it worked out that they were to be partners, not subordinates.

If the plan was executed.

And Michael was the wild card. He had to play his part or the entire plan would fail.

His burner phone rang. The only person who had this number was the general himself.

"Yeah," he answered.

"What happened?" the general asked, his voice low and rough.

"I told you Michael was a threat. He escaped."

"The feds are all over your house."

"That ain't my problem."

"It is if your stupid brother talks."

"He won't." Jaime wasn't so sure of that, but he couldn't let the general know George was trouble. "And if he does, he doesn't know anything about the plan."

"He knows enough. Mirabelle has been arrested as well."

"She probably mouthed off at the cops."

"Which leads me to the most important question. Where is Isabella?"

Jaime's face twisted in a grimace. "Safe," he said.

"She's with the authorities. You know our agreement, Jaime. I want her. Find her and bring her to me. No more waiting."

Mirabelle would never forgive him, but it was her own fault. Mirabelle had brought the general into their lives in the first place.

You made your bed, sister, now suck it up.

"I told you I would."

"It sounds like you have a lot of problems, Jaime. Take care of them."

The line went dead.

Jaime glanced at the river and considered throwing the phone in and running. But where would he go? All his contacts and friends where here. He'd be a sitting duck anywhere else in the West. He had no resources to disappear.

If he stayed, the reward would be great. But first, he would have to survive the coming war. And survival depended on finding Michael and sending him in to do his part. Jaime wished there were someone else, but it had to be Michael.

He dumped Mirabelle's car and stole another ride, took it to the warehouse on 39th. His boys were there and were happy to see him.

Andy said, "The feds are everywhere today. Some fucking sweep, ever heard of such a thing?"

Jaime shook his head. "They were at Mirabelle's. They have her and George. I need a kit and a clean car."

"Got it ready. Ben went underground. They hit his place, but he'd already heard about the sweep and disappeared."

"When he checks in, have him tag me. I need his help."

Jaime looked over the car Andy had stripped and rebuilt. There were hidden compartments for drugs and guns, but Jaime didn't need drugs right now. He packed up the weapons he could use, and cash. "Keep your eyes open," he said. "I'll check in later."

Jaime drove off, heading south. He couldn't leave the city until he had Bella, but he had a safe house just outside town where he could lay low for the rest of the day and have his people search for Michael. There weren't many places the kid could go.

As soon as he had Michael, he'd grab Bella and head south of the border. Once the general had her, Jaime could rest easier, buy some more time.

The feds might have his niece now, but finding her would be a piece of cake.

CHAPTER 3

Watching Brad Donnelly work, Lucy realized he'd done this a hundred times. He wasn't that old—in his late thirties—but he was comfortable giving orders and executing a plan. He pulled a unit from another team to transport George to a holding cell, assigned Officer Wyatt and his partner to stay with Bella and CeCe through CPS processing until they were secure in the foster home, and left two officers to stake out the Sanchez-Borez home in case Jaime returned. Within an hour he had a new staging area set up half a mile from the hardware store that, according to George Sanchez, fronted for Jaime's drug and gun storage facility.

If George was lying, they'd gambled and lost, but all that would be wasted was time. Donnelly seemed optimistic, but with detailed preparation he wasn't counting solely on George Sanchez's intel.

There were nine of them now, with a tactical backup of six watching the perimeter and manning the communications van. Donnelly had everyone gear up. Six were SWAT-trained, including Donnelly and Ryan and SAPD Officers Butcher and French, who'd been part of their team from the beginning. Two other DEA agents had joined them as well. Donnelly split them into three teams of three, and Lucy was assigned to Donnelly and Ryan.

Donnelly had week-old satellite pictures of the block, and he highlighted the hardware store and all its ins and outs. He marked the two primary entrances. "My team is Alpha, we're going through the front. Beta, you're in the rear. Delta, you're covering the parking lot. Any packages, get them clear immediately. Questions?"

There were a few, which Donnelly answered. Then he said, "As soon as the warrant gets here, we're moving."

Ryan turned to Lucy. "Are you ready for this?"

Donnelly interjected. "You have a problem, Quiroz?"

"Kincaid isn't SWAT. Neither are Rollins or Crane. You just outlined a SWAT operation."

"This is a raid, pure and simple. According to our drive-by, there are only two cars in the lot, and SAPD intelligence reports on the area list this as a low-level facility. They don't even have it confirmed as a drug house, but Sanchez swears up and down that it's for storage. And it makes sense they'd keep it low-key, to not trigger our interest." He turned to Lucy. "You want out?"

"No, sir," she said.

"Good."

It was clear from the look on his face that Ryan was still not happy. Lucy pulled him aside while Donnelly handed out communications equipment. "I'm good, Ryan."

"Donnelly's a hot dog. He's knows better than to rush an op like this."

"We don't have time. This is our best chance—if George Sanchez is being up front, we can deal a severe blow to his brother's operation and possibly gain a lead on where he's hiding. He might even be here."

"It's not *we*, Lucy, it's *him*. It's Donnelly's gig, we're just along for the ride."

"I'm okay with that."

"I don't know that I am." He glanced around at the team. "We train every week in SWAT. This is a hodgepodge of people who haven't trained together."

Lucy didn't know how to respond. She trusted Ryan; he was the most cop-like agent on the Violent Crimes Squad, largely, she suspected, because he'd been a big-city cop for so long. But this situation required speed. If they waited, they'd lose the edge.

"But," Ryan continued, "I have your back."

"I have yours, too. I might not be SWAT, but I've trained for this."

Ryan was acting protective, and she didn't know if that had more to do with her being a rookie, or her being a female agent. He didn't really know her, her history, what she'd done or what she'd been trained to do. If their roles were reversed and she were the agent assigned to a rookie, she might have similar concerns.

She added, "Ryan, when this is over, remind me to have you to the house for dinner. I have some stories for you. Maybe then you'll trust me."

He glanced at her. "I trust you. It's *him*"—he jerked his finger toward Donnelly, who was on the phone—"I don't trust. Not completely." Then he gave her a half grin. "I was wondering when you'd get around to an invite. Nate said he's over there all the time. Says your place is awesome."

"That's all Sean. He has too much time on his hands." Which was becoming a problem. Not for Lucy—she loved coming home every evening to Sean—but she sensed that Sean was getting restless. Starting a new PI business in a city where he didn't have many contacts was proving more difficult than he'd thought. He was looking into local private security companies, but he didn't want to work for anyone else. It was his chance to make a clean break from his brother's company, and he wanted to do it on his own. So he'd spent all his free time updating and decorating the house he'd found while Lucy spent New Year's with her family in San Diego.

While she loved her job, she loved coming home even more. For the first time in her life, everything was working together. A job that was her vocation, a home that she felt was truly her own, and a man she loved beyond anything else.

Which made Sean's sacrifices for her all the more noble. He'd given up his position with his brother's company, and though he wanted to leave, it still meant he had to create something from the ground up here. Because he loved her.

"Ready, Kincaid? Quiroz?" Donnelly said. "Finally got the damn warrant."

They nodded, and the three of them bumped fists. Even with the tension between Ryan and Donnelly, the operation came first. They were a unit.

They rode into the red zone via the tactical truck, cramped in a narrow space that was dominated by communications equipment. The van followed. They parked directly in front of the entrance and exited immediately. Speed was essential in case there were external security cameras that announced their presence.

Donnelly used his hands to signal each team, and everyone moved out seamlessly. Lucy had only trained with SWAT as part of rescue scenarios, years ago when she'd been an intern with the Arlington County Sheriff's Department. Because she was a certified EMT, she'd trained as the team medic. She was very comfortable with the process.

Donnelly was lead, and he silently counted down, then shouted, "Go, go, go!" and kicked open the door.

"DEA! We have a warrant to search these premises!"

Lucy surveyed the main room. It was a hardware store with several long, narrow rows of supplies, but there was more open space than shelves. Several Hispanic males were lounging on couches, and they jumped up as soon as Donnelly breached the entrance. Two ran toward the back.

Ryan shouted, "Down, down, down!" The three remaining men slowly sank to the ground. "Keep your hands up, above your head."

Donnelly nodded to Ryan. "Got them?"

"Yes, sir."

Into his mike Donnelly said, "I need backup to secure three hostiles in front." Then he motioned for Lucy to follow him in pursuit of the fleeing suspects.

The two on foot hadn't left the building. Lucy motioned to the floor. She'd felt a vibration beneath her, but hadn't heard a door closing.

Donnelly understood. In his mike he said quietly, "I need plans on this building. Is there a cellar?"

As he waited for information, they searched all potential hiding places, but came up empty. Beta team, from the rear, entered. "They didn't come out this way, sir," the Beta team leader said.

Donnelly slid over the counter. There was an old manual cash register. He motioned at the floor. Lucy saw exactly what he did: The wood was different from that in the rest of the store.

He took out his cell phone and read something, then said into his mike, "Expand the perimeter, possible tunnel escape."

He gestured to Lucy. "Get that door open." He trained his gun on the opening.

Lucy slung her rifle strap over her back and felt around the boards. The hinges were on top, flush with the wood, but indicating that the door would swing out, into the store. On the opposite side where the opening should be the boards were wider apart and discolored. A small handle was barely noticeable. She tried to open the trapdoor; a faint sound of scraping metal came as she pulled.

"They have it locked from the underside," she said.

"Stand back."

Lucy complied. Donnelly fired two bullets at the lock. The lock gave and the door sagged. Donnelly reached down, pulled it up, and leaned it against the counter.

Dull-yellow lights lit the cellar below. There was no movement and no sign of the two suspects, but that didn't mean they weren't waiting to ambush anyone who came down. A ladder lay on the packed-dirt floor below. In addition to the lock, they'd taken away the stairs. But the drop wasn't far. Rows of shelving revealed hundreds of firearms, from handguns to illegal automatic weapons.

"Shit, that's a lot of weaponry," Donnelly muttered. He grabbed a box of bolts from the counter and dropped it into the hole. No one fired.

"I'm going first. Crane, guard the door, everyone else follow me."

Donnelly didn't hesitate. He slung his rifle over his back, unholstered his sidearm, and eased himself into the hole, dropping almost immediately and landing on his feet. He searched the immediate area and said, "Clear. It's only an eight-foot clearance," he added. "The drop is easy."

Lucy dropped down, followed by two others. They fanned out and quickly searched the remainder of the basement. There were six rows of shelving with at least three hundred guns of all types, plus hundreds of boxes of ammo. A door led to a room that was mostly empty, except for a money-counting machine and a computer. A stack of unused plastic bags sat on the small table.

"Shit," Donnelly said, "this is bigger than I thought, but they haven't cleared out. We definitely caught them unaware. Either they're waiting for a new drug shipment, or they just released their last." He glanced at the guns. "I didn't expect the gun operation. The Sanchezes have always been about the drugs, this means—" He stopped for a moment, as if running through a list of scenarios.

"Someone else?" Lucy offered. "Or expanding his operation?"

"I sensed something was up. The last gang that Sanchez hit, it didn't make sense—now it does."

One of the Beta team members, Johnson, motioned to a hall that led east. It was poorly lit. Donnelly put his hand up to halt them, then asked the tactical team on the street if they'd found the exit to the tunnel.

"Affirmative," Lucy heard through the mike. "We have two men on it. No one has exited."

Johnson said, "It could be a maze down here."

Donnelly considered, then said, "Delta team, stay on the tunnel exit. I'm going through this end with Johnson. Be alert for us, no one gets caught in the cross fire, got it? Stay up on the com." He said to Lucy, "You and Rollins stay here, complete the search, secure this door, wait for my orders."

Lucy watched them enter the tunnel, then walked the perimeter of the room.

Nicole Rollins said, "No place to hide here."

True. The room off the main storage area had no door. They'd already been in there. Lucy paced, assessing the guns and space. "I'm from California. Most houses don't have basements. My brother had one in DC, but we didn't do anything with it."

"I lived in Kansas until I was fourteen," Nicole said. "Spent lots of time in the cellar during tornado season. My dad fixed it up with a television, radio, games—my brothers had an extra game system down there. Lots of batteries."

"I've never been through a tornado."

"Just wait, you'll experience it soon."

Her stomach lurched. Lucy had gone through many earthquakes, but tornadoes freaked her out. It was like God put His finger down on each individual house that was destroyed, whereas earthquakes were just big shakes of temper and everything crumbled.

"Donnelly will bring in a team to catalog and impound everything," Nicole said as they finished the second sweep of the room to verify there were no more trapdoors or hiding places.

Lucy went back into the smaller room where it was obvious that drugs had been packaged and money counted. The computer was new; the electronics team would seize it and analyze the data. She was good with computers and itched to turn it on, but refrained. Instead she looked under all the shelves, for anything that might be helpful to the investigation.

"How long have you worked with Donnelly?" Lucy asked Nicole conversationally.

"Awhile," she said.

"Why doesn't he like rookies?"

She hesitated. "What makes you think that?"

"He said so."

"Well, you're here, aren't you?"

"I sensed there was something more to it."

Nicole stood in the doorway at such an angle that she could see the main room, her back to Lucy. She was shorter than Lucy, but more muscular, as if she worked out daily with weights. She was also older, late thirties or forties. The fine lines around her eyes were getting deeper, though she wore a thick layer of makeup to hide them. "Few years ago, before I transferred here from Atlanta, he lost a rookie in an operation. I don't know much about it, but he blamed himself, blamed the kid, blamed the cartel that set them up. He never works with rookies anymore. He wants five years' experience before he'll let you on his team." She glanced at her. "So I'm surprised you're here."

So was Lucy. She simply said, "My experience is a bit different from most."

She squatted and looked under the desk. The floor had been scraped, like the desk had been moved back and forth numerous times. She holstered her gun and pushed the desk to the right.

"Hey," Nicole said, "don't touch anything."

In the ground was a metal box. It was level with the floor, small enough to be completely concealed by the desk.

"It's a hidden box."

"It could be booby-trapped."

As Nicole spoke, there was commotion on the com. Then Lucy heard, "Both suspects are secured. We're coming back through to the store, be ready."

Several minutes later Donnelly and Johnson walked through the tunnel opening with two cuffed suspects. "Sit," Donnelly ordered in Spanish.

They complied. They were dirty, and one had blood on his nose.

"Well, that was fun." Donnelly grinned. "You good, Johnson?"

"Yes, sir."

"I need to show you something," Lucy said.

Donnelly motioned for Johnson and Nicole to watch the suspects, then followed Lucy into the smaller room.

"I saw the scraping on the floor, pushed the desk, and found that. I didn't touch it."

Donnelly squatted. He checked for triggers and wires, anything that might injure them if they disturbed the box. "It's clear," he said. He picked it up and put it on the desk. There was a combination lock on the front. "Shit," he said, "I'll have to wait for our techs to open it."

"May I try?" she said.

He tilted his head, skeptical. "If you can."

She put her ear to the lock and closed her eyes. Sean had taught her to pick locks in more ways than one. She wasn't as good—or fast—as her boyfriend, but a simple mechanism like this was a breeze. In a minute she had it unlocked, but she didn't open it.

"Done."

"Open it," he said. "Carefully."

She did. Inside there was a black leather ledger. "Holy shit," Donnelly said. He pulled it out and turned the pages. "Beautiful. It's in code, but I know what this is—records. Buyers, transfers, locations. The works. Our code breakers will figure it out." He grinned widely and slid the ledger into a plastic evidence bag, then walked through to the main room.

"Good work," he said. "No shots fired, no one got hurt, guns seized, the ledger and computer seized, five suspects in custody. I'd say this operation was a success. Now let's get these two assholes locked up and find Jaime Sanchez."

Michael watched Mrs. Pope water her flowers on the large porch attached to the small house. He remembered sitting cross-legged on the old planks transplanting dozens of small plants from a tray of seedlings Mrs. Pope had bought at a big discount at the hardware store. They all looked dead to him, but she said nonsense, they just needed love and food and a gentle hand.

He squeezed his eyes shut, blinking away tears. He would not cry. He didn't have the time to feel sorry for himself.

What are you going to do now?

He didn't know why he'd come here. He'd planned to head south, back to the border to rescue the others. But he'd barely gotten out of the Sanchezes' neighborhood.

Jaime was looking for him, and Michael thought he saw him everywhere. So he laid low, hiding in an alley behind a Dumpster, fear eating at him more than his hunger.

Bella had packed him tortillas and water, and he ate one and drank an entire water bottle, even though he knew he should save it. But he kept the empty container; he'd refill it when he could.

It was while he sat there, trying to ignore the stench, trying to make himself invisible, that he thought about Hector and Olive. Just as Michael knew that Jaime would kill him, he knew that Hector and Olive would help him. He wanted to sit in their kitchen, the smells of snickerdoodle cookies and homemade *carnitas* and spices that he equated with love and a full stomach.

He couldn't remember a time in the last fourteen months when he hadn't been hungry.

At dawn he found himself walking across the city, keeping to the shadows, using alleys when he could. Staying off the main roads, staying out of the neighborhoods where one of Jaime's people might recognize him. It took him hours, but he found himself in this neighborhood—across the street from the house that had saved him. Across the street from the woman he loved as much as a mother.

Olive had lost weight. She'd always been a plump woman, with warm folds that smelled like the vanilla lotion she liked so much. She was still plump, but no longer like a Mexican Mrs. Claus. Her hair was short and streaked gray. Were there more gray hairs than before?

He'd never wanted to hurt Olive. He respected Hector, but he loved Olive. Hector was a man who worked long hours, a man who never raised his fist or his voice. He remembered one night Hector had come home with daisies. They were yellow and fresh, a little wilted from the heat; he'd bought them from a street vendor. He gave them to

Olive with a smile and a kiss on her cheek. She had tears in her eyes, happy tears she told him.

Michael had said, "It's not your birthday."

She shook her head. "It's an anniversary."

"Your wedding anniversary?"

"No. The day he saw me, working behind the counter of the Dairy Queen. He said it was the day that changed his life."

Michael didn't understand what that meant, but he knew that Hector and Olive loved each other, that she couldn't have children for some medical reason she didn't explain to him, and that Olive had more love to give than anyone Michael had known.

Olive stood at the top of the stairs and looked out onto the street. Did she see him? No way, he was too well hidden. And she didn't have on her glasses. She could barely see without them. She wiped her hands absently on her apron. Then she slowly turned and went inside.

Michael couldn't risk going to the Popes for help. They would love him and hug him and call CPS because he was a runaway. CPS would take him away from them, no doubt. Michael didn't trust anyone with CPS or the government or the police. Someone there had to have told Jaime where Michael lived. How else would he have been able to track him down? This wasn't a neighborhood anywhere near the ghetto where Michael had grown up. The Popes had sent him to Catholic school, something they could scarcely afford, but they knew the priest and Michael suspected Olive volunteered many hours just so Michael didn't have to go to the public school where people from his past might hurt him.

Not your past. Your father. You didn't do anything. It was him.

Didn't matter. He was still running from his father's

crimes, his father who refused to sign away parental rights even though the first chance he might get out of prison Michael would be over thirty. He did it out of anger, spite, the belief that Michael was his property. He didn't want Michael to have anything, not even parents who loved him.

Michael couldn't risk Hector and Olive. He couldn't return to the only house he'd ever thought of as a home.

Not until he saved the others.

He dug around Bella's backpack and tore a page from the back of a book. He wrote with a broken pencil, folded the paper, and waited until Olive had been in the house for ten minutes before he risked exposure.

He left his hiding spot and ran across the street. He didn't hesitate, but ran up the porch steps. He heard water running in the kitchen. He wanted to go inside. To see Olive. Instead he slipped the paper through the mail slot and, as quietly as possible, left.

CHAPTER 4

By the time the investigative unit arrived at the hardware store to take over for Donnelly's team, it was after three in the afternoon and no one had eaten since five a.m. Brad Donnelly brought pizza back to DEA headquarters for everyone, excited that they had a lead on Jaime—as thin as it was. He was working with the AUSA to write up the paperwork on George Sanchez's deal and set up interrogations of the five men they'd arrested. The only hiccup so far was that the prisoners weren't talking—they'd all lawyered up. But Brad didn't seem too frustrated. He had the computer, the ledger, and George Sanchez.

All in all, a damn good day, he'd said more than once.

The good day ended for Lucy when she and Ryan sat down with a mountain of paperwork. They had to write up not only reports for the sweep and the raid, but then separate reports for their boss, Supervisory Special Agent Juan Casilla.

"This is going to take half the night," Ryan grumbled. "At least we didn't have to discharge our weapons—that would be another mountain of paperwork, plus a debriefing, plus a psych eval."

"Sounds fun," Lucy said. She dreaded the potential of a

psychological evaluation. She'd been through so many of them she thought they might *make* her crazy.

They worked in silence for a few minutes; then Sean returned her call from earlier. "Hi," she answered.

"You rang?"

"When I was on my break."

"Whoops. I was talking to Patrick."

"How's my brother?"

"Working a case for Duke at my old alma mater."

"Which one?"

"The one where I actually got my degree."

"He's at MIT?"

"He needed my technical expertise."

"You love it when he asks for help."

"I do," Sean admitted, the grin in his voice. "And I'm going to savor the call from Duke when he gets my bill."

"You're *billing* him?"

"I warned everyone at RCK; I'm no longer working for free."

"He probably won't even notice. Isn't Nora's baby due any day?"

"The littlest Rogan is technically due in two weeks, but Nora's on full bed rest. It's driving both her and Duke insane, I'm sure. She's almost as much of a workaholic as you."

"Speaking of being a workaholic, I'm stuck at DEA headquarters doing paperwork."

"How late?"

"Six, seven? Tex-Mex is fine." Sean had sampled many of the local restaurants and already had his favorites.

"Rib House it is, then."

She laughed. "Can I bring Ryan? He's here working with me, and Nate's been blabbing about how he's been over to the house several times. Ryan's jealous."

Ryan shot her a dirty look, but then nodded, eyes wide. She laughed.

"The more the merrier. I'll get plenty."

"You always get too much."

"Leftovers taste even better. Work fast. I love you."

"Love you, too." She smiled as she hung up.

"Tex-Mex?"

She shook her head. "Sean discovered this place called The Rib House. He's addicted."

Ryan practically licked his lips. "Best BBQ in Texas."

"Do you have the boys this weekend? You can bring them."

"No." His face clouded, and he focused on their paperwork. Ryan was going through a nasty divorce and had two young sons. His wife had moved ninety minutes north to Austin, making it difficult for him to visit the boys during the week. He had custody every other weekend.

"Well, they're always welcome. We have a swimming pool and Sean has a game room. He's a big kid himself, at least when it comes to his toys."

They chatted as they worked. Some reports had to be handwritten, most input in the computer. Donnelly walked in just after five. "Almost done?"

"Getting there," Ryan mumbled. "Maybe thirty more minutes. Hour, tops."

"Can I borrow Kincaid for a minute?"

Ryan grew suspicious. Even though Lucy had explained to Ryan about Donnelly's strategy at the Sanchez house, Ryan thought it had gone too far and accused Donnelly—at least to Lucy—of being a hot dog who took unnecessary risks.

But he shrugged. "Up to her."

"You both did great work," Donnelly said. "I'm putting it in my report to your SSA."

"Thank you," Lucy said when Ryan didn't answer. She followed Donnelly from the room, giving Ryan a look. He simply shook his head and waved her off.

"What's his beef?" Donnelly asked.

"It's nothing."

Donnelly assessed her. "It was about this morning. At the house."

"It's fine. I should have briefed him better."

"I've worked with Ryan in the past, and he's a good cop, but he's a straight arrow. Doesn't like games."

"It wasn't a game," she said.

"And that's why we work well together. You get it."

She wasn't exactly sure what he meant.

"I need you to talk to a guy from CPS. He came around about the kid, Michael—he thinks he knows who this Michael is. I don't have time to deal with it, and your boss already said the FBI is lead on the missing kid."

That was news to Lucy, but she and Ryan had been processing paperwork for so long she hadn't even thought to call in or check her email.

Donnelly walked her down a long row of interview rooms. He opened one and said, "Hey, Charlie, good to see you again." He extended his hand. "Charlie DeSantos, this is FBI Special Agent Lucy Kincaid. She's been working with me on the Sanchez case, and is point on the missing boy."

Charlie extended his hand to Lucy. He was tall and lean with permanent scaring from long-ago acne, but a warm and friendly smile. "Agent Kincaid." He glanced from her to Brad. "I didn't realize the FBI had already been called in."

"Kincaid's part of Operation Heatwave."

"I heard about that."

"Kincaid and her partner are staying on for a few more days, until we figure out what exactly is going on with the kid. I'd sit in on the meeting, but I need to debrief my boss.

If you and Lucy can figure out if our cases intersect, that would help me."

"Of course," Charlie said. "Good to see you again, Brad."

"Call if you need anything." Then Brad was gone, leaving Lucy alone with Charlie DeSantos.

Lucy motioned for him to sit and took out a small notepad.

"Are you new?" he asked her. "I've worked with several agents in the FBI, but don't remember meeting you."

"Yes, I graduated from the academy in December. Been here for nearly three months now."

"And already on a major task force."

"Trial by fire," she said with a half smile. "Brad said you might know who Michael is?"

"I'm afraid I might," he said. He sighed and rubbed his face, looking both angry and defeated. "I got a call this morning from one of my foster families. The woman thought she'd seen a boy who'd run away from their home last year. At first I thought it was wishful thinking on her part—she and her husband wanted to adopt this boy. His name is Michael Rodriguez. CPS was alerted about the DEA sweep— often, as you know, children get swept up, too, and need a temporary bed, so we work behind the scenes to make sure there are enough places to take them. When I heard that the DEA was looking for a boy named Michael who may have been held captive by a drug dealer, I wondered if it was more than a coincidence that Mrs. Pope thought she saw him. It took me some time to figure out who was in charge, but when I found out that Agent Donnelly had been the team leader, I called him."

"Why do you think that your Michael Rodriguez is the Michael in my case?"

"I have no reason other than the call I had this morning, and the common name. But I needed to follow up. It may be a coincidence—it may not be."

He was obviously worried about the boy, and maybe his information could help Lucy track Michael.

"I don't have information about him," she said, "other than what a witness told me."

Charlie was surprised. "A witness? The report didn't say there was a witness."

"A minor in the house saw the boy, attests to the fact that he was kept against his will. Confirmed his name was Michael, that he'd been locked up for about a month."

"What about anyone else? Donnelly said there were arrests."

"I really can't share any information about the case without clearing it with Donnelly."

DeSantos sighed heavily. "And that's why I wanted to talk to him, not a junior agent."

She raised an eyebrow.

"I didn't mean it like that, Agent Kincaid. I'm sorry. It's just I understand how information is disseminated, and I'm sure you dislike bureaucracy as much as the rest of us."

She leaned forward. "Perhaps if you give me a reason to believe that your Michael and our Michael are the same boy, I can ask him to clear you."

He slid a file over to her.

She opened it. On the left was a photo of Michael Rodriguez at age eleven. He'd turned thirteen last month. When he disappeared fourteen months ago, on the last day of January, he'd been five feet one inch tall and weighed in at one hundred pounds. He'd been in the foster care system for three years when he ran away, but had been placed in the same family for the last fifteen months before he bolted.

"He ran away?"

"That's what we all thought, but I don't know now. And at the time, the Popes were certain he hadn't run away."

"Runaways aren't uncommon in foster care."

"I know, unfortunately. His foster parents were going through the process of adopting him."

Lucy turned the page. His mother was dead, his father was incarcerated, twenty-five-to-life for murder.

She looked up at DeSantos. His expression was unreadable, but his dark eyes scanned hers in the hope of answers.

"This was your case?"

He nodded. "Michael had been in and out of bad homes for nearly two years. It was just dumb luck that he landed with the Popes and they clicked. I need to talk to your witness, show her Michael's picture, confirm what I already suspect. She might know more."

Lucy thought that as well.

"I'll talk to her, show her the picture."

"I need to see her."

"I don't think that's possible."

"Then who can make it possible?" he demanded.

Lucy wasn't going to let him bully her. "Mr. DeSantos," she said firmly, "I doubt it's the same boy. My Michael was locked in a basement for four weeks. Your Michael has been gone for fourteen months. But since the ages and basic descriptions match, I'll talk to my witness. I'll share with you what I learn. That's going to have to be good enough."

He wanted to argue with her, she could see it in his eyes; then he capitulated. "I understand," he said. "But turn the page."

She did. Behind Michael's official records was a page torn from a paperback book. At the bottom was scrawled in faint pencil:

I'm sorry I had to leave. I want to come home more than anything, but I have to do something important and I might not be able to come back. Thank you for wanting me in the first place.
—M

Lucy's heart twisted.

"Olive Pope found this through the mail slot in her front door and called me. I've known Donnelly for a while, so when I found out it was his case, I came here. Then Brad hands me off to you. I'm sorry I'm a little frustrated."

"Brad referred you to me because he's hunting for a fugitive and my partner and I are looking for Michael."

"Let me help. He trusts me." Charlie rubbed the back of his neck. "Fourteen months ago I assumed like everyone else he ran away. Except—the Popes wouldn't let it go. So I might have let their faith affect me. I want to find him. For them. They never believed he ran away, and this proves it. But obviously something else is going on with him, if as you say he was held as a prisoner."

A boy like Michael, in the system with no hope of being reunited with blood relatives—why would he leave a home that seemed to be working for him?

"I think he left because he felt he had to. Maybe he was threatened or the Popes were threatened." Lucy was thinking out loud, but it felt right to her, looking again at the note.

"How can you get that from his few words?"

"He said he had to leave. He's been gone for fourteen months." She flipped back a few pages and read the brief notes on Michael's father, Vince Rodriguez. "His father—he's in prison for murder?"

DeSantos nodded. "He killed a liquor store clerk and paralyzed a customer while robbing the place. Hard man. Abused Michael. His wife—Michael's mother—died under suspicious circumstances when Michael was eight, but there were no charges filed."

"This address—is this where Michael grew up?"

"More or less."

The address where Michael grew up was only blocks

from the hardware store on 39th, where Sanchez and his gang had set up shop. Coincidence? What were the chances that they knew each other? The older Rodriguez and Jaime Sanchez? Or someone affiliated with Sanchez?

"Agent Kincaid?" DeSantos asked. "What are you thinking?"

"Nothing," she said. She wasn't going to share with De-Santos unless Donnelly cleared it. "I'll follow up on this, call you as soon as I can confirm one way or the other that we're talking about the same kid. If we are—"

"You'll let me help find him."

"It's up to Donnelly, but I'm sure you can be a help."

"Of course I will be," he snapped.

Hot and cold. She didn't know what to make of DeSantos, but she wrote her cell phone number on the back of her FBI business card. "Let me know if Michael reaches out again to the Popes, or to you. I'll do the same once I confirm his identity." She was about to walk him out when she said, "Michael wasn't the first boy kept in captivity. There was evidence that others had been in the basement. Do you know of any other missing boys like Michael?"

He shook his head, then seemed to reconsider. "I don't know specifically, but there are a lot of runaways in the system. You can't always blame them—some foster parents are good, some are not. They have problems—parents in prison, abuse, violence, even drug use—and they're not always willing or able to accept help. Could some of those runaways have been kidnapped? It's possible."

Lucy was going to ask him for a list, but realized that was bringing him into the investigation, and right now she wanted to confirm that he even had a stake in it before she gave him more. Besides, she could get the information through the FBI and their channels.

"I'll be in touch."

"I hope that's not the brush-off."

"It's not." She held on to the file. "Can I keep this?"

"Sure, it's a copy." He touched her arm. "But I'm going to hold you to your word that you'll let me know the minute you have his ID confirmed."

"I promise."

Father Mateo Flannigan sat in the confessional at St. Catherine's waiting for the next penitent to enter. It had been a long day, made longer because it was Lent, and many Catholics took the season as a time to go back to church. Many came for a few weeks and then left again, but some stayed, their faith renewed.

Mateo was tired. He was a faithful man, young, healthy. He'd been called to the priesthood as a child, knew this was what he was meant to do. He never doubted the call.

What he too often doubted was humanity. He used to enjoy the Sacrament of Confession; now it had become a chore, a punishment. He had nightmares about his parishioners. He'd been thinking of asking for a sabbatical because he didn't know if being a parish priest was his calling. There were other ways to serve. Ways that didn't leave him with sleepless nights.

He didn't like the secrets he was forced to keep. He understood that it was Jesus who forgave, that he was only the vehicle, but he couldn't unhear sins. He prayed and begged God to take the images that were in his head. Sometimes it worked.

Mostly, it didn't.

The light went on as the next parishioner stepped in. "Forgive me, Father, for I have sinned. It has been fourteen months since my last confession."

The voice was young, male, and familiar. One of the students at the school.

Mateo said a brief prayer and asked the boy what he wanted Jesus to forgive.

"My friend was murdered and I didn't stop it."

Mateo's stomach clenched. This wasn't the first time he'd heard a child confess to witnessing a violent crime.

"What happened, son?"

"I can't tell you."

"You're not telling me. You're telling God."

"I stole something that didn't belong to me. I gave it back, but my friend was killed because of what I did."

Killed? A child was killed?

"Have you gone to the police? Told a parent?"

"I can't. That's why I'm here. I'm going to die and I don't want to go to Hell."

"Son, you did not kill your friend."

"I've killed others. Other people. People I didn't know. I was weak. I should have said no but I was so scared. I would have died if I said no. I'm not scared anymore."

Michael. It was Michael, Mateo knew it was the boy who had run away. What had happened to him?

"Son," Mateo said, trying to keep his voice calm. "Are you confessing to taking a human life?"

"Yes. Six. I didn't want to. I don't deserve forgiveness. I don't know why I'm here."

"Because you want to repent."

"I can't."

"Yes, you can. We all deserve forgiveness. God forgives."

"I have to go."

"Please—Michael—"

"Don't, Father. I don't want anyone else hurt. You can't tell anyone I was here. You can't!"

"Your mother, Olive, she's worried."

"You can't say anything!" He was crying, and Mateo

wanted to go to him, but he couldn't. He was trapped in this damn booth. He almost cursed God for what he had to endure, what he had promised to uphold. He understood the principle, he respected the reasons, but this was a boy who was suffering, and Mateo couldn't do anything but talk.

"Okay, Michael, I won't say a word. God knows what's in your heart, He knows that you're repenting. Pray for guidance, pray for strength. You only need to ask for my help and I will give it."

Michael didn't say anything, but the light was on, so Mateo knew he was still there.

"I left Olive a note," Michael finally said. "Father, I am sorry for everything I've done. I didn't want to hurt anyone. But I'm not scared anymore."

He sounded terrified.

"I have to go back. There's only one thing I can do to fix this."

"You've done it. You've asked for forgiveness."

"You don't understand."

But Mateo did. He understood more than Michael could know.

"Please give me absolution, Father."

Mateo gave the boy absolution. Then he said, "Absolution is for past sins. Not future sins. Michael, think about what you plan to do. There is always someone who can help."

The light went out. Michael was gone.

CHAPTER 5

Ryan followed Lucy to Olmos Park, an older, exclusive neighborhood only ten minutes from FBI headquarters. She pulled into the garage, then walked around the front to greet Ryan on the tiled front path. Ryan whistled softly. "Nate was right."

"About what?" she asked as she typed a code into the keypad next to the door.

"Nice digs."

"Sean picked it out," she said. "He surprised me." The door unlocked and Lucy stepped in.

"Neither of my ex-wives would have trusted me to buy a house without them." Ryan eyed the keypad. "I don't think I've seen one of those on a house before."

"Sean is security-conscious."

Ryan whistled again at the sweeping terra-cotta tile staircase that curved up to the second story. Alternating cobalt-blue and hand-painted Mexican tiles accented the foyer and stairs. In the summer—and on warm spring days like today—the tile kept the house cool.

"We were lucky we could move in quickly," Lucy said. "I didn't even know I was being assigned to San Antonio until three weeks before I had to report in. Sean contacted a realtor, then a couple days after Christmas he flew out to look at a few places. He sent me pictures of three, but I loved them all so told him to pick."

The smell of Texas barbecue filled the house. Her phone vibrated and she looked down. He'd sent her a text message.

I'm in my office on the phone. Offer Ryan a beer.

She laughed. "Sean told me to offer you a beer."

"Sounds great. I need it after today." He glanced around. "How did he know you're here?"

She pointed to the camera in the corner of the foyer. Ryan squinted. "I would never have seen it."

"We have reasons to be cautious."

They walked down the wide, tiled hall, past the open dining room she and Sean had yet to eat in, to the kitchen. The kitchen had been remodeled by the previous owners to fit the Mission-style architecture. That's what Lucy loved most about the place—it looked old, but everything was new. All the details fit the period, from the tiles to the tall, arched windows to the wood beams in the ceiling. The house was too big for them, but as Sean pointed out, she had six brothers and sisters, he had four, and they had friends who now had a place to stay.

"*Plus,*" he'd added, "*we have two nieces or nephews on the way and someday we'll adopt a few of our own.*"

Lucy couldn't have children. That Sean was not only willing but excited to adopt in the future gave her a contentment she didn't know she needed until he'd said it.

She said to Ryan, "We have Samuel Adams, Dos Equis, and Harp."

"American, Mexican, and Irish?" He laughed. "Sam Adams, thanks."

Lucy didn't care much for beer, but she picked up a Harp for herself, which she'd grown to enjoy. She gave Ryan a tour of the downstairs, which included the media room where Sean had created a theater and game center. "Now I know why Nate loves this place. You guys have every video game known to man. And movies."

Lucy smiled. "Sean spoils himself."

"What does your boyfriend do?" Ryan asked.

"He was a principal in a security company for the last few years. His brothers founded it, and two of my brothers joined later. My brother Patrick was Sean's partner. Now Sean's renewing his PI license in Texas."

"Personal security?"

"Not so much. Computer security, mostly. Companies hire him to break into their networks or buildings and find weak spots, then Sean plugs the holes."

"Smart guy."

They sat in the sunroom. The sun had gone down—it was nearly seven—and the temperature had fallen enough to make it comfortable. Sean came in through the side door. He smiled when he saw Lucy and leaned over to kiss her. Twice. Then he reached over and took Ryan's hand. "Good to finally meet you, Ryan," he said. "I told Lucy to plan a party, but she's not much of a party planner. *I'm* starving, and I didn't just take down a major drug operation."

Lucy looked at him. "Where'd you hear? I didn't give you details."

"No, but Nate did. As much as he knew, anyway."

Lucy had to remember that Sean and Nate had hit it off and apparently talked a lot more than she'd thought. She shouldn't be surprised: They were close in age, had many of the same interests, and Nate—like Sean's brother Kane— had been a Marine. Nate, like Lucy, was still an FBI rookie. It took two years to lose the rookie label. Nate had one year in.

"I invited Nate to come by, but he has a date." Sean grinned.

"Michelle or Kendall?" Ryan asked.

"Trista."

"Trista? Who's that?"

"Don't know. I offered to run a full background on her, for free, but Nate hung up on me."

"If you don't mind," Lucy said, "I'm going to run upstairs and take a fast shower."

Ryan said, "I used the gym at SAPD. You know they have a women's shower, too."

"I didn't have time," Lucy said, though that was only partly true. She didn't like showering in public areas, even if they were semi-private showers. She hated the feeling of being watched, even when she wasn't. She leaned over and kissed Sean. He understood. That's another reason why she loved him so much.

Sean watched Lucy leave. He'd seen the exhaustion in her eyes, but she wouldn't slow down. It wasn't in her DNA. At the same time, this move had been good for her. For both of them. Lucy loved her job, and Sean loved when Lucy was happy.

He gave Ryan a discreet once-over. He'd met Lucy's boss, as well as Nate Dunning who'd been in the office the day Sean had taken Lucy for lunch on her birthday last month. Since then, Nate had been over several times. Not only common interests, but Nate was comfortable to be around, as if Sean had known him for years instead of six weeks. The only other person Sean felt that way about was Lucy's brother, Patrick.

Lucy had talked a lot about Ryan, mostly because they'd been working together on Operation Heatwave. She liked him, and Lucy was a good judge of character. But Sean still wanted to know who was watching her back when he wasn't.

"I'm going to grab a beer," Sean said. "Ready for another?"

"I will be." Ryan followed Sean back to the kitchen. He gestured toward children's drawings on a bulletin board in the breakfast nook. "Lucy said you didn't have kids. Nieces? Nephews?"

"No," Sean said. "We have two on the way—my brother's wife is expecting any day, and Lucy's sister is expecting in June. Those are from a kid we helped out of a jam last fall."

"Lucy's good with kids. We had two minors, girls, during the sweep today. Mother made it difficult, we had to arrest her."

"Micah and Tommy's mom got involved with the wrong guy. She ended up dead. They're living with their grandparents in Florida now." Micah wrote to Lucy every two or three weeks and included drawings from his six-year-old brother, Tommy. The boys seemed to be adjusting well. "Lucy said the sweep was a success, but that your team got reassigned? I got some details from Nate, but he didn't know much."

"Missing kid. He was locked in the basement for a couple of weeks and one of the minors let him out. The DEA was leading our team, so all our warrants were related to drugs. Lucy and Donnelly, the team leader, flipped one brother against the other. We've already gotten some good intel on the drug pipeline and shut down a storage facility. Guns, drugs. It's going to be big."

"What kind of drug pipeline?"

Ryan hesitated. Suspicious, maybe, or just cautious.

Sean said, "The kids, Micah and Tommy? Their mother's boyfriend was cooking meth in the middle of the woods. National forest. His brother was a ranger, in on it. Good-sized lab in a trailer, DEA figured it was a multimillion-dollar operation that supported the entire DC area."

Lucy stepped into the kitchen. She looked a million times better, her face bright, her wet hair pulled back into a ponytail. Sean loved it when she was fresh out of the shower, no makeup, just her beautiful self. He kissed her. "Telling stories, Sean?" she said with a grin.

"Just trying to get Ryan to spill the beans on your operation today." He opened the oven and pulled out a tray of BBQ.

"There's something more going on here than simple drug dealing," Lucy said. "I didn't tell you about the conversation with DeSantos from CPS."

"No," Sean and Ryan said simultaneously.

"DeSantos thinks that Michael, the boy Bella helped escape from the basement, is Michael Rodriguez, a thirteen-year-old from foster care who ran away last year. Allegedly ran away."

"Allegedly?" Sean brought plates to the kitchen island, which had stools all around. "Okay to eat here?" he asked.

"Absolutely," Ryan said.

"Help yourself." Sean loaded up his plate.

While they ate, Lucy continued.

"Michael's father is in prison and might have a connection to people connected to Sanchez. I'm going to dig around." She frowned, licked spicy BBQ sauce from her fingers. "Here's the thing that's been bugging me since I talked to CPS. Michael Rodriguez has been gone for fourteen months—no word from him until he left a cryptic note for his foster parents only hours after Bella let him out."

"So you *do* think it's the same kid?" Ryan said.

She nodded. "Too much of a coincidence not to be. I'm going to show Bella his picture tomorrow. We need the confirmation."

"Why didn't he go inside? Talk to the foster parents?" Sean asked. "Were they abusive?"

"I read their file," Lucy said. "And the note. He's scared of something, but it's not the Pope family."

Ryan said, "I dealt with a lot of street kids in Houston,

and most are working their way up the wrong side of the law. Sounds like this kid is doing the same. Can't say that I don't understand how—his mom's dead, his dad's in prison, it's what he knows."

Lucy shook her head. "Sometimes, not always. And he was locked up for four weeks. Maybe longer. That makes this different."

"I gather your prisoners aren't talking about Michael," Sean said.

"Sanchez will, I'm pretty sure, but Donnelly is focused on working out the deal with the AUSA. Donnelly wants Jaime Sanchez bad. His sheet is long and violent, so I'm not surprised, but I think there's more."

"What's with that guy?" Ryan said. Sean slid him over another beer, opened one for himself. Lucy shook her head, and Sean gave her water and a kiss. "What was going on this morning?"

"I explained that," Lucy said.

"Explain to me," Sean said. "Since I have no idea what you're talking about."

"It's nothing—it was an interview tactic to get the brother to talk."

"Donnelly stepped over the line," Ryan said.

"I agreed to it," Lucy said.

"Agreed to what?" Sean asked.

"Good cop, bad cop," Lucy said. "I was the good cop, the bleeding heart, challenging the big, bad angry Donnelly. It worked. We got what we wanted."

Ryan snorted. "He yelled at you, threatened you, and attempted to humiliate you."

"It was an act," she said again. "Ryan, I appreciate your chivalry, but I was cool with it." She glanced at Sean. "It was *fine*."

She didn't like the look on Sean's face. It was subtle—Ryan might not even notice—but Sean was protective of her. She understood it, and loved him for it, but at the same time, he sometimes said or did things that could get him into trouble.

"You got what you needed?" Sean confirmed.

"Yes. It was a good day. Now we just need to find Michael, track down Jaime Sanchez, and decode the ledger we found."

"Ledger?" His ears perked up.

"It's in the hands of the DEA," Lucy said. "I couldn't show you if I wanted to."

"Hmm. Maybe I need to point out to the local feds here that I have security clearance to consult."

"You're impossible," she said with a smile.

She started to clear the plates, but Sean took them from her. "You worked all day. Nearly fifteen hours by my count. Sit."

"You're spoiling me."

"You'll make it up to me later."

She laughed. Her phone vibrated on the counter and she picked it up.

"It's Donnelly," she said and answered. "This is Lucy."

"It's Brad Donnelly. George Sanchez was murdered. I need you and Quiroz at SAPD immediately."

CHAPTER 6

Lucy walked into the main San Antonio Police Station flanked by Ryan and Sean. They each signed in and were assigned visitor badges, then ushered into the briefing room. Donnelly was there with several other cops, both uniformed and plainclothes. From the heated conversation, Donnelly was demanding to know how George Sanchez had died. He wanted logs, cameras, interviews. His partner, Nicole Rollins, stood to the side, taking notes.

Lucy stood on the periphery, and after a couple of cops left to get information Donnelly wanted, she said, "You don't know what happened?"

"Poison," Donnelly said.

Rollins said, "We don't know."

"What else could it be?" Donnelly snapped. "He was served a late dinner at eight fifteen because the AUSA and I were with him before that, and twenty minutes later he's dead? No blood, no visible trauma, he's found on the floor of his cell? I'll bet my pension he was poisoned."

"Do you have his medicals?" Lucy asked. "Was he allergic to anything?"

"An allergy that kills someone in twenty minutes?"

"Severe enough allergies—some people with peanut or

seafood allergies in particular, if they don't get immediate treatment, can die because their airways constrict. They suffocate."

"His skin was reddish," Donnelly said, considering. He nodded to Rollins, who went over to a computer and started typing.

"Possibly hives," Lucy said. "A skin reaction is common."

"It can't have been a fucking accident," Donnelly said. "Not when we just cut a deal. I don't believe this!" He stared at Sean. "Who are you?"

"Sean Rogan," Sean said.

"He's with me," Lucy said.

"Rogan?" Donnelly tilted his head and stared. "Any relation to Kane Rogan?"

"My brother."

Recognition and surprise crossed Donnelly's eyes. Sean had seen it before. His brother was rather infamous, especially with federal law enforcement who worked the border or drugs. Some loved him, some hated him, most respected him. Sean couldn't tell which side of the line Donnelly was on, but he hoped it wouldn't be a problem for Lucy.

Donnelly said to Lucy, "Why didn't you tell me your brother-in-law was Kane Rogan?"

"He's not my brother-in-law," Lucy said.

Yet, Sean thought.

"And I haven't even met him," Lucy added. "Why?"

"Nothing."

It wasn't nothing. "How do you know Kane?" Sean asked.

"An op I was on a few years ago." Donnelly didn't elaborate, nor did he ban Sean from the briefing room. He said, "We're waiting on the ME. No way it can be done tonight, but he's expediting first thing in the morning."

"No cameras?" Lucy asked.

Ryan shook his head. "Not in the holding cells for arraignment. There're cameras on the corridors and common areas, but not individual cells."

"What about his lawyer?"

"He didn't ask for one until tonight, to go over the papers the AUSA drew up. A public defender. So far clean, only met briefly."

Nicole approached. "Sanchez's meds indicate he has a severe shellfish allergy. He was served hamburger, an apple, and milk."

"Do you have the food?" Lucy asked.

"What was left has been bagged," Donnelly said. "This isn't my first rodeo." He took a deep breath. "Sorry."

"We're all frustrated," Nicole said.

Donnelly continued. "We kept him isolated because we knew he'd be in danger as soon as word leaked he was turning state's evidence—but there should have been no way that anyone could have known he was helping us yet. The public defender is clean, though we're going to look deeper."

Ryan said, "The raid tipped them."

"No one knew Sanchez gave us that information."

"It's deductive reasoning," Ryan said. "Maybe not many people knew about the hardware storefront. They could have learned real quick that Sanchez is in custody. We snatched him before eight this morning. If he was poisoned he could have been poisoned anytime today."

"Not if it was anaphylaxis," Lucy said. "A severe allergic reaction is going to show up within minutes. Thirty, tops."

"We don't know if that's what it was," Donnelly said.

"He would have felt something, known he was having a reaction," Lucy said. "None of the guards noticed anything? Heard anything?"

"Maybe," Sean suggested, "it wasn't a food allergy, but a more deadly poison."

"We have everything bagged and tagged and I'll flag the allergy for the ME," Donnelly said. Whether he was irritated with Sean for his comments, or just frustrated with the situation, Sean couldn't tell. "I have my team running deep backgrounds on every guard on duty tonight, everyone who had access to his meal. Because it was after hours, the food was brought in, not made on-site." He rubbed his face. "Dammit. He was cooperating!"

"Maybe it was natural," Rollins suggested.

"Twenty-nine-year-old healthy adult male dying spontaneously of natural causes on the eve of turning state's evidence against a notorious criminal?" Donnelly pointed to Lucy and Ryan. "I need a complete time line from the minute we took custody of Sanchez until he died. You weren't alone with Sanchez, Quiroz, but Kincaid was. I need to know who talked to him, who was in the room, anyone who might have had an opportunity to slip him something. We cover all the bases here. It may have been in his food, it may have happened earlier. I'm not ruling out suicide, either."

"Guilt," Lucy said. "He might have had second thoughts about turning on his brother. Realized he'd dug a hole and thought killing himself was the only way he wouldn't talk."

"I'm getting a lot of heat over this, as should be expected. If it was someone else losing a key witness, I'd be giving them shit, too."

"You need to put a guard on Mirabelle Borez," Ryan said. "If Sanchez was targeted because of the threat of him spilling his guts, then she may be in danger."

Donnelly pointed at Nicole, and she left the room. "Done." He handed Lucy a file. "This is everything on Sanchez from the sweep this morning until his death. I need you to double-check my facts and the time line, and include your own. I want every minute of his day documented." He glanced from Lucy to Sean. "Sorry to ruin your date night."

"Every night is date night," Sean said.

Donnelly nodded. The subtle exchange was between him and Sean. Lucy didn't see it, but Brad got it. Lucy was off-limits.

How Lucy could be so clueless that men found her attractive, Sean would never understand.

"I'll bring in the coffee," Sean said.

"There's coffee here," Donnelly said.

"I'm sure it's not edible," Sean said. "There's a Starbucks down the street. My treat."

Lucy smiled at him. That was all the thanks he needed.

It was well after midnight when Jaime got word that his brother was dead.

He sat in the back of a bar off an alley with no name, a place he'd hidden before when the heat got too hot. It was a place where people killed and people died, but no cops ever walked through the door. The bodies were moved and dumped, far away, so this place became a sanctuary, of sorts. Unless you were one of the dead.

But Pablo, the owner, was getting jumpy. Because the 39th Street store had been taken down by the feds. The feds had arrested Pablo's brother-in-law. He was afraid they could track Pablo down here, and Pablo didn't want the cops anywhere near him. George and Mirabelle were in prison.

Correction: Mirabelle was in prison. George was at the morgue.

Jaime drained another shot of cheap tequila. Damn George. He should have come with him to look for the kid. Jaime was pissed; he thought George didn't lock the rat up proper. He'd warned him, time and again, that the kid couldn't be trusted, but George had a soft spot.

He poured another shot and raised his glass. "To George!"

"To George!" tired, drunk voices repeated.

He drained the shot, no longer feeling the fire in his belly after so many. He needed to be thinking clearly. But how could he think about anything when his big brother was dead.

The man slipped onto the stool next to him, nodded toward the bottle.

"You heard."

"I loved my brother."

"Blame the feds. They worked him over."

George was weak. Jaime knew he'd cave under pressure. But he'd held up so well last time, Jaime thought—hell, he didn't know *what* to think anymore. "He was my brother." He glanced at the older man. "Who's in charge?"

"Donnelly."

Jaime scowled. That fed had been a fucking problem from day one. Putting his fat, self-righteous nose into every damn business Jaime had. "He killed George?"

"Might as well have."

"Who else? I want all their names."

"Slow down, *amigo*. Vengeance must wait. There is too much at stake to go after a federal agent right now."

"Donnelly, maybe." He was high-profile. Taking him out now would bring in far too much attention. "Someday I'll have his head."

"I'm working on that. It'll take a while, but he'll be at the wrong place at the wrong time." He shrugged. "Right place, right time, depending on how you look at it, and who ends up dead."

"Is there someone else? Someone who would hurt the bastard?"

"There's a new Latina working with Donnelly. Pretty. Smart. He thinks highly of her, what I've heard."

"New? Rookie new?"

"Seems that way. She might be the weak link."

"They doing the dirty?"

The man shrugged. "Won't matter. Not with Donnelly's past."

Jaime agreed. Young, female, rookie. Definitely the weakest. And it would get under Donnelly's skin. Jaime had done it before. Well, not him, personally, but his people had taken out one of Donnelly's rookies and watched the results. Donnelly made mistakes, lost his focus. Grief and anger clouded the fed's judgment. Back then, it gave them time to regroup, reorganize, solidify their operation.

It could work again.

"I know what you're thinking. Stop."

"Someone has to pay for my brother's death." It wasn't George's fault that he was manipulated; he'd always been trusting. And dumb. But he was Jaime's brother, he was *blood*, and Jaime promised his mother on her deathbed that he would always take care of the family.

His partner said, "Wait, Jaime. We need a backup plan. They have the ledger."

Jaime barely resisted the urge to throw the half-empty tequila bottle across the room. "Fuck. Stupid idiots."

"No one is talking. They know better."

George should have known better. "Maybe we don't kill her. Just scare her."

"I don't know if she'll scare easily."

"Then don't try for easy."

"First things—the girls know too much. You have to bring them back into the fold. Especially Bella. The general will not be pleased if we lose her."

"I don't know where they are." He fidgeted. He knew he had to turn Bella over, but he didn't have to like it. Mirabelle wouldn't forgive him. But dammit, it was Mirabelle's fault that they were aligned with the general in the first place! She should have some humility over her part in this clusterfuck. If she lost her kid, so what? She made her bed, she damn well needed to lie in it.

"Leave that to me. Just be ready when I call. We can't afford any more screwups, or the general will have our heads, too. And I'm not ready to die."

Because the bar was a haven for criminals, crime lords, drug dealers, and other scum, no one paid attention to the janitor with the jagged scar marring his old, weathered face. He'd been working here longer than many of them had been alive, and most thought he was mute.

He was neither mute, nor deaf.

CHAPTER 7

Lucy stretched in bed early Sunday morning, dawn cutting through the windows of the master bedroom she shared with Sean.

"Good morning, princess," Sean said and kissed her neck.

She snuggled into him. Sean's nearly naked body generated intense heat. How did he do that? She could wear flannel pajamas and be freezing. The best thing about living in San Antonio was the weather. It would be too hot in the summer but she'd take the heat of Texas over the cold of DC any day.

"I have to go into the office this morning."

"Not for a couple hours. It's only six."

She groaned. "Why is it that no matter how late I've been up I can't sleep past six?"

He pulled her to him and grinned. "We don't have to get up." He nuzzled her neck, planting light kisses over the sensitive skin behind her ear, down her neck, until his mouth reached her breast and she sighed.

"I feel decadent," she whispered.

"You feel perfect."

Lucy closed her eyes as Sean woke up her body. Slow,

easy morning sex was exactly what she needed to feel alive.

But it was more than the comfortable merging of her body with Sean's; it was *him*, the man who'd seen her at her best and her worst, the man who loved her unconditionally. Who had moved cross-country for her, who had captured her heart when she didn't even know she had a heart to give. One look, she melted. One touch, she sighed.

"Sean," she murmured, her breath catching, as their rhythm, so perfect, so in tune, brought them both up and over the edge.

He held her close to him, his hard body wrapping her tight. "I could go back to sleep about now," he whispered.

"Me, too," she said. "Don't let me."

She held him as he held her, and she savored the few moments of peace they had before the day officially began.

Her stomach growled.

"Lucia Kincaid!" Sean exclaimed.

She buried her face in his chest, halfway between laughter and mortification. "I can't believe you heard that."

"The neighbors could hear that grumble." He rolled her on top of him and kissed her. "Go, shower, I'll make breakfast."

"You don't have to do that," she began.

He lightly slapped her naked bottom. "It's an order."

"Bossy now, aren't we?"

He kissed her again, longer, teasing. "Go, before I keep you in bed all morning."

She smiled and crawled out of bed, stretching. He watched her, his head propped up on his hand, grinning. "You look at me like that and I won't get the breakfast you promised."

"You stretch again like that and neither of us will care." He got up and kissed her again, his hands molding her body like clay. "Go. Now," he said, his voice rough around the edges.

She reluctantly pulled away and went to shower. When she stepped back into the bedroom, Sean wasn't there. She dressed in black slacks and a simple white top with black blazer, pulled her thick hair back into a wide clip, and put on just a touch of makeup. She carried her low-heeled black boots downstairs, her stomach growling again at the aroma coming from the kitchen. "Your cooking skills have improved," she commented as she walked in.

Sean was wearing a blue-and-white-checked apron and nothing else.

"Dear God, Sean."

"You like?" He grinned mischievously as he set a plate of scrambled eggs with ham and cheese in front of her.

"A half-naked man cooking for me in a beautiful house after good morning sex?"

He frowned. "Just good?"

She kissed him. "Very good. Extremely good."

"Hmm, we're going to have to work on that. Tonight."

He poured her coffee, then helped himself to a plate of eggs. Lucy loved watching Sean. Not just because he looked like the Irish version of a Greek god, but because he enjoyed life. From the little things like cooking for her to the big things, like his work.

"Are you okay?" she asked, surprised that she'd spoken out loud.

"Okay about what?"

"I don't know—you've done everything for me since we've moved here, and I haven't given you anything in return."

"You just gave me 'very good' morning sex."

"You know what I mean."

"No, I don't."

"Are you happy?"

"Where is this coming from?"

"I don't know. Just—last night—you were in your element."

He blanched. "I was *not* in my element. I was surrounded by cops."

"But you were helping. Your instincts—they're right on. And then I was thinking about Patrick, and how good you and he worked together, and then—"

He put his hands together in a time-out gesture. "I'm happy. I wake up every morning with you. This is exactly what I want."

She frowned. "Okay."

"You think I'm lying?"

"No, I just know you miss it."

"Miss DC? Definitely not."

"Miss the excitement. RCK sent you all over the world fixing problems."

"There are plenty of problems to fix right here in the Lone Star State." He picked up her plate and his and put them on the counter. He took her hands and squeezed. "I don't know where all these insecurities are coming from, Luce, but I'm telling you now, and I'll tell you every day if I have to, I love you. My life is where your life is. Hell, I can go back to designing video games again if I want."

Her brows dipped in surprise. "You want to design video games?"

He shrugged. "Not really, but it's fun. And I'm working out a consulting relationship with RCK. Not working for Duke, but being hired case by case."

"Really?"

"I was serious yesterday about billing them. I'm going to talk to JT later this week. With Nora on bed rest, I don't want Duke thinking about anything but her and the baby."

"Okay." She kissed him. "I don't know how late I'll be, but I'll call you."

"Maybe I'll make dinner for you."

"Breakfast *and* dinner?" She kissed him again, this time lingering over his lips. "You must want something in return."

"Only you." Sean smiled. "But I'll think of something *very* fun we can do that involves you, me, and water. Clothing optional."

Sunday morning at the FBI office was quiet. *Too* quiet. She didn't see anyone but the desk guard, though the sound of a copy machine cut through the silence.

"You beat me," Lucy said when she rounded the aisle and saw Ryan.

"You stayed later with Donnelly."

She poured coffee from the pot in their squad room. Violent Crimes had been relegated to the far corner of the FBI offices. With the shifts in FBI priorities to counter-intelligence and white-collar crimes, the agents assigned to the Violent Crimes Squad had been cut 75 percent across the board. They had an eight-agent squad, plus their supervisory agent and an analyst. Juan had an office, but rarely closed the door; Zach Charles, the analyst, had a double-sized work space at the front of their section. The rest of them had small cubicles, personalized against the generic government workroom. Lucy was in the middle, directly across the aisle from Ryan.

She sat in her chair and swiveled to face him. "With George dead, the only lead we have on Jaime Sanchez is this missing boy, Michael. I have a call into Bella's CPS caseworker in the hope that she knows more."

"What about the guy who came by yesterday? DeSantos? Can he help push things along?"

She shrugged. "He might be able to help, but I think Bella would be more comfortable talking to me at this point. She's seven, her life has been turned upside down." Lucy knew exactly how she felt. When she was seven, her nephew and best friend had been murdered. They were born only weeks apart, but Justin's death had had a permanent impact on the Kincaid family. "She's small and quiet and hears everything," Lucy said, remembering that her family hadn't talked to her about what happened to Justin, but she had figured it out by being, essentially, invisible and listening. All the grief from her family pouring out, suffocating her. "It's a matter of asking the right questions. I've interviewed children before. It's a touchy area because if the court gets involved, they'll screw everything up."

"It's the process."

"Yes and no. There are ways around it. But picture being seven, your mother in jail, your uncle dead, your other uncle wanted by the police, and you're being brought into a giant marble building to face an old man or woman in a long black robe in an intimidating room filled with adults and huge, dark furniture? She'll be even more scared. I want to talk to her where she feels safe. If her CPS counselor doesn't call me back, I'll talk to Donnelly, see if I can read in DeSantos." Switching gears, she said, "Did you get the time line I emailed you? Did I miss anything?"

"I reviewed it, added a couple of details, and emailed it back to you and Donnelly, right before you walked in. It's tight. He was never alone, until he was put in his cell. Donnelly is interviewing the defense attorney first thing this morning; she was the last person, other than the guard, who saw him. But she has a squeaky-clean record." He glanced at his watch. "We should head over there," he said. "Donnelly wants to debrief at oh-nine-hundred. He's sending someone to babysit the coroner so he knows exactly when there's something to know."

Juan Casilla stepped into the narrow lane between cubicles. "Agent Donnelly can wait. Fill me in first."

Ryan leaned back and gave Juan a rundown of what had happened since they'd filed their own reports yesterday afternoon.

Lucy greatly respected her boss. He was calm, reasoned, and disciplined. He was also a family man, with five children and a sixth on the way. She and Sean had been over to his house shortly after she arrived in San Antonio for Sunday dinner. It reminded her of growing up in a large family. She'd said as much to Sean, because he also came from a large family, but he shook his head. "Every family's different, Luce. The Rogans were never as close as the Kincaids."

Sean fit in with her family. Not only was her brother Patrick his best friend, but her parents loved him and treated him like one of their own, and Dillon and Jack respected Sean's unique skills. Carina hadn't been quite as enamored with Sean, but they hadn't met under the best of circumstances. She'd come around. Everyone eventually did.

But it pained Lucy that Sean's childhood hadn't been as idyllic as hers. Sean's family had far more money than the Kincaids ever did, but his parents traveled extensively for business and pleasure, and Sean was essentially raised by his siblings. He was fourteen when his parents were killed in a small-plane crash, and his older brother Duke became his guardian. Sean loved his brother, especially because he had stuck around when his other siblings had done their own thing, but there had been a lot of friction between them as well. They seemed to have developed a truce, and she hoped it lasted.

Family was complicated. It didn't matter who you were. The Sanchezes were family, albeit on the wrong side of the law, but they still behaved as family, warts and all.

Would one of his own kin kill George Sanchez? The thought made Lucy wonder—George had made a sacrifice for his nieces, thinking he was protecting them. What if Jaime or even Mirabelle didn't think that sacrifice was warranted? Both of them were far more jaded and knew how to manipulate the system. They would believe that their lawyer could get them out of the mess, find a loophole, or get them out with a low bail. Mirabelle might think it best that CeCe and Bella cool their heels in juvenile detention for a few days, no problem. But George was about family, and he couldn't bear the thought of the girls being in a potentially dangerous environment. If he cared that much, he learned it from someone. His parents? His brother? Maybe Mirabelle could still be brought around to help.

If someone else, someone associated with the Sanchezes, had ordered the hit on George, Jaime might want revenge. He was already violent; given a cause he could be ruthless. And from his rap sheet, it would fit his personality, give him a justifiable reason, in his head, to start a war.

And then there was the original reason that George and Jaime were wanted—attempted murder on a rival gang member. Maybe George's murder wasn't related to his turning state's evidence at all, but retaliation by the other gang.

"Kincaid," she heard in the back of her head.

"Yes, sorry?"

"Where did we lose you?" Juan said.

She blushed. "I was thinking about family. I'm sorry, really. I was thinking that Jaime and Mirabelle didn't kill their brother. Family's too important to them."

"Family kills each other all the time."

"It doesn't feel right to me. I think Jaime is going to get revenge on his brother's killer, or whoever he thinks is responsible. Either who they work for—if whoever's in charge believed George was a threat—or someone in the gang that the Sanchez brothers hit two months ago. Ryan—were any

of the gang Donnelly arrested at the hardware store in jail
with Sanchez?"

"Donnelly already ran them. They're all there, but they
were in a different holding wing."

"But they could have spread the word. If they thought
that Sanchez had ratted on them, they could have gotten
the word out to the rest of the prisoners. Or if there was
another gang at play, slip them the information."

"For what it's worth," Ryan said, "I think you're right to
wait until the autopsy comes back. If we know what killed
him, it'll help narrow the window. But we should definitely
talk to Donnelly about other gang affiliations. The prison
system does a damn near impossible job of keeping rival
gangs separated, but mistakes happen."

Juan said, "We need to shift focus. You two, work with
Agent Donnelly, but your priority is finding the missing boy.
He's a child at risk, under fourteen, and a witness. I talked to
Donnelly this morning, and he's okay with it. I read your
report, Lucy—you have a possible identification on the
child?"

"A CPS officer approached with a file, and the basics
match. I want to take the photo to the minor girl, Bella Borez,
but I reached out to her CPS caseworker and haven't heard
back."

"What do you need, an address? Donnelly would have
it."

"I'll talk to him. If we get a hard ID, we can narrow the
search, go back to his foster parents, his old neighborhood,
family, and friends. He could be hiding out with someone
he trusts."

"Good angle. Work it."

"I think I should stick with Donnelly," Ryan said. "Lucy
can handle the interviews on her own, Donnelly is spread
thin right now."

Juan considered for a moment. "Donnelly wanted you both assigned to him for the duration but I didn't feel comfortable with that. Donnelly is a good agent, has an outstanding reputation, but he's a maverick, and you both have maverick tendencies. Donnelly can take care of himself, but Lucy, you're still a rookie, and there are many eyes on rookies." He turned to Ryan. "You stick to Donnelly's team for now, but back up Kincaid."

"Absolutely."

"When we find the boy, we'll reassess. And Lucy, if you need help, tag Ryan. He's your partner in this, and the senior agent. Keep him in the loop."

"Yes, sir."

"Donnelly's unit may be spread thin, but so are we. I asked Zach to come in this afternoon to get debriefed and pull records or whatever you need. Copy him into all future reports. Are we good?"

"Yes, sir," Ryan said.

Juan nodded. "If you have time, Nita will have dinner on the table at six thirty tonight. You're both invited. And Sean, of course," he added. He glanced at his watch. "Nita's going to have my hide. I'm going to be late to Mass." He nodded good-bye and left.

"Dinner with the boss," Ryan said. "Always makes me nervous."

"I love his family. Reminds me of my own."

"We should get to SAPD for the debriefing."

"I need to send Zach what we have, and I have some records I'd like him to access," she said. "I'll meet you there."

After Ryan left, she sent Zach a long email about Michael, asking him to run statistics on missing children in foster care, breaking it down by race and comparing San Antonio with the rest of Texas. Maybe Michael was an anomaly, or maybe there was something bigger and more horrific than drug running. At-risk youth were called at-risk for a reason. Not just because they might turn to a life of crime, but because others used and abused them.

She also asked him to pull the records of all foster parents and CPS staff assigned to any boys who'd gone missing within the last two years and fell into the target demographic: male, ten to fourteen years of age, Hispanic, one or both parents incarcerated.

Her cell phone rang. It was Donnelly. "Where the hell are you?"

She bristled. "I'm at my desk. Ryan is on his way to the briefing now. What's your problem?" She winced at her tone. She needed to remember that she wasn't in her old world anymore, with people who knew her and had worked with her.

He let out a long breath. "Not enough sleep. Sorry. I need you here. I want your help interviewing Mirabelle Borez. We need something to shake loose, and we made a good team yesterday with George. I have another tactic we can take with Borez."

"I'll be there in thirty minutes. I also need to talk to Bella Borez about Michael. I have a photo that might be the kid."

"I'll get her file copied and have it ready for you. But let's nail Mirabelle down now. I have an idea, and maybe we can get what we both want."

CHAPTER 8

Lucy missed the debriefing, but Ryan filled her in on the highlights as soon as she arrived. Essentially, they had nothing. The autopsy was being performed on George Sanchez, but tox screens could take days or weeks to get back, even with the rush. Jaime Sanchez's gangbangers were still in custody and a team was going over their records and backgrounds, but no one was talking and all had requested lawyers. They were certainly more scared of whoever they worked for—either Jaime or someone higher up the food chain—than they were of prison.

"I told Donnelly," Ryan said, "that the hit on George might have been a way to keep the others in line. Talk, you're dead. It's classic."

"No sighting of Jaime?"

"Nada. He's deep down the rabbit hole. May have left town, but Donnelly seems to think he's close. Did he tell you about Mirabelle?"

"He wants to tag-team her, see if we can break her."

"They're bringing her in from holding now."

Donnelly walked into the room with Nicole Rollins on his heels. "Kincaid, come with me. Quiroz, where are we with the known associates?"

He held up a sheet. "I have the list, last address of each of Jaime's people. Half are in prison."

"Take the other half and you and Rollins shake them down. Find out what they know, if anything. Listen to what they don't say as much as what they say. Watch your back. Pull anyone you need, Rollins will make it happen."

"Yes, sir. I cleared it with my boss to pull in someone from my squad for today, since you have Lucy."

"Who?"

"Dunning."

Donnelly swore under his breath. "Another rookie?"

"Ten years in the Marines, Special Forces, on SWAT with me, I'd rather have him cover my ass than anyone."

"Fine," Donnelly said, but he didn't look happy. Lucy considered what Nicole had said yesterday about losing a rookie in the line of duty. She wanted to ask him, but now was not the time. While Donnelly was working out details with Ryan, she sent Sean a text message.

If you're not busy, can you look up something for me? Donnelly lost a fellow agent in the line of duty, a rookie DEA agent. I don't know when or where. I'd like to know what happened.

Only a few seconds later, Sean responded.

I'm at the gym. Will do when I get back.

She smiled. He always answered his messages, even at the gym. Might as well have his phone implanted in his palm.

Thanks. Love you.

"Ready?" Donnelly asked.

She followed him down the hall, out the back, and into the adjoining building, which housed the county jail. They signed in, turned over their weapons, and were escorted to a room generally reserved for lawyers and their clients.

"Can you give me a heads-up about what you want from Mirabelle?"

"I want Jaime Sanchez," he said, "but I doubt she'll give him up. I want you to watch her. Assess her reactions. She's not going to talk, she'll have her lawyer here, but I'm going to try to get her to slip, to do or say something that'll give us a direction. If you see an opportunity, take it. If I discipline you, don't take it personally."

"I won't. It would help if I knew what you were looking for."

"I don't know," he admitted. "She knows where Jaime is, I'm certain of it, but she's not going to tell me. So I'm going to talk around it. Ask about the boy. See if she'll spill something about him. About Jaime's plans. I'm winging this right now. We have nothing, and I won't tolerate having nothing."

Donnelly pushed himself as hard as his team—or harder. And here, now, she saw it clearly. He was beating himself up, either because George was dead or because Jaime got away. But there was something else under the surface, a deep craving to stop Jaime that went a lot deeper than an active warrant sweep. She'd seen it earlier, and now she didn't know how she'd missed it from the beginning.

"Jaime Sanchez was more than just part of the sweep, wasn't he?"

He glared at her. Angry. Then he sagged against the wall, a moment of weakness showing more than a hint of frustration. "I put them on the list. I wanted to take them down big because that's the only way to keep them in a cage. Jaime Sanchez is a vicious gangbanger. He's gotten away with drug running, kidnapping, attempted murder, conspiracy, and more—and I've never been able to nail him. We don't have him on murder one, but I know he's responsible for hits on rival gangs, likely pulled the trigger himself on several, and thinks he's invincible. And dammit, he has every reason to think that because nothing sticks to him. It's like he has a fucking evil angel getting him off, like disappearing before the sweep this morning."

"Could he have been tipped off?"

"I don't know," he replied honestly. "I don't think so. I put him on the list at the last minute because, like you said, he's more than just a guy who skipped bail." He ran his hands through his short hair, locked his fingers behind his neck. "Last year, someone in his gang was killed in a shootout that also took the life of an innocent fifteen-year-old girl walking to her grandparents' house for dinner. The hit was in retaliation for Jaime stealing fifty thousand in heroin from his rival. And that's not the first time people have died around him." He hesitated. Lucy knew there was something more, but Donnelly didn't continue. Instead he said, "The violence isn't going to stop until we stop people like Jaime Sanchez."

The door opened and Donnelly pushed off from the wall.

Mirabelle came in wearing handcuffs. Her lawyer, a short, older white male, walked in after her. "Agents," he said, shaking their hands. "I'm Keith Glum, Ms. Borez's counsel. I've spoken to Ms. Borez, and she's distraught over her brother's death. I'm sure you can understand. I've petitioned the court to release her on her own recognizance so that she can make arrangements for her brother's funeral."

She looked more smug than grieving, Lucy thought. Maybe a little of both. Her eyes were rimmed red, and if Lucy's guess was right—that George cared about family—then maybe Mirabelle did, too, in her own twisted way.

"If your client cooperates, then we'll go to the judge

with my blessing. But for the last twenty-four hours, she's been a pain in my ass."

"My client doesn't have any information about the whereabouts of her brother, Jaime Sanchez."

"Okay, then let's start with something easy. What time did he leave the house Saturday morning?"

Mirabelle whispered in her lawyer's ear. This was going to take forever, Lucy realized.

Glum said, "She doesn't know. She was sleeping."

"But she knew she was harboring a fugitive."

Again, whispering. Again, Glum answered. "Ms. Borez didn't know that her brothers had missed their court date. She didn't know they were fugitives."

"Bullshit," Donnelly said.

"If you're going to yell at my client, I'll be leaving with her."

"I'm not yelling," he said. He leaned forward. "I'm investigating additional charges, and I have until tomorrow to file them. Including kidnapping and unlawful imprisonment of a minor."

"You're fishing," Glum said.

"Ms. Borez, your daughter gave a statement that she has knowledge of at least one boy, approximately thirteen years old, who was chained in the basement. We found evidence that supports her statement. We found additional evidence that suggests more than one minor child was held against their will."

Mirabelle spoke rapidly in Spanish. Lucy picked up most of it—particularly that she spoke of *Isabella*, even though Donnelly hadn't mentioned which daughter talked.

The lawyer put his hand on Mirabelle's arm. "Nothing a minor child said will be admissible. She was without counsel, without an advocate, and I plan to level charges against you for interviewing a minor child in violation of the child's rights."

"I didn't interview her," Donnelly said. "She volunteered the information."

Technically, Lucy *had* asked questions. But it was a gray area, and one Lucy had felt comfortable swimming in.

"I hardly believe a seven-year-old would volunteer information. Besides, she's a young child with a vivid imagination."

Lucy took out the photo of Michael Rodriguez and slid it under Mirabelle's gaze. She watched her expression turn from disinterest to shock. Then she locked it up tight. "Is this the boy from your basement?"

But she already had the answer.

Glum said, "No."

"You didn't ask your client," Donnelly said.

"She already said that she was not keeping anyone against their will."

"But Jaime was," Donnelly countered. "Mirabelle, if you're scared of your brother, I understand. We can protect you, and your daughters—"

"Like you protected George?" she screamed, pounding her fist on the table. And for the first time, Lucy saw the debate in her expression, the uncertainty that the course of action she'd chosen was the right one.

"Help us help you," Lucy said. "You don't want your daughters to grow up in the system."

"I won't be here tomorrow. I'll have my babies back. Go to hell, *puta*."

Donnelly turned to Glum. "You need to explain to your client that if she cooperates we'll help her. If she doesn't, my hands are tied."

Glum said, "You have no case. Misdemeanor at most, and no judge is going to separate a mother from her two daughters on a misdemeanor charge. She'll get time served, probation. Drop this farce and release her now."

"Felony kidnapping, felony unlawful imprisonment of a minor, harboring a fugitive, possession of drugs, possession of illegal firearms, resisting arrest, and I'm just getting started. Make a deal, and it all goes away."

"It's all going to go away because you can't make those charges stick, and you know it," Glum said.

"Watch me," Donnelly countered.

Mirabelle glanced at her lawyer, then said to Donnelly, "I'm not saying anything else."

Donnelly slapped his hands on the table and walked out.

Lucy picked up her folder and said to Mirabelle, in Spanish, "Your girls need their mother. I hope you know what you're doing, because right now they'll only be seeing you behind bars for the next five to ten years."

Glum turned red as Mirabelle's face drained. Lucy followed Donnelly out.

"I need to do some legal wrangling to keep her inside after tomorrow," he said. "I have enough to set the bail high but it might not be high enough. She'll be out by Tuesday."

"She's waffling," Lucy said.

"I don't think so. Glum is convinced a judge will give her leniency."

"She was surprised we ID'd the boy. She's scared."

"She should be scared. And you think she recognized him?"

"She covered it up well, but you told me to watch. She has a telltale twitch in her eye. She knows him. She's scared, and I don't know if it's Jaime or someone else. I need to talk to Bella, then maybe I can come back at Mirabelle, especially if you can get an insurmountable bail. She thinks she can manipulate the system, she's not scared to push, but she doesn't want to lose her girls."

"What about yesterday? When she didn't care what happened to them?"

"That's the short term. She's willing to play when she

thinks she has the upper hand, but the longer you can keep her behind bars, the greater chance she'll flip. Not on Jaime—I think there's a family loyalty there, especially with George gone. But she'll give you something worthwhile if it means she's reunited with her daughters."

Donnelly watched Glum leave, and then Mirabelle was escorted out by a guard. He waited until she was out of sight before he said, "I'm meeting with the AUSA this afternoon. We'll work on additional charges and bail issues, but it's really a matter of getting the right judge."

"I still need to talk to Bella."

"I'll get you the information on the Borez kids, but you'll have to contact the CPS officer to make an appointment. You can't talk to Bella alone, not this time."

"I've been trying to reach the woman, but she hasn't returned my calls."

"I'll track her down and set up the meeting. Be ready, no one likes to be ordered."

"If she had simply returned my calls, I wouldn't need to ask for help."

Donnelly snorted a half laugh as he led Lucy back to the main police station. "Right. Because everyone is like us."

"What does that mean?"

"I know a kindred spirit when I see one. People like us, Kincaid, we *are* our job. Don't even think about denying it. You're not the type who lies to herself, so don't lie to me."

"I wasn't going to."

Donnelly was right. Not everyone was like them.

Maybe if more people were, they wouldn't have thirteen-year-old boys held captive by violent drug dealers, or little girls forced into foster care because of criminal parents.

CHAPTER 9

Jennifer Mendez was young, attractive, and—as Sean would say—had a stick up her ass. She was overdressed for a Sunday afternoon—unless she was coming from church—and obviously irritated that she'd been ordered to meet Lucy at the foster home where Bella and CeCe Borez were staying.

"I don't appreciate anyone going over my head," Mendez said in lieu of a greeting when she showed up a full twenty minutes late.

"I'm sorry about that, it wasn't my call," Lucy said, trying to be friendly.

"Hmph," Jennifer muttered. "Let's get this over with, I have someplace to be."

"Do you have any background on the foster family?"

"Of course I do," Jennifer said. "Karl and Anna Grove. They take temporary, at-risk placements. Karl is a retired SAPD officer; Anna is a retired teacher and bilingual. I know how to do my job, Agent Kincaid."

"Call me Lucy."

Jennifer glanced at her and frowned, as if trying to assess the situation and not sure what to think. "Couldn't this have waited until tomorrow?"

"The younger Borez, Isabella, has some information we need to track another missing child. She met me yesterday, knows me—"

"You mean because you arrested her mother?" Jennifer snapped. "She probably *loves* you."

"I didn't have anything to do with her mother's arrest, and made sure she knew it. I built a rapport with her, I just need her to identify a boy for me."

"Let me see." Jennifer stopped walking before they went up the porch steps.

Lucy took the file out of her satchel.

Jennifer said, "This is one of ours. Where did you get this?"

"Charlie DeSantos gave me a copy."

"DeSantos?" She frowned, flipped through it. "Why'd he give this to you?"

"Michael—the one here—made contact with his foster parents yesterday, with a note. DeSantos found out about my case and talked to DEA Agent Brad Donnelly. Because I'm lead on the missing boy, Brad sent him to me."

She returned the file to Lucy. "Your case?"

"Donnelly is looking for a fugitive. I'm FBI; I'm looking for the minor."

Jennifer was skeptical, and while Lucy didn't blame her for being protective of her charges, she also didn't understand why she was putting up this roadblock.

"If I tell you to stop the interview, stop the interview, got it?"

"Yes."

Jennifer walked up the three steps to the small, clean, wood porch and knocked on the door. A moment later a tall, broad-shouldered bald man answered. He still looked like a cop, with suspicious eyes and stern expression.

"Ms. Mendez."

"Hello, Mr. Grove. I want to apologize again for the

short notice, but the FBI has an urgent matter and they believe Isabella Borez can help them. We won't be but a few minutes."

He nodded. "It was a rough night for them, as you would expect. It's not an easy situation."

He opened the door to let them in. The small foyer led to a living room on the right and a dining room on the left. The house was immaculate. So clean Lucy didn't want to touch anything. But the delicious smells coming from the kitchen reminded her it was well past the lunch hour.

"Anna is baking with Isabella. She's a sweet kid."

"And CeCe?" Jennifer asked.

"Hasn't left her room. Angry. Scared. Defiant." He said it in a way that told Lucy he was familiar with this behavior.

"I'll talk to her before I leave," Jennifer said.

They walked into the kitchen. Bella had flour on her face and wore a checked apron that was several sizes too big for her. She was watching Anna roll dough with big eyes, asking questions about why she put flour on the rolling pin and how long it was going to take to bake and why there was salt in pie when pies didn't taste salty.

"We have company, Anna," Karl Grove said.

Bella looked, her face frozen for a brief moment, and then she burst into a smile that melted Lucy's heart.

"Lucy! You came!"

"I told you I'd try."

"I'm so glad!" Every sentence was an exclamation. Lucy loved young children. They adapted to changes so much easier than the older kids, like CeCe. "We're making apple pie! And apple cobbler for the people next door. Mr. Pa-pa-paop—" She glanced at Anna.

"Mr. Papapoulous," Anna said.

"Yeah, he had a heart attack last week and just came home from the hospital and we're making sugar-free apple cobbler for him with homemade ice cream. Can you believe that you can have something taste good without sugar? And I never had homemade ice cream."

As she spoke faster, she reverted to Spanish.

"I'm sorry I'm going to miss that," Lucy said.

"Why? Why are you going to miss it? Aren't you visiting?"

"Yes, but we can't stay long."

Jennifer smiled. "Remember me?"

"Yes. You brought us to stay with Mr. and Mrs. Grove until my mama isn't in trouble anymore."

"How do you like your room?"

"I miss my toys."

"If you make a list for me, I'll bring you what you want."

Bella frowned. "Does that mean I can never go home?"

Lucy's heart twisted. But before Lucy could say anything, Jennifer said, "I know you want to see your mom and sleep in your own bed. And everyone is working hard to make that happen. But I don't know when, and I want you to have everything you need while you're staying here with the Groves."

The little girl bit her lip, but nodded.

Lucy began to like Jennifer, her attitude outside notwithstanding.

"Agent Kincaid has a couple of questions for you. You're not in trouble, Bella. But Agent Kincaid thinks maybe you can help her find someone who needs help."

Bella nodded.

"If you want to stop, just say the word, okay?"

She nodded again and straightened in her chair. "It's about the boy," she whispered.

"Yes," Lucy said.

"I might get in trouble."

Lucy took Bella's hand and said, "I promise you, cross my heart, that you will not get in any trouble."

"Not from *you*," she whispered.

Jennifer said, "You're safe here. No one is going to get you in trouble."

Bella looked pained.

"How about this," Lucy said. "What if you don't have to talk at all, but I'll ask questions and you can nod or shake your head?"

She glanced at Anna, then nodded.

Lucy took out a photo of Michael Rodriguez. "Is this the Michael who was in your basement?"

She stared at the picture and nodded.

"Good," Lucy said. "That's great."

"Can I finish the pies now? Mrs. Grove needs my help."

"In just a minute, promise."

She sighed but didn't move.

"You told me yesterday that you thought Michael had been in the basement for three or four weeks. Right?"

She shrugged, then nodded.

"Had you ever seen Michael before then?"

She shook her head.

Lucy asked, "You told me that sometimes there were other boys who lived in the basement. Do you know how many? Three? Five? More?"

She shook her head, then bit her lip. "Lots," she whispered.

"Were any of them recent? Like, while Michael was there?"

She shook her head, then shifted uneasily in her seat. She kept looking at Anna Grove, as if to beg her to let her get up. Lucy wanted to ask more questions about Michael and what he did for Jaime, but Bella was getting skittish.

Jennifer said, "Bella, you've done good. I'm proud of you for being so brave. Agent Kincaid and I just want to find Michael and take him home."

Her eyes grew wide. "His daddy's bad. He said so."

Lucy said, "His daddy is in jail, and will be there for a long, long time. Michael has a new mama and papa. They love him and miss him."

She still looked worried. "He was afraid of the bad place."

"Do you know where the bad place is?"

She shook her head and seemed to crawl into herself. Jennifer said, "Bella, you're safe here. And we want to make sure that Michael is safe, too."

Karl Grove sat down next to her with a glass of apple juice. It was clear he wanted the conversation over, and hovered protectively over the girl. Bella drank. She touched Karl's arm. That's when Lucy noticed he had a long, jagged scar. Probably from a serrated knife. "That happened in the bad place."

Karl shook his head. "That happened a long time ago, when I was a policeman."

Lucy cut him off. "Did Michael have a scar?"

"Yes, right there." She tapped on Karl's forearm.

Lucy had read Michael's file. He had old scars on his back, but there had been nothing about a gash on his arm. CPS had done a full medical on him when he became a ward of the state.

"Would all scars be documented in his records?" she asked Jennifer.

"Absolutely."

Bella tilted her chin up. "I'm not lying."

"Of course not," Lucy said. She pulled out her notepad and a pencil. "Can you draw it for us?"

"How is that going to help find him?"

"Everything helps. You've already helped a lot."

She reluctantly took the paper and pencil and stared at it for a minute. Then she drew what at first looked like a capital T with an extra line like a small t and an arrow at the bottom. She frowned, unhappy with the picture. "Sort of," she said.

"That's good, Bella." She showed the picture to Jennifer, who shook her head, and to Karl, who was also perplexed.

Karl said, "It's too specific to be an accidental scar."

Bella looked from one adult to the others, then stared at Lucy. "He's going to be okay, right?"

"We'll do everything we can to find him."

Bella bit her lip again. "What's going to happen to me and CeCe? Are we going to go to the bad place, too?"

"No," Jennifer said emphatically. "No one is going to hurt you. You're safe here, with the Groves. Okay?"

She nodded, but she was uncertain. "When can I see Uncle George?"

Her uncle, not her mother. That was very interesting.

Lucy glanced at Karl and Anna. They knew about his murder, but no one had told the girls.

Anna said, "Let's talk about that, Bella. You, and me, and CeCe."

Karl walked them out. Lucy said, "I'm going to call about getting you some protection."

"We have good security, this is a nice neighborhood. Neighbors pay attention."

"These aren't people who care about being subtle."

"I understand, Agent Kincaid. I was a deputy sheriff for thirty-five years."

Jennifer said, "We're about as far as you can get from their old neighborhood without leaving the city limits. There's no way the uncle can find them here."

"There's always a way," Lucy said. "I'm going to work on it. They might simply increase patrols, but I'm going to try and get a unit twenty-four seven.

"And," Lucy continued, "one more thing—CeCe is

young, but she might have great loyalty to her uncle Jaime and her mother."

"I've already taken away all the phones in the house," Mr. Grove said. "I'll do everything in my power to protect those girls."

CHAPTER 10

Donnelly and Ryan were both gone when Lucy arrived back at SAPD headquarters that afternoon. She sat in the conference room that had been set aside for the task force and reviewed Michael Rodriguez's file again.

She kept coming back to the father, Vince Rodriguez. She used the federal criminal database to pull up his record, and while there was no direct connection to Sanchez, there were many common associations. They had to have known each other—same neighborhood, same friends. Even though Vince was imprisoned four hours away, she wanted to talk to him in person. She'd need Brad Donnelly's blessing first, and barring that she'd go to Juan Casilla. Her gut instincts told her Michael's disappearance and captivity was at least loosely related to his father and it would be worth their time to talk to him. Sometimes, what *wasn't* said was as important as what *was* said.

Lucy sent Donnelly a text message asking him to call her when he had the chance, then put the file and her notes aside. She wasn't going to get anywhere until she had more information to plug into the holes.

She'd promised Charlie DeSantos that she would let him know when she had a confirmation on Michael Rodriguez's identity. She left a message at the number he'd given her, relating only the basics, and telling him to contact Brad Donnelly if he needed more. She wasn't going to get in the middle of some jurisdictional issue, and Brad was in charge. She'd learned the hard way that when possible, play by the rules or you'd get bitten in the ass.

Officer Crane walked by the open door. She called out, "Do you know where Donnelly is? He and Ryan didn't sign out."

"They took a team to follow up on a lead. I don't have details."

She itched to be there, but she also had something else she wanted to do. She asked Crane, "How easy is it to get a sit-down with a prisoner at McConnell?"

"Have your boss call the warden's office. Or Donnelly can do it. It shouldn't be too much of a problem." He eyed her stack of paper with curiosity. "Something come up? It's not a pretty place."

"We ID'd the boy who was kept in the basement. His father is in prison, and I might have found an indirect connection between the father and Sanchez."

"Definitely talk to Donnelly."

She thanked Crane then turned back to her notes. She had nothing else to do except wait for Donnelly and Ryan, so she looked yet again at the limited information they had.

Had Sanchez kidnapped Michael as payback for something his father had done? Why now, four years after the father went to prison? Michael had been in foster care since he was eight; he'd turned thirteen last month. He'd disappeared the month before his twelfth birthday. What was she missing?

Where had Michael been for the thirteen months before he was held in the basement?

Lucy had a vivid imagination, created through her own

experiences and those of being a cop. She knew what horrors adults inflicted on children. She thought of the scar on Michael's arm. She looked again at Bella's crude drawing, then made a copy and posted it on the board. It had to mean something, and Donnelly might know. If not, they could consult the gang task force to see if this was a gang marking. It might not be a scar; it could be a tattoo. Bella was a little girl. She might not have been able to tell the difference, especially if the tat was homemade.

Brad would ask her what she hoped to gain from Rodriguez at the prison, and she had to convince him that they could gain insight into Sanchez. It was a long shot, so maybe they could develop an incentive to get Rodriguez to talk—particularly if Sanchez had, in fact, hurt his son.

She bit her lip. Would Rodriguez care? He'd abused Michael, had abused his wife, killed a man—was family important to him? If he had killed his wife, did he resent or hate the son she'd borne?

She wouldn't know until she met him face-to-face.

She was staring at the whiteboard Donnelly had used to post information and leads on Jaime Sanchez, practically willing a clue to leap out at her, when her cell phone rang. It was Charlie DeSantos, returning her call.

"Hello, Mr. DeSantos. You got my message?"

"Yes. Thank you. What else did you learn?"

"I simply confirmed his identity. I sent a report to my supervisor as well. Michael's file is very thin. Is there anyone from his past you think he might contact for help?"

"Only his foster parents. As far as I know, he cut all ties to his old neighborhood."

"How much do you know about Vince Rodriguez?"

"The father? He's in prison, twenty-five-to-life. It's in Michael's file."

"Rodriguez and Sanchez are from the same neighborhood." She was musing out loud, trying to get information from DeSantos without giving him more than she was allowed.

"I didn't see any connections in the file. Rodriguez wasn't affiliated with a specific gang, at least as far as I knew."

"Fourteen months is a long time for a thirteen-year-old to stay in hiding. Do you have any idea where he might have gone?"

"None. I assumed, like the police, that he'd run away."

"If you hear from him, please call me."

"Likewise. And Agent Kincaid—Lucy—I want to help."

"Talk to his foster parents again. Make sure they call you or me if they see him, if he makes any contact."

"I've already done that."

"Then maybe, since you were his counselor, if there's anyone from one of his previous homes that he might have reached out to?"

"I can pull those records."

She almost said her good-byes, then asked spontaneously, "Did Michael have a scar on his forearm that isn't in his medical records?"

"What kind of scar?" he asked.

She looked at the picture Bella had drawn. "A double-crossed T, maybe, possibly with an arrow at the bottom."

"I never saw anything like that. An accident?"

"I don't know, it was described to me verbally. I'm just trying to put it all together. Do you think his father might have information that could help us track him down? I assume he knew his son was missing and presumed a runaway."

"Yes," DeSantos said. "I didn't notify him, but I'm certain someone must have."

"Maybe he knows something not in the records that might help us find Michael."

"Vince Rodriguez has nothing but contempt for his son and the system. Even if he knew something, he wouldn't share. Michael hated his father, never visited him in prison."

"It was just a thought," she said. Brad and Ryan walked in, faces long and tired. "I have to go, Mr. DeSantos. I'll call you if I get a lead." She hung up and turned to her teammates. "Bad news?"

"We're chasing our tails," Donnelly said, then walked out to take a call.

She looked at Ryan. "What happened?"

"We got a warrant and dumped all the phone data from the five gangbangers we arrested yesterday. Found a pattern of usage and targeted a run-down apartment building four blocks from the hardware store. Thought it was a hot lead, but there was nothing. If Sanchez was there, no one's talking, there's no cameras or other security, and there's no sign of him. Donnelly has his analysts going through the data to see if they can pick any more potential leads, but it's a long shot."

"Why didn't he send out uniforms to check it out?"

Ryan glanced behind him, then closed the door so they could have a modicum of privacy. "My guess? He wants the collar. Personally. He has a stick up his ass about Sanchez. I think there's something more here than what we know."

Lucy had suspected the same thing, and was glad to have Ryan's confirmation.

"Personal?"

"I don't know. But something's going on with him and Sanchez. He wants him bad."

"Maybe it has to do with the rookie who was killed while on one of his ops," Lucy said, almost to herself.

Ryan scowled. "What? What rookie?"

"Something his partner, Nicole Rollins, said to me. About why he doesn't like working with rookies."

"I don't know anything about it. Must have been before

my time." Ryan ran both hands over his drawn face, took a deep breath and slowly released it. "I don't like this. I need a plan of action, and right now we're just reacting."

"I have some news." She told him what she'd learned from Bella about Michael, and the information she was gathering about his father. "Do you think maybe Vince Rodriguez might have information about Sanchez?"

"Long shot," Ryan said. "He's been in prison for four years. But it's definitely no coincidence that the kid was raised in the same neighborhood as Sanchez's hangout. You found other connections?"

"Not directly between Sanchez and Rodriguez, but between Rodriguez and some of Sanchez's people."

Donnelly walked in alone. He took off his tactical vest and dropped it on the table. "What about Sanchez?"

He didn't look at them, but was staring at the information Lucy had added to the board.

Lucy repeated everything she'd just told Ryan. Then she said, "I'd like to talk to Vince Rodriguez. About his son," she added.

"It's too long ago, too many variables. But it's another angle. I'll contact our DEA unit there and have them send two agents to talk to Rodriguez. Write up what you have and get it to me by tomorrow morning."

Lucy tried not to show her disappointment about not being the one to talk to the father, but she had to admit, it probably wasn't the best use of her time, especially when it was a two-hour trip each way. She said, "See if you can get someone with psychological training. Someone who might be able to manipulate information out of the father."

"Someone like you?" Donnelly said.

"I said I'd go."

"I need you here."

Ryan bristled. "We work for Casilla, not you. If Lucy thinks this is a lead, we should follow it up."

Donnelly shot Ryan an angry glare. The tension was rising between the two men. Lucy intervened before it escalated. "Let's see what Donnelly's people can get from him and depending on what he says, decide if we need to visit ourselves."

Before Ryan could say anything else, Donnelly tapped Bella's drawing. "What's this?"

"A scar or tattoo on Michael's arm. Have you seen something like this before?"

"No. Is this from the girl?"

"Yes."

"Gangs and drug cartels tat or brand themselves with symbols all the time," he said, "but I haven't seen this one. They start them young."

"Maybe Michael wasn't a willing participant."

Brad didn't say anything.

"He was held against his will," Lucy said.

"We don't know that. Maybe it was a gang-related punishment because he didn't do something Sanchez wanted. We can't assume that this kid is an innocent victim."

"He *is* a victim."

"You don't know that. Don't go all soft on me now, Kincaid. Kids can kill just as easily as adults, especially if they're brought up to be killers."

"You don't have to explain what we're up against, but this kid is different. I can't explain why, except that Bella let him go because she was worried about his safety. If he was violent, I don't think she would have trusted him."

"Her uncle is Jaime Sanchez. The kid's been raised around hardened criminals."

"And she warned me about Jaime. She said that her uncle George was nice and sometimes made mistakes, but that her uncle Jaime wasn't nice, and she was scared of him. Kids get it, even if they can't explain it in big words."

Donnelly looked back at the board, whether because he

was irritated with her or in an attempt to wrap his head around the information they had, she didn't know.

"Gangs recruit young," he said, but his tone was much softer. "Maybe this kid was enticed with money, or maybe he was threatened. All we know is that Jaime Sanchez is on the run and has something big coming down, that there's a missing teen who allegedly ran away from a good home fourteen months ago and wasn't seen until he turned up in the Borez family basement, and that our witness is seven years old. And someone got to George Sanchez, which makes me think that there's someone on the inside." He obviously hadn't meant for that to slip. He glanced from Ryan to Lucy. "That's not a public theory."

"It's the only theory that makes sense. Someone who turned his back so Sanchez could be poisoned. Did you get the autopsy report?"

"Preliminary. The guy had an allergic reaction, but the ME thinks there was a secondary factor, and is rushing some tests."

"He has to have a guess." Lucy had worked at the morgue for a year as a pathologist. MEs always had a guess, and were usually right. They just didn't routinely share with the investigators until they confirmed their findings.

"He said the allergic reaction seemed to be far too extreme—it happened too fast. There're some drugs that may have increased the reaction, or a poison that killed him but the allergic reaction to fish was a red herring." He stopped, then suddenly his entire body relaxed and he smiled. "I can't believe I said that."

Lucy relaxed, too. They needed to all take a step back and reassess.

"We're running all the guards who were on duty, the food prep, anyone who potentially could have come in contact with Sanchez or the food. But it's not going to be easy to prove without physical evidence."

He glanced away and then Lucy saw it, the familiar focus in Brad Donnelly's eyes. She was well aware of how fixated a cop could be when pursuing a violent predator. Focus was important, but there was a fine line between being committed to the job and being obsessed with the job. Lucy had been on both sides of the line. She knew the signs better than anyone.

Brad Donnelly was obsessed with Jaime Sanchez. Lucy needed to know why.

Sean said he had a meeting and couldn't make it to the Casillas' for dinner. He didn't elaborate on it so she didn't push, but it seemed odd to her that he had a business meeting late on a Sunday afternoon.

She and Ryan drove to the Casillas' house north of the outer loop, in an older neighborhood filled with families in simple one-story ranch-style homes, no fences; all of them looked like they'd been built in the early 1960s. Instead of being crammed together, each house had a large lot and established trees. Kids of all ages rode their bikes up and down the street, and Lucy had to stop for a football pass that required the kid to run into the middle of the road to make the play.

Ryan stared wistfully at the kids as they waved their apology. Lucy said, "You miss your boys."

"I don't want to talk about it."

Lucy didn't know exactly what had happened between Ryan and his second ex-wife, but Nate said it was a combination of Ryan's job and his ex-wife's desire for more than Ryan could afford. He didn't say it that kindly, either, and since the divorce had just been finalized at the beginning of the year, before Lucy arrived, Nate had gone through much of it with his friend.

Lucy parked in the driveway and they walked up to the house. It was six fifteen, and the street started clearing off

as bells were rung and voices raised throughout the neighborhood to bring the kids in for dinner. Lucy smiled, remembering that her mother had a whistle. If you weren't in
the door within five minutes, you had kitchen cleanup duty
for the week. Lucy remembered a summer when she was
six and her sister Carina was seventeen when Carina had
cleanup duty for nine weeks straight. Before that, their
older brother Connor had the record at six weeks.

A handsome ten-year-old boy rode his bike up the
driveway and parked it against the wall. Chris was the oldest of the soon-to-be-six Casilla children, and the only
boy. "Lucy!" he exclaimed. "Where's Sean?"

"He had a meeting," she said.

Chris's face fell.

"Next time," she promised.

Boys loved Sean, and Lucy knew that was because Sean
was a kid at heart. Video games, electronics, computers
were only part of it. He also played ball, told slightly inap-
propriate jokes (cleaned up for the religious Casilla clan),
and talked to them like people, not children. The last time
they were here, Sean had rallied not only the older Casilla
kids, but another half a dozen kids in the neighborhood,
for a game of street hockey that went on until it was dark.
He'd had as much fun as anyone.

When Lucy saw Sean with kids like Chris, she felt the
pang of regret that she was unable to have children. He'd
make a great dad.

Someday, she thought. *Someday we'll adopt.*

But someday was far from now. She was barely used to
being responsible for herself; she didn't want to think
about being responsible for anyone else, not yet. Especially
someone wholly and completely dependent on her.

Chris led them inside, where there was organized chaos.
Melina, the oldest girl, was setting the large dining room
table with the "help" of three-year-old Beth. Nita, Juan's

very pregnant wife, greeted them both warmly, asked about Sean. She offered drinks and told them that Juan was in the kitchen, they should join him.

Juan had two faces—his professional, serious work profile, and his relaxed, happy family-man face. He wore jeans and a white polo shirt under a bright-red apron. He never dressed in anything less than an impeccable suit at FBI headquarters. His hair wasn't perfectly combed—the humidity and lack of product made it curl even though he kept it trimmed short. He looked younger than his forty-one years.

"Lucy, Ryan. So glad you could come."

"Did you get my message?"

"Sean's busy, and you want to debrief me. You have five minutes. No cop talk at the table."

Juan was dishing food into bowls, and Lucy fell into step. She'd done this for years at home. Her father wouldn't have been caught dead in the kitchen, which was a good thing because on the rare occasions when the colonel did attempt to cook, they ended up with sandwiches or a rare night out for dinner.

Lucy and Ryan filled him in on the big picture, and then Lucy said, "I want to talk to the Popes tomorrow morning, see if they saw Michael again, and check his room."

"Will it be the same as last year?"

"I don't know, but they probably kept his belongings. They had planned to adopt him, and they haven't taken in another foster child since he ran away."

"I would do the same."

"Donnelly is sending a local team to interview his father in prison, because there might be a connection to Sanchez, but I might want to follow up."

Juan glanced at Ryan, then said to Lucy, "Only if you have good reason to believe he has information about Michael's whereabouts. That would be a full day going to

McConnell, interviewing him, getting back. Your time would be better spent here. You don't have any other leads?"

"The old Rodriguez neighborhood, which is in Sanchez's territory. Except—I don't think he would go there if he was running from Sanchez. Based on the note he left for the Popes, he's planning to do something specific."

Ryan said, "Donnelly thinks the scar on his arm might be a gang tat, but he hasn't seen it before. It's not one of the larger, known drug gangs. He's sending it to his analysts, but we also sent it to Zach."

"Good. If the kid is in a gang, he's not going to turn on them."

"He's barely thirteen," Lucy said.

"I've faced younger criminals. Keep your mind open, Lucy."

She did, she knew what abused kids faced, she knew how killers were created. But she couldn't forget the way Bella spoke about Michael. There was something else there, something kind and protective in the boy. Lucy needed to find him; she needed to save him. She didn't believe he was beyond redemption.

Dinner lasted nearly an hour with rapid-fire conversation and plenty of good food. Juan walked them out while the kids cleared the table. "If you stay much longer, you'll be roped into a game," he said.

"I would," Lucy said, "but it's been a long day."

"I'm glad you both could come. I know this case is all-consuming, but everyone needs a few hours' downtime. You'll come back to the case fresher in the morning."

"How long have you known Agent Donnelly?" Lucy asked.

"Years, mostly by reputation and a few cases that crossed jurisdiction. Is there a problem?"

"No, nothing like that."

"I meant what I said this morning. Donnelly's rep is

solid, but he's a maverick. If you have questions about anything, call me, day or night. I mean that, too. I can't protect
my people if I'm kept in the dark."

"Thank you, sir," Ryan said and shook his hand.

"Next week, bring your boys with you, Ryan. As you
can tell, we always have plenty of food."

CHAPTER 11

Lucy dropped Ryan off at his car at SAPD, then drove home. She pulled into the garage, surprised that Sean's black Mustang was still gone. She sent him a message that she was home, then went upstairs to the master suite.

She was hot and tired, but wonderfully satiated from the home-cooked dinner. She called her mom, just to say hi, while her shower warmed up. Rosa Kincaid couldn't talk long, because they had a houseful of company.

Going home for Christmas and spending an extra ten days with her family had reminded Lucy what she'd given up when she moved to DC eight years ago.

Those had been rocky years. She had her family back now, but then it had been so difficult being around them. Every time they looked at her, she knew what they were thinking—what they remembered. About her kidnapping at her high school graduation. Being raped, repeatedly, for the sick enjoyment of perverts who paid to watch her attack on the Internet. And then Patrick's long coma, and knowing that he had been injured because he was coming to save her.

Her family tried to hide their pain, but she saw it in their eyes, not just the pain and anger, but the quiet regret, the silent accusations that somehow it was her fault.

Over time she realized it wasn't their accusations, but her own. They'd forgiven her—probably didn't think she needed to be forgiven. She would never completely rid herself of the guilt that part of what happened to her was because she'd been stupid. She'd let herself walk into a trap and she should have known better. The events that unfolded had hurt not only her, but her entire family. Being raped wasn't her fault, but few rape victims could stop thinking about the *if only* . . .

If only I hadn't flirted online . . .
If only I hadn't agreed to meet him . . .
If only I'd fought harder . . .
If only . . .

She shook her head to rid herself of the negative thoughts. She'd worked hard to keep the past in the past and not let it control her life. She was healed, mostly. She wasn't a victim anymore. She hadn't been for years. Because of her family. Because of Sean.

Lucy stripped off her clothes and stepped into the hot shower. It didn't matter how hot it was outside; she loved the heat and steam of the shower.

Family, she thought as the water rolled down her body, family was complicated. She loved her family and missed them. But they also knew all her weaknesses and flaws. They loved her in spite of her flaws. Just like the Casillas, the Kincaids were a close group—the tragedies and heartbreak they suffered had brought them closer together.

Lucy recognized that what she had growing up was special, that some other families could be cruel. Instead of support, or good-natured teasing, weaknesses and flaws could be used against others for manipulation and control. They could pit one member against another. Family was loyal, but how far did that loyalty go? Lucy would do anything for her family—but they would never ask her to do something that was evil. They would never ask her to hurt someone, to break the law—unless it was for a very good reason. A just reason.

She used to believe in black and white, right and wrong, but sometimes there were gray areas and those gray areas were dependent on the who and what and why. Her brothers worked for a private security company that often tread into gray areas. Sean was the poster child for working in the gray.

She thought back to some of her decisions, choices she'd made knowing that they could change her future. She'd been up before the Office of Professional Responsibility twice while she was at Quantico because she'd made choices that were right on the one hand, but didn't conform to the rules on the other. But they were choices she would make again if she had to, because doing what was right had to come before doing what would save her butt.

It had taken her a long time to get to this point, she thought as she turned slowly under the spray of water. She let it wash over her, burn her skin in a way that both hurt and cleansed.

A long time to grow up. To forget the pain. To be whole again. To fall in love and live with a man who made her happy in ways she'd never thought she'd see. Though he didn't admit it, it was a sacrifice for Sean to give up RCK and move to San Antonio with her. He'd wanted to go out on his own, but it would have been easier in a city where he'd grown roots. And part of her was hoping to be assigned to New York because they had friends there—mutual friends they'd cultivated together.

San Antonio was like being a world away. The crimes were violent, the community poorer; crimes tended more toward drugs and gangs than white collar and the standard homicide. As if any murders were standard. But Lucy knew why she was here—she wanted to be on the Violent Crimes Squad, and there were few positions open since the

FBI restructured their priorities after 9/11. She was particularly well suited for the squad, though she could have held her own in cybercrimes. She was the only one in her class of thirty-seven who'd been assigned to violent crimes, and she suspected someone had pulled strings, though no one admitted to it. Her sister-in-law Kate? Her mentor, Dr. Hans Vigo? She didn't know, and she wasn't going to ask. In the past it would have greatly bothered her to think she'd gotten special treatment, but she'd learned that sometimes the extra help was necessary. She'd earned it, and wanted it, and if she needed a special recommendation to get this slot, so be it.

Yeah, she'd done a lot of growing up in the last year.

The hot water worked miracles on her sore, tired muscles. She scrubbed her body with a soapy loofah, trying to battle back the questions she still had after their busy day of interviews and information. But try as she might, she couldn't rid her head of the odd T that Bella had drawn of the scar, or tattoo, on Michael's forearm.

"Lucy," she heard Sean call from the bedroom, "it's me!"

Sean stepped into the doorway. He was wearing slacks and a button-down shirt, no tie. He said, "I didn't want to startle you."

She smiled and slid open the glass door halfway. "I would have waited, but I didn't know when you'd be home. Why are you all dressed up?" For Sean, he was practically formal.

"I'll tell you over dinner."

She frowned. "I ate at the Casillas'. But Nita made you a plate."

"I suspected she would." He raised an eyebrow. "You look pretty cooked. How long have you been in there?"

"Ten, fifteen minutes maybe. Twenty? These dual showerheads are amazing."

"You only now figured that out?" He leaned over and

kissed her as she stuck her head out. "The hot water in this old house isn't going to last if I slip in there with you, though I very much want to."

She gave him a slight pout.

"Okay, you convinced me," Sean said as he unbuttoned his shirt. "But if the water turns icy cold, don't get mad at me."

"Never," she said as she watched him strip.

"You're smiling," he said.

"You're very nice to look at."

"Nice? I'm *nice*?"

She laughed and pulled him into the shower. "*Extra* nice." She tilted her head up for another kiss. He pushed her wet hair from her face and stared at her, his eyes darkening with a desire she recognized as raw lust. A rush made her heart skip a beat, and her lips parted as he leaned down for the kiss.

Each time Sean kissed her, it was both familiar and new. There was a deep comfort in his affection, as well as a passion that excited and frightened her. How could her love for this man continue to grow? Would it stop? Was her heart going to burst with her need for him?

"I'm so lucky to have you," Lucy whispered.

"Yes," Sean said with a half smile, "yes, you are."

And with that, he took the fear and turned it to fun. He kissed her again, catching her laugh, reminding her of all the reasons she'd fallen in love with this man.

He made her smile. He made her laugh.

But mostly, he made her feel loved.

"The water is getting cold," she whispered.

"It's gone from scalding to hot," he said.

She looked directly in his eyes as her hands moved from around his neck, down his muscular arms, around to his back, and lower. She squeezed his bare butt and leaned into him at the same time.

"Luce—" He kissed her, then turned off the water.

He grabbed a towel and wrapped her in it, then picked her up and carried her to the bed.

Neither of them cared about dripping water or wet sheets. All that mattered was reconnecting after a long day apart.

Sean and Lucy sat on the floor in the family room with a bottle of wine and the remains of the leftovers from the Casillas' dinner. She picked at his plate as well, nibbling the *carnitas*, which were a favorite of hers.

"You know," she said, "we have a table in the other room. In fact, we have a dining room table, a kitchen table, and a kitchen bar."

He grinned. "This is much more fun. A picnic." Lucy was hardly spontaneous, and Sean loved surprising her.

She leaned back onto a large grouping of pillows he'd taken off the couch and nursed her glass of wine.

"This house is too big for us," she said.

"Not really." He looked around. "It's just that the rooms are big. There're only three bedrooms."

"In the *main* house. And a library, and a movie room, and a family room, and four bathrooms—"

"Three and a half."

She gave him a stern look, and he kissed her nose. She laughed. "But I love it, because you're here. I don't think I've told you enough how much I appreciate the huge sacrifice you've made to move—"

"Stop. This is the hundredth time you've gotten that guilty look on your face, like I didn't want to come. I *want* to be here. I'm happy. I'm not bored. I love this house because you're here, and it's all us. It's *ours*. It's our *home*. And believe me, I'd much rather be living with you than with your brother."

She laughed. "The way you and Patrick traveled you never saw each other."

"But having you over whenever I wanted wasn't easy."

"And now I get to stay over every night."

He raised his eyebrow. "Stay over? This is your house as much as it is mine." He touched her chin. "You okay?"

"Of course."

She put her wineglass on the table and gathered up the plates. Sean folded up the picnic blanket he'd laid down, then took the plates from her and put them on the table. "Relax, princess. I thought the too-hot shower and mutually fun sexual aerobics had turned you to jelly."

"They did."

He rubbed her shoulders. "Not anymore."

She groaned and closed her eyes. "Don't stop."

He kissed her neck. "Luce, I have to leave town for a couple of days."

She frowned. "Washington?"

He nibbled her ear. "Dallas. Not that far, but too far to drive back and forth all week. It's a job."

"Job?" Her voice caught, and he knew what she was thinking.

"Not permanent. I'm not totally happy about it, but Duke sent it my way. Patrick is on another assignment, and they need someone with my skill set. Someone is embezzling from the company, and they've narrowed it down to a department, but not the individual. They need me to analyze their data and logs, and the only way I can be certain the results aren't tampered with is to go on-site."

"I'll miss you," she said.

He moved his hands up to the base of her skull and put pressure in all the right places to relieve the growing headache. How had he known she was in pain? This connection of theirs was new and exciting, but a lot intimidating. That someone could know her so well, she didn't have to speak.

"This case of yours will keep you busy," Sean said. "And I hope to be done by Wednesday at the latest."

"Still." She rolled over and looked at him, resting her head on her propped-up hand. "I like sleeping with you next to me."

He grinned. "I like sleeping with you, too."

"One-track mind."

He feigned hurt. "Who invited me into the shower? Hmm?" He nuzzled her neck and tickled her.

"Uncle!" she exclaimed.

She scrambled up and grabbed the plates. "Let's clean up. I'm beat."

He took the plates from her and carried them into the kitchen. She sat at the island and picked bites off a crumb cake their elderly neighbor across the street made them. They'd lived in this house for nine weeks and every Saturday morning, Mrs. Ethel Dobbins brought over something she'd baked. "I'm surprised you didn't finish this," Lucy said to Sean.

"It was big enough for ten people."

She smiled and took a big bite while Sean loaded the dishwasher.

"How's the case going? Any leads on Sanchez's killer?"

She shook her head. "Donnelly is all over it. He's confident it's an inside job, maybe a guard who was paid to look the other way. But they haven't narrowed it down yet." She finished her wine and handed Sean the glass. "But Juan put Ryan and me exclusively on finding Michael Rodriguez, helping Donnelly and the DEA only insofar as helping is leading us to the kid. Separating the agencies, I suppose."

"But you think they're connected."

"We all do—and we learned why. Michael's father lived in the same neighborhood as the Sanchezes. He's older than Jaime and George, but the time line still works out. I wanted to talk to him in prison, but Donnelly is sending local agents tomorrow morning. The prison is two hours away."

"It seems a bit thin," he said. "Any other connections?"

She went over everything she knew, and all her theories. Talking it all out with Sean, who asked smart questions and kept her mind working, helped more than stewing over possibilities in the shower. And in the end, it went back to Michael.

She said, "I don't understand what he was doing for the year between when he left and when he was held captive by the Sanchezes."

"You're certain he wasn't imprisoned elsewhere before the girl saw him?"

"No, I'm not, but the note he left makes it seem that he left of his own free will. Maybe threatened or coerced, but not kidnapped."

Sean sat next to her at the kitchen bar. He took her hand. "You care about this kid and you haven't even met him."

"He's had such a rough life, Sean. Why would he leave foster parents who obviously loved him and wanted to adopt him?"

"Maybe he didn't think he deserved to be happy," Sean said quietly, then kissed her hand.

She knew how that felt. She hadn't been happy, truly happy, for years before Sean came into her life. He taught her how to live again. How to smile. How to appreciate the small things that made her happy. "I thought about that, and maybe that's part of it, but I don't think that's all of it. I can't explain why."

"Your instincts. Trust them, Luce."

"What would be the only reason you'd leave people you loved?"

"I'm not going to leave you, Lucy." He turned her face to look at him. "You know that, right?" He was both fearful and angry, his own doubts of worthiness coming briefly to the surface.

She held his face. "I know. But that's not exactly what I

meant. Put yourself into the shoes of a twelve-year-old boy who, after years of abuse and betrayal, finds two people who love him for who he is, who feed and clothe him and make sure he goes to school and brushes his teeth. Who gave him his own room with his own toys and put him on a baseball team even though they didn't have to do it, even though it cost them their own money and not the money they were getting from the foster care system. Two people who never raise their voices or use their fists. Why would you walk away from that?"

"I wouldn't." Then he said, "He was trying to protect them."

"That's the only thing I can see. There's no indication that he was kidnapped, and he was only locked in the basement for four weeks. Even though the police don't have a verified connection between Rodriguez and Sanchez, that doesn't mean there isn't one. And if Rodriguez knew Sanchez, it goes to reason that Sanchez knew Michael."

"How did he reach him? How did he find out where he lived?"

"I don't know. Michael was placed as far as you can get from his old neighborhood. He wasn't sent to the same school—in fact the Popes put him in Catholic school."

"Chance?"

"Or someone on the inside."

"The inside of where?"

"DeSantos, his CPS counselor, said that Michael's father was fighting the adoption. What if his lawyer gave him information? All he'd need is a name. It would then be easy to track down the Popes."

"That's a good place to start."

"Or it could be Michael kept in touch with old friends, maybe told someone where he lived, and it got back to Sanchez." She rubbed her eyes. This was getting her nowhere.

"I interviewed Bella this morning, with CPS."

"This DeSantos?"

"No, Bella's caseworker. Jennifer Mendez. She's difficult, but good with kids."

Lucy got up and went to her briefcase to pull out a copy of the crude drawing. She showed it to Sean. "Bella drew this. Said it was a scar on Michael's arm. Or it could be a homemade tattoo."

Sean looked, turned it around, shook his head. "I've never seen it."

"Neither has anyone on Donnelly's team. He sent it to Washington, hoping they'll have something more. Donnelly thinks it's drug-related."

"You should send this to Jack. RCK has a database of drug cartel symbols."

"DEA would have a similar system."

"They do. It doesn't hurt to cross-check. And RCK is faster than the government."

"True," she said. "Thanks."

"Thank your brother." He paused. "Or I can call Kane. I can't guarantee he'll respond or be able to help, but if anyone knows what's going on with drug issues along the border, it's Kane."

Sean didn't particularly want to call his brother. He hadn't spoken to him in months. Kane called when he needed something, never just to talk or say hi. Sean was used to it, but it didn't make brotherly bonding easy. The last time he'd actually seen Kane was before he met Lucy, and it was for a short and dangerous flight in Mexico. Duke, who'd raised Sean after their parents were killed, didn't like when Sean did jobs for Kane, even though Kane was one of the founders of RCK and their initial focus was hostage rescue in Mexico and Central America. People around Kane tended to die.

Lucy didn't know Kane. Sean admired him in many

ways, but didn't always understand him. He was blunt, he could be cruel, and if he didn't have the time or inclination to help, he wouldn't. He had his own agenda, and it didn't always coincide with what the feds wanted. Kane helped the military in many off-book operations, and fed a substantial amount of information to the DEA and ICE, but he also had some choice words to say about the government. Sean didn't think his brother had stepped foot in the U.S. more than a dozen times in the last fifteen years.

But for Sean, Kane would help. For Jack's sister, Kane would help.

At least, Sean hoped he wasn't wrong about his oldest brother.

"Sean?" Lucy asked, rubbing his arm up and down. "You don't have to talk to Kane. I'll call Jack."

"No, it's fine. If Kane can help, he'll call me. I'll send him a message tonight. And a copy of this, if that's okay."

"Of course."

"He'll probably call you directly, cut out the middleman. Just remember—he can be difficult."

"Like all the Rogans?" she said with a smile.

"Me?" He reached over and tickled her again. "I'm the easiest one of all."

She snorted and Sean laughed. He picked her up and, over her protests, carried her up to bed.

An hour later, while Lucy slept, Sean tried to reach Kane.

Jaime had the address and drove around twice to make sure no one was watching the house. His contact told him there were increased patrols, but no one sitting outside the house. Experience told Jaime to always verify the information.

His contact was right. This time. The federal sweep had made everyone in Jaime's business antsy or stupid. They either holed up and Jaime couldn't find them, or they did something stupid, like the five who'd been arrested at the hardware store and lost the ledger.

The feds didn't know what they had; if they did, the names and faces of everyone on the general's payroll would have been plastered all over the news. The general was far bigger and more powerful than anyone knew. Even Jaime was surprised at his reach sometimes.

Everyone knew that the general had never been in the military, but fashioned himself a military expert. Everyone knew he had a temper, but he was also generous. Money flowed, promises were kept . . . unless you did something to anger him.

Jaime shivered. Little scared him. *Nothing* scared him, except the general.

And now Jaime was on the hot seat, and unless he got Michael back, he would be dead.

Except for his ace in the hole.

Bella.

The general wanted her now, but Jaime needed a win. He needed Bella, he had to find Michael, and he had a plan to take care of DEA Agent Brad Donnelly and his entire team. His partner wouldn't like it, so Jaime kept him in the dark.

Jaime answered only to the general.

His phone rang.

"What?"

"Go. The patrol is fifteen minutes out."

He hung up, checked his gun, and left the car around the corner from the house where his nieces were staying. He slipped through the back gate that was now unlocked.

CeCe had gotten the message. She'd done what was asked of her. This should be a piece of cake.

He stood in the dark of the backyard. There were motion lights on each corner of the house, but they didn't go on.

He smiled.

Good girl, CeCe.

He opened the back door. Unlocked, just as CeCe had been told to leave it. The girl had always obeyed well. She was her mother's daughter.

He stood in the warm, spice-filled kitchen. This was where it would get dangerous. He didn't want to go up the stairs, where he could be trapped. And though he would kill the family if he had to, he would rather get away clean and have time to get back to the safe house before the cops started looking for him or the girls.

A small sound in the foyer made him freeze. He had his gun out.

"No," a little voice said. "No, no!" It was Bella, and she was getting louder.

CeCe hissed at her. "Yes!"

Jaime acted. He moved silently through the kitchen and grabbed Bella by the arm. "It's me, Uncle Jaime. Come."

She started sobbing and dragging her feet.

There was a thud upstairs. Jaime picked Bella up and hoisted her over his shoulder.

CeCe followed, but Jaime made sure she couldn't keep up with him. He didn't know what to do with CeCe, but the general only wanted Bella. Jaime feared what he would do to his older niece; she was safer here. And it was safer for him.

Jaime got to the car and glanced over his shoulder. The lights in the corner house were on, and CeCe was running down the street toward him.

He didn't wait.

He put Bella in the backseat, turned the ignition, and sped off.

"I don't want to go, please, Uncle Jaime, please let me out."

"Trust me, Bella. You're going to be treated like a princess."

"I want Mommy."

"I'm working on it," he lied. He didn't know what the general had in store for Mirabelle. All Jaime knew was that he was very angry with the woman who'd betrayed him.

And Jaime didn't blame him.

Family was important, but some family was more important than others.

He glanced in the rearview mirror.

Like Bella.

CHAPTER 12

Light kisses woke her up before the sun. Lucy stretched and felt Sean next to her. But he was fully dressed.

She opened one eye. "What time is it?" She sat up and yawned. It wasn't even five.

"I want to get to Stinson before the rush." Stinson Municipal Airport catered mostly to private planes, many commuters or business charters. Sean had a Cessna he housed there. "I emailed you some interesting information about Donnelly."

He kissed her again. "Go back to sleep."

"No, I'm fine." Once she had coffee.

"I wish I could stay, but I can't. Love you." He gave her a last, long kiss, then left.

Lucy got ready for work and drank a cup of coffee while sitting at the desk in her home office. She scanned the information Sean had sent her.

Brad Donnelly, thirty-nine. Four years in the Marines right out of high school, then went to college, graduated with a degree in criminal justice. Went right into the DEA, was in the first class that graduated from the new facilities that opened in 1999, also located at Quantico next to the

FBI training academy. He was initially assigned to the Phoenix Division, where he stayed for five years. He transferred to Houston and received a promotion to Supervisory Special Agent. He had a long list of accomplishments and awards, and though Lucy didn't know how Sean had found it, he also had a few dings on his record.

Four years ago, Donnelly was transferred to the San Antonio regional office in a lateral move. He was also tasked with being the interagency liaison, which made sense since he had led the recent sweep.

But it was a headline from Arizona, shortly before the transfer to Houston, that told Lucy all she needed to know.

TWO FEDERAL AGENTS KILLED DURING DRUG BUST

TUCSON, AZ. Two agents with the Drug Enforcement Administration were killed last night during a sting operation outside Sierra Valley, twenty miles north of the Mexican border.

A spokesperson for the DEA, Special Agent Margaret Neilson, said a team of agents raided a warehouse where more than a thousand pounds of heroin were recovered.

"After the drugs were seized, a well-armed gang of criminals attacked the officers who were stationed outside. Two agents were killed. After a standoff, reinforcements arrived and three members of the gang were shot and killed. Two were arrested. We suspect that two escaped and a manhunt is currently under way."

There was nothing in the article that mentioned Brad Donnelly, but Sean had found other information that put him at the scene.

Lucy looked at the two deceased agents. Both were rookies with less than one year experience. One male, one female.

Tucson was a far cry from San Antonio, but could Sanchez, or his people, have been responsible for those deaths? Was that why Donnelly was so obsessed with him? Or was it simply the situation itself, bad guys getting away with crimes over and over, and young cops dying in the process? Was there another case that impacted Donnelly? Something closer to home?

She wanted to talk to him about it, but then Donnelly would know she'd been researching him. Sean had written a note that said his contacts told him Donnelly was respected but feared within the office.

There had to be more to the Tucson case than what was in the press. Operational details, names, what really happened. A well-planned operation shouldn't have ended up with the team being ambushed. Drug dealers didn't just leave a thousand pounds of heroin unprotected.

She considered going into the office early, before going to the Popes, but decided to drive through the Popes' neighborhood to get a sense of the community.

It was an older, established neighborhood on the outskirts of San Antonio, nowhere near the Rodriquez/Sanchez area. It wasn't far from the Groves' house, maybe two miles on the other side of the loop. The small bungalows were generally clean and tidy with 1950s charm. The Popes were on the corner with a deck and a cheerful yellow coat of paint, windows trimmed in white and gray, and a multitude of flowers in the ground, hanging from the porch roof, or overflowing from pots. It was a warm house, a place a kid like Michael from the bad side of town would never expect to live.

She'd left a message for the Popes yesterday, but they hadn't returned her call. She hoped they would talk to her.

The old Chevy truck that was registered to Hector Pope

wasn't in the driveway, and on her second turn around the block, a woman of about fifty was watering the flowers on the front porch from an oversized watering pot. She wore a long multicolored skirt and loose white blouse. She was a plumper, shorter version of Lucy's mother and for a minute, Lucy was homesick.

You're being ridiculous, Luce. You haven't lived at home for eight years.

It was that she'd spent so much time over Christmas with her family that she was nostalgic for what she used to have, before her life was turned inside out by a monster.

She took a deep breath and got out of the car. She approached Mrs. Pope with a smile. "Hello, Mrs. Pope? I'm Agent Lucy Kincaid with the San Antonio FBI. I'm hoping you have a moment to talk about Michael."

The woman stared at her with a deer-in-the-headlights expression.

"I need to call my husband," she said as Lucy walked up the stairs.

"I only have a few questions—he's not in trouble."

"Why would the FBI be here? What do the *federales* want with my boy?"

"I'm trying to help him."

She frowned, confused.

"Did Mr. DeSantos talk to you yesterday?"

She relaxed, just a bit. "I called Mr. DeSantos about the note Michael left me. He said he would look into it, find out what he could."

"And you haven't talked to him since?"

"No, why? Is something wrong?"

DeSantos might not have wanted to get their hopes up. Lucy appreciated that concern, but right now she needed information.

She motioned to the chairs that were positioned between pots of flowers. "Can we sit a minute?"

Mrs. Pope hesitated, then nodded. She put down the watering can and clasped her hands together in her lap as she sat in the chair closest to the door. Lucy took the other cushioned seat and smiled. Mrs. Pope didn't return the smile; she still looked worried.

"The police never come here. We never have trouble, Agent Kincaid."

"No one is in trouble," Lucy said. She wanted to put Mrs. Pope at ease. "Call me Lucy, *por favor?*" She didn't get a response, so she continued. "I want to help Michael, and I think you can help me find him. I think he's in trouble, that some bad people might be trying to hurt him."

Mrs. Pope looked skeptical and worried at the same time. "Why would anyone hurt him? He's a good boy. A sad boy, but a good boy."

"I read his files, all his paperwork. I know about his father."

"Evil man." Her eyes widened. "He's not out of jail, is he? Mr. DeSantos would have told us."

"He's still in prison," Lucy assured her. "I'd like to know about Michael in the days before he ran away. Did he seem different? Aloof? Maybe quieter than normal? Secretive?"

"He didn't run away," she said defiantly. "I know he didn't. He loves us, he told me that. Not one week before he disappeared, he told me while we were cooking. 'Olive,' he said to me. I told him not to call me Mrs. Pope. I had hoped some day he would call me Mama, but I wasn't going to push him. 'Olive, do you think my dad can stop this?' He was talking about the adoption. I said to him, 'No, Michael, he can't. The family rights lawyer said we have the best case she's seen and all he's doing is delaying the inevitable.' And he asked me, 'Olive, do you really want me to be here forever?' I said, 'Yes, I couldn't love you more than if you came from my womb.' And he said, 'I couldn't love you more if you were my real mom.' " She teared up. "And then I cried, like I'm doing now, and he hugged me. And . . ." She stopped.

"And what?"

"Just—well, I didn't think about it until now. He said one more thing. I guess I didn't think it was odd, because I was emotional, but he said, 'I'll take care of you.'"

She sniffed. "He probably meant if anything happened to Hector. My husband works hard. Long hours. Six days a week. He's a good man, a good husband, and good father to the boys we've had here through the years."

"I'm sure he is."

"But he works too hard sometimes. The Christmas before Michael disappeared, Hector had a scare. A heart problem. But he's fine now."

"My father had a heart attack last Christmas. That must have been awful for you."

"Michael was a rock. He told me, 'Olive, Hector is the strongest man I know. He's going to get better.' Michael never left my side, except to get me tea or food. He's a good boy."

"Olive, help me help Michael."

"I still don't understand why the FBI is asking questions."

Lucy weighed how much to tell her. She wasn't going to lie, but she also didn't want to worry the woman.

"On Saturday morning, the FBI and several other law enforcement agencies arrested wanted fugitives. Criminals who didn't show up at court when they were supposed to, or were wanted on a warrant of some sort."

She nodded once. "I heard about it on the news."

"One of the fugitives is a man by the name of Jaime Sanchez. He wasn't at his house, but a witness identified Michael."

"I don't understand."

"The witness said Michael had been kept there against his will for the last month."

Olive didn't say anything for a long minute. Then she shook her head. "Michael's been gone more than a year."

"You called Michael's CPS counselor Saturday and showed him a note Michael had left you. Mr. DeSantos shared it with me. He's helping me find Michael," she added, hoping that would help put Olive's mind at ease.

She didn't say anything but looked at her tightly clasped hands.

"I think Michael left last year because someone from his father's former life found him."

Olive closed her eyes. "To protect us."

Did she know something?

"What do you know about that?"

"Nothing. Just that Michael is always protective. Always worried about something. His mother was abused," she added. "He told me he felt so helpless. What could he have done at six to save his mother's life? Nothing. I told him that, many times, but it doesn't always help."

No, it doesn't.

Olive brushed away tears. "If Michael is in trouble, why wouldn't he talk to me? He knows I'll protect him. We could go to the police, to the church. We have people who will help."

"Because he's a thirteen-year-old boy who's scared and doesn't know who to trust."

"He trusts me. He trusts Hector."

"Yes, but he wants to protect you. Is there anything else about those weeks?"

She shook her head, her face fallen. "I've told you everything."

"What about friends?"

"Michael was slow to make friends. I asked Father Flannigan at the church, since Michael seemed to like him especially. He was also Michael's math teacher. Michael was very good in math. Advanced, they told me. Father was distraught about Michael going missing, as upset as we were."

Lucy's instincts twitched. "Did the police talk to him?"

Olive shook her head. "You don't understand. The police thought Michael was a runaway. They didn't do anything. They treated Michael like he was a nobody. Even Mr. DeSantos, God bless him, thought Michael ran away."

"Olive," Lucy said, leaning forward and catching her eye. "I promise you, I will not stop until I find Michael." As she said it she feared that she was making a promise she couldn't keep. Then she added, "Michael is somebody. I don't care who his father is, or what happened to him, or even why he left. He's a scared, brave thirteen-year-old boy who needs you. I will bring him back."

Olive stared at her for a long minute. "Thank you."

"I need one more thing from you. I'd like to look at his room."

Olive nodded. "I haven't changed it. Only clean it once a week. He needs a room when he comes home." She stood up, straightened her spine. "He will come home."

Lucy didn't find anything in Michael's room that told her why he might have left, but she did find a clue that sent her to St. Catherine's, the Catholic church and school where Father Flannigan was an associate pastor.

Michael had hidden a prayer card with MATEO FLANNIGAN written in small block letters, along with a phone number.

San Antonio was overwhelmingly Hispanic, and church attendance was high. When Lucy was growing up in San Diego, they had associate pastors come and go; church attendance had been down and while Rosa Kincaid insisted they go to Mass every Sunday, most families weren't as consistent. In San Antonio, families attended regularly, and St. Catherine's had a full schedule of Masses, more

Spanish Masses than English, and two permanently assigned pastors.

St. Catherine's was an old parish but the grounds were well maintained and the school was undergoing expansion. Lucy almost felt guilty for thinking the influx of cash had a nefarious source.

She avoided the school and headed to the main church office. The old cathedral called out to her and she realized she hadn't been to church since she moved to San Antonio. She wasn't as devout as her mother, but she'd gone regularly when she lived in Washington. Church kept her grounded, reminded her that for all the evil in the world, there was still hope.

Maybe it was time to go back.

She showed her identification to the secretary and said, "I need to speak with Father Flannigan."

If the secretary was surprised or suspicious, she kept it to herself. "Please sit, I'll call the father for you."

Lucy continued to stand, walking around the small lobby looking at the art, icons, and photographs. There were church picnics, school events, baptisms, and more. St. Catherine's was a young, active parish, and the bulletin board highlighted the events.

She was reading the bulletin when a priest approached her. "Agent Kincaid?"

She looked up and was surprised to note that Father Flannigan looked familiar, but she'd never met him before. Mateo Flannigan. He was half Hispanic, half Irish, just like her. Her Hispanic half came by way of Cuba, but Mateo Flannigan would have fit at her family table without question. Because of that, she felt immediately comfortable, and feared her ease would jeopardize her impartiality.

"Father Flannigan?" she asked formally.

"Yes. What can I do for the FBI?"

"I'm here about Michael Rodriguez."

He didn't say anything for a long moment. Then: "Let's take a walk."

Father Flannigan was young, no more than thirty-five, and shorter than Lucy, but he had a presence that spread beyond his stature and age. He wore small, wire-rimmed glasses that Lucy suspected ingratiated him with the kids because they resembled Harry Potter's spectacles, and his hands were rough and worn, as if he were building the new school himself.

They walked to a small but well-cultivated rose garden hidden in the back of the parish, behind the rectory. Father Flannigan was silent. He stopped in front of a statue of St. Jude and murmured a prayer.

St. Jude. The patron saint of desperate causes.

Then he sat on a stone bench, under a willow tree, and motioned for her to do the same.

"Thank you for meeting with me, Father."

"Did I have a choice?"

"Of course. I'm conducting an investigation. You don't have to talk to me if you don't want to."

He smiled, reminding her of a shorter, slimmer version of her brothers. He had the hybrid good looks of a Hispanic male with distinctly Irish features, including green eyes.

She must be missing her family. Everything and everyone was reminding her of them.

"Most FBI agents wouldn't admit that."

"Have you been interviewed often by the FBI?"

"Often enough."

That made her curious, but it was nearly ten, and she was already late for her meeting with Ryan and Donnelly.

"I just spoke with Olive Pope. She may not have told you, but Michael left her a note Saturday morning. I was working another case, and now I'm tracking Michael."

"Why?"

"Because he's in trouble. Possibly in grave danger."

"Why didn't you care last year when I tried to get people to help?"

"I wasn't here last year."

"I went to SAPD."

"I'm sure they tried, but there are many runaways. It's not fair, but it's true."

He stared across the rose garden, not looking at anything in particular.

"Why now?"

"Why not now?" She was getting frustrated with Father Flannigan. She showed him the prayer card she'd taken from Michael's room. "Olive told me Michael and you were friendly; then I found this hidden in his room. Michael made some cryptic remarks to Olive the week before he disappeared. Do you know what was going on in his life when he left fourteen months ago?"

"I can't talk about it."

"Why?" she demanded.

He didn't say anything for a moment. "Do you understand the sanctity of the confessional?"

"Yes."

He raised an eyebrow. "Then you know my hands are tied."

She wanted to scream with frustration, but then realized that if he did know where Michael had gone, he would have gone after him—he might not be able to tell anyone what Michael had told him during confession, but that didn't preclude him from trying to help.

She shifted tactics. "When you found out Michael had run away, who did you talk to?"

"I was with the Popes when the police arrived. I suggested they go back to Michael's old neighborhood, specifically the apartment building where his father lived before he was sent to prison. See if they could find him there."

"Olive didn't tell me that."

"She and Hector weren't in the room when I said it. I don't want to hurt them."

"I understand your dilemma, but time is critical. Jaime Sanchez, a wanted fugitive, is connected to Michael's father from their old neighborhood. I haven't found a direct connection, except that I have a witness who told me that Jaime kept Michael locked in his basement for the past month."

Father Flannigan was distinctly surprised.

She pulled out the drawing of the double-crossed T. "Do you recognize this?"

He stared for a long time, then shook his head. "Not specifically, but you're going to tell me that Michael has this mark."

"So you have seen it."

"Not that one. But others. Children, marked because of birth. Relegated to a life they did not ask for. Michael was a child of two worlds, his father's and the Popes'. He wanted a clean break. He didn't get it. And that's all I can say."

"No!" Lucy exclaimed. She sighed. "Forgive me, Father, but I need your help."

"I can't tell you what Michael told me, but I can tell you who I saw him with the day before he disappeared. I told the police as well, but they interviewed the kid and nothing came of it."

"Who?"

"A boy by the name of Richard Diaz."

"Do you have an address?"

"No. He was a friend of Michael's from his old life, came here with Michael a few times. A year or two younger. I haven't seen him since Michael disappeared. Richard may have been upset that I told the police about him, I don't know."

"Father, I respect the confessional. But Michael is alive and he is in danger. Help me."

He wrestled with his conscience; she could see the debate. He wrestled with his vows. The vows won.

"I can tell you only what Michael and I discussed outside the confessional. I shouldn't even do that, but it was in my role as a teacher, not a priest. Michael wrestled with anger over what his father did, and a deep shame over his father's life, as well as a belief that he was somehow to blame for what happened to his mother."

"They were both abused, mother and son."

Father Flannigan nodded. "And do you think that reason always wins over emotion?"

He was right, of course. "Michael was six when his mother died. There was no proof Vince Rodriguez killed her, but it was a suspicion."

"Michael doesn't trust the police." He looked at her. "He trusts me."

"Have you seen him since he disappeared?"

He didn't say anything for a long minute. "No, but I heard him."

And it became clear to her he was talking about the boy coming in for confession.

"When was the last time you heard him?" she asked quietly.

"Late Saturday afternoon." He hesitated and looked out into the garden. "You were right in that Michael wasn't himself before he disappeared. You said it yourself when we first sat down. A name. An old family associate. Michael saw him before he left fourteen months ago and it changed him. Then he was gone."

"Why didn't you go to the police? Give them something, even if you couldn't give them everything?"

"Agent Kincaid," he said as if he were reprimanding a child. "The police didn't care when he disappeared fourteen months ago. Why would they care now, when I can't even tell them where he is or what he is planning to do?"

He didn't say anything for a long time, just looked beyond Lucy into the rose garden. Then he reached around his neck and removed a chain with the medal of St. Jude. He handed it to her.

"If you find him, give him this. He'll know it's from me. It may help you earn his trust."

She slipped it over her neck. "Thank you."

"I'm scared for him, Agent Kincaid. What I told the police then was that they should look in his old neighborhood. Two days before he disappeared, he went to his old apartment building."

"How do you know?"

"I can't say."

"Is there anyone else who Michael might have confided in? A friend?"

The priest shook his head. "Only that boy, Richard Diaz. But I don't know where he lives, and I haven't seen him since Michael disappeared."

He stood up, signaling the conversation was over. "I'll call you if I hear anything else, Agent Kincaid."

"Thank you. And, please, call me Lucy." She stood and gave him her card. "If he comes back, if he calls, let me know. I will do everything in my power to protect him."

"I believe that, Lucy. But you may not be able to protect him from himself."

Lucy was practically jumping with anticipation as she left St. Catherine's. She called Zach as she drove and asked for more information about where Michael and his father lived prior to Vince Rodriguez's arrest. That was the key. Vince Rodriguez was connected to Jaime Sanchez, and now she had proof. Not proof for court, but proof enough for her to follow the lead.

While waiting for Zach, she drove toward the closest Starbucks, needing a jolt of caffeine. And a muffin. She'd become spoiled with Sean making her breakfast in the morning, and had skipped it because he'd left so early.

A tingling on the back of her neck made the hair on her arms rise.

She didn't believe in psychics or anything that couldn't be explained scientifically, but she did believe that the human senses were more advanced and sensitive than most people understood. It was well known and scientifically proven that those who lost one sense—like eyesight—had better-developed remaining senses.

When she'd been held captive eight years ago, she'd developed an intense fear of being watched. Now it was like a sixth sense to her; when eyes were on her back, she just *knew*. At first, when she was still prone to panic attacks, it could be anyone. But over time—with a lot of training and self-discipline—she'd been able to distinguish between people simply glancing at her and people actually watching her.

Her heart started thumping loudly in her ears as she looked in all her mirrors. She was on a busy street, midmorning traffic still thick. She couldn't distinguish any vehicles, nothing looked familiar, she saw no one giving her undue attention. She took deep breaths to force her heart rate to slow. It worked. Two years ago, she might have had a full panic attack, but it hadn't happened in a long time, and she wouldn't let it happen now.

The car directly behind her was a gold minivan with a female at the wheel and a teenage boy in the front seat. There were other kids in the rear. Behind the minivan was a shiny dark-blue foreign sedan. She couldn't make out the driver. In the lane to the right was a white cargo van with a Hispanic driver wearing a work cap with the same logo as the van. A plumbing company.

Starbucks was two blocks up on the left. She'd planned on going through the drive-through, but that would trap her. She considered going straight to FBI headquarters, but if someone was following her, they wouldn't put themselves at risk. She wanted a glimpse, an idea of who was behind her. She decided to circle the block a few times and park on the street outside the coffee shop.

She pulled into the left-hand turn lane and waited for the light. The white van passed, as well as the foreign sedan. It was a new Honda with tinted rear windows. The driver was female, but her head was turned as if she was playing with the radio. All Lucy could get was that she was Caucasian or light-skinned Hispanic. There was no license plate on the back, simply the advertisement for the dealership where the car had been bought.

The minivan was behind her, and another sedan behind the van. The mother honked and Lucy realized the light had turned green. She turned, drove past the corner Starbucks, and went down two blocks. The minivan turned into the Starbucks drive-through. The second sedan—a dark-green American model—followed Lucy.

She turned left again. So did the green car. She turned right. So did the green car.

She was in the middle of a residential neighborhood. Modest, middle-class homes, some in bad need of repair, lined the narrow street. She turned right at the stop sign and found herself on a dead-end road. Damn, damn, damn. She didn't know San Antonio well enough yet.

But the green car didn't turn right. It turned left, went down the street, then pulled into a driveway.

Lucy slowly turned around at the end of the dead-end road and drove past the green sedan. An older man, in his sixties, was walking up the broken front walk carrying a small suitcase. A little boy ran out the door, no older than four, and greeted the grandfather with a hug around the legs. His mother stood in the doorway while the boy half carried, half dragged the suitcase inside.

"You're paranoid," Lucy told herself as she made her way back to Starbucks.

She parked on the street nonetheless. She might be cautious, but she wasn't paranoid. Someone had been following her. Not anymore—she didn't have the same creepy feeling on her skin, but someone had been staring while she'd been driving from St. Catherine's.

Who else knew about Michael's relationship with Father Flannigan? Had Jaime Sanchez or one of his people staked out the place, hoping to catch the boy there? Had someone recognized her from the sweep? Her visit to St. Catherine's had been spontaneous. Her office and Donnelly knew she was going to visit the Popes, but she'd only had the strange feeling after leaving St. Catherine's.

She walked inside, looking at every car on the street and in the lot. Nothing jumped out as familiar. The minivan pulled out of the drive-through and back onto the street. She went inside and ordered, then stood against the wall and looked at the people sitting and waiting. No one looked familiar. No one was giving her undue attention.

She took her drink and muffin and returned to her car. She headed back the way she'd come, toward St. Catherine's. If someone was staking out the place, they may have returned.

But before she arrived at the church, her phone rang.

It was Donnelly. "Where the hell are you?"

She bristled at his tone. "I have a lead," she began, but he cut her off.

"Jaime Sanchez kidnapped Isabella Borez. Kidnapping trumps your lead."

CHAPTER 13

Because the interagency sweep was technically over, operations had moved from SAPD to the San Antonio DEA regional office. Brad Donnelly was in his element, and everyone seemed to get out of his way as he ushered Lucy through the bureaucracy of getting temporary credentials and setting her up in the conference room he'd taken over to hunt for Sanchez.

Ryan was there and gave Lucy an odd look—if he was going to say anything, Donnelly didn't give him a chance.

"At two this morning, Bella's sister CeCe got her out of bed. The foster parents heard the girls arguing downstairs, then Bella cried out. Karl Grove told his wife to call nine-one-one while he came downstairs in time to see Jaime Sanchez running through the back gate carrying Bella over his shoulder. CeCe was trying to keep up. Grove caught up with her, but Jaime disappeared in an old Ford sedan, partial license plate S-one-seven-W. He thinks the last two letters were the same, an L or T or F."

"How did—" Lucy began, but Donnelly cut her off.

"CeCe had a hidden burner phone, police found it under her mattress. We have no idea how she got it, who gave it to her, if she had it with her things and it was missed in the search, or what. There was a deleted message our tech people pulled out, sent from an untraceable burner phone at midnight." He handed Lucy a printout from the message, which had been in Spanish and also translated.

Turn off outside lights. Unlock back door. Be downstairs with B at 2.

"Let me talk to her," Lucy said.

"Can't. She has a court-appointed advocate. She's in juvenile detention right now, she's already been interviewed and isn't saying anything. In addition to the phone, she had a homemade shiv she'd made out of a toothbrush—just like they do in prison." He shook his head, as if to say he was both stunned and not surprised at the same time. "She attempted to stab Mr. Grove when he caught up with her on the street, but he caught her wrist in time and sustained only minor injuries.

"Based on his statement, Bella didn't want to go with Sanchez." He pounded his fist on the table. "Dammit, I should have put them in protective custody."

There was a knock on the door and Donnelly barked out, "What?"

The door opened and an agent escorted Jennifer Mendez in. "This is CPS Officer Mendez," the agent said, then stepped out.

"Great," Donnelly muttered.

"I need to know what's going on," Jennifer said. "I haven't gotten a straight answer from anyone."

"The FBI is handling the kidnapping," Donnelly said. "That's not DEA's purview."

"That's bullshit," Jennifer said. "A seven-year-old was kidnapped by a violent criminal and you're passing the buck?"

"Maybe you can answer how CeCe Borez got a burner phone? Aren't you supposed to search your wards?"

Jennifer bristled but didn't back down. "They were

searched according to procedure, but we don't strip-search minors who aren't in detention. You should have had an officer on the house if you even suspected that your drug dealer was going after his nieces."

The veins in Donnelly's neck throbbed but he didn't comment. Lucy felt for him. He was beating himself up, and now Jennifer was adding to it.

Lucy said, "We increased patrols in the neighborhood, but Sanchez must have been watching. He saw a window of opportunity and took it."

"How do I know you didn't lead him there?" Jennifer turned to Lucy.

"What?" Lucy had no idea what Jennifer was talking about.

"The Groves operate a safe house. We've never had problems. You walk in Sunday morning and Sunday night one of their charges is kidnapped. I don't think that's a co-incidence."

Ryan slowly leaned forward. "You'll need to watch your next words very carefully, Ms. Mendez."

Jennifer seemed to realize what she'd implied, and back-tracked. "What I meant was—"

"I know what you meant," Lucy said, "and I can assure you I wasn't followed to the Groves's house."

"How can you be so sure?"

It wasn't easy explaining to someone about Lucy's in-tense awareness of her surroundings, so she didn't. "I am. We don't know that anyone was followed. We *do* know that CeCe had a burner phone, and she alerted Sanchez. She may have told him."

Donnelly frowned. "There were no incoming or outgo-ing calls on the burner phone. Only the messages to CeCe."

"GPS on the phone?"

"No."

Jennifer said, "Who knew where they were?"

Ryan interjected, "We should be asking you the same thing."

"If you're implying—"

"I'm not implying," Ryan said.

Lucy put her hands up before this got out of control. "We have to assume that there's someone with access who gave Sanchez the information. Either at CPS or at a law enforcement agency."

Donnelly shook his head. "Only a handful of people knew on my end, but we can't assume that it was an inside leak. I know how CPS operates. Everything is in their database. It wouldn't take much to hack into the system."

Jennifer opened her mouth, then closed it. "I'll talk to my boss and see if the IT people can trace any unauthorized access to the files. But I think you're grasping at straws."

"We're *all* on edge," Lucy said.

Ryan said, "We have a debriefing at FBI headquarters in less than thirty minutes."

"I'd like to be there," Jennifer said. "Is that going to be a problem?"

"No," Donnelly said before anyone else could. "Meet us there. I need a minute with my team."

He waited until she left, then sat down, his head in his hands. "This is fucked. I wish—"

"Brad," Lucy said, "wishing isn't productive."

"Do you know that Mendez is clean?" Ryan asked. "Maybe she's on Sanchez's payroll."

Lucy didn't buy it. "It would be very stupid of her to leak information about her own CPS wards."

"Or very smart. Because it looks stupid."

"I didn't get that vibe from her," Lucy said.

"Her name has never come up in any of my investigations," Donnelly said, "but I'll put Nicole on it. I'm not going to wait for Mendez to talk to her boss. We'll light a fire under CPS and get them to look for security breaches on their end, send over one of our cybercrimes experts if we have to."

"You should also run a background on Mendez," Ryan said. He looked at the clock. "We've got to go."

"Just—give me a minute. I'll meet you there."

Donnelly walked out.

"I need to talk to Brad," Lucy said. "I'll get a ride with him over to headquarters."

"What's going on?" Ryan asked. "Donnelly's rep is solid, but he's losing it. I don't think he's slept since the sweep, and he's taking a time-out when the SSA of Violent Crimes is expecting him at a debriefing?"

"He knows Jaime Sanchez better than anyone on the team. He'll be there."

"Watch yourself with him," Ryan said. "I know cops. He's going to snap."

"He knows he's on edge. Cut him a little slack on this, Ryan."

Ryan didn't comment. Her partner was suspicious, and the most important thing on a task force like theirs was trust.

"Don't be late," he said to her and left.

Lucy asked one of the agents outside the conference room where Donnelly had gone, and he said he thought the locker room. She hesitated, then stepped inside.

"Brad," she said quietly.

"This is the boys' room," he said without looking at her. He was facing the wall, head down, hands above his head.

"Casilla wants us in for a debriefing. We need you there."

"I should have known Jaime would try something like this. There's been something off about this whole thing from the beginning, but I have no idea what it is. It's making me crazy trying to figure it out."

"Finding out he'd imprisoned kids—"

He cut her off. "It's not just the boy in the basement."

"I have a lead on Michael." She didn't tell him it was old—fourteen months old. It was more than they'd had two hours ago. "If we find Michael, he can lead us to Sanchez. I'm almost certain of it. I have to convince Casilla that I'm right. You can help with that, and then we both get what we want. We save Michael, find Bella, and put Sanchez in prison."

"I should have put them in protective custody. I should have protected them myself! Is this your way of saying *I told you so*?"

"I don't do that."

He grunted and leaned against the lockers, head down, his hands still fisted above his head.

"They're family," she said. "I don't think he plans to harm her."

"Jaime Sanchez is violent. You read his file. He fucking beat us. It doesn't matter that those girls are his nieces. He's not his brother George."

"You're right. But hurting them is his last option. Right now he thinks he's winning. He has Bella."

"Why? Why her? Why not CeCe who was helping him?"

"I don't know. Leverage? She's easier to control?"

"It makes no fucking sense to take a kid when every cop in southern Texas is looking for him."

"Brad, he won this battle. So we go at him from another direction. Shake every tree. You said from the beginning that something big was going on and Sanchez was at the center—you focus on that."

"No one is talking. They're too scared, and not of us."

"We talk to Mirabelle, find a way to convince her to help."

"Maybe she's in on this,"

"I don't think so. Maybe—"

Brad cut her off. "The logical reason for Jaime to take Bella is to keep his sister in line. He has her daughter, not us. We have no more leverage. He does. She talks, her daughter dies. Every time I think *Why Bella*, that's what I come back to."

Lucy's stomach burned. Brad's scenario made sense.

"We have to find a way."

"You're pulling at straws, Kincaid."

"I never thought you would be defeated."

He didn't say anything.

"I'm going to take a run at her. I don't need your permission, Brad, but I want your blessing. If you're right and she's scared of what Jaime might do to Bella, we'll know. She could let something slip. Or maybe I can convince her that she needs to help us to save her daughter."

Again, he remained silent.

"It's one more angle," she continued. "You have every law enforcement agency looking for him. The border patrol has been alerted. You took down his supply house. If you were him, what would you do?"

Brad thought for a moment. He'd calmed down after his outburst, and Lucy was relieved. He was a good cop, but far more emotionally involved in this case than he should be.

"I'd lay low. Regroup. Send my most trusted allies out to do my work for me."

"And you know who those are, right?"

He nodded, for the first time excited about a possibility. "Stick to them. Talk to them. Haul them in if there's a warrant."

"Exactly. Disrupt his process. Force him to show himself. Force him to make a mistake."

"We have some leads on the next shipment—which is supposed to be the big one. But nothing solid. We don't know where it's going to cross, or how. Truck, car, plane, foot."

"Foot? From the border?"

"Best way to do it. Small quantities brought in through couriers."

"The boys," Lucy said before she realized she'd said it. "Like Michael."

Brad's eyes widened. "That's it. It's why he's been so successful. He has young boys hauling his heroin across the border. They're under the radar. They're American. They're not going to be treated the same as if they're teenagers or adults."

He paced in front of the lockers. "They can blend in, practically carry the drugs in the open because they've found a way to not be inspected, something. Bribes. Holes in the system. They could move hundreds of pounds of drugs, especially if they rotate—" He stopped.

"What?"

"Until we find Michael we don't have anything on them. I can't prove this. No one is talking, Jaime Sanchez is in the wind, and now we have a missing seven-year-old."

Two uniformed cops came into the locker room and glanced at Lucy. "We're done," she said with a slight smile. She turned to Brad. "We're going to get him. It starts with Michael."

"I hope you're right. Because I'm telling you, Kincaid, I've met my fair share of thirteen-year-olds who would shoot me in the back without remorse."

The FBI conference room was half full when Lucy arrived with Donnelly. It was clear that nearly everyone knew him and greeted him warmly. She spotted Jennifer sitting at the far end of the table, away from everyone else, looking out of place, her chin up. Every cell in the woman's body was screaming *Stay away* and Lucy wondered what her story was.

Donnelly immediately approached Casilla. "I'm sorry we're late, Juan, but can I have a minute alone?"

"Of course. Ryan, start the debriefing. Nate, Kenzie, and a team from the cyber unit who specialize in child abductions need to be brought up to speed. They're on the task force now, use them."

Lucy didn't know what Brad wanted with Juan, but she followed Ryan's lead and sat near the head of the long conference table.

Ryan ran through the status of Jaime Sanchez and Bella Borez quickly. "The cybercrimes unit already has the burner phone that CeCe Borez used, and they're tracing it. The girl is distraught and refuses to talk. A child psychologist is working with her, but we're not holding out hope. It's clear that she's been in contact with either her uncle or an intermediary."

He also gave them a brief rundown of the sting, the raid, and what they'd found in the basement of the hardware store that fronted Sanchez's drug and weapons storage facility.

"DEA Agent Brad Donnelly called the shots, and he was right on. We dealt Sanchez a major blow." Ryan motioned to Lucy. "Agent Kincaid will fill you in on her parallel investigation."

She frowned. "What?"

"You said you had information about Michael Rodriguez."

She cleared her throat. This was the first time she'd had to formally speak in front of her colleagues. As she spoke, Casilla and Donnelly walked into the back of the room and remained standing.

"The girl Bella Borez confirmed that the boy kept

chained in the basement for the past four weeks is Michael Rodriguez. Michael was a suspected runaway fourteen months ago, leaving his foster family in what I believe was his attempt to protect them from a threat.

"Based on interviews with Bella, Michael's foster mother, and Michael's priest, it seems that about a week before his disappearance, Michael started behaving strangely. He went to his old neighborhood and was seen with a younger boy known as Richard Diaz."

"A classmate?" Kenzie asked.

"No, Father Flannigan didn't know much about the boy, but suspected he was from Michael's past. I don't have all the details yet, I literally just learned about this right before I heard about Bella Borez's kidnapping. However, there are several indirect connections between Jaime Sanchez and Michael Rodriguez, primarily through his father Vince and common associates.

"Sometime after Michael first disappeared, he was scarred or tattooed with a symbol that appears to be gang-related. No one has identified it yet." She pointed to the copy on the master board. "He was missing and unseen by anyone who knows him until Saturday, when he left a note for his foster mother"—she pointed to the copy—"and then was at his church, St. Catherine's."

"His priest saw him?" Ryan asked.

"He took his confession, and I couldn't get any details out of him about that, as you might expect. Father Flannigan told me what he told the police when Michael first disappeared, and I think some of the leads might still yield information.

"I also believe," she added, "that if we find Michael, he can lead us to Jaime Sanchez."

Kenzie said, "I don't understand. I thought this kid was locked up by Sanchez. Why?"

"It may be that Michael was aiding Sanchez under duress, but at some point Sanchez felt he was a flight risk and kept him under lock and key. Bella implied that she let him go because she feared for his life."

"Why didn't he talk to someone about this?" Tony, the head of the cybercrimes team, asked.

"He doesn't trust the police. Neither do the Popes, because they don't think the police took Michael's disappearance seriously. Treated him like just another runaway foster kid."

"But he wasn't," Ryan reiterated.

"No. There's a lot more here and if we're going to find Bella, I think Michael is our best bet."

Juan cleared his throat. "We're going to tackle this investigation from three angles. With Agent Donnelly's agreement, the FBI is taking point. Agents Kenzie Malone and Nate Dunning will join Agents Kincaid and Quiroz specifically on the child abduction. Jennifer Mendez from CPS will be our contact person with that agency."

Everyone turned to look at her, and Jennifer got the deer-in-the-headlights look, though it disappeared almost immediately. She nodded but didn't say anything.

Juan continued. "Agent Donnelly is running the op. We have the full cooperation of the DEA when and if we need it." He nodded to Brad, who took over the conversation.

He said, "I've been tracking Jaime Sanchez for years. He's good at getting others to take the fall for him. He's violent and will not hesitate to kill anyone who gets in his way.

"But because of the Michael Rodriguez situation, we now believe that he's not using the traditional gang-related drug distribution structure. We believe he's using minors to move product across the border. If we can find this kid, we can learn how the operation works.

"We all know that Sanchez is not the one calling the shots. He's a high-ranking operative, but we have no intel on who he answers to. We're hoping the ledger Agent Kincaid found at the Thirty-Ninth Street gang headquarters will lead us in the right direction, but so far we've had no success in decoding the information."

He looked around the room. "It very well could be that this boy has the information we need, not only on Jaime Sanchez, but also on who he answers to. The gang didn't seem overly worried that we seized the weapons in the hardware store facility, and it could be because they have more coming in. It's also clear that at one point there were drugs in the facility, but they were removed prior to our sting. We have known for some time that something big is going down and Sanchez is involved, which is why he and his brother were added to the sweep this weekend." He glanced at Lucy. She wondered if he would have revealed that information if she hadn't already called him on it.

He continued. "I have a full squad of DEA agents currently shaking down every known associate of Jaime Sanchez. We're making it hard for him to hide. We have border patrol on high alert, and now that we have the kidnapping, they're fully engaged. We don't know why he took Bella and not his older niece—who helped him get Bella out of the house—but we suspect it's to keep his sister from talking. He doesn't do anything without a reason."

"And you don't know how he found out where CPS had stashed the kids?" Tony asked.

"We're working on it," Donnelly said.

Juan turned to Tony, "If you and your team can get together with Ms. Mendez and the CPS technology department and see if you can find a breach, that may answer our question."

Lucy glanced at Donnelly. Good call; the FBI cybercrimes unit was bigger with more resources than the DEA unit. Even though Donnelly was borderline obsessed with Sanchez, he was willing to delegate.

"Sanchez could be in Mexico by now," Nate said.

"We alerted border patrol within an hour of the kidnapping," Donnelly said. "He couldn't have reached the border that fast. And ICE is cooperating." He glanced at his watch. "It's thirteen hundred hours. Fuel up and let's find this bastard."

CHAPTER 14

Ryan tossed a file at Lucy while he slid into the driver's seat. They were heading to Michael Rodriguez's old neighborhood. "That's from Zach," he said. "You asked him to run a list of foster kids who went missing in the last two years, or something."

"Kids in Michael's demographic," she said.

"Gotta love Zach. He always comes through."

She flipped through the information. Not only had Zach pulled all the missing foster kids, but he'd highlighted several who had been in the same foster homes as Michael, though not all at the same time. "There are a dozen kids who went missing over the last two years who had been in at least one of the same foster homes as Michael."

"Together?"

"No—except for one. Richard Diaz. He went missing six months ago. The first home they were in together for three months." Richard Diaz. The same name that Father Flannigan had mentioned.

Lucy's phone rang. It was Sean.

"Am I interrupting something?" Sean asked.

"No. Ryan and I are driving, following up on a lead."

"I talked to Kane. It was very one-sided."

"One-sided?"

"Kane's like Jack."

"Ah." Jack wasn't a talker.

"I told him about the scar, sent him the photo. All he said was that I didn't need to call him; kids were recruited by the cartels all the time, it's nothing new. But I think he's interested. He'll call you if he learns something. Just don't expect much from him."

"I appreciate it, whether or not he finds something. How's the job in Dallas going?"

"I know who it is. I just need to set the trap."

"That was fast."

"It took me three hours. I'm getting rusty."

She laughed. "I love you."

"Back at ya, princess." He hung up.

"You share everything with your boyfriend?" Ryan said.

"Yes. His brother Kane knows a lot about the drug cartels. I wanted him to see the mark on Michael's arm. The DEA is stumped. I thought Kane might know what it means."

Ryan winced.

"What?"

"You shouldn't have done that."

"I'm just following a line of investigation."

"Yeah, but, isn't Sean's brother a mercenary?"

"Not exactly."

"Well, *not exactly* isn't going to cut it when Donnelly finds out you're talking about his case behind his back."

"Sean didn't tell him about Sanchez." Though Lucy wasn't certain of that. "We thought that Kane might know something about the mark that would help us track down Michael."

"You don't have to sell me. But you need to at least cover your ass with Casilla."

"You're right." She bit her lip. She'd meant to tell Casilla about being followed from St. Catherine's, but it had honestly slipped her mind. "Ryan, I may have been followed today."

"Why didn't you say something?"

"Because I didn't have anything to share except a feeling. I went through evasive driving maneuvers and no one tipped their hand. It was more a feeling I had of being watched. I get them sometimes."

"Hey, I get it. I worked undercover for three years in Houston. One of the reasons my first marriage failed. You get that sixth sense. Saved my ass more than once."

She was relieved he understood. "I think someone followed me from Saint Catherine's. I lost them in a neighborhood near Starbucks. Meaning, I turned into the neighborhood and whoever was following me didn't. There were two cars that caught my attention. A dark-blue, new-model Honda without plates driven by a white female and a white panel van driven by a middle-aged Hispanic male. There was a plumbing logo on the side; I'd recognize it if I saw it again. But that doesn't mean there wasn't someone else that I missed."

"Watch your back, Kincaid. And tell Casilla." He pulled over on a street crowded with beat-up cars and a few shiny rides. "It's that place, across the street."

The apartment structure was brown and sagging behind an equally sagging chain-link fence. Kids played in the front; men and women of all different ages, mostly Hispanic, sat on stoops and watched as the two feds approached.

"Do you have a plan?" Ryan asked. "This isn't a neighborhood we want to stay in."

"Michael came here the week before he disappeared. There has to be a reason."

"Over a year ago," Ryan said flatly. He obviously didn't

think they'd find anything after this long, but Lucy was more optimistic.

"Let's start with the old Rodriguez apartment."

Michael and his father had lived in apartment 110, in the back corner. The old woman who lived there now refused to open the door. She spoke in rapid Spanish, and Lucy responded in kind. The woman still didn't open the door, said she'd been here for three years and didn't know anyone who lived here before.

Lucy tried several of the neighbors. No one answered their doors. Whether they were home or not was uncertain.

"Why would he come here?" Lucy asked almost to herself. "Wait—"

She walked back to the front office, which was one unsecured room with mailboxes. The manager, a scrawny Hispanic man of fifty with sleeve tattoos and a telltale prison tat on his wrist, was behind a filthy glass window in a tiny, cramped office littered with tools and food wrappers. A loud fan blew air but did nothing to rid the room of the foul stench of sweat and cheap cologne.

He glared at them. Lucy showed her badge and said in Spanish, "How long have you worked here?"

"I don't have to answer no questions."

"I can bring you to FBI headquarters and ask them."

"Bullshit, *chica*."

"There are two missing children."

"No one's missing. I'da heard."

"How long have you worked here?"

"Two years," he said.

She showed him Michael's photograph. "Have you seen this boy?"

He didn't even look at the picture. "No."

"Look at it."

"I ain't seen him."

"What about this man?" She showed him Sanchez's picture. Right in front of his face, plastered against the glass.

"No."

But there was a flicker. Lucy was certain he knew both Michael and Sanchez.

"It would benefit you if you cooperated."

He didn't say anything.

"Lucy," Ryan said under his breath. He was standing by the mailboxes. Most had last names, some scratched out, some barely legible. A partial name at apartment 210 read:

D Z

At first she didn't see it; then she nodded.

She turned to the manager. "Thanks for nothing."

"Don't harass my tenants, if you know what's good for you!"

Ryan stepped up to the glass, all six feet of solid cop muscle. "Is that a threat? Because I haven't reached my quota today for arresting assholes."

The manager gave Ryan the finger. Ryan stared for a long minute. The manager glanced away first.

They left the building. "I hate pricks."

"He recognized both Michael and Sanchez."

"He won't say anything. He's more scared of Sanchez than us."

Ryan looked up the address and any information on Richard Diaz's mother. "Teresa Diaz. Never been married. Several arrests for drug possession, public intoxication, prostitution. Five children between the ages of four and sixteen, four different fathers, all in foster care."

"That's awful."

"That's reality. When I was in patrol in Houston, I wasn't just a cop. I was a fucking family counselor dealing with people just like her. I swear, if I had one wish it wouldn't be for world peace, it would be to make drugs disappear. Poof. Solve half the damn problems in this country. Stealing, murder, abuse. My prediction? Four of her five kids will be dead or in prison by the time they're twenty-one."

She glanced at Ryan. A darkness had spread across his face. "That's pessimistic."

"No, optimistic. I'm holding out for the youngest kid. Maybe he or she will make it out of the cycle, now that the mother is out of the picture."

Unlike the other neighbors, Teresa Diaz opened the door almost immediately. She was an impossibly skinny woman who looked fifty, but her file said she was thirty-three. Her stringy brown hair hung limp around her once pretty face that now had several open sores. Her eyes were red, from lack of sleep or drugs or both.

The apartment was a pit, worse than most Lucy had seen, but Ryan barely noticed it. Rotting food coupled with stale beer and the fresher scent of marijuana. That's when Lucy noticed the joint between her stained fingers.

Ryan showed his badge and said, "Put that out."

"Fucking cops," she said and staggered into the living room. She took a long drag on the joint before putting it in an overflowing ashtray.

"What are you on?" Ryan said, walking into the dark room.

Lucy followed but left the door open. There were three mismatched couches crammed into the room, and a three-legged coffee table propped up by telephone books. It was littered with drug paraphernalia including used needles and one impressively large bong. A flat-screen television was mounted on the wall. There were no real decorations, except along the hall leading to what Lucy presumed was the bedroom or bedrooms. Pictures of kids, some in cracked frames, some tacked up.

"What's it to you? Go ahead, arrest me. At least I'll get a decent meal."

"We're not going to arrest you," Ryan said. "We're here to talk about your son, Richard."

"My Richie? He do something? Not my fault. He was a good kid till you people took him away. All my kids were good kids, they did nothing wrong."

"When was the last time you saw your son?"

"My son? Richie?" She blinked, confused. She was definitely high on more than marijuana. "Tommy? You arresting babies now?"

"Richie," Ryan said. "When was the last time you saw Richie?"

She waved her hand. "Dunno. I used to get visitation, you know? But the pigs stopped that. Fucking assholes. I was a good mama. Better than my mama. I never hit my kids. Not once. Never." She pulled up her sleeve. "See this?"

"The needle marks?" Ryan said calmly.

She poked a long jagged scar that went from her elbow halfway to her shoulder. "My mama did that when I was eleven. Blood everywhere. I don't do that to my kids, but you assholes took them anyway. So arrest me, whatever." She stuck her chin out defiantly.

Ryan retained an eerie calm when he spoke, though his body was tense. He held out Michael's picture. "Is this a friend of Richie's?"

She grabbed the photo and stared. "Michael. His asshole father is in prison with Richie's asshole father."

Definitely not a coincidence. Lucy prompted, "They visited last year, together."

"Richie used to visit me every week, even though I was only allowed to visit him and my other babies once a month. He used to bring me food and money, sometimes. He's a good boy. I haven't seen him in months. They said he ran away. That's not my fault, it's theirs. They were supposed to protect him, right? Protect him from *me*?" She barked out a laugh. "I protected *him*, now he's run away. Is that why you're here? Because you found him? No one cares, you know. No one cares about my babies but me."

"He brought Michael here."

She shrugged. "Once or twice. Not in a long time." She suddenly sat heavily on the couch. "You think you can get me to see my kids? They said no more visitation, which is just bullshit. They're my kids, and they lost one. I should get them back, the rest, because they'll just lose them, too."

"Thank you for your time," Ryan said through clenched teeth. He turned to leave.

Lucy had one more question. "Ms. Diaz, who's the CPS caseworker for your family?"

She shrugged. "Hell if I know. They're all assholes."

Lucy and Ryan walked out. Ryan was walking fast to the car. Lucy had to jog to keep up. Ryan had the car running by the time she slid into the passenger seat. As soon as she closed the door, he sped off.

He didn't talk driving back to FBI headquarters. Lucy let him stew. She sent Zach all the information they'd learned, and asked him to find out who Richard Diaz's CPS caseworker was as well as the caseworkers for all the runaways who fit the profile.

Why had Michael still associated with kids from his old neighborhood? Had he been seeing Richie Diaz all along, or was it recent, right before he ran away?

She also asked Zach for the files related to Richard Diaz's disappearance. It couldn't be a coincidence that both Michael and Richie, from the same old neighborhood, both in foster care, both with incarcerated fathers, had been listed as runaways. But Michael had been gone more than a year, and Richie only six months.

"It seems that Michael kept at least one of his friendships from his old neighborhood, a relationship that even the Popes didn't know about," Lucy said.

"You saw that woman. Kids who grow up in places like that don't turn out well."

"They can."

"Rarely."

"I know you're angry—"

"Angry? Yes. *Furious*. And depressed. It's because of people like Teresa Diaz that I quit the force. I couldn't do it anymore. I couldn't stand back and let shit happen." His hands were tight on the steering wheel. "At least here, in the FBI, I thought I was making a difference."

"You are."

"Not when I have to go through this shit again."

She suspected there was more than just Teresa Diaz and her five children bothering Ryan. But he wasn't talking, and she didn't want to pry even more. She would, though, when the time was right.

"The question is," she asked several minutes later, "why did Michael return to his old neighborhood fourteen months ago? What were he and Richie doing? Were they working together?"

"And the missing kids keep piling up," Ryan said. In the parking lot of FBI headquarters, he said, "Can I have a minute? I'm going to call my boys. They should be out of school by now."

"Of course." And that was the crux of the problem. Ryan wanted to be with his kids and he couldn't.

Being forced to work for Jaime Sanchez for so long, Michael had learned many survival skills. He could hot-wire a car, pickpocket tourists, and hide in plain sight, among other things.

He was nervous about stealing a car because though he

could drive, he looked thirteen. Instead, he walked all Sunday night, taking back roads and quiet neighborhoods, until he reached the Riverwalk. Monday morning it was crowded, which enabled him to grab several wallets from unsuspecting tourists. Purses left open while window shopping. Carts in the grocery store unattended. In less than thirty minutes, he had over three hundred dollars in cash. He dumped the wallets in a mailbox; he had no need for the credit cards. He already felt bad about stealing money from people who might need it, but he was desperate. He couldn't walk to the border, and he didn't want to steal a car. He worried about the buses, because Jaime could be staking out the bus station. But that was the best, fastest way to get out of town.

Michael made his way to the main bus depot. He cleaned up in a public restroom. His clothes were stained, but he couldn't do anything about that. He looked around, half hiding by leaning against the wall and pretending to listen to music. He'd found broken earbuds in a trash can, but putting them in his ears he fit right in with any other teenager and no one suspected the cord wasn't connected to an iPod.

People saw what they expected to see.

He watched not the crowd, but individuals. Jaime's people were mostly young guys, in their twenties, some teenagers. Michael knew most of them by sight, but there were always new thugs coming in.

A crowd of kids walked through. Five girls, a little older than him, chatting at the same time about taking the bus down to the lake. They were playing hooky.

He took a risk and followed them. They bought their tickets; he bought a ticket on the same bus. He could transfer later, but if he got out of the city, he could breathe a little easier. He still hoped to make it to the border before dark.

He didn't know what he would do then. He didn't have a plan to rescue his friends. He had no weapons, no vehicle—

though he could remedy both when he reached Hidalgo. He hoped. He prayed.

God forgives.

Father Flannigan didn't know what he'd done; if he had he would never have told him that. Some things were unforgivable. Michael didn't know why he'd even gone to St. Catherine's . . . it was dumb. Maybe . . . he just wanted someone to listen. He didn't know what to do, because he was so scared that if he did what he must, he'd get them all killed. And no one would be able to stop the general.

You know what to do. You're a killer. You can do this.

Michael shuffled his feet behind the girls as they waited in line for the bus. He kept his head low, but moved closer to them, hoping if anyone was watching they would think that he was part of the group, not alone.

Ten minutes later he was in his seat. And no one stopped him.

It's a sign, Michael. A sign that you're on the right path. Follow it. Hidalgo. Steal a gun. Kill the general.

It's the only way to save them.

CHAPTER 15

The FBI desk was staffed by a security guard 24/7, and an FBI civilian secretary from eight to five. The on-call desk rotated through all special agents, who worked it in pairs roughly one night every two months.

Zach's official hours were from eight to five like the other analysts and support staff, but he often stayed late, so Lucy wasn't surprised to see him at his desk at five thirty. Likewise, she wasn't surprised to see half her squad gone, their desks cleared for the next day of work. The workaholics were her, Ryan, Nate, and Kenzie. Kenzie was in the National Guard and had been gone all weekend for her monthly training. Either she and Nate were following up on a lead, or she'd bailed early to catch up on sleep.

The others in her squad weren't slackers, but they viewed their job as forty hours a week, with the occasional overtime. Lucy had been raised in a family that worked hard and played hard; she didn't know what she would do with free time. She'd been trained by an agent in DC who didn't know the meaning of time off. And Sean? He loved to play, but like her he grew bored if he wasn't continually challenged.

Though she missed him, she was glad he had this job in Dallas. He'd sounded happy on the phone, and that made

her more relaxed in their relationship. They'd been together for nearly fifteen months, but it still felt new to her
because they'd spent so much time apart—Sean's previous
job kept him traveling half the time, and she'd spent nearly
five months at Quantico where she'd been lucky to see him
every other weekend. The last ten weeks had been the long-
est consecutive days they'd seen each other since they
first met.

Zach's fingers were flying over his keyboard. He didn't
look up but said, "Hey, Lucy. You read the file I gave Ryan?"

"Yes."

"Great. I have something big for you. Sit, I'm almost
done."

He took only another half a minute, then sent off an
email and reached over to grab a file behind him. He handed
it right to her.

"Open."

She did. Inside was an autopsy report for a twelve-year-
old John Doe. He'd been found one month ago, shot in the
back of the head and left in a ditch off Interstate 69, near
state route 141. Even though he had good dental work and
evidence of a break that had healed properly, he was malnourished. He appeared to be Mexican American, but the
top of his head was gone, making a visual identification
nearly impossible. The coroner thought he might have been
from an affluent family in Mexico. His image had been sent
to authorities in border towns, as had his dental impressions.

"Poor kid," Lucy said.

"Look at the photos."

Lucy had worked for the medical examiner in DC for
over a year and was hardly squeamish about autopsy photos, but she took a breath before turning the page. It was
never easy to look at a dead child.

And she hoped she would never find it easy.

At first, she didn't see it. Then it was clear as day.

"The scar. It's similar to what Bella drew."

Zach nodded. He handed Lucy another file. "I think I identified him."

"You're amazing."

"I made some assumptions that paid off." He popped a couple Peanut M&M's in his mouth and offered her the bag. She took one.

"Don't be overly humble."

"It was more you than me, I just took it a step farther." He went on, "When you asked me to run all the kids who may have known Michael within the foster care system, you also asked me to look at runaway statistics. I put the two together."

"That's why you highlighted the missing kids on the list," she said. "And it helped."

"Good. I think this is one of those kids. I checked the missing kids database and plugged in very limited parameters. Wards of the state are given annual dental visits, so I compared dental records of Hispanic males between nine and thirteen, who were wards of the state and went missing within the last two years. I started with nearly a hundred thousand missing kids but was able to narrow it down to less than ten thousand. Only ten percent of them are active cases—runaways are lower priority than abductions, for example."

"What you're trying to say is that there are a lot of cases."

"Yes, and I started broad, but then made a few more assumptions. If I was wrong, it would have been a lot of wasted time."

"But you weren't wrong," she guessed.

"No. I called in a favor at the lab and had them visually compare the dental records of John Doe against the six missing boys who knew Michael in the foster care system. They won't put it in writing until the forensic tests are complete, but they confirmed he's Richard Diaz."

Lucy's heart skipped a beat. "Richard Diaz? Are you sure?"

"I'm sorry. I know you'd rather have better news."

"This is no coincidence," she said. "He and Michael knew each other, they were in the same foster care for three months, they had lived in the same apartment building for several years. And he was seen with Michael the week before Michael disappeared." She glanced at her notes. "He didn't go missing until six months ago. Long after Michael. I met his mother today. She was high, but coherent enough. She said Richie and Michael had been friends, and more or less confirmed they'd been there the week before Michael disappeared."

"I pulled his records," Zach said. "Richard was taken from his mother after she was arrested for possession and drug use. She's been in and out of rehab. Did jail time. Mostly petty stuff—stealing to feed her fix. She put 'unknown' under father on the birth certificate. But she hooked up with a guy named Gregor Molina, a low-level drug dealer, when Richard was three. Never married, but she's on Molina's visitor list at McConnell."

"The same prison Michael's father is at."

"Might be a coincidence, because Molina was convicted two years ago and Rodriguez has been there four years. Molina will be getting out soon—it was a drug charge. Possession with intent, fourth conviction so he got more than a few days."

Zach handed her a computer printout. "After I ran the narrow parameters, I broadened the search again. You'd said something else yesterday about kids with parents in prison."

"I did?" She honestly didn't remember.

"That maybe it was the felons' relationship with Sanchez that put their kids into the position of being forced to run drugs. Anyway, I identified seventeen boys who might be in a similar situation. Of those seventeen, nine of them have one or both parents in prison for drug-related offenses. Mostly violent—attempted murder, murder, assault. But I focused on cases that had a drug angle, narrowed to San Antonio, and further narrowed to kids in foster care. There could be more than seventeen, but this is a good start."

She spontaneously hugged him. "You're amazing. It would have taken me days to figure this out."

"I doubt it, but this is my job." He grinned and ate another handful of candy before putting the bag in his bottom drawer.

"Don't ever let me take you for granted, Zach. You're indispensable."

She took the file to her desk and pulled out the names that Zach had flagged. She reviewed their records, their placement history, their parents, and created a time line of when they'd gone missing. It started eighteen months ago, and Michael was the fourth boy who'd allegedly run away. The most recent was Javier Marshal, a ten-year-old who'd been in three foster homes in nine months before he was presumed to have run away six months ago, almost the same time as Richie. He'd be eleven now.

She was writing up a report for Juan with the information Zach had uncovered and the additional analysis she did when Ryan approached quietly and startled her.

"Sorry," he said. "I didn't know you were still here."

"I thought you left."

"Yeah, me too. But I wanted to get some paperwork done while it was quiet."

"I was just leaving," Lucy said, though it was the first time she'd thought of it, "as soon as I send this report. Zach's still here, I think, and I saw Nate come in and out a while ago."

"Zach's been gone for hours. It's after nine."

She looked at the clock on her computer. "Well, dammit."

"Sean going to be worried?"

"He's in Dallas." She rubbed her head. No wonder she had a headache—she'd skipped dinner.

"Give me fifteen minutes, then I'll walk you out."

"You don't have to do that."

Ryan shot her a look. "My mom raised a gentleman. Of course, my two ex-wives wouldn't agree, but that's another story."

Lucy had just hung up from saying good night to Sean when her cell phone rang. It was an unfamiliar number.

"Kincaid," she answered.

"Agent Lucy Kincaid? This is Sergeant Jim Younger with the Bexar County Sheriff's Department."

"Yes, Sergeant?"

"The alert you put out Saturday on Michael Rodriguez came up with a hit."

She sat up, her fatigue disappearing. "You found him?"

"No, ma'am, but he's been captured on video at the Greyhound bus terminal in central San Antonio."

"Is he there now?"

"No, it's a recording from this morning. We know what bus he boarded and where he got off, and have sent a unit to Braunig Lake Park. They spoke to the kids he appeared to have travelled with, but none of them claimed to have known him. One witness remembers seeing a boy matching his description hitchhiking on Interstate Thirty-Seven at dusk, but couldn't swear it was the same boy."

"North or south?"

"He was on the southbound side of the turnpike. I have a patrol in the area but we haven't spotted him. Either he was picked up or he got off the road."

"Can you send me the video?"

"I already sent a copy to the FBI, SAPD, and the DEA, they'll arrive first thing in the morning. Because he's a minor, I wanted to call you with the update. I'm sorry we didn't have it earlier, but there are a lot of feeds to sift through."

"No apologies necessary, I appreciate your help, Sergeant."

She hung up. Their first solid lead on where Michael had been and where he was going.

She looked at a map and found the lake, then traced the interstate south. There were several small towns off Interstate 37. It led all the way to Corpus Christi on the coast. Or he could turn off to State Route 281 and head to McAllen, then the Mexican border.

Where was Michael going? Corpus Christi? The border? Did he plan to disappear in Mexico? Why?

She squeezed her temples. She didn't know what his plan was, or why he wasn't trying to get help. She understood not trusting anyone—but there had to be *someone* he trusted for help. Is that what he was doing? Heading south to get help? And who?

Lucy fell into a troubled sleep.

The old couple who picked up Michael on the interstate were going home to Corpus Christi. It was out of Michael's way, but it would be a good place to hide for a day or two. And if anyone was trying to find him, they would have no reason to look there.

The couple, Mr. and Mrs. Valdez, reminded Michael of Hector and Olive, except they were much older. He sat quietly in the back while they listened to Mexican music. They didn't speak much English, and he spoke less Spanish, but they were kind. Mrs. Valdez had a hamper in the back with homemade sandwiches, and she told him to eat one. He did. Years ago, he would never have eaten food from strangers. Now it was better than garbage.

And the sandwiches were very good.

He made up a story. It was close to the truth. His dad

was a deadbeat in prison and his mom had to take odd jobs where she could. She'd found a permanent job in Corpus Christi at a restaurant, but didn't have a car to get him there. He took a bus partway, but didn't have enough money to go farther.

He was in truth hoarding his money, because he might need it to get information. Or buy a gun. Or both. But he also knew that if he took a completely different bus from a completely different town where Jaime wouldn't know to look, he might be able to sneak into Hidalgo without anyone knowing. He wouldn't even take the bus there, because Jaime might have people watching the bus depot. He could get a bus to Harlingen, then walk the rest of the way. It was only twenty miles. Or he'd steal a car and dump it in McAllen, then walk to Hidalgo.

He wasn't sure yet. He wasn't sure about anything. Except he had to save his brothers. If he couldn't, he didn't deserve to live.

He didn't know he'd fallen asleep until Mrs. Valdez gently shook him. "Javier?" she said.

Michael had almost forgotten he'd given a false name.

"Sorry," he mumbled.

"Where do you want us to take you?" she asked in broken English.

He blinked. They were in a city. Right off the freeway. Mr. Valdez was pumping gas.

"Javier, do you need help?" she asked kindly.

He shook his head. "I'm okay. You can let me out here."

She frowned. "We drive you. To your mother."

He shook his head again, wiped his face with the back of his hand. He'd dreamed about his mother, for the first time in months. He missed her so much, even though she'd been gone for nearly half his life. He still remembered how pretty she smelled, and how much she loved daisies.

He'd pick daisies from a yard the neighborhood over just to see the look on her face.

"I'm good," he said. "I gotta go."

He got out of the car. Mr. Valdez tried to stop him. "*Amigo*, let us—"

Michael shook his head.

"Javier!" Mrs. Valdez said. She came after him with a brown paper bag. "You eat. Okay?"

He took it and nodded. "*Gracias*," he said, then turned and walked south, in the dark, ignoring the eyes that followed him.

Dawn had barely broken when Jaime's cell phone rang. Only three people had this number, but this was the person he trusted the least.

"The kid left town. Heading south."

"Where?"

"You know where. He's going to fuck everything up. You need to stop him."

"He'll be dead before he gets there. And even if he manages to cross the border, there's no way he can get to the camp without our people seeing him."

"Make sure of it. Or I'll tell the general you're the one who fucked this up."

"Don't threaten me."

" 'Don't threaten me,' " the voice mimicked and hung up.

CHAPTER 16

Lucy was in FBI headquarters before eight that morning to review the security disk Sergeant Younger sent over. Ryan walked in while she was watching it for a second time.

There was nothing of value on the tape, other than confirmation that Michael Rodriquez had boarded a bus headed for Braunig Lake, and had gotten off. Lucy called Sergeant Younger to find out if his deputies had any information about hitchhikers on the interstate. Nothing yet. No one had come forward saying they'd seen a boy getting into a car anytime the evening before.

"But," Younger added, "we're going to send a patrol to talk to people who work in the area, see if we can learn anything new."

"Thanks—you have my cell phone, call me if you learn anything."

She called Donnelly on his cell. "Did you see the security footage?" she asked.

"Nicole and I just finished watching it. There's nothing useful."

"Did you recognize anyone in the feed from Sanchez's organization? Maybe someone who followed Michael?"

"Negative. I have my guys going through it more carefully, but so far it doesn't tell us anything."

"It tells us he's heading south."

"Does that help me find Jaime Sanchez?"

Lucy bristled. "Sanchez is looking for Michael, so it stands to reason that if we are looking for him our paths will eventually cross."

"I can't count on it." He put his hand over the phone and spoke to someone in the background. "Sorry," he said a moment later. "I just forwarded you an email from DeSantos with CPS. He wants a status on Michael. Call him back or get Mendez to do it. I have a debriefing I should have started five minutes ago and two of Sanchez's men in lockup I need to interview."

Lucy agreed. Jennifer didn't know as much about Michael's case as Bella's, so Lucy called DeSantos back herself.

"Hello, Mr. DeSantos, it's Special Agent Lucy Kincaid from the FBI. Brad Donnelly said you wanted a status report."

"Yes—I thought you were going to keep me in the loop on this."

"We've been swamped these last few days."

"I heard. A girl was kidnapped from foster care Sunday night. It's related to Michael."

"Why do you assume that?"

"Assume? It's all anyone here is talking about. A cybercrimes unit from the FBI has been working with one of my co-workers to see if we were hacked, and we have the bulletin about Isabella Borez and the man who kidnapped her."

Of course. Lucy rubbed her eyes. "I'm sorry, I haven't gotten a lot of sleep."

"I want something to tell the Popes. Do you have anything?"

"Michael was seen at the Greyhound bus station yesterday, and the sheriff's department is trying to pick up his trail from where he got off the bus."

"Which was?"

"Braunig Lake. Did he have any friends or family there? Maybe a foster family in the area? He may have been hitchhiking to Corpus Christi."

"No connection to either place. Are you sure it was him?"

"Yes. Maybe the Popes have friends or family in Corpus Christi, someone Michael would trust."

"I'll ask them, but I don't want to give them false hope," he said. "I saw a request come through from your office to pull records on runaway boys. There were several names on the list, including Michael."

"Yes." Zach was fast. She had to remember to thank him again. Maybe get him a bag of the Peanut M&M's he seemed to live on. "According to your file on Michael, he was assigned to you from the beginning."

"Yes."

"Do you remember Richard Diaz? A year younger than Michael. They were in a foster home together for several months, and they're originally from the same neighborhood."

"I don't recognize the name, but I'd have to check my files to see if he was one of mine. Diaz is a very common name."

"Richie's mother's a junkie, stepfather's in prison on drug charges. He ran away from his last home six months ago, and we have reason to believe that a twelve-year-old John Doe in the morgue is in fact Diaz."

"What? How? Why didn't CPS hear about this?"

"Bullet to the head. He was found a month ago, but had no ID and didn't match missing persons reports. The analyst here matched up CPS dental records to the John Doe, but we're awaiting forensic confirmation."

Lucy realized then that Richard Diaz was found dead at about the same time Michael was imprisoned in the basement. She made note of the timeline.

"Let me help get the information you need," he said. "I know the system, I can access it faster than having your office request it through proper channels."

"Your colleague, Jennifer Mendez, is assisting us."

"You could have asked me."

"She's been involved because of the kidnapping, but the more eyes the better. Maybe compare them with anyone Michael would have known, either from his neighborhood or foster care." She snapped her fingers. "Oh! Just thought of this. Richie disappeared six months ago. Someone he knew in his last home may be able to help us piece together his last week."

"Kids move in and out of these homes often. It's certainly not ideal, but we often don't have control over it." He started typing into a computer. "Okay, I have Diaz's file here. I'll send it to you. It'll list all the homes he's been in."

"Can you cross-reference that list with other children in the same houses at the same time? Particularly in the home he shared with Michael and when he disappeared."

"I'll send what I have now, but the rest will take a while. Let me know if you want to meet later and compare notes."

"All right," she said, though she had no intention of doing so. When would she have the time? "Thanks for your help."

The email from DeSantos popped up in her inbox as soon as she hung up. She opened it and skimmed, then did a double take when she saw that Jennifer Mendez had been Richard Diaz's CPS officer.

Why hadn't she said anything about him during the debriefing yesterday?

Lucy jumped out of her chair and ran to Zach's desk, where she impatiently waited for Zach to get off the phone.

"Wow, I'm so popular," Zach said.

"Jennifer Mendez. CPS."

"She was the officer assigned to the Borez girls. Wasn't she here yesterday?"

"I need a background on her. DEA said they're doing one, but I want you to look at it. She was also the officer assigned to Richard Diaz, the John Doe you ID'd yesterday."

"Okay," he said, with a glance toward Juan's office.

"I'm going to write up a report, promise."

"I know, just make sure you do, because I answer to Juan, and I need to cover my butt."

She went to her seat and quickly wrote up a report from her conversation with Charlie DeSantos.

Jennifer Mendez. Could she be part of Sanchez's operation? Someone had to tell Jaime where to find the girls. They'd assumed that it was CeCe because they'd found the phone, or that Jaime had followed someone to the Grove house, but Lucy had also suggested it might be a leak. Maybe even accidental, but right now a leak was looking more likely. It could have been Mendez. And then there was the issue of how CeCe had gotten the phone. That could have been Mendez in an effort to cover her trail.

Lucy didn't want to believe the young CPS caseworker was corrupt, but she'd seen enough corruption among people in positions of authority that she would believe it if she found proof.

She got a note back from Juan on her memo. It was brief and to the point.

Tread carefully.

Zach approached her with a file. "Here's a quick background on Jennifer Mendez. No criminal background, but she has a sealed juvie file. Not unheard of."

"Thank you."

"If you need more, let me know—but more will take time, unless it's directly connected to the Borez kidnapping."

"It might be."

She opened the file. It was basic information. Jennifer Mendez was only a few years older than Lucy. She was born and raised in San Antonio until the age of thirteen, when her parents were killed in a flash flood. She was one of three girls, the middle child. They were placed in foster care because their only living relatives were a grandmother who lived in an assisted living facility, and an aunt out of state who didn't want custody of the girls.

Lucy wrote out the time line. The oldest, Grace, had been sixteen and a year later got her GED and was emancipated. She went to a state college on a full scholarship and was now a county prosecutor. The youngest, then eleven, was currently a cop in San Antonio. And Jennifer became a social worker two years ago. Only a short time before Michael Rodriguez disappeared.

Could a girl who had lived in the system, who had a cop and a lawyer for sisters, be involved in something as horrific as boys being used as couriers for drug cartels?

But there was no doubt that Diaz had been one of Jennifer's responsibilities. Jennifer had access to information, she was one of the few people who knew where the Borez girls were staying, and she knew Lucy was interested in information Bella may have about Michael. Maybe the kidnapping wasn't to keep Mirabelle in line, but to stop Bella from talking.

After watching Jennifer with Bella and the way she

looked out for the girl's interests, Lucy had dismissed her initial dislike for the caseworker. But now she wondered if the woman had in fact turned Bella over to her violent uncle? Everything in Jennifer's background told Lucy that she was a do-gooder. But it could all be a lie. It wouldn't be the first time Lucy had encountered someone who on the surface did great things, but underneath was corrupt. Just because Jennifer was a young, pretty female didn't mean that she didn't have a hardened heart.

Lucy wanted to talk to Jennifer about Richard Diaz, but she was nervous about tipping her hand. If she was right, it gave Jennifer time to contact Sanchez. If she was wrong, she could damage the woman's reputation, as well as the tenuous working relationship the FBI had with CPS in this case.

Except . . . Lucy had a reason to see Jennifer. Diaz was her charge. She needed to be notified that he was dead. The ME would notify CPS when the ID was confirmed, but Lucy could go see her first.

No one was around, except Juan in his office. She knocked on the open door.

"Come in," he said.

"Sir, I have an angle I want to pursue. To rule out someone as a suspect."

"A suspect for what?"

"Someone told Jaime Sanchez where Bella was staying."

"I have two of our best tech people at CPS working on their security. Donnelly thinks they were hacked."

"They could have been. But that's going to take time. The logical place to start is with the CPS officer who was assigned to the case. She would know who else had access to the information."

"Or," he said, "you think she's the one."

"No, sir." She paused. "Maybe."

He raised an eyebrow and didn't say anything.

She backtracked, though only a bit. "I need a sit-down with her. Face-to-face, inform her about Richard Diaz, and then assess her reaction."

"Take Quiroz with you. Or Dunning if Quiroz is still at the DEA."

"Sir, with all due respect, I need to do this one-on-one. We met when we interviewed Bella. If I bring backup and she's guilty, she'll be suspicious and I won't get anything out of her. If she's innocent, she'll be defensive and I won't get anything out of her. This will be a public meeting. I'll call her, set it up at her office as routine, in public."

He considered, then nodded. "Keep me in the loop. If you get any vibes that there's something off, call it in. If she knows anything about where Jaime Sanchez took the girl, we will interrogate her here. Understood?"

"Yes, sir. Thank you."

She didn't release her breath until she left Juan's office.

She went back to her desk and called Jennifer Mendez, relieved that the social worker picked up her phone and was amicable to a meeting.

Lucy signed out and drove to Child Protective Services, which was a good thirty minutes outside the city. But it gave her time to think and figure out how to interview the woman without Jennifer knowing she was, essentially, being interrogated.

Lucy parked in visitors' parking and walked around to the front of the building to check in. Jennifer came out for Lucy immediately. "Can we walk?" she asked.

Lucy hesitated, then agreed. "Sure."

"It's going to be hot this afternoon, but right now it's beautiful, and I need to get out of the office." She pushed open the glass doors and led Lucy to three benches under a canopy of trees. Smokers used the place, but it was surprisingly clean.

Jennifer lit up a cigarette, took a long drag, then put it out in one of the sand-filled pots. "I'm quitting," she said, "but it's not easy, so I don't want to stay here. Too tempting." She started walking again, along the perimeter of the parking lot, shielded by trees. By the worn dirt, it looked like the path was well used.

Lucy asked, "Do you remember a boy named Richard Diaz?"

Jennifer stopped walking and turned to face Lucy. "I thought you were here about Bella."

"I didn't say that on the phone."

"I assumed." Her brows dipped in concentration. "Richard Diaz? That's the boy you were talking about yesterday at the briefing."

"He was murdered. We identified his body this morning." Lucy waited a beat, trying to read Jennifer's face. She looked wholly confused.

"You were his caseworker."

"I don't think so."

Lucy handed Jennifer a printout of Richard's file. She stared at it for a long minute, then tapped the bottom.

"I inherited this boy from someone who retired last year. I never even met him."

"You didn't remember that he ran away six months ago?"

"Runaways are not unusual. I—I let him slip through the cracks." She stopped walking and stared at the paperwork. "I know this house—I try not to place kids there anymore. I didn't like them."

"Do you have a say?"

"Not usually, but I've learned to manipulate the system. It helps that I used to be part of it."

She didn't say it with anger or resentment, just a statement of fact.

"Did you know that he and Michael Rodriguez were acquainted?"

"No. I mean yesterday I listened to everything you and Agent Quiroz said, but I didn't know then that this boy was mine. I'm truly sorry. When Maggie retired last year, I inherited half her wards. Because of budget cuts, we couldn't bring on another counselor, and because I was new, I didn't have as full a plate as the senior staff. But it was a lot to absorb at one time. I can look at my notes and see if I have anything that might help."

"I would appreciate that," Lucy said.

Jennifer flipped the pages of Richie's file, slowly shaking her head. Then she tapped a handwritten note. "I wrote this. I remember this case."

"What does it mean?"

"It's an internal code, but I added my own shorthand. It's coming back to me. Richie ran away several times, always went back to his mother. He had a very mature sense of obligation to her. I never met him, but after he ran away I talked to his foster parents who said he often visited his mother's to make sure she had food, clean up after her, check in. The woman is a drug addict, he was removed by the courts because she couldn't take care of him or his siblings. She didn't abuse him—that was his stepfather—but she didn't feed him, she didn't clothe him, she didn't make sure he went to school or had his vaccinations or do anything a mother is supposed to do. She didn't protect him. But . . ." Her voice trailed off.

"But he loved her."

She nodded. "That was the sense I got. The system isn't perfect. When he ran away, I was certain he went to her apartment. I checked a half dozen times over the next two weeks, but he never showed up. She wasn't helpful, either."

Jennifer closed her eyes. "I can't believe he's dead."

"He was murdered, Jennifer. A month ago. At about the same time Michael Rodriguez was taken prisoner by Jaime Sanchez."

"I don't understand what this all means. Is Richie dead because of Sanchez? The same man who kidnapped Bella?"

That's what Lucy thought, but she didn't say it.

Jennifer sat down. Right where she was, in her pretty blue dress, on the grass under an elm tree. Lucy sat next to her.

"I try, every day I try to make lives better for kids who have lost all hope. You couldn't possibly understand what it's like to have everything you know taken from you. Even though it's usually bad, often unsafe, it's familiar. And then it's gone. You're put in a house with people who don't know you, who pretend to care about you or, worse, pretend you don't exist." Jennifer glanced at her. "You have no idea what it's like to have no hope."

"You don't know me, Jennifer."

"Jenny." She closed her eyes. "I had a wonderful childhood and then it was taken away. I saw an underbelly I had no idea in my perfect childhood even existed. Parents who abused their kids. Drug addicts, child molesters, kids who at fourteen were just as hard and violent as the people who spawned them. I had to try to stop it. And sometimes, I win. Sometimes, I get a victory. But mostly? I get shit. I get kids who are shuffled from good homes into bad because beds need to be found. Kids who are split up from their families because a foster home can only take one, not all three."

Can only take one, not all three.

Very specific. Very personal.

"I failed that boy. I didn't follow up. I didn't know he was in trouble, but I should have. Now he's dead and no one cares."

"I care and you care," Lucy said. "I need your help."

"Why does the FBI care about the dead kid of a junkie and drug dealer?"

"Why do you?" she snapped. "You had a chip on your shoulder when I met you Sunday, and it's still there. *We care.* It has to be enough."

Jenny looked at her for a long minute, took a deep breath, and said, "What do you need?"

"You're already helping by working with us, but the faster we get those files the FBI requested, the faster we find Michael. I believe that."

She nodded. "I can do that."

DEA Special Agent Brad Donnelly had wasted the entire morning. He'd gone back and forth between two Sanchez lowlifes trying to get one of them to break. Nicole had taken a stab at each of them as well, but nothing. They weren't talking, they weren't helpful, and one even went so far as to say he hadn't seen Sanchez in over a year.

"We're not hanging with the same *amigos, comprende?*"

No comprende. Gangs didn't just change loyalties. If these two assholes weren't talking to Sanchez, that meant they were lying or Sanchez didn't trust them.

He'd also planned to interrogate again the five gang-bangers who'd been at the warehouse, but three had been released on bail. Brad had gone through the roof when he heard. Their lawyers had gotten their bail set low, claiming that they didn't know there were guns and drugs in the basement; they were just hanging out with friends. Brad didn't buy that for a minute. But the two who'd fled through the tunnel had their bail set higher, and they were still in jail.

He buzzed Nicole. "Hey, can you set it up for me to interview the two pricks from the warehouse? Guiterrez and Hansen."

"Do you really think we're going to get anything more from them?"

"We've got nothing, I'm willing to go at them again."

"Okay."

He'd just hung up when his private cell phone rang. It was an unknown number. This was the line he used for snitches.

"Hello," he answered.

"It's Dixon. Ten minutes, usual place."

"I'm in the middle of a huge investigation. I can't drop everything right now."

"It's related."

He hung up.

Brad holstered his gun and ran out of the office.

CHAPTER 17

It took Brad twelve minutes to get from headquarters to the San Antonio Botanical Gardens. Brad didn't know what Dixon did for a living, if anything. He suspected the old man was an illegal immigrant, but doubted that he was breaking any other laws.

They'd met shortly after Brad started in the San Antonio field office. He'd busted a meth distribution network and during the cleanup, Dixon had approached him.

"You didn't get them all."

The old man handed him a slip of paper with an address and walked away.

The address had led to another meth house, bigger than the first, and the arrest of the ringleader of the operation. It was a good bust all around.

Brad didn't know if Dixon was the scrawny Mexican's first name, last name, or a fake name. He didn't even know how old the man was, or where he lived. He dressed like a bum, but had expensive leather shoes. His face was like well-worn leather, pinched around the faded, irregular scar that ran from his temple to the middle of his cheek, as if he'd been hit with a broken bottle; his teeth were straight and white. Brad would have thought they were dentures, except he'd seen a flash of fillings when Dixon first sought him out. The man spoke fluent Spanish and fluent English, but had no accent.

He had to be over sixty, but he might have been eighty and Brad wouldn't be surprised. Once, Brad had followed him into a modest middle-class neighborhood to see if he could figure out where he lived and how he always seemed to find verifiable information. But the old man had lost him, and Brad wondered if the entire excursion had been a wild goose chase.

Unlike most of Brad's snitches, Brad had no way of contacting Dixon except through an anonymous email. Brad had traced one of Dixon's responses to a public library and, on occasion, staked it out, but had never seen Dixon come or go.

More often, Dixon called when he heard something valuable, even before Brad put the word out. Brad suspected that he was the grandfather or great-grandfather of a gangbanger, someone who seemed invisible to others, but heard everything. Or maybe he hung out at a bar, sipping draft beer and listening. Dixon would never say. Probably to save his life.

Brad liked him. He'd offered money for information, but Dixon always refused. So Brad stopped offering.

Dixon was sitting on a bench feeding the ducks. The day turned out to be nice—eighty degrees, clear sky, low humidity. As soon as Dixon spotted Brad, he started walking down one of the trails. Brad followed.

"I almost didn't call you," Dixon said.

"I appreciate it."

"You might not." He walked a few steps and when they were out of view of any other passersby, he stopped and looked up at Brad. Brad towered over him, but Dixon looked neither intimidated nor scared. "I only heard part of a conversation, but because there's a missing girl, I decided to tell you."

"Where?"

"That's off-limits. And it wouldn't matter, he's not there."

"Who's he?"

"The man you've been after."

Brad's heart raced. "Whatever you have."

"McAllen. All I heard was that he left in the middle of the night, with the little girl, for a safe place in McAllen. If I knew more, I would tell you."

"Do you know him?"

"No. But I've seen him from time to time."

"Where?"

"I can't. Mr. Donnelly, you've never asked me to say more than I can. If I told you where I heard, where I saw, the wrong people would know I talked. I must go." He turned to leave.

"Why do you do this? Why risk it?"

He stopped, didn't look back. "If not me, who?"

Brad went immediately back to the DEA office. The San Antonio field office was small, an offshoot of the main Houston office, so he wasn't surprised when his boss, Assistant Director Samantha Archer, was standing in the lobby talking to Nicole.

"Brad, I didn't know you went out," Nicole said. She gave him an apologetic look over Sam's shoulder.

"I just needed fresh air."

Sam said, "Brad, a minute please."

He nodded, because what else was he going to say? "Your office or mine?"

"Doesn't matter."

"It does. Your office means I'm in trouble. Mine means I'm not."

She almost smiled. Then she said, "Yours is fine."

He led the way. The office wasn't large, but his office was on the opposite side of the suite from Sam's.

Samantha Archer had the title of Assistant Director, but she was also a good field agent. She only had five years' seniority on him, but he was a year older—he'd spent time in the military before college, and she'd joined the DEA right out of college. She'd always had her sights on being in charge, and with her brains and political savvy, she'd be up for a major national appointment within the next five years.

He was her Achilles' heel, he knew, and he used it whenever he could. Maybe in some ways he resented that she'd been quickly promoted. It wasn't that she didn't deserve it, it was because she was both a great agent *and* cautious, but she'd forgotten that sometimes in the field, dirty work was necessary.

Too many times they'd played fair, and their friends and colleagues had been slaughtered.

Drug cartels never played fair.

"Do you need to step away?" she asked as she closed the door.

"No." He sat behind his cluttered desk and picked up a stress ball. Squeezed.

She stared at him for a minute. She had worry lines around her crystal-sharp blue eyes, a few strands of gray in her sunstreaked blond hair, but she was still as beautiful as when they'd first met. And smart. He had a thing for smart blondes. "I understand why you're obsessed with Sanchez, but—"

He bristled. Except when they tried to play shrink with him. "I'm not obsessed. No more than you."

"When was the last time you slept?"

"He kidnapped a little girl!"

"And the FBI is running with it."

"Sam, something big is going down, I feel it. You do, too."

"We have no proof. All this could be because of one typical drug shipment."

"It's not. You'd agree if you weren't—"

He cut himself off. Insulting Sam wasn't going to get her to see the truth.

"I want Jaime Sanchez as much as you do, Brad. If he falls, a lot of dominoes fall. I like that. But I don't want you to risk your career over this."

"I haven't crossed any lines."

"We can't keep Mirabelle Borez."

"Like hell we can't."

"The most we have her on is harboring a fugitive. The fact that one of her brothers was killed in jail and her daughter has been kidnapped is in her favor. She has a hearing tomorrow morning in front of Axelrod. She's going to be released."

He tossed the stress ball into the trash can. "We have to stop it."

"I don't know that we can. I'm not going to fight it. The AUSA doesn't want to, in light of what's happened to her daughter."

"Does Mirabelle know?"

"She doesn't know we're not going to object. The AUSA is going to move for a strict probation, but that's it."

"Then I want another run at her beforehand."

"Her lawyer isn't going to let her talk."

"I have another idea." He had none. But he wasn't going to tell Sam that.

"What?"

"I'm going to bring in FBI Agent Kincaid—she's a psychologist, she got info from the girl, I think she can push Mirabelle's buttons."

"Is Casilla okay with us using his people?"

"I talked to him in person yesterday. I sent you the report."

He was grasping at straws, he knew it, but he didn't know what else to do. And he had the info from Dixon.

Not a huge tip, but it was something. If he could push Mirabelle on McAllen . . . maybe she would give them something more to work with. A name, address, any straw.

Sam was watching him, and he kept his face as tight and blank as possible. He retrieved his stress ball and squeezed it once before putting it back on his desk.

"All right," she finally relented. "I'll have the AUSA work it out, tell her to keep it zipped about tomorrow until the hearing, and maybe you'll have some leverage. If you and Kincaid can get her to give us *anything* I'll take you both out for beers when this is all over."

"I need one more thing."

She sighed. "Brad—"

"It's legit. I have a tip that Sanchez might be heading to McAllen. Might already be there."

"Where?"

"An informant. He's been reliable in the past."

She mulled that over. "I can call the SSA down there, find out what they might know. They already have an alert on him, they would have called me if he'd been spotted."

She started to leave, her hand on the doorknob, but before she opened it she said, "Brad, we've been colleagues for fifteen years, as well as friends. You're my best agent, you know that, but you're also the only one who truly worries me. Don't let Sanchez destroy you."

"He won't."

She wanted to say more. He looked her in the eye, almost daring her to bring up their past. If things had been different—if he hadn't been transferred under her command, if she hadn't suspended him for two weeks last year when he disobeyed orders, if they didn't see the job from different angles—maybe they could have made it work. But there were too many obstacles, and too many fundamental disagreements. She wanted to fix him. He didn't need fixing.

"Let me know what happens."

"You know I will," he said, standing.

"Why don't you take Rollins with you instead of the FBI agent?"

"Nicole is good in the field, but Kincaid has a knack with people."

Sam nodded. She, of all people, appreciated when strengths were used. "Remember, Nicole is part of your team, don't shut her out."

Sam left. What did she mean by that? Did Nicole feel he was keeping things from her? Ridiculous. He'd shared everything with everyone on his team.

He dry-swallowed three aspirin and left to track down Nicole. She was on the phone. He wrote a note.

Off to run at Borez one more time. Sanchez might be in McAllen—Archer is calling down, follow up with her. Text me if anything breaks.

There. He wasn't a control freak, or obsessed. He'd just delegated an important task.

He walked out and dialed Lucy Kincaid's cell phone.

"Kincaid? I need you to help me break Mirabelle Borez. Meet me at the jail in thirty minutes."

CHAPTER 18

Brad was practically bouncing on his heels when Lucy walked into the county jail where Mirabella Borez was being held.

"Thanks for coming," he said.

"Of course." Lucy eyed him, half suspicious. Brad was both distracted and excited, an odd combination. "I was surprised, though, considering the first interview with Mirabelle."

"I told you yesterday we might do this."

"Yes, but—"

"Push her on the danger to her daughter. You're the shrink, I think you can do it. You said you wanted another run at her."

"I'm not a shrink."

He dismissed the comment. "Look, Lucy, I've read your files. I know you have a master's in criminal psychology, and your brother is a respected forensic psychiatrist. You understand her, right?"

"I think so, but—"

"You said she didn't care about her daughters, and that might be true—"

"That's not exactly what I said. I said that she would be fine with them going into the system because she didn't think that she'd be held for longer than a few days. She was weighing the situation, calculating."

"Look, I'm going to be honest with you."

She tilted her head. "That would be nice."

"They're going to cut her loose tomorrow. She doesn't know, but the AUSA isn't going to fight the defense's motion. I don't know the legalese, I suspect they're going to try to have everything tossed, use the grief card, we'll get probation, time served, some such thing. But she doesn't know. I want to push her as hard as I can to get *something* that will lead us to her brother. Get her to slip up."

Lucy was shocked. "What about Michael? She had a child locked in her basement."

"And she'll say she didn't know. Or that he wasn't held captive, he was living down there."

"That's bullshit, and you know it!" Lucy rarely swore, but she was seeing red right now. "Her daughters both knew."

"CeCe isn't talking and Bella is missing. This is our last opportunity to compel her to talk. Anything we can get is better than what we have."

"I'll do my best." But Lucy was not happy with the situation. There was no doubt in her mind that Mirabelle knew all about Michael being held against his will.

"We need an idea about where Sanchez might be holed up. Safe houses. Friends, family we don't know about. I got a tip that he's already in McAllen. I have locals there following up on it, but I can't go down myself unless I have something tangible."

A corrections officer approached. "The prisoner wants a minute with her lawyer. You good here?"

"Yes," Brad said. He waited until the guard was gone, then said, "I'm going to observe. You're in there with just her and her lawyer. Keep your earpiece in, I may have some questions for her if you get her to open up."

"More likely I'll get her to slip up than open up," Lucy said.

She filled him in on her meeting with Jennifer Mendez and the possibility that there were many more boys from the foster care system who'd been marked as runaways, but were in fact coerced to work for Sanchez. "There're too many similarities. The scar on the forearm is only one. There's at least one common foster home between Richie Diaz and Michael, both of their fathers are in prison, they don't have a mother in the picture. Different CPS counselors, they've been gone different lengths of time, and Richie was murdered—but the fact that they both originally came from Sanchez's neighborhood tells me that they either knew him, or their fathers knew him."

Brad absorbed the information. "That's all good. Are your people running it down with CPS?"

"Yes. Both from the director's end, and from my end. Jenny is going to try to get the information we need faster."

The guard approached again. "They're ready for you, Agent Donnelly."

They followed the guard down a locked hall, were required to leave their weapons with another guard, then proceeded down yet another locked corridor until they reached the small interrogation room. Donnelly slipped into the narrow adjoining room where he could observe and listen.

Lucy walked into the interrogation room alone. Mirabelle's attorney, Keith Glum, glared at her and said, "Where's Agent Donnelly?"

"I'm Agent Lucy Kincaid from the FBI," she said. "We met the other day."

"What do you want? We were waiting for Donnelly."

She sat down across from them. She looked directly at

Mirabelle. "Donnelly is focused on finding your brother. I'm focused on finding your daughter. Kidnapping is under the FBI."

"My client has nothing more to say."

"Good. Then she can listen." Lucy sat down and looked Mirabelle in the eye. The woman maintained eye contact, possibly trying to intimidate her, but it wouldn't work.

"You're not safe and neither are your daughters. Your brother took Bella as leverage. Over you, over someone else, I don't know. But she's in danger, and you know it."

"Family does not betray family."

"I agree. I have a large family and I would do anything for any one of them. I would die for them. I would kill for them, to save their lives. I know where you're coming from. Jaime is your brother. But Jaime is in deep with the wrong people, and now he's put Bella in harm's way."

Mirabelle snorted.

"You think it's funny?"

"Jaime can handle himself."

"The people he's associating with killed George."

"Your people killed George."

"You don't believe that." Lucy shook her head. Donnelly was talking in her earpiece. *Find a way to drop McAllen. Like a bomb.*

"If you didn't lock him up, George would be alive today."

Lucy ignored that and continued. "If the people your brother is working for will kill George to keep him quiet, they'll kill Jaime. And then where will Bella be? Where will your sweet, beautiful seven-year-old daughter be then? Stranded with violent predators? Sold to an old man who likes to screw little girls?"

"You're sick!"

"*They're* sick! Bella is in danger, and Jaime will not be able to protect her if he's dead." She paused. "Why did he take her in the first place? To make sure you wouldn't talk?

Or because she knows about the boys locked in the basement."

A flicker in Mirabelle's eyes, but her attorney said, "My client has already told the DEA and the AUSA that Michael Rodriguez was not locked in the basement, but was living there."

"I spoke to Bella, and she told me the truth," Lucy said, ignoring the lawyer.

Glum said, "You spoke to her without an advocate. She's a seven-year-old child, hardly more than a baby. Nothing she said will hold up in court."

"And now your brother took your little girl out of the city." Again, something in her eyes alerted Lucy that she was going in the right direction. "We've confirmed they're in McAllen."

She shook her head. "He wouldn't. He would never hurt Isabella. We're *family*."

"Right now, she's safe with him, because he loves his family. That's why he does all this, to give his family—you, your daughters, George—a better life. Food. Money. A house. I honestly believe that Jaime will protect Bella if he can." Lucy didn't know that for certain, but Mirabelle believed it, and Lucy had to work with that.

"But," Lucy continued, "what happens when these people think he's risking them? It's a war out there, and Jaime is in the battlefield, which means that Bella is in the battlefield. What happens if he takes her across the border? Does she have a passport? Anything to help her get back?"

It was evident she didn't, and Mirabelle paled.

"McAllen is minutes from the border. Once they cross, she's gone forever."

"Agent Kincaid," Glum exclaimed. "Enough with the threats."

"I'm not threatening anyone. I want to find a scared little girl who cried and begged not to be taken. A little girl who is in the middle of a dangerous situation, taken away from her family and home, on the run. Do you want her to be caught in the crossfire? Because that's the kind of life Jaime leads, and you know it. Every cop and federal agent in southern Texas is looking for him. Is he going to give up willingly or go for the gun battle? And where will Bella be when he does?

"Help us find Bella and I'll help you."

Mirabelle was thinking. Lucy could practically see the gears in her brain turning. Yes, Mirabelle was selfish, a criminal, had no qualms about locking Michael up in the basement, but she did it for her family. She would use her daughters, but she didn't want them hurt. Lucy finally understood this woman and what made her tick. What she would be willing to do for her family.

"You don't understand," Mirabelle said, but she'd lost some of the venom. "He wouldn't. He knows that—he just wouldn't."

"He wouldn't what?"

"Leave the country. He wouldn't."

"To save himself? Yes, he would."

Now Mirabelle was visibly scared, her eyes wide and searching. She didn't want to believe Lucy, but she *did* believe her. Because she knew something.

"Save Bella."

"Jaime will protect her. That's all. I'll say nothing."

"And what about CeCe? Why did he leave CeCe behind and only take Bella? CeCe wanted to go with him, but he didn't take her."

Mirabelle frowned, but didn't speak.

"That's enough," Glum said. "You're fishing. My client has nothing more to say. She doesn't know where her brother is, or where he took her daughter."

Lucy leaned forward, focused solely on Mirabelle. "You know where he's going. You're scared. For him, for

Bella. You can save him, Mirabelle. More, you can save your daughter."

"What do I get?" she asked quietly. "You're still holding me here. You're still going to keep me here."

"If you cooperate, I will stand up for you in court."

They stared at each other. Thinking. Plotting? Lucy waited.

Brad's phone vibrated in his pocket. He didn't want to answer it—Lucy was good, she had Mirabelle close to giving them intel—but when he glanced down he saw it was Ryan Quiroz. He wouldn't call if it wasn't urgent.

"What?" he answered.

"Our people were going over backgrounds on the Borez family," Ryan said. "There's something that doesn't quite match up with the time line, and since you're planning on interrogating her again, maybe this will help."

"Kincaid is in with her now. What is it?"

"Isabella Borez was born in early February. The earliest she could have been conceived, even if she were a week or two late, would be May. Mirabelle's husband was in prison from April sixteen until July thirty-first on a minor drug charge."

"So? Maybe she was early by a few weeks."

"It just seems slightly off."

"Thanks."

Donnelly hesitated. Lucy was going good, he didn't want to mess with her rhythm, but Lucy and Mirabelle were at a standstill. They were staring at each other, and the lawyer was getting antsy. Maybe the info would help.

Mirabelle leaned back in her chair. "Your promises mean shit."

"Let your daughter be raised in Mexico then," Lucy said. "With drug dealers and killers."

"That's not going to happen."

"Yes it is. Because Jaime is not going to be able to get back into this country without being caught. You know it, I know it. Jaime sure as hell knows it. He took Bella for something specific, and you know why!"

Mirabelle just stared. The lawyer started blabbing, but Lucy kept eye contact with Mirabelle.

"Help me save Bella," Lucy repeated.

"Jaime won't hurt her. I have nothing to say."

The lawyer started talking about the hearing tomorrow, and then Donnelly spoke in her earpiece.

Ask her about Bella's father. Her real father. Ryan has a hunch it's not Borez. He was in prison when she most likely conceived.

Lucy waited until the lawyer took a breath, then said to Mirabelle, "Tell me about Bella's father."

"He's dead."

"Her real father, not the name on her birth certificate."

Mirabelle said nothing.

"Jaime knows who it is, doesn't he?"

"No. No." Mirabelle started crying. "Leave me alone!"

"You help us, we can help you. Help you so you can be with your daughters. So you and CeCe can be together to-morrow."

"It's too late. Damn you, bitch! It's too late!"

Mirabelle made a lunge for Lucy. The guard pulled her back. Mirabelle was crying and swearing and cursing Lucy.

"Let's get you back to your cell, wildcat," the guard said.

"No," Lucy said. "I'm okay. Mirabelle, calm down and tell me where your brother is."

Sobbing, she half collapsed into her seat. "I don't know. I swear, I don't know."

"But you know why he took Bella."

"He wouldn't. He wouldn't take her to Mexico. He knows what will happen."

"What will happen in Mexico?"

She shook her head, tears falling freely down her gaunt cheeks.

"Anything you can give us will help. Anything, and I'll talk to the judge for you. So you and CeCe can be together."

Through the tears, she said, "Why would you help me?"

"Because I don't want your girls to grow up without their mother."

Mirabelle was wrestling with her divided loyalties, between her brother and her children.

The children won.

"I don't know where he is, I swear," she said. "But there's one person in McAllen he would go to for help. Someone who would hide him. His ex-girlfriend, Benita Peña."

"Where does she live?"

"I don't know. But last I heard, she was working at Alberto's. It's a diner in McAllen. I think the owner is her cousin or something." She looked Lucy in the eye. "I love my brother, but I want my daughter back."

"I'll get her back." And Lucy prayed she could.

Donnelly was practically jumping for joy when she stepped into the room adjoining the interrogation room. He gave her a high five. "We're going to get him. I already have my people tracking down Peña and the diner."

"We need to be careful. If Peña sees cops, she'll tip him off."

"They're good, Kincaid. First thing in the morning, we're heading to McAllen. I want to be there when we take the bastard down."

"We?"

"Casilla will let you go. I'm going after Jaime, you're

going after Bella—she's going to need a familiar face. We don't know what's happened to her in the last two days."

"Is it true that Borez isn't Bella's father?"

"It was an educated guess. He *was* in prison, but the timing's iffy. Jaime knows who Bella's real father is, and that's why he took her."

"From his own sister?"

"If there's enough money involved, Jaime would sell his own mother."

When Kincaid left for FBI headquarters, Brad went to talk to his boss. He knocked on her open door.

Sam waved him in, then finished her call. When she hung up, Brad said, "I was right about Kincaid. We got info from Mirabelle. Jaime Sanchez has an ex-girlfriend in McAllen. Benita Peña."

"Why don't we know about her?"

Brad shrugged. "She works at a diner and Mirabelle doesn't know where she lives. There's a ring of authenticity to it, I don't think she's bullshitting us, but I want to send Nicole to work with our people down there."

Sam leaned back and visibly relaxed. "You're delegating. Good."

"I want to go tomorrow. Bring Kincaid and Quiroz. I'm sure Juan Casilla will clear them."

"I guess I hoped for too much, that you'd let Nicole ride this out."

"I need to be there. I know Sanchez better than anyone. I know the way he thinks. I know the way he operates. But I also recognize that sometimes, another set of eyes, a different way of looking at a situation is good. Nicole has proven herself, and we have a good team down there."

"You don't have to sell me. Fine, I'll clear it, both Nicole and you. You deal with Casilla—if he balks, don't push it. He's already given us more time and manpower than he should have, and I've already been called twice by Naygrow. Superficial inquiries, but that tells me the higher-ups are also watching our alliance closely."

Ritz Naygrow was the Special-Agent-in-Charge of the San Antonio FBI. He rarely got involved in the day-to-day management of his agents, delegating to the three Assistant SACs. If he was calling Sam, that meant someone in Washington had their eye on the situation. That alone made Brad uncomfortable. Not because he couldn't justify everything he'd done, but because he didn't trust bureaucrats.

"Understood," he said. He started to leave, then glanced over his shoulder. Sam was staring at him. "And thanks."

CHAPTER 19

Lucy didn't get home until after nine, again. She foraged for leftovers while she called Sean. It was noisy where he was.

"A party?" she asked.

"Dinner and drinks with the company president, others."

"Celebrating, I hope."

"The job was a lot easier than I was led to believe. I'll wrap it up in the morning and be home tomorrow before dark."

"Good. I've been spoiled, coming home to you every night."

"You certainly have," he teased. "I miss you, too. How's the case?"

"Baby steps."

"No word about the little girl?"

"She may have been taken out of San Antonio to a border town."

"Shit."

Succinct and to the point.

"We have some leads. I may be going to McAllen tomorrow."

"I'll try to get back before you go."

She hesitated, then asked, "Have you heard from Kane?" Stupid question. Of course he'd tell her if he had.

"He has your number. Don't get your hopes up, Lucy. It's a long shot. He's not going to reach out just to tell you he doesn't have anything. Honestly, he can be a jerk, but he's my brother."

"Family. It's complicated."

"Some more complicated than others. If he has intel, he'll call you. I love you, princess. I'm going to head back to the hotel in a bit."

"Love you, too."

She hung up and looked around the big kitchen. Yes, she missed Sean more than she wanted to. She'd grown to depend on him, not just for comfort and sex and companionship, but to complete her. She was happier when he was around, more relaxed, safe. She looked at him and saw his love for her in his eyes, and it never failed to take her breath away. Before they moved in together, she missed him, but it wasn't the same. She wasn't lying when she said she'd grown spoiled having him to herself every night.

But the Dallas job was a good thing for him, and it was only for a couple of days. She had to keep telling herself that. She still hadn't received confirmation from her boss that she was cleared to go to McAllen. She suspected she and Ryan would be sent because of Brad's tip that Bella was down there, but Juan could decide to use agents from the McAllen field office rather than sending a team from San Antonio.

Lucy rinsed her plate, grabbed a water bottle from the fridge, and walked around the house making sure all the doors and windows were locked and the alarm set. Sean was a stickler for security, because it was his bread and butter. She was a stickler because she knew what could happen when you let your guard down. Even if you didn't let your guard down.

Brad Donnelly called her while she was finishing her rounds. "I'm sorry to call so late," he said, "but I thought you'd want to know. Agents in McAllen tracked down Benita Peña. We don't have her address yet—the one in the motor vehicles database was a dud, she hasn't been there in two years. But we found her place of employment and we have an undercover team on it."

"That's terrific." One small step closer to finding Bella.

"I talked to Casilla and told him how instrumental you were in pulling the information out of Mirabelle, and how much I need you on this op. Bella trusts you, we don't have a shrink in McAllen—no one in the DEA or the FBI resident agencies. Our best hostage negotiator is at a standoff up in Houston. Casilla said you have training in hostage negotiation, and cleared you and Quiroz to join us. We're leaving at oh-eight-hundred. Prepare for at least one night, but expect two. I don't know when it'll wrap up."

"I'm not a shrink," she said, but realized that after the third time, Brad just didn't want to hear what she said about it.

Still, he was right about one thing—she'd worked hostage negotiation, and she had experience. Being bilingual was another benefit. And she wanted to be there.

"And we have one more lead," Brad said. "I sent Nicole to McAllen this afternoon, and she and the crew down there have identified a warehouse that associates of Sanchez have been using for storage, but there's been chatter of a major deal going down there. Initially we were thinking drugs, but based on the weapons we uncovered in the hardware store, some of the team are thinking we're looking at guns. If they're bringing them in, that's street warfare we're ill prepared for. If they're shipping them down to

Mexico, we'll have international diplomacy shit to deal with. But it's the same kind of chatter I heard before the sweep, so my money is on drugs, guns on the side."

Lucy would have laughed at the phrase if it wasn't such a serious situation.

"How did they get the information?"

"Same way we get a lot of our intel—snitches plus police work. The McAllen office already had the warehouse in the files because of previous surveillance, so it's not out of left field. It has all the tactical benefits for a deal—in the middle of nowhere, abandoned in a row of abandoned warehouses, down a long road, bordered by the desert on one side and a junkyard on another. I'm thinking they changed locations once we started arresting their people. This is the best time to go after them. They're down in numbers, had to change their operation on the fly, and Sanchez is a well-known and wanted fugitive. He's making mistakes—starting with kidnapping his niece."

That all made sense to Lucy, though she trusted Brad's instincts more than hers on this. She was more familiar with killers and kidnappers than she was with drug running, but psychologically she could see Sanchez's desperation.

Brad continued, "We're working on a plan to take it down, but we want to go at him from two directions simultaneously. If we can take down the warehouse and raid Peña's residence, we up our chances of finding Sanchez and rescuing Bella."

He paused. "Are you with me?"

"I'll be ready."

Lucy packed her overnight bag and put it at the end of her bed, then tried to sleep. She closed her eyes, but her mind was working overtime. She got up, stretched, and decided a cup of hot chocolate would settle her nerves. Her phone rang before she'd left her room.

It was after eleven at night and the number was blocked.

"Kincaid," she answered.

"Kane Rogan. Sean said you had a picture of a tat. I need more than what he had."

No *Hi, how are you*. All business. "There's another victim marked with the same tat that was on Michael Rodriguez."

"Email me the picture." He hung up. A moment later, a text message popped up with an email address.

"Sure, no problem," she said to no one. She walked down the hall to the small alcove she used as her in-home office and emailed Kane the autopsy photos of Richard Diaz. She added key facts about the case, some Sean probably already told him, and information about Bella's kidnapping and the likelihood she was in McAllen.

He called her back almost immediately.

"Where was the boy found?"

"In a ditch at Interstate 69 and Highway 141. My contact told me the cartels often leave bodies there because of scavengers."

"Only the American side. There are far more efficient ways to dispose of a corpse."

Lucy felt a chill. It wasn't what Kane said—she knew he was right—it was his tone. She couldn't reconcile Sean, her fun-loving genius lover, to his brother the cold-blooded mercenary. Kane sounded like her brother Jack—except colder, with more than a hint of disdain in his voice.

"You know this mark."

"I do."

He didn't say anything more, so Lucy pushed. "Who did this?"

"Why do you need to know? You can't do anything about it."

"I'm working a case. I am doing something."

With a shrug in his voice, Kane said flatly, "The mark is the brand of Vasco Trejo, an American expatriate living in Mexico. A self-appointed general of a drug army that has slowly been taking over smaller operations to merge with his. He's about a year away from becoming a major player and on the US radar."

"Why doesn't the DEA know about the mark?"

Kane didn't answer her question. "Until last year, Trejo was nothing. He's had several key victories. American authorities will know of him soon enough, after much bloodshed."

"What can you tell me about him?"

"There's no reason for you to know. You can't touch him. He's on my side of the border."

Lucy's slow-rising temper started to churn. "This dead boy is Richard Diaz whose only crime is that his mother's a junkie and his father's in prison. Richie isn't the only one he's branded. There's another American, Michael Rodriguez, who was forced to work for Jaime Sanchez. He was kept imprisoned for fourteen months. He also had this mark."

"Fourteen months before he was killed? Strong boy. Most don't last six months. And it's not Sanchez these boys work for. It's Trejo, the general. Never forget that."

Kane knew exactly who she was talking about—and he knew Jaime Sanchez. "Michael isn't dead. I need to find him."

"He escaped?"

"Yes. He was held by Sanchez in the basement of their house and escaped early Saturday morning. He was spotted outside the home of his former foster parents, and at his church, and at a Greyhound station, but I suspect he's on his way to McAllen or he's already there." She hadn't thought about it until she said it, but it made sense. Michael might know where Sanchez was hiding out, especially if he'd been working for him for the last fourteen months. But why would he go back?

She continued. "Michael and Richie were friends before they both disappeared. According to a witness, Sanchez is desperate to find him, but we don't know why. I suspect he has information about—"

"It's common," Kane interrupted.

"What?"

"Forcing boys to be couriers. Forcing them to fight in wars. Turning them into killers. This Michael cannot be trusted. Fourteen months? He's already lost."

"I don't believe that."

"I don't care what you believe. Kidnapping orphans and throwaway kids to fight, steal, transport drugs, send on a suicide mission. Take children no one wants and condition them."

"These aren't unwanted children. Michael's foster parents planned to adopt him. They—"

Kane cut her off. "It doesn't matter, the system doesn't care. Fourteen months is plenty of time to condition a twelve-year-old. Most break in days."

"I care." She spoke louder than she intended, but Kane had made her angry. The de facto *This is the problem, there's nothing we can do* irritated her. "Brad Donnelly, DEA, has intel on Sanchez's girlfriend in McAllen. His team is watching her. They're still in the United States for now and we're working on a plan to take him out, but my responsibility is to find the hostage—the seven-year-old niece he kidnapped—and Michael. Anything you can tell me about this mark and this Trejo will help me save them."

"Tell me about this op."

She hesitated, then told Kane about the ex-girlfriend and the warehouse, because she wanted information from him, and she wanted him to trust her. But she knew that trust would be rare from Kane.

"I don't have specific details yet," she said, then told him what she did know. "By the time I get down there, we'll know more."

"It's a trap," Kane said simply. "One or both of them."

"How do you know?"

He grunted. "It's a diversion. These people aren't that stupid. I'll get back to you." He hung up.

She stared at her dead phone. *That* could become extremely annoying.

Vasco Trejo, who preferred to be called the General, loved all things Mexican. He loved the country. He loved the women. He loved that life was cheap and people lived with fear. Understanding that fear, using that fear, helped him build a small empire in the seven years he'd been living on this mountain.

He'd perfected creating fear and using it for his greater plan. A greater good, he thought, for those who were on his side.

In Texas, where he'd been born and raised, people didn't fear. They had food to eat and television to watch and video games to play. They were lazy and bold and too independent. They weren't easily controlled because they had too many ways out. They could run. They could go to the police. They could hide behind their job or their family. They didn't have enough fear of him, or anyone, to do what they were told.

Until they lost everything. Until they were part of the system, in prison, bent to the will of whoever had the most power inside the bars.

The general recognized that his power was precarious. Too many people were involved, too many thought they could play games with him for information or money. He had an endgame, as soon as the Vallerjos were destroyed. Once he took out the gang considered bigger and better than his, all their routes and suppliers would be his, and he would have the alliance with the Texas Mexican Mafia that was necessary to take him to the next level. They would be equals. TMM would *need* Vasco because Vasco would then control more than half the smuggling routes into Texas.

To think it had almost been destroyed because of one boy, one *gringo* child who couldn't be broken. The general should have killed him when he saw his eyes, but he craved breaking him. Needed to break him, as he once had been broken.

And the boy pretended. He lied. And he stole.

He would make Michael Rodriguez suffer. He would wish he were dead. But the general had no plans to kill the boy anytime soon.

He would know fear. He would know pain. He would beg to die, but death would not come. Not until the boy knew what real suffering was.

His secure phone line rang, the one only he answered.

"What?"

"The bait has been dangled."

"And he will bite?"

"Most certainly."

"My men will be ready."

CHAPTER 20

Her conversation with Kane kept Lucy up well past midnight. She curled in a chair in the small den off the master bedroom with a large mug of hot chocolate, her comfort food. It was one of her favorite rooms, and the place she liked best when Sean was out of town. It was small, cozy, and filled with her books—her fun books, not her work books. She'd hoped immersing herself in high fantasy would make her drowsy, but the story was about family betrayal, at its core, and all Lucy could think about was who had betrayed all those boys. Was it their parents, incarcerated and unable to continue their illegal activities, who'd turned their sons over to the business? Did their children think that was the only option they had? And what evil would subject young kids to a life of violent crime? The drug trade never ended well, especially for those on the streets. They died young, and they died hopeless.

Lucy yawned. She needed a couple of hours' sleep before travelling to McAllen. Could Kane be right and this entire excursion be a setup? How? Mirabelle gave them a name, but she had no way of communicating that she had shared the information. She could alert Sanchez tomorrow when she was released, but would she?

Lucy suspected that she might call him just to find out about her daughter, talk to Bella. She sent Brad a text message.

You may have already thought of this, but is it possible to tap Mirabelle's phones in case she calls Sanchez when she's released?

Less than thirty seconds later he replied.

Already have the warrant.

She smiled. Mirabelle might be too smart for it, but there was genuine fear for her daughter, and she would want to talk to her, make sure she was okay.

How could Kane possibly know that the operation was a setup or diversion based on the very little information she had told him? If Sean didn't trust Kane, she wouldn't. It also helped that Kane and her brother Jack were tight. They had worked together, Jack trusted him. And Jack's instincts were always dead-on. Lucy wanted to trust Kane the same way . . . but he wasn't her brother. She hadn't worked in the trenches with him. She didn't *know* him like Sean and Jack did.

Finally she put down her book and stretched. She wasn't getting anything done except giving herself a headache. She kept the bathroom light on. It was childish, she knew, and she didn't need it when Sean was here, but when she was alone, she didn't like sleeping in the dark. Sean had put in floor lighting under the stairs on the main staircase, and they kept the light above the stove on as well. And even though her mind was mulling over everything that had happened that day, she felt herself drift off.

A loud triple beep woke her. She sat up and reached for the gun on her nightstand. Her heart pounded, and the triple beep sounded again. Someone was on her property.

She walked over to the tablet that Sean had hooked up to monitor house security. Most people thought Sean's security was overkill, but considering they'd both come up against people who would do almost anything to kill them, Lucy was glad for the added safety measures. *Especially* when she was alone.

She brought up the camera feeds and saw there were two men, in masks, in the backyard. One was trying to pick the lock on the door that led into the breakfast nook; the other pushed him aside and used a hammer to break the glass.

The alarm changed from the three warning beeps to a long, high-pitched wail that the intruders heard. They argued, and one bolted. Lucy pressed the panic button that would immediately call the police. If she waited, they would be called if the alarm wasn't turned off in sixty seconds, but she didn't want to wait that extra minute. People could die faster.

She swiped the pad to bring up the household controls. She turned on all the lights in the house simultaneously. Then she went back to the video feed. The intruder was standing in her entryway, staring at the camera mounted in the corner. He hadn't noticed the cameras outside—they were very well hidden—but the ones in the house were in corners. He pointed to the camera, then made a slicing motion across his throat with the knife he held in his hand.

Did he really think that he could find her, disarm her, and kill her before the police got here?

She was both scared and angry. Furious that someone had broken into her house and threatened her. She was also torn—between confronting him (she had a gun, after all, which would trump his knife) and staying in her room to wait for the police.

She rubbed her shoulder where a tranquilizer dart had incapacitated her only a few months ago. She'd been kidnapped before, overpowered. She would kill to defend herself and others, but she didn't go looking for trouble. And the police would be here any minute. She could hold any-one off for a few minutes, right?

Her phone rang. She almost didn't hear it over the alarm. She grabbed the phone. It was Sean. He had the security synced to his phone. If the alarm went off, he was notified.

"Lucy? Why is the alarm going off?"

"There's an intruder." She watched on the tablet as the guy ran back the way he came. Then she heard distant sirens. "They're gone now. The alarms scared them off. The police are almost here." She hoped.

"I'm coming home."

"You don't—"

"Don't say it. I need to." He hung up.

She put her phone down and after checking all camera angles to make sure that the intruders really had left the house, she turned off the alarm. Her ears were still ringing when the doorbell rang, followed by knocking.

"San Antonio Police Department! Answer the door or we will come in."

The entry camera showed two uniformed officers. She ran down the stairs and opened the door. "The intruders left," she said. "The first about six minutes ago, the second one about three minutes ago."

"Keep your gun down," one of the officers said. "Did you discharge your weapon?"

She almost forgot she still had her gun in hand. She shook her head. "I'm a federal agent. FBI."

"Stay here, we'll search the place," he said.

"We have cameras everywhere. They were recorded, but wore masks."

"We'll search the grounds," he repeated. He told her to stay in the living room and they searched the entire house, then the grounds. By the time they were done, another pa-trol had arrived. And Nate Dunning. The police asked to see his identification, even after Lucy said he was a friend and FBI agent. He came over to her. "Are you okay?"

"Yes—why are you here?"

"You're shaking."

She looked down at her hands. Damn, she *was* shaking. "I'm okay."

"Sean called me," Nate said.

"He shouldn't have woken you up."

"He didn't."

"It's two in the morning."

"I have insomnia."

She didn't know whether to believe Nate or not, but she was glad to see a friendly face.

Nate had hard ridges like her brother Jack—former military, Special Forces. Though Nate was more happy-go-lucky than Jack, and quicker to laugh, he still had the edge, the tension, that told Lucy he was always hyperaware of his surroundings.

She squeezed his hand. "Thank you for coming."

One of the officers approached. "Agent Kincaid? I'm Sergeant Morales." He glanced at Nate.

"This is FBI Special Agent Nate Dunning, a friend."

Morales nodded. "The house and grounds are clear, and you know about the window in the back door."

"Yes. I watched through our security system as they broke in—that's when I hit the panic button. I can make you a copy. They might not have had their masks on the entire time they were outside, maybe you'll get something off it."

"Thank you. Do you know if they took anything?"

"When he saw the camera in the entry, that's when he left, back out the way he came.

"Do you live here alone?"

She shook her head. "Sean Rogan, my boyfriend, is out of town on business."

"What kind of business?"

"Computer security. For private businesses as well as government."

"So that's why you have so many cameras and security pads installed?"

"Yeah," she said. Easier to agree to his statement than to admit being paranoid.

He made a note in his pad, then said, "You need to see something, outside."

She wanted to ask what, but instead just followed him, Nate at her side.

He led her to the garage. The doors were visible from the street, even though the house was set nearly a hundred feet from the sidewalk. Painted in red was a T with the second cross and an arrow at the bottom. But this arrow looked more like a dagger, maybe because it dripped blood.

Not blood. Red paint. It's red paint.

In Spanish was written MUERTE.

She'd been marked for death.

Then she smelled the sickening, familiar scent, and realized she was wrong.

"That's not paint, it's blood."

"It's done," Jaime's contact told him over a secure phone line.

"Good."

"I'm getting some heat up here. You need to take care of it."

"You're not in a position to give me orders."

"She's way too close."

"She doesn't know anything."

"She has spies everywhere. They're pulling records and making connections. Connections they shouldn't be making, but they are."

"That's not my problem. You should have done a better job getting rid of records."

"You should have killed that little bastard when you had the chance!"

Jaime didn't like to be reminded of his failings. Everyone had failed Jaime. The people he worked with, his brother, his sister. He still reeled that Mirabelle had told the feds about Benita. They were all over Alberto's. Benita was very angry at him.

He was going to have to stay in Mexico for a while. That did not make him happy. He was on the top in southern Texas; he would be climbing up from the bottom if he had to work directly for the general.

But it was better than dying.

His contact continued. "Just remember it was you who set this ball in motion. I had everything under control until you grabbed the kid. If you hadn't done that, the FBI wouldn't be in bed with the DEA. They don't care about guns and drugs, but take a kid and they're all over that. We have twice the problems because of you."

Jaime had no reason to explain that snatching Bella was mandatory. There was far more to this deal than moving two tons of coke. *He* would rather have just dealt with the merchandise, but the general wanted Bella, and therefore the general would get Bella.

And considering Mirabelle had turned on him, he no longer had even an ounce of remorse.

"You're forgetting the endgame, *amigo*," his partner hissed.

"Don't tell me how to do my job. You find Michael before the feds. That's on *you*. Because I'm not going down on *anything*."

Jaime slammed down the phone.

Bella cried out from the adjoining room. He unlocked the door and went inside. He didn't *like* locking up his niece, but he also didn't trust her to stay put.

He turned on the light. Bella was huddled in the corner of the small bed, clutching her doll. It was the only thing she'd had with her when he grabbed her.

"I want to go home," she whispered through her tears.

He sat on the edge of the bed. She didn't come to him. She used to crawl into George's lap and listen to his stories, or just watch television with him. She didn't do that with Jaime. Of course, Jaime was the one who had to make the money to feed the family, her and George and Mirabelle and CeCe and his gang. He was in charge. So he was short-tempered with them, so what? What did a kid understand about the pressures and responsibilities of being the head of a family?

"Everything is going to be better tomorrow."

"I want Mommy."

"I'm working to make that happen." That was solely up to Mirabelle. When she found out what she'd have to do to see Bella again, well, she might just stay in San Antonio. That wasn't his problem.

"Why can't we go home?"

"Because the *federales* took that away from us. You can't trust the police. They took you and CeCe away from your mama. They killed your uncle George. My brother."

She whimpered. Good. She needed to grow up and realize that she was a Sanchez *first*.

Better, she had to realize who her father was.

"Tomorrow night, you'll be with your papa."

Her eyes got wide. "I'm going to Heaven?" Her voice cracked and her lip quivered.

"No. I'm talking about your *real* papa. Your mama told you a lie. Your real father lives in a palace in Mexico. He wants to meet you. He wants you to live with him."

She whimpered. "My daddy's dead. Mama told me."

"No, she just told us that so we didn't know she was a

wh—" He hesitated. He needed Bella with him, not fighting him. "Your mama has some secrets. And this was one of them. You're going to be fine. You know I'd never hurt you, Bella. But you're going to meet your real papa, and you're going to live with him, and if your mother wants to join you, that's up to her."

"I want to go to sleep."

"Good, do that, because we're leaving first thing in the morning."

He closed the door; locked it. He couldn't wait to get Bella off his hands.

Mirabelle fucking made her bed, now she had to lie in it.

He stared at the phone for a long time, weighing what he needed to do. It took him all of thirty seconds to make the decision.

His contact at CPS had crossed the line. Now it was time to slit his throat.

He dialed.

The voice answered immediately and hissed, "I told you never—"

"He went too far." Jaime relayed what he knew, then there was silence.

"Did you give him that order?"

"No," Jaime lied.

"I knew he was going to be a problem when he started weaseling in on the investigation. Order the hit."

"How much?"

"I should take it out of your hide."

He bristled. "You don't want to make me angry."

Silence, again. Then, "Hundred K if it's done before noon."

"Five hundred."

"Three. Before dawn. Two before noon. And your people had better make sure he has *nothing* that will steer Donnelly or Kincaid to us. *Nothing.* If that fucking FBI agent finds out he's involved and gets to him first, you know damn well he'll talk. Then we'll have a war, and you'll be first on the casualty list."

"Don't threaten me."

But the phone went dead.

CHAPTER 21

Three hours after Sean had been alerted that his home had been broken into, he was driving down his street, a bundle of nerves and anger that the woman he loved had been threatened.

It was still dark, just after five in the morning, but there was a police car and two unmarked federal cars, as well as Nate's four-wheel-drive truck. No ambulance, no coroner. He knew she was okay—he'd talked to her on the phone—but that wasn't the same as seeing her, touching her, holding her.

He stared at the garage door, frozen. His fists clenched and unclenched and he felt physically ill.

Lucy hadn't told him about the death threat.

He strode up the front walk and a uniformed officer stopped him at the door.

"I live here," he said through clenched teeth.

Nate was standing at the edge of the living room, his back against the wall, and saw Sean. "Officer, let him in," Nate said.

Sean put his hand on Nate's shoulder as he scanned the room. Nate, Juan, Ryan, Kenzie, Brad Donnelly from the DEA.

And Lucy. Sitting in a chair, pale with dark circles under her eyes.

He walked right over to her. He wanted to carry her upstairs and make her sleep, but knew she wouldn't go.

When she saw him, her entire body relaxed, and there was a hint of a smile under the layers of worry. That made the night flight worth it. It made coming home worth it.

"Lucy said you were in Dallas," Juan said.

"I flew in."

"You caught a plane in the middle of the night?" Ryan asked.

"It's my plane," Sean said, not taking his eyes off Lucy. He sat on the edge of the chair and took her hand. She squeezed, and he didn't let go. He looked around the room, but his eyes settled on Donnelly. "Who did it?"

"You saw the door," Brad said. "It's connected to Sanchez."

"No shit," Sean said before he could stop himself. "How'd they find out where we live?"

"They must have followed Lucy home," Ryan began.

"No," Sean and Lucy said simultaneously. Lucy added, "I wasn't followed home. I would have known."

It was clear no one believed her, except Sean. He knew.

Lucy said, "Someone followed me from Saint Catherine's on Monday, but I lost them. I put it in my report."

"But you didn't get a description of the car or a license plate," Juan said. "How do you know?"

"I just . . . it was a feeling. I trust my instincts."

Juan said, "We're going to keep a patrol out front, and if you want an agent inside, you can have it."

"I'm here," Sean said.

"Of course, no offense meant."

"None taken." He was still watching Donnelly. This was his case, his responsibility. "Have you seen this before?" he asked the DEA agent.

"Years ago," he said. "They went after my team at their homes."

"Sanchez?"

He nodded. "They were threats only, no one was hurt, but one of my rookies resigned. And I'm sorry, Lucy, I should have warned you. I didn't think they'd target you because you're not DEA."

Nate said, "It's standard drug cartel intimidation tactics. Go after whoever they think is the weakest link. Lucy is FBI, she's not trained with the DEA, she doesn't have the background with the cartels, they figure she's the weak link."

"They went after the wrong agent," Sean said.

"Sean," Juan said, "I can't have you going off the reservation."

Lucy squeezed his hand and said, "What he means is, Sean's family and my brother are well versed in fighting the drug cartels. They may think I'm the weak link, but they definitely disturbed the hornets' nest."

Donnelly slowly stood up. "I can't have your brother in the middle of my operation," he said to Sean. "I know Kane, by reputation. I'm not passing judgment on his methods. But this is Texas, not the Mexican backcountry, and I'm responsible for my people. He interferes and many could be exposed. My informants, my team."

"Then you don't know Kane," Sean said, not breaking eye contact.

Juan cleared his throat. "It's clear they're trying to scare us, and it's not going to work."

Sean glanced at Lucy. She'd been terrified, but now she had stubborn determination on her face. He wanted to take her away until this was over, but he knew better than to suggest it. This was her career, her vocation. If she ran away she would never forgive herself.

It was one of the many reasons he loved her.

"If you want out," Donnelly said to Lucy, "just say it."

She shook her head. "They don't know me."

Sean's heart twisted. Lucy was in that body, he knew it, but she'd put up her shields, her cold exterior that helped her survive the past. He'd spent a year helping her ease out of that hard shell, and there it was, as if she'd never smiled or laughed or relaxed. A defense mechanism. It made Sean ache, even though he understood.

"I'm going to McAllen," she said.

No one contradicted her. But she wasn't going without him. Sean simply didn't feel the need to share that fact just yet.

"I want to know how they found me," she said. "Anyone have an idea that isn't them following me home?"

"Hand me your phone, Luce," Sean said.

She reached into her pocket and handed it to him. He went through all the settings. "No, not hacked." He handed it back to her.

Juan frowned. "There's GPS on all federal phones. For security. Someone could have found our codes."

"I disabled them on Lucy's phone," Sean said.

"What?" Juan was obviously surprised and not happy.

"I can remotely activate it, but what you call security I'd call a beacon."

"We need to talk later," Juan mumbled and rubbed his eyes.

Nate spoke up. "GPS. That has to be it. What about your car, Lucy?"

"I disabled the GPS on that, too," Sean said.

"Someone could have planted a device," Donnelly said.

Sean almost said *no*, but Donnelly was right. It was all too easy. He'd done it himself many times when he worked for RCK.

"I'll check," he said and walked through the house toward the garage. Nate followed him.

"She's okay," Nate told him when they were alone.

"She's not. She hides it well." Sean turned on all the lights and pulled out his own phone. He ran an app he'd written that was essentially a bug-detecting device, but had the added benefit of detecting any system that sent a signal, including GPS.

His phone alarm went off.

"Bingo."

"That is hot," Nate said.

"But it can't tell me where, just that it's here some-place."

"You check inside, I'll check the outside," Nate said. He pulled on gloves and started feeling around the bumpers and undercarriage.

Sean sat sideways in Lucy's driver's seat and inspected the dashboard, the controls, searched under the seats and the glove compartment. Nothing.

"Sean," Nate said. "I found it. In the wheel well, and it's a good one."

Sean was partly wrong: the device under Lucy's car wasn't a simple GPS tracker.

He itched to dismantle it himself, but Juan called in SWAT to make sure it wasn't something more dangerous. No one wanted to say *bomb*. Sean was certain it wasn't a bomb, and so was Nate, and so was Donnelly—the other two people in the room who had experience with bombs. But Juan wasn't taking chances.

It was after dawn by the time the bomb squad determined that the device wouldn't detonate if removed. They secured and analyzed it in their van. Sean finagled his way into the periphery of observation, but he figured out before the bomb tech exactly what the device was.

"That's a boosted GPS tracker," Sean said. "It has a small detonation to take out the electrical system, which could cause a serious accident but isn't designed to blow up the vehicle."

Juan didn't take Sean's word for it, and though Sean couldn't blame him he was irritated. "Leo?"

The SWAT team leader, Leo Proctor, was also the FBI's leading bomb tech. He'd served three tours in Afghanistan with the Marines. "Rogan's right. But that doesn't make this any less dangerous. It's designed to take out a single target on command—it has a cell phone trigger. It's track-able twenty-four seven, but you have to call the device to ignite it. It would spark and send a surge into the car's electrical system, cause it to completely shut down. Just stop. If the target was on a freeway going sixty-five, for example, the shutdown could cause a serious accident. The device also has a self-destruct mechanism, so once it does its job, the plastic melts."

"But it would be detectible," Juan said, "in an investigation."

"Yes, if you know what you're looking for. It's not that big—essentially the size of a small cell phone. The car diagnostics would be fried, and it would take smart techs to see that it was something other than a massive and unexpected electrical failure."

"We track the device, we'll know who planted it."

Leo considered. "Possibly. It's homemade. I haven't seen anything like it, but I'll send the specs out to law enforcement, make some calls." He glanced at Sean but didn't say what Sean knew he was thinking.

Does RCK have a lead on this?

Sean didn't regret quitting his brother's private security company, but now for the first time he wondered if he should have found a way to make it work. RCK's access to information was unparalleled.

Of course, he could get anything he wanted. Lucy was a Kincaid, Jack and Patrick were both principals in the business, and they would do anything to find out who had threatened their sister.

"Do what you need to," Juan told Leo. He glanced at his watch. "I need everyone at headquarters for a briefing at oh-eight-hundred. Wrap this up, I want a pair of agents on Kincaid at all times."

Sean followed Juan out of the tactical van. "Juan, I'll protect Lucy."

"I'm aware of your background, and therefore I won't post agents in your house. But when she leaves this property, she's under *my* protection."

Sean wasn't going to argue with Juan, but there was no way in hell he was letting Lucy out of his sight now that the drug cartels had threatened her.

They only had an hour before Lucy needed to leave. Juan told Lucy he would have Nate bring her to the office for the debriefing, and then he left.

"This is fucked," Sean muttered to Nate as they watched everyone leave. "Where's Donnelly?"

"Inside," Nate said.

"I dug around."

Nate raised an eyebrow, but didn't comment, and Sean didn't elaborate. Nate knew what RCK did, and what Sean had done for them.

"He hasn't been completely honest with us," Sean said. "He will be now."

Twelve miles away, in a quiet, middle-class neighborhood filled with quiet, middle-class houses, the man's screams could not be heard because he had duct tape over his mouth. He could not move because his torso was tied to a chair.

He stared at the walls as the flames roared higher and higher, bright and violent, fueled by the gasoline. They surrounded him, his skin reddened, blistered. The stumps where his hands had been dripped blood. He wished he'd bled to death first. He was living in Hell, and he would die in Hell.

But he'd known, as soon as he hung up the phone, that he was a dead man.

He would get his vengeance from the grave.

Then the ceiling collapsed and the fire consumed him.

CHAPTER 22

Lucy poured coffee for herself and Brad. There would be no sleep this morning. "I'm still going to McAllen," she said. "I'm not letting them scare me off."

"I won't think less of you if you wanted to sit this one out."

"*I* would think less of me."

She was exhausted, but she wouldn't be able to sleep even if she tried.

"I'm sorry about this," Brad said. "I should have seen it coming."

"Why?"

Sean and Nate stepped into the kitchen. "Because he's been lying since you met him."

Brad turned to stare at Sean. "I haven't lied."

"Lies of omission."

Lucy walked over to Sean and wrapped her arm around his waist. He was rigid, simmering with anger. "Sean, I know."

"He told you about what happened in Tucson?"

"Not in so many words, but I picked up on it."

Nate helped himself to coffee. Sean didn't move. Lucy

stood next to him. She didn't think he'd go after Brad, but they were all running on fumes.

"I lost a rookie five years ago when I was on a major undercover op in Tucson."

"I know," Sean said. "And?"

"You running a background check on a federal agent?"

"I'll bet my security clearance is higher than yours."

Lucy squeezed his biceps, wanting him to take it down a notch. Fortunately, Brad deflated, physically and emotionally, right in front of them.

"They threatened her, too. Just like this. It'll be pig's blood, not human."

Sean said, "Sanchez was in Tucson."

It wasn't a question. Lucy wondered what else Sean had dug up. Information was his bailiwick.

"No—but he's hooked up with people who were responsible for what happened there. And I know in my gut that Sanchez was responsible for assassinating my rookie. But there was no evidence, nothing to tie him or his gang to the shooting."

Lucy was confused. "This wasn't related to the two agents killed in Tucson?"

"Yes, but it was someone else. Before the raid, no proof that it was connected. And because of it, I let my emotions affect my judgment. Never again."

"What else?" Sean demanded.

"Look, Rogan, I get it—Lucy's your girl, you want to protect her. I told you everything. Sanchez is an evil bastard and he deserves to die. But all I can do is arrest him unless he shoots first."

Sean stared, then shrugged Lucy off and pulled food out of the refrigerator. He started making breakfast, eggs and sausage, not talking.

Brad said to Lucy, "I'm sorry this landed on your

doorstep. I've been wondering if you might have done something, talked to someone, learned something you might not realize is important. I don't know if you were targeted just because you're the rookie here. It could be, but I think there's more to it."

"We'll go over all the reports again." She hesitated, then said, "I had a long talk with Jennifer Mendez yesterday. She knows I connected Michael and Richie Diaz, the boy in the morgue. She was helping me run reports, going through the back door since official channels were taking too long."

"We ran a background on her. She's clean, though she has a sealed juvie record."

"We found the same thing," Lucy said.

"Who else knows?"

"The boy's mother. The landlord saw us, but we only showed him Michael's picture. He could have learned from the mother about her missing son, but I don't think so. Michael's CPS officer, Charlie DeSantos. I didn't tell the Popes about Richie, but I don't know if DeSantos might have. The priest at St. Catherine's gave me Richie's name in the first place. Everyone who's been in any briefing or had access to the files knows what we know."

"The FBI and DEA operate the same way—the files are eyes-only," Brad said.

"There are corrupt cops," Sean said. "And feds."

"Not on my team," Brad said. "Except for Lucy, I've worked with everyone on the task force in the past, some going back years."

Nate said, "It's more likely that Lucy did or said something that made the players involved very nervous."

Lucy frowned. "Sanchez is supposed to be in McAllen."

"How do you know?" Sean asked as he put plates of

eggs, sausage, and packaged muffins on the counter. Lucy brought out plates and utensils.

"Confidential source," Brad said.

"And you trust him?"

"He's been giving me information since I arrived in San Antonio. Not once has he been wrong."

Lucy couldn't think of what she might know that no one else knew. "CPS's security isn't as tight as the DEA or the FBI."

"From here on out, we don't talk to Mendez or DeSantos," Brad said. "If they want a report, we shoot them up to Juan or Sam. I'm not saying the leak is one of them, but their offices don't afford much privacy or security. It could be a secretary, another agent, or hackers."

"Agreed," Lucy said.

Lucy picked at her food, mostly to please Sean, and drank a third cup of coffee.

"I'm going to shower," she finally said. "I need to wake up. I won't be long, Nate."

Sean watched her leave the kitchen, then he said to Nate, "If you want a shower, you know where the guest room is."

Nate grabbed a muffin and a full cup of coffee. "Thanks, bro. Go easy on the drug cop." He said it lightly, but Nate understood Sean as well as any of his brothers.

Brad stared at him. "Spill it, Rogan."

"I think you're obsessed and you should have told Lucy from the beginning how far back you go with Sanchez. Even now, you only touched on it."

Brad glared at him. "Bastard."

"I'm not the liar."

"I did everything by the book."

"Last time you went after Sanchez, two cops died. The time before that, in Tucson, two DEA agents died. And the rookie they took out in her own home." Sean hesitated. "I think they targeted Lucy because of something she knows, as well as to hit *you*. After the last sting, you were suspended for running unapproved ops, nearly got yourself and your team killed—"

"Hold it. That's classified."

Sean ignored that. "I'm going to McAllen with you. Don't fight me on this, because you will lose."

"It's not my call. You're a civilian."

"I can get cleared. Or I'll run parallel to you. I think you would do anything to take Sanchez down, and I'm with you on that. He's a vile bastard who deserves to rot in jail or six feet under. But you're blinded by your obsession."

"I'm not." Brad rose from the stool. "You don't know me, Rogan, and I've always owned my mistakes. I've made them, and I've cleaned up other people's. But I have the best damn record in Texas, and I'm going to get Sanchez and find out who he's aligned with. I will take them down. I don't have a death wish, and I sure as hell am not going to send anyone else in to do anything I'm not willing to do myself."

Sean believed that. He had mixed feelings about Brad Donnelly, but his record was solid—except when he'd gone rogue, which was more than a couple of times. He should have been running the San Antonio office, not taking orders. And—ironically—Brad Donnelly was the type of cop that RCK liked to recruit. Former military, ten or more years in law enforcement, independent thinker.

But he still wasn't certain Brad wouldn't lose it if the op went south. And if he did? That put Lucy in the crosshairs.

Sean walked Brad to the door. He glanced at the security panel; all was well. Brad said, "I'm really sorry about what happened last night."

"So am I."

"Lucy's tough."

Sean nodded. "More than you know."

Sean watched Brad leave, then pulled his phone from his pocket. He dialed Kane's number, irritated when voice mail immediately clicked in. He hadn't expected Kane to answer, but he'd hoped.

He left a brief, two-word message. "Call me."

Lucy took a fast, hot shower, then sat heavily on the end of the bed, wrapped in a towel.

Stop feeling sorry for yourself.

"I'm not," she said out loud. This had nothing to do with pity. She was angry. It was a simmering anger. She was usually the calm one, the reasoned voice among her brothers or Sean or sister-in-law Kate. She'd learned to control her emotions, her reactions, through years of working with her brother Dillon, the forensic psychiatrist. Keeping her emotions even and steady had saved her from going into rages or depressions after she'd been raped. Now she felt almost normal, at least as normal as she was going to get.

But she knew what the anger felt like; she'd felt it before, long ago when she'd killed her rapist. The narrow vision, the sole focus, the determination.

She wasn't panicked, though. Wasn't that improvement?

Sean came in and closed the door behind him. "Nate's going to take you to headquarters in thirty minutes." He sat next to her, wrapping his arms around her.

"I'm fine," she said, shrugging out of his hug. She didn't want him to feel the coiled anger. He'd be more worried about her. "I'm not going to let Juan remove me from this case."

"Of course you're not," Sean said, watching her. Did he see that she was on edge? That she wanted to throw something against the wall?

"I just have to convince him that I'm an asset." She paced. She wasn't a pacer; she usually froze before she moved. Kate paced, and for a brief moment Lucy felt a flash of kinship with her sister-in-law who was two thousand miles away in Washington, DC. Kate paced because she couldn't stop moving, and pacing helped her work things out. Lucy had always thought better if she stopped, stared, focused on something small. Then the big picture would reveal itself.

But maybe this time she needed to take a page from Kate's book.

"Obviously, you found something so important that they consider you a threat." Sean tracked her with his eyes.

"I went over the day for Juan when he got here. I need to write it all out, have it ready for the briefing."

"Good idea."

And still he watched her, which was making her very nervous.

"What?" she said.

"I'm waiting for you to walk out your nerves."

"I'm nervous because you're watching me."

He shook his head. "You're nervous because you're mad."

"I'm not mad!"

She sounded angry, and she knew it. She sat heavily in her reading chair and sighed. "How do you know?"

"Because I know you. You're the most calm, even-tempered person I know."

She almost smiled. "Even when you met me in the pouring rain half hysterical when I found out my family lied to me?"

"Half hysterical?" Now he did laugh. "You had every right to be angry, but you were so calm about it." He walked over to her and sat on the arm of her chair. "It's okay to be angry. And scared."

"Not for me," she said. The anger was still there—the anger that someone had broken into her house, the house she shared with Sean; anger that someone had threatened her, using pig's blood to try to intimidate her; anger that she might be pulled off a case when she was so deeply invested in it. In the people, the investigation. It wasn't fair, and she didn't know how to convince her boss that she needed to be involved. Maybe she wouldn't have to. Maybe he'd already come to the same conclusion.

But she also felt a layer of calm over the heat.

Not *needed*. The only way Juan would let her stay was if she explained—calmly—why she was an *asset* to the team. Why they couldn't let these criminals intimidate a federal agent, why letting them control the players let them control everything.

She sat down next to Sean but didn't touch him. She said, "Do you know why I usually act so cold?"

"You're not cold."

"Yes, I am. I know it. I have this layer, a protective layer, that makes me come off as calm and cool."

"It's a defense mechanism, and it helps you do a damn good job."

"Yes—but not in the way you think. If I don't have the calm, the cool, I fear the pit of anger I've been harboring for so long will escape. I have to ice myself down to keep it from exploding. It's so hot sometimes," she whispered.

Sean stared at her as if he were only seeing her for the first time.

"Don't," she said, turning away.

"Don't what?"

"Look at me like that."

"Like what? Lucy, what are you scared of?"

"You know me, but maybe you don't."

"You're sounding silly."

"Am I?" How could she explain? She'd come to not only expect, but maybe *need* Sean to understand her without her having to explain. Explaining meant confronting the pit of rage deep in her soul. She didn't want to put words to anything so dark, so dangerous.

"Do you think I would be upset if you got mad? On the contrary, I'm glad you do. Sometimes I worry that you keep everything *too* closed up, too much inside."

"I have to, Sean, don't you understand that? If I let it out, it might consume me."

He took her hand. She tried to pull away, but he kept a firm grip on her. "Lucy, I love everything about you. I love the calm, I love the heat. Never hide from me. If you want to scream in frustration, I want to hear it. I'm not going to worry if you need to explode. You *should* be mad at what happened here. If you weren't—maybe then I would be concerned."

"But what if I can't control it? What if I let it out and can't stop it?"

"Trust yourself, because God knows I do." He stared at her and she wanted to stay here, locked in his deep-blue eyes, where she felt the most safe, the most at peace, the most *normal*. "If you need the heat, use it. If you need the ice, use it. They are tools at your disposal. You think you can't control it, but you do. Every day." He frowned. "What are you scared of, baby?"

"I'm not scared," she said. "I mean, I am, but that's not what this is about. I wanted to shoot that guy. I could see myself, standing at the top of the stairs, and putting three bullets into his chest."

"But you didn't," Sean said.

"But I wanted to."

"Hell, *I* want to."

"I'm angry that they made me scared. I'm angry that they violated our home. That they broke our window, dumped blood on our door. That they made me, for one minute, feel like a victim again."

She stood, needing to pace again. Now she understood

why Kate had to move all the time. It was the adrenaline, and it was pumping through her. She didn't know if it was good or bad, but she felt better.

"I'm *not* a victim."

"You're not."

"I'm an asset to this team. They need me. Obviously, Sanchez and his people think that I'm close to uncovering something they don't want us to know. I'm going to figure it out, then I'm going to help stop him."

"Of course you are."

She finally stopped walking and stared at him. God, she loved this man. "I'm sorry you had to leave Dallas. I don't know what I did to deserve you, but I'm so glad you're here."

"I'm done. All I was going to do today was gloat when the embezzler got axed. I can write the reports for their attorney from here. And *you* are more important than anything, especially a short-term job."

She strode over, put his face in her hands, and kissed him. "Thank you. I can do this."

Sean watched her go into the closet to get dressed. He was both relieved and worried. Relieved because she was fine, she would be fine; worried because someone had threatened her. The device under her car wouldn't have killed her, but it sent a message. If she got too close, they would follow through.

He pulled out his cell phone and called Kane again. Again, it went to voice mail.

"Dammit, Kane, call me back. It's important."

CHAPTER 23

Though Juan had ordered everyone into the office at oh-eight-hundred, he wasn't in the conference room when Lucy, Nate, and Ryan walked in at five minutes to. Neither was Brad Donnelly. The SAC's door was closed and there was a quiet buzz in the office. Lucy felt eyes on her from colleagues she didn't work with on a day-to-day basis, the agents who made up the squads in the other divisions.

She hated being the center of attention—especially, *this* kind of attention.

Once she was in her sanctuary, the Violent Crimes Squad, she relaxed. She wasn't going to get a chance to plead her case. Her boss might be taking that away from her, with this closed-door meeting.

She had to trust Juan. They were federal agents, after all. If they cowered when the bad guys struck, who would be left to stand for justice? No one—and that wasn't acceptable. She wasn't going to be intimidated, she wasn't going to be locked in an office simply because she was doing her job.

Her phone rang and she grabbed it.

It was the secretary to Special-Agent-in-Charge Ritz Naygrow.

"Please come to the director's office."

Lucy hung up and stared at the phone. "Dammit."

When Nate gave her a questioning look, she explained. He said, "Don't sweat it."

"I'm not." But she was.

She walked back down the long hallway to the front of the building and turned into the administrative wing. A large bull pen, of sorts, was in the middle—eight cubicles of support staff for the ASACs. Three ASAC offices along the far wall, then human resources, the media information officer, accounting, and in the corner the small suite for SAC Naygrow.

The SAC had as many responsibilities outside of the office as in it, partly political, partly community building, and he had the reputation of trusting and relying on his ASACs to keep the office running smoothly. He had little field training, having moved up in the ranks administratively through the main FBI headquarters in DC until he was transferred as an ASAC five years ago. Two years ago, when his predecessor retired, he was promoted. Juan had said, during a family dinner at his house when he was relaxed, that it had all been planned by headquarters when Naygrow was first transferred. Lucy didn't know what Juan really thought of the SAC, but he had always been professional and respectful.

Naygrow was considered smart, trusted his field agents, and fair—but he expected every squad to run smoothly. He didn't like surprises, and he particularly didn't like bad press.

His administrative assistant, Thomas Xavier, said, "Go right in, Agent Kincaid."

She did, hesitating only momentarily before knocking and turning the knob.

SAC Naygrow sat at the head of his small conference table. He was an impeccably dressed man in his late forties with graying, conservatively cut hair and dark eyes. He looked more like a businessman than a cop. Next to him was ASAC Abigail Durant, whom Juan reported to. Juan, Brad, and SWAT team leader Leo Proctor were there, as well as two people Lucy didn't know, a man and woman who both wore guest badges.

"Agent Kincaid, please have a seat," Naygrow said.

Juan nodded to the seat across from him, between Brad and Leo. Lucy clasped her hands, forcing herself to remain calm and detached. The two strangers—both from DEA—introduced themselves. The woman was Samantha Archer, assistant director and in charge of the San Antonio DEA office.

Naygrow said, "Juan filled us in on not only what happened last night, but your current case, Agent Kincaid. I called you in to let you know that no one gets away with going after one of my agents."

"Yes, sir," she said.

"This is an unusual situation, as you've been working on a joint task force with the DEA. SSA Donnelly has asked that you stay on the case, even though you've been singled out."

Lucy glanced at Brad, but he wasn't looking at her.

Naygrow continued. "I don't like my agents being attacked, and I like less that they've been compromised. But as my colleague Assistant Director Archer reminded me, when the bad guys start going for us, it means we're doing something right. And apparently, you've done a lot right this week."

He smiled. Lucy didn't think it was anything to smile about; nor did she understand the direction of this conversation. But she nodded.

"If the DEA didn't want you on board," Naygrow said, "I'd pull you. You're a rookie, you've been a sworn agent for barely three months, and you have no training with this level of criminal. No drug background, no organized crime. I don't want to see you injured, or worse. But there's no time to bring in someone else and get them up to speed, and because we have a missing child, every minute counts."

"Yes, sir."

"I'm not going to order you to do this," he said. "It's your choice. You've been singled out by one of the cartels, and that is terrifying."

"With all due respect," Lucy said—stunned she had the courage to speak at all—"I'm not terrified. I'm not going to back down just because someone comes after me. If I were scared of the criminals I pursue, I wouldn't have become a federal agent."

Naygrow nodded. "I guess that's your answer."

"Yes, sir, it is. I want to see this through."

"Very well, I'll authorize it. You and—" He looked at his notes. "—Agent Quiroz will be assigned to SSA Donnelly for the duration of this operation."

"Thank you, Ritz," AD Archer said. "I'll personally keep your people in the loop."

"Report directly to Juan Casilla, please," Naygrow said. "These are his people, and his concerns. Juan will personally run the investigation into the attack on Agent Kincaid. I expect equal cooperation with all information your office has related to like crimes."

"Yes, sir," Archer said. "I've assigned an agent to focus on pulling relevant information, plus we have our tech working with Agent Proctor on the device found on Kincaid's car."

Naygrow turned to Juan. "I know you need to brief your people. I think we're done here."

"Thank you, sir," Juan said formally and walked out.

Lucy followed the line of people. Outside Naygrow's office, AD Archer came up to her. "Lucy? I wanted to introduce myself. I'm Sam Archer." She pulled Brad over to them. "Brad says you've been an asset, and I want to tell you how sorry I am about what happened at your house."

"I appreciate you letting me stay on the task force."

"We're really close, and Sanchez knows it," she said. "I think Brad's right in that this is our best chance to find out who he's working for."

The conversation Lucy had with Kane the night before came back to her, but she didn't have a chance to comment before Ryan pulled her and Brad into the briefing room. Juan had already started, and she stood in the back with Brad.

"Thank you," she whispered. "I appreciate you going to bat for me."

"Your boss isn't happy. I'm sorry about that. If that changes your mind—"

She shook her head. "I'll fix it." She hoped she could.

The briefing went fast. After Juan, Brad gave the bullet points of the investigation to date, then assigned tasks.

Nate called out, "I thought I was sticking to Lucy like glue."

"That's now Ryan's job. He's been her partner in this op from the beginning. We don't have time to fully brief you before they leave for McAllen."

Juan was about to dismiss the group when Lucy raised her hand. "I have some new information."

"The floor is yours."

Lucy went to the front of the room and with Zach's help brought up the images of the tattoo on Richard Diaz's forearm and the one Bella drew. "I've been researching this symbol, along with Zach and the DEA. Until last night, we had no leads. I went to a source that has experience with these sorts of things, and he indicated that the mark is the brand of Vasco Trejo, an American expatriate living in Mexico. He's a relatively new player, has brought in or destroyed smaller groups to build his base. Sanchez appears to be his primary American contact. He brands his couriers with this mark. Apparently, this is common—using young boys as drug couriers, similar to how gangs use them as killers. But what we're still working out is how. Both Michael Rodriguez and Richard Diaz appeared to have run away, but in all likelihood were coerced into working for Jaime Sanchez. The fathers, both incarcerated, have a connection to Sanchez, and it may be that Sanchez used that connection to lure the boys away."

There was silence. Lucy looked around and added, "This gives us a direct connection from Sanchez to one of the smaller cartels."

Again, silence. Juan rose and said, "Dismissed."

Brad immediately approached her as everyone else filed from the room. His eyes were dark with anger. "Where did you get that information?"

Before she could say anything, he said, "It was Rogan, wasn't it? Your boyfriend's brother. Shit!"

"It's good intel."

"I didn't say it wasn't, but you should never talk about my case without telling me first. I need to make some calls." He looked at his watch. "We're taking a military transport to McAllen. Archer arranged it, we leave in ninety minutes. Be at my office in forty-five minutes."

Lucy followed Juan to his office. "Sir?"

"Shut the door."

She did. "I apologize if I stepped on your toes. I didn't know what was going on in the meeting, but it seemed you don't want me with the task force anymore. I can assure you, I'm not reckless. I understand the risks and I'm willing to take them. There are two children in jeopardy, sir. And I think—"

He put up his hand, then sat heavily at his desk. "Lucy, please sit."

She did, though her back was rigid.

"You misunderstand. It's true, I had second thoughts about your involvement with Donnelly's operation. Not because I think you're incapable; on the contrary, you've exceeded my expectations in the three months you've been assigned to my team. But you're part of *my* team, and this situation has gotten out of *my* control. Donnelly wasn't straight with me, and I wanted to pull you and Ryan because of that, not because I didn't believe you'd be a valuable addition.

"Donnelly has been after Sanchez for years. I didn't realize Operation Heatwave was targeting some of Donnelly's biggest cases. The fugitives on Donnelly's list were from drug cases, not just rounding up gangbangers who slipped through the cracks. While we work closely with the DEA, the FBI does not routinely involve itself in drug crimes. There's a completely different set of skills, risks, and training. You're not there. I didn't like that Donnelly had kept important information to himself; I didn't like that you have become a target for whatever cartel Sanchez is working for."

"Sir, if I may." Lucy cleared her throat. "I should have told you earlier that I guessed that Donnelly had another agenda. It was clear after working with him Saturday that he was a bit . . . *obsessed*, for lack of a better word . . . about Sanchez. But rightfully so. And knowing what we now know about his connection to this new group is going to help the DEA shut down Sanchez, find his source, and help us find Bella and Michael."

Juan nodded. "You were vague about where you came by that information in the briefing. Did it come from RCK?"

"Yes, sir." Technically, it was Kane, but since Kane was still part of RCK there was no reason to go into specifics.

Juan rubbed his eyes. "It's a slippery slope, Lucy." It

looked like he wanted to say more, then didn't. "Until this is over, don't go anywhere alone. You and Ryan are partners; stick together. Even if it's a routine interview, you need backup. I would tell any of my agents the same thing if they had just been threatened as you were. Understood?"

"Yes, sir. Thank you."

"Be careful, Lucy. For agents, the FBI is safer than most law enforcement organizations. Working for the DEA is probably the most dangerous."

Lucy and Ryan arrived at the DEA office ten minutes early, and Assistant Director Archer greeted them. "Brad will be back in a minute. I'm glad to have you both on board."

"Thank you, ma'am," Ryan said.

"Let's find some place to talk," she said. She ushered them into a small conference room and closed the door. She didn't sit, nor did she invite them to. "Where'd you get the information about Vasco Trejo?" Archer asked.

"Kane Rogan. He's a principal at Rogan-Caruso-Kincaid and—"

Archer said, "I know who they are. Donnelly didn't tell me you were *that* Kincaid."

"It's not important."

"Damn straight it's important. We run up against RCK all the time and sometimes it's not friendly. They don't play by the same rules we're forced to."

Lucy bristled at the tone, but kept her face impassive. "I know what they do."

"I assume Jack's your brother."

"Yes."

She smiled and shook her head. "Small fucking world. My first assignment was down in McAllen. I was as green as they came, but had the fire in the belly. One day my partner said, 'We got a delivery.' I had no idea what that meant.

He took me outside and in the parking lot was the right-hand man of one of the cartel leaders. Trussed up like a pig. My partner grinned ear-to-ear and said, 'Major Kincaid comes through again.'" She laughed. "That was years ago. I knew he'd moved back to California, got himself married or something. Never thought he'd be one to settle down. And you're his sister."

"Yes." It was clear that at some point, before Jack left Texas five years ago, he and Samantha had some sort of relationship.

"The intel was good. Very good. Vasco Trejo has been on my radar for months, but until now I had nothing on him and put him at the bottom of the shit pile. Not many people here know much about him. He's wanted for murder—and we knew he'd fled to Mexico. As far as we know, he hasn't crossed to our side of the border in seven years, so he hasn't been on our active list. He was a low-life gangbanger who offed a rival gang member, then fled with money and drugs. Not a peep until one of our contacts said he'd been seen in Monterrey, about two hours south of the border. So I put him back on the list, just to keep him in my face. We haven't heard a word until you mentioned him this morning. Brad's all over it. But this changes the game somewhat. I'm going to join you in McAllen, because if we have a chance to nab him, we will, and I can deal directly with border issues."

Brad walked in. "We need to make a stop. Mirabelle's lawyer just called me. She's out, reunited with her daughter, and she wants to talk to Lucy."

"Do we have time?" Archer asked.

"I'll take Lucy to meet with her—she's still at the courthouse. She refuses to leave, wants protection. The AUSA is working on something temporary, but they want something from her."

Ryan said, "I'm going, too. Sorry, Luce, but Casilla made me swear to watch your back. No offense, Donnelly."

"None taken."

Archer nodded. "I can hold the transport a few minutes, but don't make me wait too long."

CHAPTER 24

Mirabella Borez was sitting with her daughter CeCe in a small conference room adjacent to an office used by the Justice Department on the third floor of the courthouse. They held hands, their damp, streaky faces evidence of tears.

The AUSA left them alone with Mirabelle, who glared at Donnelly. "I'm not talking to you. I don't have to, my lawyer said I don't."

"That's right," Lucy said. "You don't have to talk to us at all, but you requested this meeting because you want police protection. To get it, you have to convince us that your life is in danger."

CeCe squeezed her mother's hand tighter. Her bravado from Saturday was gone; she was a scared eleven-year-old, confused, perhaps feeling manipulated by her uncle. Her hair was pulled back into a ponytail and hung limp down her back. Her clothes were clean, but her eyes were swollen from crying. She stared at Lucy as if she hated her, but then looked away and all Lucy saw was the scared little girl inside.

Mirabelle nodded. Lucy gestured for Ryan and Brad to take seats at the other end of the table, not to crowd Mirabelle. She wanted her to feel comfortable enough to talk freely.

"Mirabelle, I think I know why you wanted to talk to me. It was about our meeting yesterday."

Mirabelle nodded, and fresh tears streamed down her face. "I've made a lot of mistakes, Ms. Kincaid. But I love my girls. I really do."

"I know you do."

"You said something about Bella's father—I told CeCe the truth, and she told me what happened when Jaime took my Isabella. That he deliberately left her. I know why, and I'm scared."

Lucy took a risk, because there was a chance that she was wrong, but she'd been mulling over Bella's parentage all night. And when Sam Archer said that Trejo had left San Antonio about seven years ago, it clicked.

She said, "Vasco Trejo is Bella's father, isn't he?"

Mirabelle nodded. "I don't know why Jaime is doing this, I don't know why he would betray me—his own sister—but taking Bella, he's going to give her to Vasco. I'll never see her again."

"Are you certain?"

This time CeCe spoke. "Uncle Jaime told me once when he was mad at my mama that we could all live in a palace in Mexico if only Mama would agree."

"My husband's name is on Bella's birth certificate, and I think of her as Pablo's daughter. Vasco is cruel. He likes to own people.

"Tell me what happened, Mirabelle."

"I can't." She gave a sidelong glance at her daughter, and Lucy understood there were some things she would never say in front of her children. "But he left, and he didn't know I was pregnant."

"He must have figured it out."

Mirabelle said, "Jaime knew. George always believed

me, but Jaime knew the truth. I . . . um . . . I didn't want what happened. He . . ." She glanced at CeCe again.

Lucy said to Ryan, "Can you take CeCe to get a soda or something?"

Ryan took the girl out and then Lucy asked, "Did Vasco Trejo rape you?"

She nodded and closed her eyes. She wiped her nose with the back of her hand. "The first time. And then he said I was his, and after that I just went along so he wouldn't hurt me."

Lucy dug into her purse and came out with a small package of tissues. She slid it across the table to Mirabelle, who clutched it in both hands.

"It's not your fault, Mirabelle," Lucy said. She'd had enough experience working with rape victims to know what Mirabelle was feeling. The confusion, the conflict, the guilt, the anger, the sorrow. "And it's not Bella's fault."

"But I never said no, not after that first time."

"The first time counts. Okay? I'll hook you up with a great crisis counselor I know, but just believe me, okay? If you want to believe in your heart that Bella is Pablo's daughter, believe it. Vasco has no claims to her."

"He wants to possess her, to own her, to punish me for not going with him. But I couldn't—no matter how much money he had, I couldn't go with the man who killed my husband."

Lucy remembered reading that Pablo Borez had died in a prison fight.

"You know that?"

"Jaime was upset and told me. He said he had to work for Vasco now, because of what I had done. It was my fault—I met Vasco in the bar where I worked. He was smart and charming and cute and I thought he had the answer for everything. But I didn't do anything!"

"Tell me about the boys in the basement," Lucy asked, shifting the direction of the conversation.

"Jaime brought them. I told him not to, but he did. They never stayed long, just a few days, until the last one. He took something that belonged to the general . . ." Mirabelle stopped. She stared at Lucy. "Don't tell me—"

Lucy nodded. "Vasco Trejo is the general."

"He knew! He knew from the beginning! Why would my brother betray me like that? Betray his nieces? He knows what that man did to me. To my Pablo. Pablo was his best friend. How could Jaime betray his sister and his best friend?"

"We think that Jaime has someone in law enforcement feeding him information."

"He does."

Donnelly leaned forward and said, "Who? Who is it, Mirabelle?"

"I don't know! I swear to you, I don't know! Does this mean you can't protect me and my daughter?"

She looked at Brad. Brad said, "Ms. Borez, I can put you in protective custody for a few days, but we need something you can testify to against your brother or against Vasco Trejo."

Her bottom lip quivered and she looked from Brad to Lucy. Then she sighed deeply, almost a cry. She pulled several now-crumpled tissues from the package Lucy had given her and blew her nose.

"I was there, seven years ago, when Vasco killed my boss at the bar," she said quietly. "In cold blood, for no reason, except that he thought my boss was skimming the protection money he paid Vasco."

Lucy and Brad exchanged looks. Mirabelle probably had a lot more information than she even realized would be valuable.

Brad said, "I'll make the call," and stepped out of the room.

Mirabelle reached across the table and grabbed Lucy's hands. "I know you don't like me, but you don't want to hurt my daughters."

"I will do everything I can to find Bella and bring her home."

"I believe you. But if I go home, he'll find me there. He'll kill me. But first he'll make me watch him kill CeCe. He told me he would hurt her if I ever told about my boss, and I never told anyone until now. No one. Please don't let him hurt my babies."

"We can protect you," Lucy said. *I hope.* "But from here on out, you have to be honest. Because if the government attorney catches you in a lie, all bets are off. Do you understand what that means?"

She nodded and wiped her face again. She smoothed down her hair. "I won't lie. But, Lucy, what about this cop my brother has? What if they find out? Get to me like they got to George?"

Lucy straightened. "Do you know who killed your brother?"

"It has to be the cop. Who else could get to him?"

Mirabelle was right. The way George was killed—poison or allergy—wasn't typical of a gang-related homicide, where a prisoner could be bribed to kill another prisoner. Gangs also liked to take credit. It helped them keep others from talking, helped them earn street cred. But George's murder was more sophisticated. More difficult.

"We'll keep the information you give us on a need-to-know," Lucy assured her. "And make it clear you don't know the identity of any law enforcement on your brother's payroll. They won't have any reason to go after you or CeCe."

Mirabelle looked skeptical, and Lucy wished she were

more confident. If there was a corrupt cop, that made everyone more vulnerable.

"What is the big endgame?" Lucy asked. "Bella is in danger. What is your brother supposed to do for Trejo?"

"I don't know the details," she said. "All I know is that they plan to steal a shipment of something, drugs probably, from a rival group. When that happens, Jaime said the circle would be complete because that group would be killed for not delivering and his hands would be clean. Their last big rival will be dead. I don't know when, but soon."

"And why did they need Michael?"

"Like the others, he delivers things. Anything Jaime needs done. I don't know why Jaime needed him for this job."

"Where is Michael now? I believe he can lead us to Trejo and therefore lead us to Bella."

"I don't know!"

Ryan and CeCe reentered the room.

CeCe said in a small voice, "I know why Michael left. He said he was going to get out and go back to the bad place. I asked him once, why would he want to be in a bad place?

"And he said, 'To kill the bad people.'"

Sean was on his way to the private airport he used when Lucy called. "We're about to board at the Air Force base," she said.

"You could always fly with me."

"Sean—you don't need to do that."

"Need and want are two different things. I'm working on reaching Kane right now. You need all the information you can get."

"Thank you—but let's keep it quiet for now. I told Brad and Juan about what Kane already gave us. They seemed . . . I don't know, not completely comfortable. Especially Juan."

"I like your boss, Lucy, but this is not a murder investigation. These people are not like people you know."

"I get that," she said, irritated.

"I didn't mean to be insulting."

"I know. I'm just tired. Brad's boss, Samantha Archer, knows Jack."

"I'm not surprised, considering what he used to do, and he lived outside McAllen for years. If Jack knew one of the cartels threatened you, he'd put you in protective custody so deep even *I* might not be able to find you."

"Jack would understand I'm doing my job," she said.

"Sleep, okay?"

"I will."

"Let me know where you're staying. I'm sure it'll be a dive, the FBI doesn't spring for five-star hotels."

"Is there one in McAllen?"

"Funny. I'll be less than an hour behind you, princess. Be careful."

As soon as he hung up, his phone vibrated with an unknown caller. "Rogan."

"It's Kane. It's not always easy, or safe, to answer a call."

Sean didn't respond to that comment. He said, "Sanchez or whoever he works for sent two thugs to break into our house while Lucy was there alone."

"I'm sorry," he said flatly.

"Dammit, Kane, what do I have to do to get you to help?"

"What is it you want me to do?"

"Information."

"I gave it to your girlfriend last night."

"We need more. I want to know where Vasco Trejo is right now and how to get to him. I want to know if there are any other boys like Michael Rodriguez who are being forced to run drugs and guns from the border north. I want information so that Lucy and her team don't walk into a trap."

"I already told her that the operation the DEA has planned is problematic. Tell her to walk away. Half those people are idiots."

"Jaime Sanchez kidnapped a seven-year-old girl. Would you walk away?"

"I'm not most people."

"Can you, for once, drop whatever the fuck you're doing and help your family?"

Silence. Damn, he'd pissed Kane off. "I thought I was," he said quietly. "I have an ally in Hidalgo. Padre Cardenas. He was Special Forces with Jack, now he's a priest. He gets information for us, helps when needed. Is your girlfriend still going down to McAllen?"

"Yes."

"I'll make contact with Padre. He'll reach out to you when he knows something. But under no circumstances should you seek him out. He has to be extremely careful. He walks a dangerous line."

"Thank you."

"If I were you, I would get down to McAllen and keep an eye on the situation."

"I'm already on my way."

There were two faces to every city. The ugly and the pretty. The good and the bad. As Michael had learned long ago, maybe before he could consciously think about it, people were blind. He didn't know if it was a choice—if they saw the desperate and dying but turned their heads, or if they were truly blind and *didn't* see.

It helped him now. Getting down to McAllen had been easy; he'd snuck into the back of a truck at a rest stop south of Corpus Christi. He'd crept out, only miles from his destination, when the truck stopped at a light. Once he got to Hidalgo, then it would get dangerous.

He walked the rest of the way, at night, hiding in the

shadows, drinking water he collected every chance he got. He had three water bottles, and he filled them up at a church, then at a gas station with tepid, unclear water, then at the rest stop. The night was cold, but he didn't care.

Once he was in town, he staked out a Laundromat and waited until dawn when a harassed mother with four young kids started two loads of laundry and put two more in the dryer, then walked her kids to school. At least, that's where Michael assumed they were going because three of the four had backpacks. The oldest was a boy, just a little smaller than Michael. The youngest, a girl, reminded him of Bella. He hoped Bella was okay. He hoped she didn't get in trouble for letting him go. But he knew, family or not, Jaime would punish her if he knew the truth.

Michael squeezed his eyes shut to block out the image of Bella being beaten. It wasn't his problem right now. He couldn't go back; he could only do what he'd set out to do. When it was done, if he lived, he would go back and help Bella. Because when he was done, her uncle would be dead and no longer be able to hurt anyone.

Michael waited. The heat rose, but the sky darkened. There would be a thunderstorm today. He was sweating, and not from the heat. The air was wet, moving in and out of his lungs, making him wheeze. He cleared his throat, spit into the dirt. And waited.

People came and went. Some stayed to guard their clothing, but most left it. It was an old neighborhood, with a thick layer of dust that was as much a part of the peeling stucco paint as the paint itself. As if the paint had been wet and a dust storm came and stuck to every building, every inch of concrete.

He walked inside with purpose. His clothes stank and were filthy, covered with sweat and dirt and dried blood. He opened the dryer the mother of four had used and pulled out jeans and a T-shirt that looked like they would fit him. They were still damp, but he couldn't wait. He stuffed them in the small pink backpack and walked back out, as if he had every right to be there. An impossibly old woman approached, looked like she was going to say something to him, tell him he was a thief, tell him to put the clothes back. Then she just shook her head sadly and went back to her own laundry.

Michael walked behind to the alley and stripped. He used one water bottle to scrub his face and hands, then put on the damp clothes. The jeans were too wide in the waist—he had lost weight—and a little short, but they wouldn't stand out as being wrong. The orange T-shirt was worn and faded with a barely discernible logo for a soft drink on the front. Crush.

He used to love orange soda. He didn't remember much about his mother, but she'd take him to the corner store and, for a treat, buy him an orange soda and one of Mrs. Jessup's homemade chocolate chip cookies she sold for fifty cents from her front porch. She was always sitting there, in her rocking chair, blind as a bat. How had she made such delicious cookies when she couldn't see? But she had good hearing, and if she didn't hear those two quarters, her hand would reach out so fast and take the cookie from your grasp.

Michael missed her. And his mom.

Tears burned his eyes. If he could kill his father, he would. The urge to see him dead, to be the one doing the killing, overwhelmed him, and he knew he was going to Hell. It didn't matter that Father Flannigan told him he was forgiven; he planned to kill. There would be no absolving him of his sin. And maybe he didn't care. Maybe there wasn't even a God. How could there be when his mother was dead and his father got away with killing her? How could there be a God when people like Jaime Sanchez could threaten to hurt good people like the Popes? When devils like the general could beat and hurt and kill boys like Javier?

But the Popes believed, and Michael's mother believed, and Michael *wanted* to believe, but he didn't, not really. He pretended because he loved Olive and he respected Hector; he pretended because Father Flannigan truly listened to him. He pretended because maybe, deep down, he hoped there was something better, where every kitchen smelled like Olive's cooking and every girl was as sweet as Bella and every man as gentle as Hector.

Michael tossed his clothes into the overflowing Dumpster and set out for the tunnel. Fat, isolated raindrops fell sporadically around him.

This began the most dangerous part of his journey.

The tunnel wouldn't be guarded, as people standing around would draw attention. There were three routes the general used, but this was the closest. Michael knew the system very well. He knew how to avoid border patrol—much easier going from Texas into Mexico. He knew how to blend, whether in Mexico as a Mexican, or in America as an American. That's why the general liked boys like Michael. They blended. And they feared.

He would prefer to do this at night, but at night was when he would most likely be caught. Night cloaked them, the dark, the shadows, but there were predators everywhere. Now he was a boy on his way to school, heading into a neighborhood that looked like all the other broken-down neighborhoods in southwest Texas, hurrying because it was starting to rain.

He reached the abandoned building, and for a minute Michael thought the tunnel was gone. That when he'd escaped, they'd buried alive everyone who was left, buried them under the Rio Grande, where no one would ever find them. Where no one would know the truth.

He wished he could have told Olive. Or Father Flannigan. But Jaime did not issue idle threats. He said he would kill them; Michael knew he would. Escaping put a target on their backs, but Michael hoped they heeded the warnings he'd tried to give them.

If he could just get back to the camp. Kill the general. Kill Jaime. Free his brothers.

Kill the general . . .

His heart raced. He was no better than his father. He reached into his pocket, felt the cool steel of the switchblade he'd lifted from Jaime's car while still in San Antonio. Was this the knife that had sliced Javier's throat? Was this the knife that had carved the mark into his flesh?

He absently rubbed his forearm as his eyes looked left and right. He didn't see anyone, but someone was watching. Someone saw him as he hesitated in the increasing rain.

Move, Michael! Move!

He went around to the back of the empty warehouse and the door was still there, still camouflaged. He was close.

So close.

Then a policeman stepped into view. And smiled.

There was no humor in his face.

And Michael knew he was going to die.

CHAPTER 25

Lucy had, surprisingly, slept during the forty-minute flight to McAllen. Not enough, but by the time they landed she was more relaxed. A team of agents met them, and Samantha Archer took charge. Lucy said quietly to Ryan, "Is it odd that the assistant director is on this op with us?"

"She's supervising. Not odd, but unusual. I'm not DEA, though. You won't see one of our ASACs—her comp level—in the field, unless it's a major operation, and then they'd be in the tactical tent. But since she runs a field office under Houston, she has more autonomy. And I heard she misses fieldwork."

"I wouldn't like sitting at a desk, either."

"You and me both."

They followed Archer and Brad into a hangar where the two DEA agents promptly moved aside to confer with their McAllen staff, leaving Lucy and Ryan on the side, distant observers. Lucy put her bag at her feet, retrieved her Glock from the side compartment, and holstered it. She then pulled out a Kahr PM9 and fitted it into her pocket holster. She wasn't supposed to carry a second weapon that wasn't regulation, but nothing about this assignment seemed to fit with the regs, so she wanted the extra piece. Fortunately,

Ryan didn't say anything and she wondered if he, too, had a backup piece.

Her phone rang—a blocked number. She knew, even before she answered, that it was Kane.

"You should have told me about the death threat," he said without identifying himself.

Lucy said, "You didn't seem inclined to help us any further, above the information you already provided. I understand your dilemma—"

"Listen to me. I've asked around. That mark is reserved for slaves. Those boys were taken to serve Trejo. My source tells me the boys were given up by their incarcerated parents as a sign of loyalty to Trejo so they would be protected in prison. A couple of dead inmates is all it took for the others to fall into line."

Lucy had no time to reflect on the horror of the situation, though it was close to what she'd thought. She asked, "And they're forced to be couriers."

"In part. They're compelled by a system of reward and punishment. They're essentially reprogrammed, retrained to be loyal to their captors. They may have gone in as young boys, but they come out just as dangerous as the men who took them."

"I can't believe—"

"I don't care what you believe, Lucia, I've lost men to these young killers. Are you so ignorant that you don't know that what has happened in Africa has happened on our own continent? You don't have to look far to find evil, little girl."

Lucy snapped, "I don't need you to lecture me on evil, Rogan. Michael hasn't been reprogrammed, he's out for revenge. He's going to get himself killed because he doesn't care about his life, he cares about hurting those who hurt him. I understand him more than you can possibly know. And I can save him. There are children at risk, not just

Michael, but a little girl kidnapped by her uncle. I will find her and bring her home. I won't let her suffer."

"You need to know that this situation is unlike anything you've ever handled."

"I get that." She glanced at Ryan; he was listening to everything. She asked Kane, "Do you know DEA Agents Samantha Archer and Brad Donnelly?"

"Yes."

Nothing more. So she asked, "Are they good?"

"Not as good as me."

He sounded just like Sean—except when Sean said it, there was a smile in his voice, a sparkle in his eye. Kane's tone was flat and straightforward.

"Send me a picture of the girl," Kane said.

"Why?"

"You don't take orders well, do you?"

"Not from you."

"I've already talked to one of my most trusted contacts. He's doing the work your beloved law enforcement agencies can't or won't do. He'll reach out when he learns something."

"Who?"

"I'm having a difficult time trusting you, Lucy. You told the DEA and the FBI where the information I gave you came from."

"You didn't say not to."

"I didn't think it had to be said."

"And you don't want me to share the name of your contact."

"It could get him killed."

"I won't say anything."

Kane hesitated, then said, "Padre. Father Francis Cardenas, but everyone calls him Padre. He's tight with Jack."

Lucy had never met Father Francis, but she knew of him.

"Now send me the picture of that little girl and I'll get back to you."

He hung up, even though Lucy had more questions.

Then he called back ten seconds later. She said, "That was fast."

"You distracted me. I have information. If you're marked, it's because you're close."

"I figured that out. But close to what?"

"Someone thinks you know how to shut their operation down. That means you found the key."

"Are you talking metaphorically?"

He sighed. "I forget you're a damn novice."

"Not as much as you think," she mumbled.

"An operation like Trejo's—small, tight—has a key person. That person connects everyone else. Without them, everything comes to a halt. It's always someone on the inside. A cop, usually."

"Or someone with access to the boys?" she asked.

"How are the boys connected?"

"They were all in foster care."

"Same home?"

"No. Not even the same counselor. But all CPS caseworkers can pull any records from the system. They have access to the kids and to the parents. I have to go."

She hung up this time, sent Kane the photo of Bella, then turned to Ryan. "I think I know who the key is. Who I got close to. Charlie DeSantos."

"Michael's CPS caseworker?"

"It has to be him. He had access to my car while I was talking to Jenny. Or maybe he even planted it while I was in Starbucks, after being followed on Monday." She frowned, thinking. "Or while I was at Saint Catherine's."

"I'll call Juan, but we'll need evidence. Do you have anything but your gut?"

"No." But it was the only thing that made sense. He'd

come to them, insinuated himself in the investigation. She'd kept him at arm's length, but also filled him in on the status of Michael—and she'd told him about Richie Diaz.

And he'd been the one to tell her that Jenny Mendez was Richie's counselor. There was no reason to do that, except to divert her attention. To make her doubt Jenny.

Ryan typed into his phone. "Okay, I sent Zach a message. Deeper background, surveillance starting now, and I'll call Juan when we get a second." He looked up from his phone. "So what was that call about?"

She didn't know what she should say. She hated being deceptive, but Kane had been upset that she'd told her boss that he'd shared information. It wasn't a secret what RCK did, or that she would have access to the information through Sean, her brothers, or Kane. Still, she kept it vague. "My contact wanted Bella's picture."

"Kane Rogan."

"I guess I shouldn't have told Juan and Brad he was my contact."

"Yes, you should. You can't play that game. And he shouldn't ask you to. You work for the government, he doesn't."

"He has access to far more intel than we do."

"That is true. But it's a big dark-gray area."

Brad walked over to them. "Sorry that took so long. The guys down here tracked down the ex-girlfriend's place. The problem is that we stand out. Two agents are dressed down and hanging in the area and confirmed that Sanchez was seen going into the house at dawn this morning, and he didn't come out."

"Did they get a visual on Bella?"

"Negative. The girlfriend left for work at ten; he should be there alone with his hostage. We have Nicole and a local guy sitting in the restaurant and they have eyes on Peña. We're going to do this now."

The situation was far from ideal. If they stormed the house, they put Bella in harm's way. Sanchez could use her as a shield. If this turned into a standoff, Bella's life was in greater danger.

They started toward the tactical van. Lucy told Brad her theory about DeSantos.

"Proof?"

"No, but my squad is working on it."

"I've known DeSantos practically since I've been in the San Antonio office. He seems solid. What about the girl? Mendez? I've never worked with her before, she's new. Started two years ago, right? About the time Sanchez started recruiting these boys."

"DeSantos insinuated himself into the investigation. He was on the scene real quick—the same day we put the BOLO out on Michael Rodriguez. And something he said to me that day seemed off—he was in the office on Saturday? Not usual working hours for CPS. Jenny was extremely put out that I wanted her to meet with me on Sunday afternoon. He also gave me information that was only partly accurate, about Jenny being Richard Diaz's counselor. She inherited him, and he disappeared shortly thereafter. She said she'd never met him, and I believe her. And," she added, almost as an afterthought, "Jenny works for CPS because she used to be in the system. She has two sisters, one a prosecutor and one a cop. I don't see her working with the drug cartels."

Brad absorbed everything she said. "And her past also makes her prime recruitment material for people like Trejo." He paused. "I don't want to believe it, but I've seen it before." He pulled open the doors from the back of the tactical van.

"Seen what before?" Archer asked.

"Corrupt public officials. Cops. Even federal agents. Mostly bribes, turning to look the other way, but there've been more active cases."

"Are you talking about anyone in particular?" Archer asked.

"Charlie DeSantos from CPS. The FBI is looking at him now."

"Does he know anything important?"

Lucy responded. "He knows we connected Michael and Richard Diaz, and he knows we're focused on the double-T scar on their forearms. He also knew I was running all runaways that fit the profile. He called me, met with me, seemed to be involved from the very beginning—like he knew more than he should have. It's a subtle thing, and not anything I picked up on until I started thinking back to when my car could have been tampered with."

Ryan said, "Zach's calling."

He took the call as the van pulled away from the airplane hangar. He didn't say much, and a minute later hung up.

"Charlie DeSantos's house burned to the ground early this morning. There's a body inside, unrecognizable, but they believe it's DeSantos."

"Arson?"

"Preliminary report is yes—the fire burned hot and fast and there's evidence at the scene that suggests fuel was added. They're saying gasoline. But here's the kicker—he was tortured first."

"How do they know?" Lucy asked.

"His hands were cut off."

CHAPTER 26

Jaime's ex-girlfriend Benita Peña lived on the outskirts of McAllen, close to the small, depressed border town of Hidalgo where Lucy's brother Jack had lived for a decade. Lucy'd never been here when Jack was; he'd been estranged from the family at the time. But she could picture him in the disheartened community, living light and cheap, a mercenary for hire who primarily rescued Americans who'd been kidnapped for ransom, or working on off-book operations where the American government had no business being.

Jack still had his fingers in such operations through RCK; the firm was often hired by companies to serve as protection for executives negotiating in countries where life was cheap, but most of the south-of-the-border work went to Sean's brother Kane and his team.

They drove up to the staging area, several blocks from Jaime's location. Because of the area, their vehicles—though undercover and as worn and old on the outside as others in the area—might stand out. Sam Archer had filled them in on the way. The undercover agents with eyes on the house had seen no movement since the ex-girlfriend left for work.

Brad had been quiet during the drive. Now he said, "I don't think he's there."

"There's no reason to think that," Sam said. He came in late last night, alone. He's there."

Lucy asked, "No one has seen Bella?"

"Correct. We're going in with the assumption that she's inside. Donnelly, the lead goes to the local SWAT team. You and Quiroz will be part of Beta team. Kincaid, you're with me. We're staying back until SWAT clears the building."

Waiting. At times like this she wished she could be part of the team instead of listening two blocks away on the com.

DEA announced themselves outside and asked the occupants to come out. No movement. As Lucy listened, they surrounded the house and forced entry. Reports of *clear, clear, clear* came at regular intervals for the next five minutes. Then Donnelly came on the com. "Director, they're gone. They were here—we found girl's clothing in a small room with an external lock. There's a tunnel in the basement, just like the fucking hardware store."

He was angry, and Lucy didn't blame him—though there was no way to have known there was a tunnel under this small, ramshackle house. They didn't have enough intel when everything was moving so fast.

Lucy joined Archer as the director walked down the street and up the short dirt walk to the crumbling one-story wood house. They met up with Brad and Ryan. Ryan had a doll in his hand and handed it to Lucy.

"It's Bella's," Lucy said. "She brought it from her house on Saturday."

"How long?" Archer demanded.

"He could have bolted with her anytime after two in the morning until five minutes before we arrived," Donnelly said.

"We need a better window than that. Canvass the area. Maybe someone saw something."

Ryan said, "No one here is going to talk to us."

"We have to try."

The canvass was a bust. No one would say anything. Everyone who said a word said the same thing: they'd seen nothing and no one. Didn't know who lived there. Never saw the man before. No one admitted to seeing a little girl.

Ryan and Brad tracked down the tunnel exit, one block over.

"Border patrol has been on alert for Jaime since Saturday morning," Archer said, "and I just called in an update and the director is going to reiterate that Sanchez is wanted for kidnapping a minor and may be fleeing to Mexico with her. The higher the BOLO, the more they pay attention."

Brad shook his head. "You know as well as I do that there are plenty of border holes they can slip through. Especially going south."

"Then go search and find us something to work with! Where did he go? Which way? Did he leave in the middle of the night or in the morning? Are we nine minutes behind him or nine hours?"

Lucy sent Sean a message with the status. He responded:

I just landed. I'm working on something for Kane.
I'll call you when I can.

What was Sean doing for Kane?

Ryan ran out. "We got something," he told Archer and Lucy. As they followed him around to the back of the house, he said, "I went through the garbage—disgusting. And found a burner phone. Your techs are going through it now, but it looks like he tossed it on his way out. The last message coming in was at eight thirty this morning."

"That puts him only three hours ahead of us," Archer said. "Good work."

A SWAT tech had the phone in a bag and said, "I can get more off it in the lab. He didn't wipe it. I retrieved a series of text messages from this morning." He handed Archer the phone. "I set it up so you can scroll from the first one, at eight ten this morning, down to the last message nineteen minutes later."

Lucy looked over Samantha's shoulder.

The first message was incoming.

Unknown: *He's here. Tracking him now.*
Sanchez: *fucking time. when? where?*
Unknown: *In town. Heading to the tunnel.*
Sanchez: *send D 4 him. get guys & wait 4 call*
Unknown: *Is it still on? Even with the heat?*

And the last message came five minutes later, presumably from Jaime:

Sanchez: *fuck yea gen aint scared*

"I hope you have something more," Sam said, frustrated. "This doesn't tell us where they are or even their plans—just that they're going through with whatever it is because they don't think we're onto them."

"I do," Donnelly said as he came out of the house. "The key to the ledger." He handed Sam a torn sheet of paper.

"Decipher," she said.

Donnelly pulled from his pocket a copy of a page of the ledger. "We quickly figured out that each page encompassed a week, and this page is for this week, so I made a copy. But we didn't know what the symbols meant. Until now. This paper was in the tunnel, in the corner like garbage. It tells us that today, at three p.m., they'll be at location *gato*. *Gato* is a warehouse in Hidalgo, in a heavily industrial area that the local guys say is mostly abandoned. Location *polla* is a bar in McAllen, *casa* is Mirabelle's house in San Antonio. We can't figure out the entire code, but we have enough to give us *something* to track them. And this coincides with what the McAllen team gave us earlier."

Sam considered. "Where was this?"

"In the tunnel mixed with a bunch of trash."

Lucy said, "I think we should be cautious. My source thinks it may be a setup."

"Source?" Brad said, turning on her. "You mean Kane Rogan?"

Archer asked, "Did he have specifics?"

"No, just he's suspicious about—"

"Nothing solid. And why did you tell him about the op in the first place? That was last night—things change rapidly."

"He understands this area and these people. He identified the general as Vasco Trejo. He knows what he's doing."

Archer put her hand up to stop Brad from arguing. "I agree we need more intel, but I trust the people down here. I'm not stopping a key operation because a mercenary has a suspicion. If he has something solid, give it to me and I'll listen."

Lucy shook her head. She trusted Kane's instincts, but there was nothing solid to give. She glanced at Brad, then said, "Mirabelle said earlier that Jaime had someone on the inside."

Sam said, "Brad told me. And we're proceeding with caution. But you think it's DeSantos, right?"

"Yes, but that doesn't mean there isn't someone else."

Sam turned to Brad. "Thoughts?"

"We've kept this as close to the vest as possible. If

there's a law enforcement leak, the chances are it's some-one in SAPD. Our teams in San Antonio and McAllen aren't new."

Sam considered, then said, "It's my call. We'll send a recon team to the site. I'm going to leave a team of six here to continue searching and make sure Sanchez isn't coming back. I'll have Rollins detain the girlfriend. Everyone else, we'll head to *gato* but we do *nothing* until we confirm the intel we have. Got it?"

"Yes, ma'am," Donnelly said.

Bella had never seen such a huge house. And it was pink. Not bright pink like her Barbie house, but light pink, like the roses in Abuelita's backyard.

Uncle Jaime was mad at her because she cried too much. She tried not to cry, because she didn't want to make him mad, but sometimes she couldn't stop. She missed her mama. She missed Uncle George. She even missed CeCe.

Men she didn't know had stopped them at the bottom of the mountain, then drove them up to the gigantic house. The road was bumpy and went around and around. She leaned into her uncle because even though she was scared of him, these other men were even more scary. And they had guns, big guns over their shoulders, and knives on their belts and they didn't smile at all, not *once*.

"I wish CeCe were here," she whispered as the Jeep stopped and her uncle lifted her out of the backseat.

He didn't say anything. He hadn't talked to her hardly at all since they left the dirty house where that woman he kissed a lot lived.

Bella didn't like Uncle Jaime's voice anymore. He'd never really been nice, but he sounded meaner now. He didn't give her a toothbrush. And he only gave her food in wrappers. Her mama didn't like that food, she said it was bad for you even if it tasted good. Bella liked her mama's food, especially when she let her help make tamales.

"Uncle Jaime?"

"Be quiet. Okay? Just stop talking."

She was shaking by the time they walked all the way up the stone path to the big wood front door. It had a glass window with colors, like the church.

The men who walked with them knocked on the door. It was opened by another man with a gun. Bella stepped behind her uncle.

"You're late," the man in the doorway said. He didn't smile.

But he let them in, and that was good because Bella was hot and tired and really, really thirsty.

The house was cool with tile floors and big ceilings and lots of space. Bella's eyes grew wide as she looked all around. She'd never, ever seen a house this big or beautiful. She felt so small.

They went into a room that was as big as her whole house. It had couches and books and a big table and glass doors that went right outside. She could see a pool, big and blue, shimmering in the sunshine.

A man stood in the middle. He wasn't a big man. There was nothing scary about him and he didn't have a gun. He was shorter than her uncle George, but taller than her uncle Jaime. He wore white pants and a white shirt and was very pretty.

Girls are pretty, boys are handsome, stupid.

It was like CeCe was talking in her head right there. That made Bella homesick all over again.

No one said anything. The man in the white shirt walked over to her and squatted down. He had a mustache. He smiled. He was the first person who had smiled at her since Uncle Jaime took her from Mr. and Mrs. Grove.

"Hello, Isabella," the man said. "I'm so happy to finally meet you. Do you know who I am?"

She knew because Uncle Jaime had told her many times. "You're my father?" Her voice was small and whispery.

He smiled wider. "Yes, I am your father. I have wanted you to live with me for a long time." He took her hand, then stood back up and walked her to the doorway. A woman appeared. Older than her mama but younger than her *abuelita*. "Letitia will show you to your room so you can take a bath and put on pretty clothes and maybe sleep for a bit, okay? Then we'll have dinner together, just you and me, and get to know each other better. Okay?"

She nodded because she had to answer, but didn't know what to say.

Then she asked, "Can my mama come live here, too?"

He stopped smiling. "We'll see," he said in a tone that Bella knew meant no. Her mama used that tone a lot.

She really wanted to go home.

Jaime Sanchez has caused Vasco far more problems than he was usually willing to tolerate, but he needed the man for a while longer.

It didn't make Vasco happy.

Jaime said, "We found the boy. We have him secure, and will be transporting him to the compound tonight."

"Kill him already. He's the reason the police are so close. We'll use another kid. Why you didn't kill him when you found him the first time, I don't know. Sometimes, Jaime, I wonder about your intelligence."

"It takes time to train them. He was prepared."

"He was fooling you. Not me, but you. And you bought it. He needs to die. But we have another problem. The FBI agent who's been working with the DEA is related to a mercenary down here, someone I've managed to avoid for the last seven years. Now I can't. That doesn't make me happy."

"I don't understand."

"And that's the problem. You go after the FBI agent and the hammer comes down. If they get any closer, we're taking them all out, not just that bastard DEA agent. Understand? You don't like getting your hands dirty, but you're going to be getting dirty, Jaime."

"I didn't go after her! I swear!"

Vasco laughed. "Don't play me for a fool. DeSantos was a bigger fool for listening to you. He ultimately had to pay the price, but don't think I won't make you pay if there's one more fuckup before we destroy the Vallerjos. Once we take out that gang, we'll be on equal footing with the Texas Mexican Mafia. If we fail, I will slit your throat myself. Understand?"

Jaime nodded. He didn't have a choice.

And it didn't really matter. Vasco planned to kill him in the end, anyway.

"Now I'm going to make sure that dinner is perfect so I can finally get to know my daughter. It figures that Mirabelle couldn't give me a boy, but I'll marry her off at sixteen and she'll start having my grandchildren. She'll have babies until I get my flesh-and-blood boy."

The snitch was a hooker who went by the name of Lana. Lana had given the DEA information on occasion. She was the preferred whore to certain men who knew certain men. It wasn't that they talked to her, unless it was to tell her to get on her knees, but she was around, and being around had its advantages.

She didn't share everything, but she knew what was worth sharing—information that couldn't be traced back to her. Her mama didn't raise no fool.

So when she got a call from a friend of a man she knew,

a friend who dropped all the right names and places, she went to the meeting. She'd already been paid a thousand bucks for sharing information she'd overheard; if they wanted to give her more to keep her ears open, she'd take it.

But when she opened the door to the motel room with the key that had been left under the mat, she realized that maybe she had her daddy's pea-brain after all.

She faced a gun. With a silencer. And a person in a mask aiming it at her ample chest.

Lana realized that maybe the information she'd most recently sold had come too easily. They'd found out, and she was being terminated.

No words were exchanged, no pleas heard, because three bullets hit her center mass before Lana figured out that her initial thought was wrong.

Lana didn't see her killer step over her body and take her purse because she was already dead. No surveillance camera caught the crime because there were none pointing toward the cheap motel.

Five minutes later a small fire destroyed the leather gloves, black jumpsuit, and ski mask that the killer wore. It also burned the thousand-dollar bundle that had been used to pay Lana to set up the ambush.

The gun, however, would be hidden, to plant later when someone needed to be framed.

CHAPTER 27

The staging area for the second phase of the operation was by necessity a mile from the abandoned row of warehouses, off the main highway, down an unused, packed dirt road. Boulders provided a natural barrier, but it would be difficult for anyone to spot them unless they had air surveillance.

Two decades ago the whole area had been owned by private military contractors serving the many Air Force bases in southern Texas; after the bulk of the base closures, they shut down. Many went bankrupt, or simply walked away from their business. Over the years, they'd been leased by the city, but for the past five years, they'd been virtually untouched, their fate ruled by the economy.

Lucy stood apart from the DEA agents who controlled the scene. Ryan was silent at her side, watchful as Juan had ordered him to be. She didn't want a bodyguard, but she was grateful for a friend. "Do you think Kane might be right?" Lucy asked Ryan.

"Any op like this is dangerous," Ryan said. "But according to Tom and Clark, the source is reliable."

Tom and Clark were the two undercover agents who'd been watching the warehouse from a strategic vantage point. Unfortunately, because the row of warehouses was in the middle of open space bordered by an unused junk-yard, they couldn't get as close as they would like.

"I understand your loyalty to Sean's brother," Ryan said, "but you also need to look at where Archer and Donnelly are coming from. They're DEA, they have rules and checks and balances, and they're not going to go into a situation without as much intel as possible. Kane Rogan is making a knee-jerk response to partial information. He doesn't know the source or even the location."

"You make sense." And he did, but so far Kane had also given them verifiable information. Archer already knew about Trejo, so that information hadn't come out of no-where.

"But, that said, I'm going into this eyes wide open and expect the unexpected."

She smiled up at him. "Glad to hear it."

They stood there and watched as Sam Archer gave final instructions to Tom and Clark. The two men, both in their thirties, fit the bill of undercover agents and could have been brothers. Both Hispanic, they wore faded jeans and dirty plaid shirts. They had an unmarked undercover car, an old El Camino that had more exposed metal showing than faded brown paint. An early morning rain shower had left a blanket of humidity in the air, and the dark sky threatened to dump more. Distant thunder rumbled, but she didn't know if there'd be more rain or if it would pass them by.

Sean called her as the El Camino drove off.

"Where are you?" he asked.

"Waiting near the warehouse where we think Sanchez is going to show up."

"Based on?"

"A snitch."

"Kane thinks it's a trap."

"I know. I talked to the team about it, but they have additional intelligence on this location and think it's good information."

"I'm with Padre."

"Jack's Army buddy?"

"We're checking on a lead."

"On Michael?"

"I can't say."

"Can't? Or won't?"

"I don't know anything specific. Call me when you're done. And be careful, okay?"

"Always." She hung up and itched to do something. Standing here, waiting for Sean, waiting for information, waiting for *action*, was going to drive her batty.

The undercover agents returned fifteen minutes later, windows rolled down, music blaring, maintaining their undercover role. They turned off the car and approached Sam Archer. Lucy and Ryan inched closer so they could listen.

"Report," Archer demanded.

"Something's going down," Tom said. "Two men, young, with guns are hanging at the door to the last warehouse on the strip."

"Guards?"

"Our take, yes."

"Vehicles?"

"None visible, but there's a trucking bay that looks like it's been recently used. They gave us a look, didn't seem concerned, but watched us leave."

"Can we get heat signatures?"

"Not at this distance."

Brad approached. "We need a plan, Sam."

"We need better intelligence, and two gangbangers with guns isn't enough. You had this information on the warehouse yesterday—why didn't you have people down here?" she asked the two agents.

"It's almost impossible to set up a good vantage point," Tom said. "We were here this morning, and it was empty. It's a good setup for them—nearly three-hundred-sixty-degree visibility, if he has enough people to cover each point. Junkyard to the north, easy to disappear."

"How close is the junkyard?" Brad asked.

"Shared fence. Maybe fifty yards, max."

"Our thermal imaging unit should be able to read at fifty yards," Archer said. "Team of two, covert only, take the scan into the junkyard. Give us something to work with."

"We got it, we know the layout." Tom motioned for Clark to grab the equipment. They left in the El Camino, but went in the opposite direction so they could enter from the north through the abandoned junkyard.

"Do we have blueprints on the warehouse?" Archer demanded. "People! I asked for blueprints forty-five minutes ago!"

Brad said, "Rollins is on her way."

"I thought she was with the ex."

"Peña is in custody, and since all agents are either here or sitting on Peña's house, Rollins is the only available agent."

Minutes later Nicole Rollins drove up in a government sedan. She had a file folder and ran over to where they stood outside one of the tactical trucks. "This is all we could find on the property. The analyst is trying to track down the last owners to see if they know more, but they're no longer in business."

Archer grabbed the folder, opened it, and spread out a handful of sheets. "This was an aerospace facility?"

"Long ago," Nicole said. "Then auto parts, then leased when the county took over the property. Cops shut down a chop shop a while back, it's been empty ever since. All these places are empty. But our McAllen office had the address on a watch list, and there was a major bust here last year. No connection to Sanchez or Trejo, but—"

"It's Sanchez," Brad said with conviction. "Controlled by Trejo."

"If we're right," Archer said, "they've expanded exponentially over the last seven years. They used to be low-level scumbags—now they're running an op this big?"

"You said it yourself, Sam, back when Trejo went under—he has the balls for this."

Archer handed Nicole back the folder. "These plans are worthless. They could have done anything with the interior. Is there a second floor?"

"Yes," Nicole said. "One of the McAllen agents who was involved in the bust last year said there are four car bays on the main floor, and a staircase was added to put three offices along the south wall above a self-contained storage room. Beyond that, we don't know. I can contact the PD and ask to speak to someone who was part of the raid last year, see—"

Archer cut her off. "No. We don't know who Sanchez and Trejo have in their pocket. The new police chief is solid, but we don't know about every cop on the beat." She glanced at Lucy. "Bet you didn't know that your brother had a big hand in bringing down a corrupt cop here five years ago."

Before Lucy could comment, Brad said, "Listen, Sam, we have two teams of six, plus you and Lucy manning tactical, and two undercovers now in the junkyard."

"And we don't know how many are inside, what kind of weapons they have, or whether the little girl is with them. We have to assume she is."

"No one has seen Sanchez," Brad said.

"He disappeared this morning. He could have been here all day."

Tom's voice came over the com. "We're in position. We see a vehicle approaching. A van."

"How many subjects?" Archer asked.

"At least two."

"Can you identify the target?"

"Negative. Two males."

"Do you have thermal?"

"We have four outside, but can't get a reading inside yet. We're calibrating. We might not be close enough. They may have reinforced the interior walls."

"Don't expose yourselves."

"Two white or light-skinned Hispanic males have entered the building. Two guards still outside."

"Either one of them Sanchez?"

"Negative."

"Do you see any sort of security on the building? Cameras?"

"Affirmative. Two cameras, one in the northeast corner facing the street; one above the doorway."

"Hold your position." Archer turned to Brad. "We wait until they move. We can't go on their turf without intel from the inside. Four subjects we know of. Could be more."

More waiting, and they didn't know where Bella was. Lucy shifted nervously on her feet.

Brad paced. "What about the neighboring buildings? Can we get in through one of them?"

"Not in a vehicle, they'll see our approach." Archer considered, then said to the agents in the junkyard, "Tom, verify the angles of the cameras and see if there is any way we can approach from the rear or from the adjoining warehouse, any angle."

"Roger. Hold."

Archer said, "Brad, listen. I know you want Sanchez. I want him, too. And I damn well want Trejo. But we're going to do this right, and we're not going in hot when we don't know what they have."

She glanced at Lucy. "You know, he could have bolted, left the information so we sit on our asses here while he slips out. It wouldn't be the first time a top dog sacrifices his underlings in order to escape."

"Don't you think I know that?" Brad said. "But we have no other leads. *Nothing.* All we have is this. We're close, I know we are. If he's not here, if he's putting these men up as a distraction, we can get them to talk."

"If they know anything," Nicole said. "They could be local hires, disconnected from his inner circle."

There was mumbling on the com, then Tom said, "We may have been made. We found two cameras, camouflaged, aimed at the junkyard."

"Get out of there!"

Gunfire erupted from the com and Archer shouted, "Agent needs assistance! Team one, take the yard; team two, with me. Nicole, stay here with Brian and man the com."

Lucy jumped into the tactical van with Sam Archer, Ryan, and two other DEA agents, even though she wasn't technically part of the team. The rest of their team followed behind, while team one, led by Brad, hightailed it to the junkyard entrance.

"Tom! Report!"

"Clark's down. I have cover." More gunfire, so loud it had to be coming from Tom.

"Shit, shit, shit!"

It only took two minutes for the tactical team to reach the warehouse. They watched four males swarm the edge of the junkyard. There was a hole in the fence, and the two agents were effectively trapped behind rusting, dismantled vehicles until they could get backup.

Gunfire burst out of a broken window on the second floor, aimed at their vans.

Archer was calling for immediate backup from both Hidalgo PD and the DEA, including air cover.

"Team one, status!"

Brad responded, "Shooters have Tom and Clark pinned down."

"Tom, can you walk?"

"I'm not leaving Clark. He's injured."

"Team one, can you get to them?"

"We need cover."

Tom said, "The shooters are closing in."

Brad said, "We're almost there."

Lucy listened in horror as the firefight in the junkyard continued, and they backed out of the line of fire from the warehouse.

"The bastards aren't getting out," Archer said. "Quiroz, you and Regan get up on that roof and take care of the shooter upstairs. You're cleared to take the first available shot."

"Roger."

Ryan looked at Lucy and said, "It's going to be fine, kid."

"Just get them," she said.

Thunder vibrated across the sky, and fat drops of rain fell on the dry dirt. The four agents in the van behind them covered Ryan and Regan as they ran into the warehouse directly across from the target.

"Donnelly, status!"

"Hold," Brad whispered.

There was silence, the only sound the rain that fell suddenly and thickly all around. Sam was staring at the communications console as if willing it to speak to her.

A single gunshot was heard, then Brad said, "One down." Then, "Tom, hold tight, we're coming."

"Clark needs an ambulance. It's bad."

"It's on its way," Archer said.

Ryan's voice came over. "We're in position."

"First clear shot," Sam said.

"Roger."

Sam muttered, "They're not getting out of here. Is this a damn suicide hit? This makes no sense."

"Psychologically, Sanchez could be trying to mess with you," Lucy said.

"What the hell does that mean?"

"If you lose a man in an op, it doesn't matter if we take down the four they have, it's going to affect you."

"It'll make me go after them in force. They don't want my wrath."

"Or it's a diversion. Sacrificing four men when your a-team is engaged here, and the real deal is miles away."

Sam shot her a glare that was full of venom and Lucy realized she'd completely overstepped. She'd stated the obvious, and it sounded too much like an *I told you so.* Considering that Kane had warned that any intel they learned could have been a trap or a diversion, and it now most likely was, Sam didn't need Lucy, the rookie, to make the observation.

Lucy looked away first.

There were five known shooters—four outside and one in the second story of the warehouse. They couldn't survive against sixteen federal agents.

A spurt of gunfire in the junkyard jolted Lucy. Voices shouting on the com. Lucy couldn't make out who was talking, but something big had happened.

A single rifle shot from the roof hit the second-story shooter. His rifle fell from the opening to the ground below. They couldn't see anyone else coming in or out, and had lost visual on the attackers who were in the junkyard.

Tom's voice said, "We're out. Two down. One at large, but Clark and I made it to the van."

"Where's the team?"

"Everyone's here, except Donnelly."

"Donnelly, report!"

Silence.

Sam said, "Did he lose communication? Anyone have eyes on him?"

"No, ma'am."

She pounded her fist on the dashboard. "Dammit, Donnelly! Answer me!"

"We have to get Clark out now. He's critical."

"Back to staging. The ambulance is on its way there."

Lucy said, "I have medical training."

"We're not leaving without Donnelly. Regan!" she said into the com. "Do you have eyes on the junkyard?"

"Visibility is low, Director. I don't see any movement, but I only have about forty yards' sight."

Sirens pierced the air. The police had arrived, and Sam ordered Ryan and Regan to hold their position while she ordered her driver to back up the van and meet up with the police at the industrial park entrance.

She issued orders for the police to block off the street and her team to clear the warehouse and start a search in the junkyard for Donnelly. "We have to assume he's down and lost communication. There's one subject known to be at large, but there could be more. We clear the warehouse first. Regan, can you cover?"

"You're covered, Director."

Sam turned to Lucy. "You're cleared to go to the staging area. See if you can help Clark. Take the van."

Lucy didn't have to be told twice. She'd been listening to the transmissions, knew that Clark had been shot at least twice and was critical. She didn't know if she could help, but she had to try.

She arrived at the same time as team one's van. They

unloaded Clark and put him on a blanket in the dirt. Nicole found an umbrella and held it over them.

Clark was unconscious but alive. Tom stayed while the others went back to the junkyard to look for Donnelly.

"What happened?" Nicole asked. "I heard on the com, where's Brad?"

"They're looking for him," Lucy said. She didn't have to tell Nicole that he might have been shot and unconscious. Or worse. She focused on Clark. "Brian," she said to the agent who'd been manning the staging area with Nicole, "get the first-aid kit out of the tactical van."

"Is there one?"

"If it's like the FBI's unit, it's under the passenger seat or the—"

Tom interrupted. "It's under the passenger seat." He had stripped off his shirt and was applying pressure to Clark's gut wound. There was a graze on Clark's head and a serious wound in his upper thigh. He was losing too much blood.

"I need a tourniquet," Lucy demanded. "Now!"

Brian rushed back with the first-aid kit. There was no tourniquet, so Lucy told him to grab Sam's SWAT pack in the front seat.

Lucy took off her jacket, then her blouse and tied it tight around Clark's right leg, above the wound. "Do you know what blood type he is?"

"A-positive."

"Make sure the ambulance knows that. They'll need to get him to the hospital ASAP and get some blood in him. He's already lost too much."

"I know. Fuck, it was an ambush. They were waiting for us."

Brian came back with the SWAT kit and Lucy tore through it until she found the tourniquet. She tied it tight around his leg. He groaned and came to consciousness.

"Hey, buddy, you're going to be fine," Tom told his partner, still putting pressure on Clark's stomach.

The ambulance pulled up and two paramedics came out. Lucy said, "He's A-positive, he's lost at least two pints, probably more. He needs a transfusion immediately. The head wound is superficial, I put a tourniquet on his leg, it's slowed but not stopped the bleeding."

"I'm going with him," Tom said as the paramedics put Clark on the gurney.

Lucy watched as the paramedics got to work on Clark while they wheeled him into the ambulance. Speed would save him. She prayed they'd get him to the hospital in time.

The rain stopped as fast as it had started. Lucy found a towel and wiped as much blood off her hands as she could. Her tank top was covered with it, but there was nothing she could do. She turned to Nicole. "What have you heard?"

"The warehouse is empty. One suspect down." That would have been Ryan and Regan. Lucy didn't know who'd taken the shot.

"Have they found Brad?"

"Negative. They're still looking."

Lucy jumped back into the tactical van and put on the headphones. She listened, her heart sinking as each search team reported negative findings. Three more suspects were dead in the junkyard, and they were chasing the fourth.

Archer said in her ear, "Kincaid, report on Clark."

"He's en route to the hospital."

"Prognosis?"

"I don't know. Three GSWs. The most serious was to his upper right thigh. He regained consciousness temporarily."

"That's good, right?"

Lucy didn't say anything. It was far too early to know.

A commotion on the com had Lucy hopeful. She listened as the agents apprehended the surviving suspect.

He'd been shot, a superficial wound to his hand, and was now cuffed and in custody.

But Brad Donnelly was nowhere.

"Search the entire junkyard again!" Sam Archer ordered. "Every fucking inch, he couldn't have disappeared into thin air."

Then Sam said, "Shit."

Lucy leaned forward and listened, her eyes closed. Something was very wrong.

Sam said, "There's another damn tunnel. What are these guys, fucking gophers?"

There was some scrambling, then nothing, and Sam said, "I need a direct line to the director in DC. Donnelly's been taken hostage. His captors have made demands."

CHAPTER 28

There was a crowd and commotion with practically every cop in the city and county combing the area in and around the warehouses and junkyard. And even with all the people, Lucy knew when Sean arrived.

Lucy cleared him to cross the line. He immediately pulled her into his arms. "Tell me none of that is your blood."

His voice was strained, and she'd almost forgotten about Clark's blood on her tank top.

"None of it," she said.

He squeezed her harder, then let her go. Pools of emotion filled his blue eyes.

"I didn't mean to scare you," she whispered.

"I'm okay. Touching you helps. What happened?"

"Sanchez's people kidnapped Donnelly. No one saw Sanchez; he may not have even been here. They had a damn tunnel that went from the warehouse to the junkyard. We don't know how they got out, exactly, but they must have grabbed him, taken him under, and gotten out along the periphery. Cops are searching everywhere. Another agent is in critical condition at the hospital, two more wounded. Four of the five shooters are dead. The last is in custody."

He rubbed her arms. "You're freezing."

"It's the rain, on and off all afternoon. I wish it would make up its mind."

"Did they make demands?"

"They want the two gangbangers Donnelly arrested Saturday who are still in custody. Release them in twenty-four hours, or Donnelly dies."

"The government isn't going to release prisoners. They know that."

"They want an excuse to kill him."

"They don't need an excuse."

"I have to go after him."

"Hell, no." He waved his arms toward the dozen SWAT members securing the area. "There will be three times that many looking for him."

"Not across the border. Ask Kane. Border issues are complex as it is, they're not going to send a team of United States feds into Mexico without going through the diplomatic channels, and that's going to take longer than twenty-four hours!"

She didn't want to yell at Sean, but she couldn't help it. She felt helpless and angry.

"You don't know that they even went across the border. It would be difficult with the heightened security." But his tone matched Lucy's fears: These people were far more organized with far better planning than anyone had expected. Except for maybe Kane.

"I had a feeling this was personal," Lucy said. "Between Sanchez and Donnelly. There's something more going on between them. Like Sanchez has been taunting him. Pushing him. I think that's why they threatened me, to get to Brad. But when Trejo was identified as behind this—I think that goes deeper. Both Brad and the director knew exactly who Trejo was. There's history there as well."

"Kane," Sean whispered. He glanced around. "Kane will find him."

Lucy wanted to trust Sean and his brother, but Donnelly had been her partner in this operation; she had an obligation to do something. Still, her hands were tied. She could look from here to Mexico, but couldn't cross the Rio Grande.

"Luce? Did you hear me?"

She nodded.

"Does Donnelly have a phone on him? Anything I can track?"

"All his equipment was dumped in the tunnel."

There was going to be nothing easy about finding Donnelly, that much Lucy was certain. Her phone rang. It was a private number.

"Kincaid," she answered.

"Lucia Kincaid?"

"Yes." No one called her Lucia except her mom. When her mom was mad.

"This is Francis Cardenas, a friend of Jack's. He calls me Padre."

"Padre. Yes, Kane said he was going to call you. Sean's here with me."

"Aw, yes, the Little Rogan. I need to see you both, right now, with no other police."

"I can't," she said. "We have a situation—"

"Yes, I know. One of your agents was taken hostage. It's all the buzz right now. But Kane called me because of the boy. I know where he is, but we do not have much time. And if the federal police come with you, he will die."

"Where are you?"

"I'm right on the other side of the barricade. I'm the only one here with a cleric's collar."

"Five minutes, Padre."

"No more. Time is critical."

She hung up and said to Sean, "That was Padre. He has a lead on Michael."

"That was fast. I left him only thirty minutes ago and we had nothing."

"I need an excuse to get out of here." She looked around for Ryan and spotted him with two other SWAT. "I can't just disappear, Ryan will worry."

"I'll take care of it."

"What? I can't lie—"

"*You* can't. I said I'll take care of it"

Before she could stop him, Sean approached Ryan. "Hey, can I take Lucy to the hotel? I have a room, she needs to shower and change." He gestured to her bloody clothes. "Her shirt is with the guy who got shot."

"That was good work, Kincaid," one of the DEA agents said. "Clark's still in surgery, but he's alive."

Ryan nodded. "Go. You can't do anything else here. It's going to be dark in a couple of hours, and negotiations are completely out of our hands. Call me later."

"Have you talked to Casilla?" she asked.

"Briefly. He wants me to stick with you, but I'll tell him Sean's here and you're at the hotel."

Lucy didn't feel good about deceiving Ryan, but Sean didn't give her a chance to talk. "Let us know if anything breaks," he said.

"Of course. And I'll text you when we debrief in the morning," Ryan said. "It's been a long fucking day."

She couldn't disagree.

Because they were on the outskirts of town, most of the bystanders were support staff, medics, and police. A few people milled around, people who used these back roads to get to and from work. A pair of sheriff's deputies were stopping every car and asking to search, which created a line.

She and Sean went under the barricade and immediately spotted Padre. He wasn't tall, under six feet, and had a gnarled scar that twisted his left cheek. His eyes were dark and focused, and he smiled when he saw her. "Lucia," he said, touching her arm. "We need to go."

They wound around through the people and vehicles, Padre focused on his destination. Some of the people knew him, or maybe they didn't and simply deferred to him because he was a priest. She must have heard a dozen *Hello, Father*s as they passed. Padre would smile and nod and keep moving. If he knew the person, he said hello by name.

They walked to the far edge of a makeshift lot where cars were parked, and Padre told them to get into a jeep that had no roof. He pulled the key from his pocket and turned the ignition. "Sorry about the wet seats," he said.

"I'm too soaked to care," Lucy said. "What do you know about Michael?"

"I've been looking for him since Kane called me this morning. But I didn't learn anything until shortly after Sean left to meet with you.

"Michael was found this morning," Padre continued as he pulled out of the parking lot. "He's being held, but not for long. Now that they have your agent, they're going to want to move both of them across the border. I don't know where your agent is now, but I know where the boy is." He glanced behind them and Lucy followed his gaze. No one was following.

"A cop named Gregory Floresca put the word out that he has the boy the feds are after," Padre said. "He plans to sell him to Sanchez's people. We need to get there first."

"Sanchez is going to be there?"

"No, Sanchez is in Mexico."

"You're certain?"

"Kane is certain."

Why hadn't Kane told her earlier? She could have passed it on to Brad and Sam and maybe stopped what happened today.

"You have guns?" Padre asked.

"Yes," they said.

"Sean, open the lockbox behind you. The lock code is three-four-five-nine."

Sean rolled the numbers into place and popped the lock. Inside the box were several semi-automatic rifles.

"I hope we won't need them, but you're welcome to whatever you need."

"How did you hear about Michael?" Lucy asked. "I can bring in a team to extract him."

"There's no time to plan an operation, and the feds never move fast. Not fast enough. He's not at the police station—Floresca knows most of the previous administration's bad cops have been axed, the town is being cleaned up. My source tells me Michael is being held in the storeroom of a liquor store. The clerk will be armed. The storeroom is accessible only from inside the store."

He parked against a broken sidewalk down the street from a generic liquor store. The neighborhood was depressed and dirty, most of the signs in Spanish, not even a nod to the English language. Though the jeep was old, people looked at them with suspicion.

Padre turned to face them. "I need you both to trust me."

"If Kane and Jack trust you, I trust you," Sean said.

"First, Lucy, you need to put this on." He handed her a worn and faded flannel shirt. She pulled it over her bloodied tank. She made sure she could still reach her gun, but covered it with the shirt.

Padre continued. "Lucy and I are going to go into the store. I'm going to do my sales pitch for the church. Lucy, you go to the storeroom and get the boy. You can pick a lock, right?"

"Not as well as Sean," she admitted.

"Almost," Sean said. "What kind?"

"A padlock. The kind with a keyhole."

Sean slipped her his tool set.

"We can bring in a team," she reiterated. She didn't like the idea of doing this without backup, without Ryan and the others knowing where she was. "They can be here in twenty minutes."

"We don't have twenty minutes. We might already be too late."

Padre continued. "The trick is going to be slipping *out* of the store with the boy. I'm going to insist that the clerk pray with me. If there are any other patrons in the store, I'll have them join in. When you see that, you need to get the boy out. Walk along the perimeter quickly, but don't stop for anything. I'll make sure the clerk won't be looking."

He glanced at Sean, and Sean said, "I got it, you want me to watch and drive up when I see Lucy and the kid."

"Yes. But you must be quick. If I don't get out, leave me there and I'll meet you at the church in an hour."

"Unless they take you hostage."

Padre smiled, though it was very sad. "They won't be able to. I may be getting old—I'm five years older than Jack—but I still train. I'll just pay for it in the morning."

Padre and Lucy walked in. "Keep your head down, don't make eye contact," he whispered as they entered.

Lucy did what he said, though it was against all her instincts not to see and assess her surroundings.

"*Hola, Padre*," the clerk said. For a brief moment Lucy thought the clerk knew Padre, but of course *padre* was the Spanish word for 'father.'

"*¿Cómo estás, hijo?*"

"*Bueno.*" From her veiled eyes, Lucy noticed that the clerk was looking out the door. He said, "*Vuelve después, el padre.*"

He was nervous. He wanted them to leave.

"Mi primo tiene artículos femeninos."

He wanted her to get tampons? Fabulous. She knew she was blushing, even though this was just an act.

Fortunately, Padre knew the clerk would be just as embarrassed.

"La parte posterior. A la derecha."

Lucy moved to the back of the store, shuffling her feet, acting embarrassed—okay, she *was* embarrassed—and looked over the meager feminine supplies.

The storeroom was right there. How had Padre known?

She didn't dwell on that, and as Padre engaged the clerk in conversation about why he didn't see him at church anymore, Lucy quickly picked the lock.

Sean had taught her well. She was inside the storeroom in less than ten seconds. She quickly shut the door behind her, in case the clerk looked this way.

Michael was sitting in the far corner, his head in his lap. He wasn't tied up, which was a small blessing.

He stared at her, his eyes a mix of fear and anger.

She knew that look well. She'd seen that look in the mirror many times, before she'd met Sean.

"Michael, I don't have time to explain. We need to go."

"Who are you?" he said, his voice hoarse.

"Shh. A friend."

He didn't move. How could she get him to trust her?

St. Jude.

"I know Bella helped you escape. I've been looking for you." She pulled out the medallion, which was buried between her breasts. "I met Father Flannigan at Saint Catherine's. He gave me this, so you know you can trust me."

He stared at the medal, fear and surprise and a deep regret etched in his dirty, expressive face.

"I know you were friends with Richie Diaz, and I know Richie died at the same time Jaime Sanchez locked you in the basement. If you don't come with me now, the policeman who put you here is going to turn you over to Jaime Sanchez."

His face hardened. "Then I will kill him."

He said it so flatly, so matter-of-fact that Lucy knew he believed he would.

"Jaime kidnapped Bella. I need your help to find her. To save her."

She heard the bell above the door ding. They weren't alone anymore. Was it the cop?

She listened at the door. Someone, not Padre, said to the clerk, "We're here for the kid."

"I'll get him," the clerk said.

Lucy said to Michael, "Do exactly what I say. Okay?"

He nodded and took her hand.

She slipped out of the storeroom with Michael at her side.

People weren't discreet staring at Sean. He might have dark hair, but he was a *gringo* in every sense of the word. Terrific. He was drawing attention when he didn't want to. He found an old, worn Texas Rangers baseball cap in the glove compartment and put it on. He didn't know if it was better.

Five minutes had passed. Lucy should be coming out any moment. Sean didn't like relying on anyone but himself. Sure, Padre was a friend of Jack's, but how much Special Forces operative was left in a man who had turned priest?

A large four-by-four black pickup passed him and stopped outside the store. Three Hispanic males, all in their early twenties, jumped out. They had guns in their jeans. The driver remained in the car, and one of the boys stood outside. None of them was Sanchez.

Either they were robbing the place or picking up the kid. Whichever way Sean cut it, the situation was bad.

Sean drove the jeep, passed the truck, and tried to look inside, but the clutter and dirty windows prevented a clear view.

He turned the corner and parked where he was just out of view of the black truck. He jumped out of the jeep and put his back up against the building. He heard shouts coming from inside, in Spanish, and had no idea what they were saying. A couple of years of high school Spanish wasn't helping him here.

He had one idea. Only one idea, so he hoped it worked.

He climbed back into the jeep, made a U-turn, and pulled up in front of the liquor store, directly in front of the truck. He waved at the guy standing out front.

"Sir!" he called. "Sir! I'm lost. Can you help me?"

He had no idea what the guy said, but it sounded like the swear words Sean had been proud he'd learned when he was twelve.

"I'm trying to get to International Boulevard. I think I turned the wrong way, I can't find it. I don't speak Spanish. Do you speak English? Hello?"

The guy in the truck honked the horn at Sean. In broken English he said through his rolled-down window, "Fuck off, *gringo*!"

A gunshot went off inside the store. Sean jumped out of the jeep. The guy in the truck had a gun in hand fast; Sean shot his wrist and the gun clattered to the pavement. The guy at the door was slower on the uptake and Sean rushed him, kicked his arm as it was coming up with a gun, knocked the weapon from his hand, and pistol-whipped him twice until he fell to his knees.

He opened the door and immediately went left in case someone was planning on shooting at the first person to enter. Padre was kneeling in front of the cashier. His hands were on top of his head. The clerk held a gun on him.

The other two guys were in the far corner of the store.

As soon as the clerk's attention diverted to Sean, just for a second, the former Army sergeant rolled right, into a crouch, took a gun from his pocket and shot the clerk in the arm. The clerk dropped his gun, cursing with pain, and clutched his biceps.

"Good timing, Little Rogan," Padre said.

"Don't call me that," Sean muttered.

There were shouts from the back of the store, and one of the guys came running toward Sean and Padre, firing his gun. They both fired back and he fell to the floor.

Lucy came around from the back aisle, pulling Michael along, as the second guy chased them. Sean glanced around, saw two cameras in the corners above the counter, and prayed there were no more. He took them both out, then the security box in the back behind the tequila. It was an old-school system, and he hoped he destroyed all evidence. Then he opened the door, quickly made sure it was clear, and the four of them ran out. Padre rolled a smoke bomb into the store before the door closed.

The driver of the truck was standing on the sidewalk, blood dripping from his right hand, now holding a gun with this left hand. He fired at Sean, and there was no doubt that if his left hand had been dominant, Sean would have been dead. But he couldn't aim properly and the bullet went through the store window.

Padre shot both knees and the guy went down. Sirens were heard far in the distance.

"Keys." Padre held his hand out. Sean dropped them into his palm and the four of them jumped into the jeep.

"We're in deep shit," Sean said as Padre drove off.

"I think you disabled the security."

"I have to report this," Lucy said from the backseat.

Padre said, "We'll talk about that later."

Sean half turned in his seat. He first assessed Lucy. She

nodded that she was okay without him having to ask. Then he turned to Michael. "And you're Michael?"

The kid didn't say anything.

"It's okay," Lucy told him. "This is Sean and Father Francis Cardenas. We call him Padre. They're helping me find Bella."

"Did Jaime really take her?"

"Yes."

"I knew I shouldn't have left. She got in trouble because of me."

"I promise, it wasn't because of you. She was safe, in a safe home, when someone betrayed her. Someone else, not you. Her mother was arrested and she and her sister were placed in foster care. Someone told Jaime where she was."

Michael turned to her. "Foster care." He scowled. "Charlie. He's the one who betrayed us all."

Even though Lucy had strongly suspected Charlie De-Santos was involved with Sanchez, hearing Michael say it out loud startled her.

She said, "He's dead. Someone tortured him and burned down his house."

"Good," Michael said, and her blood ran cold. "I only wish I could have killed him myself."

CHAPTER 29

Padre drove them through Hidalgo, to the outskirts of the city, to a secluded house he said Lucy's brother Jack owned. The sun had gone down, the only light a thin red line on the horizon that disappeared as Lucy watched.

"You live here now?" Lucy asked.

"No," Padre said. He drove the jeep to behind the house, where there was a carport. The vehicle could only be seen from one angle. "It's still Jack's. I keep my eye on it, sometimes use it as a sanctuary."

For a simple house in the middle of nowhere, Texas, the security was state-of-the-art. They drove through a gate controlled by a keypad, past several outbuildings, up to the squat house that had 360-degree views of open space. They parked in the back, invisible to anyone from the road—though this far from the road, binoculars would be necessary.

Padre typed into a keypad in the back door, then unlocked the door with a key.

Sean inspected the security. "Not bad," he said.

Padre smiled. "I suppose that's praise, coming from you, Little Rogan."

Sean groaned.

Lucy had to make a call. She didn't want to—but she

had to tell Ryan she was safe. She should call Juan as well, but she didn't want to do that, either.

First, she took a short, hot shower. She had to scrub to get all of Clark's blood off her—she hadn't realized how awful she looked until she stared in the mirror and saw dried blood on her face, neck, and arms. Sean had added a change of clothes for her into his go-bag, and that he was prepared—when she'd left her overnight bag at DEA headquarters—made her love him even more.

She stepped out of the bathroom and didn't see Padre or Michael. Sean gave her a kiss and said, "They're in the back room. Michael took a shower and now they're talking."

"Good. I need to call Ryan, and I don't want an audience. Except you." She squeezed his hand, then closed her eyes. There was no more putting this conversation off.

She dialed, not quite knowing what she was going to say. "Hey," he said when he answered. "I just got to the hotel. Archer gave half of us eight hours off. Not much we can do in the dark. You going to be ready at oh-five-hundred?"

She didn't answer the question. "No sign of Donnelly?"

"None. Except, we figured out how they got out of the area. The tunnel went into the warehouse and appeared to end at a ladder leading into the facility. But when they brought in the dogs, they discovered a trapdoor. The tunnel went down. I'm surprised Brad could fit in there, it was so narrow. But they found blood that matches his type."

"Blood." Her stomach roiled.

"Not enough to be life-threatening. The tunnel exited into a drainage ditch only a hundred yards out, on the opposite side of the warehouses from where we staged. There's evidence of an all-terrain vehicle leaving the area, and we collected as much evidence as we could until it got dark. They have lights set up now, but they're not going to find anything, my guess."

"They had to have moved fast."

"They moved when we were occupied with the shooters in the warehouse and searching the junkyard. They diverted our attention."

"Why didn't we see a vehicle during surveillance?"

"It wasn't there this morning, according to the sweep."

"How did they know we wouldn't have been fanned out? How did they—'

"Lucy, I don't know. Archer will have some answers tomorrow, and hopefully news about Donnelly. I need to unwind. Want to meet in the bar for a beer? I'm sure Sean could use one."

"I'm not at the hotel."

"Dinner?"

"I'm at my brother's house."

"You have a brother in Texas?"

"Jack used to live here and is letting us use his house." She bit her lip. She had to tell Ryan. "We found Michael."

He didn't say anything for a long minute. "You found the kid?"

"It's a long story—"

"I have time."

"I can't go into it now, but I got a tip and acted on it."

"You should have called me." He was angry, and she didn't blame him.

"I know, but we had to act fast."

"Did you talk to Juan?"

"We just got to the house. I called you first."

"Shit, Lucy, you need to bring the kid in immediately. He needs to be debriefed."

"It's a delicate situation."

"I don't give a damn. I'm not a stickler for every rule in the book, but this is serious."

"I know, Ryan! And I'm sorry, but right now I can't. I

need tonight to talk to him, myself. Michael confirmed
that Charlie DeSantos was working for Sanchez."

I wish I could have killed him myself.

It was his tone even more than his words that had disturbed Lucy.

"Confirmed? Confirmed what about DeSantos?"

"That DeSantos found the boys for Sanchez's operation.
Children of prisoners. I don't have all the details, that's
why I need to talk to Michael. He doesn't trust anyone,
Ryan, I can't turn him over to the system until we know for
certain DeSantos was the only corrupt official involved."

"Well, shit."

"I don't think he's the only one," Lucy admitted.

"What the hell does that mean?"

"It means just what I said. If Sanchez and Vasco Trejo
had one government employee on their payroll, why not
two? This warehouse disaster that got Brad kidnapped, it
was set up by the McAllen DEA office. It was their snitch,
their contact, and they vouched for the person. Archer
doesn't even know who tipped us off."

"She will soon—she's with the local office right now."

"I trust you, Ryan, and I can't say that for everyone else.
Michael's life is in danger. I'm asking you—" She stopped.
What was she asking for?

"I'm not going to lie for you, Lucy. I can't cover this up."

"Not that—just let me do this my way. Tonight. Michael
isn't going to talk to anyone but me." That probably wasn't
true—Lucy suspected he would talk to Padre. They were
still in the back room; the door was still closed. "I'll call
you in the morning."

"You have to call Juan."

"I know."

"You're not going to, are you?"

"In the morning. I promise. When I have more information that we can use." And, ultimately, she didn't want Juan to tell her to come in tonight. Defying a direct order would be worse, and she didn't know that she would come in if he told her to.

Ryan sighed, weary. "You're a rookie. Juan doesn't need to jump through hoops to have you fired."

She knew that. But some things were more important than a job, so she didn't say anything.

"Let me see what I can do," Ryan said. "I might be able to smooth this over, but I'm not going to lie to Juan."

"I wouldn't ask or expect you to. I'll write up a report and send it in. And if I get anything from Michael about a potential leak, I'll call you immediately. Watch your back, Ryan."

"You too, Kincaid."

She hung up and turned to Sean. He'd heard her end of the conversation, and it was clear he'd extrapolated the rest. "Okay, he passes."

"What?"

"I wasn't sold on Ryan at first, but he's willing to bend."

"Let's hope he doesn't have to bend too much. I hate putting him in that position."

"But you're right, Lucy. We need to find out who we can trust before we turn Michael over to anyone."

It bothered her greatly that Charlie DeSantos had used Brad to get into their investigation, and then was party to getting him kidnapped. Or was he? Maybe that's why they killed him. Except . . . he'd been involved in Richard Diaz and Michael Rodriguez's disappearances, which meant that kidnapping wasn't a big deal for him.

"Brad knew DeSantos. Vouched for him. Called him a good guy," Lucy said. "The bastard weaseled his way into our investigation not only to find out what we knew, but to find Michael."

Sean walked up behind Lucy and put his hands on her

shoulders. He squeezed, leaned in, and kissed her neck. "And he's dead. Maybe he was the only traitor."

"Do you really think that?"

He hesitated only a moment. "No."

"Neither do I. There's someone here, in McAllen, who's helping Sanchez. It's the only other thing that makes sense."

"There's still no proof that DeSantos was involved, other than Michael's statement. His house is gone, he's dead, Sanchez sent his people to destroy evidence." She knew it was true even though she couldn't prove it, and that made the truth harder to say. "We think he's involved, but with no proof—"

"Don't." He kissed her. "Juan Casilla is a good boss, and he has some great staff. Nate is in San Antonio, I'm sure he's following up."

"Did you talk to him?"

"Not directly. I don't want to get him in trouble, but I'm confident if there's anything to find, he'll find it. This is about kids being used, branded, tortured, and killed. If Charlie DeSantos was part of it, he needed to pay." Sean's face hardened. No one could turn their back on kids being hurt, but Sean had a long history of battling bullies. Whenever Sean crossed the line—and Lucy knew he had—it was because of someone in power, physically or emotionally or authoritatively, bullying those who were weaker.

"He's dead. He has paid."

"Then we need to destroy his reputation and get justice for all the kids he hurt. Find out who, if anyone, was part of the conspiracy. Stop them. Have faith, Lucy, that you and your team will get what they need."

"I do." But she was still worried.

"Ryan said something about Brad."

She told him about the tunnel and how they got out.

"You're right."

She looked at him skeptically. "That's what Ryan said."

"I mean, another person was involved. Someone with detailed information about the DEA operation, when they were going to hit, where they were going to be."

"You're talking a handful of people, many of them decorated federal agents."

"And corruption always finds a way. What do you know about Sam Archer?"

"She knows Kane and Jack. Especially Jack."

Sean raised an eyebrow. "Really."

"I don't know much about her, but psychologically I don't think so. She was stunned—in shock—when Brad was kidnapped."

"Maybe she was the leak but didn't expect Sanchez would kidnap a federal agent."

She considered that. "Maybe. But I still think it's someone in the McAllen office. The information about the warehouse was cleared because it was a place already on their radar, and then we confirmed it from the trash at Sanchez's ex-girlfriend's house and a McAllen snitch."

"And that's the dead giveaway. Sanchez didn't trust that whoever put together the leak could get Donnelly to the location, so he planted the additional confirmation."

"That's . . ." What could she say? She wanted to say the whole idea was crazy, but she knew it wasn't. "Possible," she finished.

She looked down the hall to the room where Padre had taken Michael. They'd been in there a long time—nearly an hour.

"I don't know if we can save him."

She didn't realize she'd spoken out loud until Sean said, "Donnelly?"

"Michael. He just turned thirteen. He's hardened. He's seen things—maybe if we can get him to talk about it, if we can get him into counseling or—"

"Or someone like Padre?"

"Yeah. Someone like him. Who understands. And it helps that he had a good relationship with Father Flannigan."

"I called Kane," Sean said, "told him about Brad. He already knew, he was already looking. If anyone can find him, it's Kane."

"I can't leave him behind."

"You can't go for him."

"If he's not dead, Michael knows where he is. Michael knows Sanchez, where he hides, what he's up to. And I don't see Sanchez killing his prize quickly. They want information—and they'll torture Brad to get it. I doubt they care about the gangbangers Brad arrested on Saturday. This is about Brad Donnelly himself—otherwise they would have kidnapped the first two agents who went into the junkyard—or killed one and grabbed the other."

Something tickled at the back of her mind, but she couldn't figure out what was bothering her. She'd seen something or heard something that made her twitch . . . she was missing a clue.

She rubbed her temples.

"You haven't eaten," Sean said, kissing her forehead. "You have a headache."

"I'm okay."

He was about to argue with her when the lights dimmed and the security box near the front door turned from yellow to red. Someone had breached the perimeter.

Sean ran to the computer station and typed in codes to see where the breach occurred. He pulled up the camera feed. Then Lucy's phone rang with an undisclosed number.

"Kincaid," she answered.

"It's Kane. I'm here. Didn't want to set off the alarms."

"You already did," she said. Then to Sean, "It's your brother."

Sean swore under his breath and took the phone from Lucy. "You could have given me more warning. Okay, I reset the system. Come on up and I won't shoot you."

Lucy went down the hall and knocked on the door of the bedroom where Padre and Michael were quietly talking. A long minute later, Padre opened the door. Michael stood next to him. His eyes were red, but he had a determined expression on his face.

"Kane's here."

Padre nodded solemnly. "Michael has information, and we all need to hear it."

CHAPTER 30

Lucy couldn't stop staring at Kane. He looked exactly like Sean, except older and rougher around the edges. He had the same dark hair—cut shorter—and the same intense deep-blue eyes, but hardened. He had the same dimples in the same places and even the same small mole on his right temple.

They had similar mannerisms, even though Kane was fourteen years older than Sean and had been in the Marines before Sean started school. The Rogan genes were strong.

Except . . . Sean smiled more. He didn't have the hard lines etched in his forehead. Though Kane was fit, he was underweight, all hard muscle that wasn't readily visible under his black T-shirt. Sean worked out in a gym and ate well, while Kane likely ate military rations and fresh food only when he could get it. Kane was a soldier through and through, his attitude more Jack than Sean.

It was clear that Sean both admired his brother and harbored an uneasy suspicion. Why? Because Kane himself was suspicious, vague, and tense?

Kane gave Sean a hug and slap on the back, then did the same with Padre. "Good to see you," he said. He looked at

Lucy, and she couldn't tell if he was smiling or scowling. "So you're Jack's little sister."

"Lucy Kincaid," she said and extended her hand.

He shook it and said, "I'm truly glad to meet you. Jack is a good man." The comment sounded like he was saying *Jack is a saint.*

Jack was no saint, but he was one of the few people Lucy trusted beyond all others.

Kane eyed Michael.

Lucy said, "This is Michael Rodriguez. He's the boy I've been looking for, the one I told you about. Padre found him."

"We found him," Padre corrected. They sat around the small table in the kitchen, Sean within arm's reach of the security system. Padre turned to Kane. "You came alone?"

"I left my men in town for recon. We're running out of time and I need information. The raid was a setup, through and through. The entire plan was to kidnap a federal agent. They will kill him; they may already have."

"They gave us twenty-four hours," Lucy said.

Kane deadpanned her. "You think they're honest?"

"No, but—"

"However," he continued as if she hadn't spoken, "they'll kill him in a public way after torturing him for information and pleasure. This is a federal agent, they want the shock factor, the power of the capture. It'll demoralize the feds and empower the cartels. I think he's still alive, but he won't be for long."

"They didn't target just any federal agent," Lucy said. "I think they specifically wanted Brad Donnelly."

"Why?"

"I don't know."

"If it's a personal kidnapping, that might change the dynamic, but not the final outcome. Why do you think they targeted him specifically?"

"A gut feeling. I had a sense that Donnelly had more than the usual reasons for going after Sanchez. And when they learned that Vasco Trejo was behind this, he and Samantha Archer both got excited. As if the connection between Sanchez and Trejo made other things click into place for them. They didn't tell me what."

"I know Archer," Kane said, and left it at that. He looked at Michael. "You know where they took him." A statement, not a question.

Michael didn't say anything. He wasn't like any thirteen-year-old Lucy had met. He was more man, a small man, with hard, dark eyes and scars, inside and out.

Michael looked at Padre while fingering the medal of St. Jude that Lucy had given him. She didn't know what Padre said, how he made the connection, but he gave Michael a nod, then said to the others, "Michael wants to help us, but he also needs our help. Michael, tell them from the beginning. They already know about DeSantos."

Michael took a minute, drinking the water that Padre had given him. "Charlie DeSantos wasn't my original CPS counselor," he began. "I went through a couple, then had a really nice woman—" He looked at Lucy. "—like you. Pretty and everything. She hooked me up with Hector and Olive.

"Then she left, moved or something, and Charlie started coming around. At first I didn't think anything was weird. Two months before I ran away, at Christmas, Hector and Olive told me they wanted to adopt me. My dad said no, then said he'd think about it if I'd come and see him. I hadn't seen him in three years, I didn't want to." His face darkened. "He used to hit my mom. She cried all the time. I wanted to kill him." He glanced at Padre and seemed torn about whether he should have said that. "I'm not sorry for thinking that."

"You're doing fine, son," Padre said.

Michael stared at his hands as if counting the hairs, then a minute later spoke. "So I went to see him and he told me when I was twelve, I'd have to pick up the slack. I had no idea what that meant, and he didn't explain. Just that I was his son, and I would do what I was told. He said Charlie would tell me what to do."

Michael drank water, his jaw so tense Lucy could see the small veins throbbing beneath his skin.

"Charlie came to the house once when Hector was working and Olive was at the church and I was doing homework. He said my dad had made a deal with an organization that I would work for them. I told him to fuck off. He told me I had no choice. If I didn't go, my dad would be killed. I said fine by me. Then he laughed and picked up a picture of me, Hector, and Olive. And I knew that he didn't mean my real dad. Charlie said that the court had agreed to sever parental rights, and that cleared the way for Hector and Olive to adopt me, but that it would never happen because they'd be dead if I didn't do exactly what he told me to."

Michael looked at Padre, his dark eyes searching for answers that Lucy didn't know if any of them had. "I had to do it. Maybe I didn't really believe him at first, but then—well, I believe him now. I wasn't the only one. There were dozens of us."

Kane asked, "What were you required to do?"

"Harvesting. Bringing in drugs. I worked in the fields for months. Some of us, they take away, I don't know what they do with them. I never seen them again. I don't think they kill them, because when they kill one of us, they do it publicly. In front of us, to teach us to obey. To make sure we do what we're told. We're hybrids, you know. We can look Mexican or American. We can blend better than anyone. And when you know someone will die if you don't behave, well, you do whatever they want. And some of the boys—they didn't have a Hector and Olive to protect. They did it to survive."

"How did you end up in Jaime Sanchez's basement?"

"A month ago I took something from the general."

Kane leaned forward. "Trejo?"

Michael shrugged. "We call him the general. I don't know his name. He's an American, but pretends to be Mexican. Charlie worked for him. Jaime. We all work for him."

"What did you take?"

"A box. I thought—well, I wanted to escape. Me and some of the guys had a plan. I couldn't trust everyone, because some of them would rat on you so they got stuff. Like more water, a cot, blankets, stuff like that. But there were some of us who vowed to stay together no matter what. We all wanted to go home. There was this black box that the general had. He kept saying it was his future. After we did a hard job, we got to spend a night in his mansion. Eat good food on dishes at a table and stuff. So I volunteered for a job, and did it well, and got into the mansion. I stole the box, and when I was sent back to the camp I hid it."

Lucy asked, "What was in the box?

"Computer disks. CDs or DVDs, I don't know, and that's what's so stupid about what I did. I had no way of looking at anything. No computer, no television, I would have put them back if I had a chance."

"Were they labeled?" Sean asked.

Michael nodded. "But I didn't know what any of it meant. They were names and dates, but I don't remember any of them."

"How many?"

"Fifty. It was one of those CD boxes you can get at the store, with a little lock on the front with four numbers. You spin them around."

"You knew the code?" Sean asked.

"No. I played with it until I figured it out. Three-one-eight-one."

"Do you still have the box? Is that why they wanted you so badly?"

"No. I gave it back because he knew I'd taken it, and he threatened everyone. The general rarely came to our camp, but he did that day. Even though I gave him back the box, I thought I was going to die. He didn't shoot me—he killed Javier. My brother." His voice cracked, just a bit.

"Brother?" Lucy asked quietly.

"Blood brother. More than real brothers. I ran that night with Richie, just ran and left the rest of them. I can't—" He stopped, looked away.

Padre reached out to touch him, but Michael hit his hand away and jumped up. "They found us. Shot Richie and left him by the side of the road. Said they would make me watch them kill Hector and Olive, that they had one last job for me, something that would take vengeance on the general's enemies and forge a new alliance. That's what Jaime kept saying."

"What?" Kane asked sharply.

"I don't know! I just know that I would be dead when it was over. It was a suicide job, and I had no choice."

"What did you plan to do when Bella let you out?" Lucy asked.

"I was going to tell Hector and Olive everything, but . . . I sensed Charlie might be around. And I realized he would kill them if he knew I talked to them. Or he would have all my brothers over the border killed. Maybe they're already dead! I should have died with them!"

Kane stood up. He walked over to Michael. The boy flinched, but then stood straight, as if prepared to take a beating.

Kane knelt in front of him, making himself shorter than

the boy. He took Michael firmly by the shoulders and said, "These men are evil. You are not the first they have taken; you will not be the last. But if you have the stomach to save your brothers, we will save them."

"They have dozens of armed soldiers. They're across the border. There's no way to stop them."

"There is always a way. We need to know where they took the federal agent."

Michael frowned. "I thought you said you'd help my brothers."

"We will. But the agent has a ticking clock. He will be tortured and killed. I need to know where."

Michael looked at Lucy, then Sean, then Padre. Finally, he stared straight in Kane's eyes and said, "I'll take you."

Sean found Lucy thirty minutes later outside, staring at the stars. "We're ready. You should stay," Sean said.

"I'm not staying."

"You know the risks."

"You're taking them."

"I meant to your career."

She turned to face him, put her hands on his cheeks, rough with a day's growth of beard. "I can do this. I need to. I gave DeSantos information that may have—"

"Shh," he said, putting a finger to her lips. "Don't. De-Santos was part of the system, and you trusted the system. If you didn't tell him, Ryan or Brad would have."

"Do you think we'll be back by five in the morning?"

"Doubt it. You've slept very little in the last thirty-six hours. Are you sure you're okay?"

"I've slept enough. I'll buy time with Ryan if I have to, but I'm going with you. Someone needs to bring Brad back while Kane and you rescue those boys. He could be injured, we don't know."

"There's more than career danger when an American agent gets stuck in a volatile country."

"I know. That's why I'm leaving my ID here."

"Lucy, I've done this before. I don't talk about it because it's a very gray area, but Kane is my brother, and when he needs help, I go."

"And Brad is a federal agent and I knew there was something more to the investigation than he was telling me. I sensed the obsession with Jaime, the drive. I ignored it because we were making progress, and now he's being tortured. You know it's true," she said when Sean opened his mouth.

He nodded. "Luce—Kane is a difficult, arrogant know-it-all, but he knows what he's doing. Listen to him."

"Sounds like a Rogan to me."

"Hey! I'm not difficult."

She stepped forward, into Sean's embrace. Just one minute; all she wanted was one minute here with Sean, where she still felt safe and loved.

She tensed. "Someone's watching us," she whispered.

From the shadows, Kane stepped out. "It's now or never, Romeo and Juliet."

Lucy gave him a half smile. "Was that a *joke*?"

Kane winked and walked away.

"He can be a jerk," Sean said, "but he's still a Rogan at heart."

CHAPTER 31

They left in the middle of the night.

They didn't take Sean's plane, which was a four-seater, but instead used a plane Padre had access to, a Cessna Caravan that could hold more people. Technically, ten passengers, plus two pilots, but they could squeeze in more if necessary.

"The plane is Jack's," he explained. "It had been Scout's. We had many missions in this old bird."

"He called her Carrie, and Jack used to give him shit over it," Kane said. "Scout was a good man."

"He was," Padre concurred and crossed himself.

Padre sat in the copilot's seat; Lucy was in the back with Kane and Michael. Based on both a map and Kane's knowledge of the area, Kane mapped out the route he wanted Sean to take. His men would meet them at the landing spot so they could go in quickly and quietly.

"Stay low, Sean, to avoid radar, but not too low. Do you have the heat sensor activated?"

"I've done this before, Kane. I'm not going to get us caught or shot down."

"Habit," Kane said without apology.

Sean grunted.

They hadn't filed a flight plan. They were flying into Mexico illegally, using the cover of darkness and keeping low enough to avoid radar and high enough to avoid visual identification. The interior of the plane was equipped with jammers and a host of other electronics to help avoid detection. And it was clear that Kane and Sean had done all of this many times.

Michael told them about the camp where the boys lived and trained. It was an old prison, he said; he knew the general area. "I can get there on foot, but I don't know about this map."

"I know where it is," Kane replied and rolled out his own personal map. He used his finger to approximate where they where and where they were heading. "We'll be landing here, out of sight. It'll be bumpy, it's an abandoned airstrip. We need to be cautious—there could be patrols. It's two kilometers to the prison. My men will meet us at the strip. We'll have two trucks. How many boys might be there, Michael?"

"When I left, there were sixteen."

"Guards?"

"Four at all times. Usually more."

Kane handed him a pencil. "Draw it. Buildings, relative distances, and natural boundaries like boulders or trees."

From the cockpit, Sean said, "ETA, fourteen minutes."

Sean had hardly spoken since Kane arrived. Lucy didn't know how to read him. It was like he'd closed down. No, not *closed down* so much as changed focus. No jokes. No smiles. Lucy didn't realize how much she'd grown to count on his positive attitude. Was it the situation or Kane's presence? Was Sean as worried about what they were doing as she was? They were not only violating international law, but putting themselves, and a young boy, in danger.

But there was nothing the FBI or DEA could do quickly to rescue Brad. They would attempt to go through diplomatic channels while trying to get information about Trejo and his location. A military operation would require confirmed intel about where he was being held, how many threats, and they only had the word of a child.

A child who might be lying to them.

Lucy didn't want to believe Michael would risk all their lives, but it was also clear to her he was experiencing a severe case of survivor's guilt. He wanted to save his friends, but more than that, he wanted revenge. It wasn't so much what he said, but how he looked when he talked about the men who had killed his friends. His brothers.

Maybe, because Lucy knew that feeling. She lived with it.

Eight years ago Lucy had killed her rapist in cold blood. Truth be told, the man who called himself Trask hadn't actually raped her. He'd facilitated her rape, he recorded it, he showed it to thousands of people live, on the Internet. He'd planned on raping her, told her how he would kill her while he did it. Lucy called him a rapist because he'd taken everything from her, and more. Those two days in Hell had nearly killed her, literally and figuratively.

She didn't think, she acted. Some might say she acted on pure emotion, but there was nothing emotional about her taking her father's gun and shooting Trask six times in the chest, dead center.

He hadn't been armed. He hadn't posed an immediate threat, but she still shot him. She watched him bleed, she watched him die. She felt no remorse. In fact, she felt relief and anger and fear. Even dead, she'd felt the fear.

She had wanted revenge; right or wrong, she'd taken it. Premeditated, cold, calculating.

Her brother Dillon, the forensic psychiatrist, had told her that she was acting on instinct, that she wasn't accountable for her actions because of the trauma she'd suffered. Post-traumatic stress. The FBI had concurred, and sealed her file. And she'd let them. She didn't tell anyone that she'd known exactly what she was doing. She didn't tell Dillon everything, and being a shrink didn't make anyone psychic.

It was Jack who'd known. She had never told him, but he knew.

He'd come out to visit her one day at Georgetown, a year after her attack. He came east often—ostensibly to reconnect with his twin brother Dillon, but mostly to talk to her. To train her. She'd learned more about firearms and self-defense from Jack than from her FBI training.

It was a Sunday afternoon, and they'd sparred. He'd pinned her and she had a panic attack. That was when her panic attacks were far too common. Before she learned to control them, to shut them down.

She'd hated herself for being weak, and she'd hated Jack for putting her in a position that made her feel like a victim again.

"Stop," Jack told her.

"Stop what? Feeling helpless?"

"Stop feeling guilty that you have no regrets."

"I don't know what you mean," she'd said through clenched teeth.

He just stared at her. He didn't have to say anything; Jack never said more than was necessary.

"I'm numb," she whispered.

"You're healing."

"I'd do it again."

"Yes."

"I didn't feel anything." But that was a lie, and he knew it.

"Let it go. Let the guilt over how you felt then, how you feel now, go. Or you'll always be a victim."

"How dare you—"

"Is that what you want? To feel victimized? To feel ashamed? You have nothing to be ashamed about. You killed him. He deserved it. If you hadn't, he would have

*raped, tortured, and killed other women. Why on earth
would you feel guilty for ridding the planet of a man who
showed less remorse for his crimes than you have for protecting yourself?"*

*"That's not fair, Jack—" she had wanted to scream, to
cry, but she couldn't. Her emotions were gone. And that's
what she'd truly feared. That she had no feelings anymore.
Nothing. That she would never feel anything again.*

*"Put it in a box, Lucy. Lock it up. Don't let your fear
control you. If you do, you'll always be a victim, and that
bastard will win."*

At the time, she didn't believe him. She thought he was
being a soldier, teaching her to be a soldier. How could she
not feel *anything* when she took a human life?

How could she feel justified?

It was a long time before she understood.

She wasn't like most people. And maybe that was okay.
It was her defense mechanism to survive what had happened to her. It had made her who she was today. Someone
who could violate laws and rules and jeopardize her job to
save innocents. That if she had to kill again, she could do
it without hesitation. Her training gave her more skill,
more experience, the ability to decipher a situation and
know what to do and when to do it.

It didn't make her happy knowing that about her; but it
put her life in perspective. And made her appreciate how
Sean made her feel normal. She needed that so she could
live with the black hole inside her, that black box she'd
locked up but still had, the blackness that enabled her to
take a life to save a life.

And yet now, Sean was closed, stalwart, quiet. He was
never quiet. Did he sense she was opening that dark box so
she could do what needed to be done? Or did he fear she
wouldn't be able to control herself? That she wouldn't come
back?

Kane was studying the map of the prison that Michael had drawn.

"There's a small town near here," he said.

"Hardly anyone lives there," Michael said. "Except the general's people."

"Where's his mansion?"

Michael frowned. "I was blindfolded. But we went over a river, on a wooden bridge. A small river, but I heard water and it smelled fresh and clean."

Kane looked at his map. He asked, "How far from the prison?"

"Maybe an hour, at the most."

"And how far from the river?"

"I don't know. Ten, fifteen minutes?"

Kane drew an arc from a small blue line on his map. He picked up his radio and clicked it. A minute later a voice came over the speaker.

"Ranger here."

"Ranger, it's Rogan. I need the exact location of a wood bridge approximately thirty to forty minutes south-southwest of the target."

"Roger that."

Lucy looked at Kane. "What are they doing?"

"Recon," Kane said and didn't elaborate.

Michael looked worried. "The mansion is in the middle of a jungle."

"There're no jungles within an hour of the prison."

"It felt like it."

Kane thought a moment. He got back on the radio. "Ranger, check more southwest first. The mountain."

"Yes, sir."

"Do you know where it is?" Lucy asked.

"I have an idea."

"Bella will be there," she said.

"The girl?"

"Trejo is her father."

"You should have told me."

"I'm telling you now." She didn't back down from Kane's hard stare.

"Five minutes," Sean said from the cockpit.

"Go through it again." Kane turned to Michael. "Anything you remember, no matter how unimportant you think it is."

"They have a lot of guns," he said. "I want a gun."

"No," Lucy said.

Kane ignored her and said to Michael, "Have you used a gun before?"

"Yes." No hesitation. No blinking. Lucy felt ill. This little boy—this not-so-little boy—had killed before.

"I'll think on it," Kane said.

"Why?"

Kane didn't give him an explanation. He called out to the cockpit. "Padre."

Padre unbuckled himself and came back. Sean said, "Buckle up, we're starting our descent. Such as it is," he muttered.

Kane said, "Padre, you're staying with the plane. We need someone to guard it."

Padre nodded.

"Michael, you will stay with Sean. You hear that, Sean?"

"Loud and clear."

"My brother will die to protect you. I don't want him dead, so you will do exactly what he tells you to."

Michael didn't respond.

"I need an affirmative, Michael."

Padre said, "Michael, we need your help. The boys at the prison will trust you. They don't know us."

"I'll obey."

Kane looked at Lucy. "Kincaid, you're with me. If there's a threat, are you capable of taking care of it?"

"Yes."

But she wasn't happy about it.

It was two in the morning and Samantha Archer couldn't sleep. Every time she closed her eyes she pictured Brad being tortured.

She hadn't gone to the hotel—she had a team out in the field and she was in charge. Houston was sending down a team to relieve her first thing in the morning, but until then it was just her.

She was using the SSA's office in the small DEA field office in McAllen. There was a staff of ten down here, set up almost exactly like the FBI resident agency, except the DEA office was larger. They had a secure storage for drugs and guns they seized until they could be shipped to be destroyed. She was the assistant director in charge of this office, San Antonio, and two more small units—and she'd failed everyone.

Especially Brad.

The couch she lay on was hard and vinyl. She sat up, put her head in her hands, then drank a full bottle of water.

Sam's dad had been a cop, her mother had been a dispatcher, her sister was a federal prosecutor in DC. She'd been recruited by the DEA in college. She'd thought it was noble to fight the war on drugs. She thought she could make a difference. She was smart, she was dedicated, and now she had eighteen years' experience and was in leadership.

And they were losing the war. The losses that had piled up in those eighteen years haunted her.

Now she understood Brad in ways she hadn't when they were sleeping together. She understood his obsession in ways she couldn't before someone she cared about was taken.

A knock on her door made her jump, and she mentally admonished herself.

"Come in."

It was Tom Saldana. "Clark made it out of surgery. He's in the ICU. If he survives the next twenty-four hours, the doctors think he'll make it."

"Good." *Thank God.*

Tom closed the door. "I need to tell you something in complete confidence."

"Of course."

"We were set up."

"I figured that out," she snapped. She rubbed her eyes. She shouldn't be taking her anger and exhaustion out on this agent who almost lost his partner.

"But I know how." He sat down across from her. "Clark and I have cultivated several CIs. One, Lana, is a prostitute who has never given us bad information. *Never.* I don't say that lightly, because no one else is that good. She's the one who gave us the information about the warehouse."

"We also confirmed it at Peña's house."

"Yeah, but it was too neat. That had to be part of the setup."

"Tom, I'm too tired for vague. Tell me straight out."

"When all this came down on Saturday, with Sanchez, Donnelly asked us to keep our eyes and ears open. Clark and I talked to Lana, told her what she needed to know, and said there was a thou in it if she had verifiable information, five grand if it led to his capture. She wasn't interested— she knows who Sanchez is. Doesn't want to cross the wrong people.

"After we had confirmation that Sanchez was in McAllen—through Donnelly's own CI—she came to us, said she had heard about a deal at the warehouse. It was a place we were familiar with. We knew it was used by the cartels, and it fit what we knew about Sanchez."

He paused. "She's dead."

"So Sanchez killed her because she ratted him out."

Tom shook his head, and was about to say something when Sam put her hand up. It clicked. "He wouldn't kill her if he set the whole thing up."

"Exactly."

"But she could testify against him, right?"

"No. She didn't get the information from Sanchez; she said she got it from another client of hers, an associate of Sanchez. There would be no reason to kill her—if she was effective for them. She didn't know enough to be of use to us, so they'd simply let her be, using her as they needed."

"So they killed her to tie up loose ends."

"Maybe," he said. "I'm sure it's directly related to the ambush. That maybe she knew something else, about the setup. It's the way she was killed that has me suspicious. She was shot in a motel off the freeway. Shot three times center mass when she opened the door, this afternoon."

"I still don't see what you're saying."

"Three times in the chest. That's classic federal firearms training. You, me, every DEA and FBI agent use the same firearms instructors at Quantico. Her purse was missing. The clerk said she came in and paid cash. I went back tonight and asked to see the money. He wasn't happy, but he let me buy it off him. Two crisp twenty-dollar bills."

"From an ATM?"

"Maybe. Or maybe from whoever killed her. I hadn't paid her yet, that would have come after the takedown. So *someone* paid her. Look, if it's someone inside, where are they going to get the money? Money they could put back?"

"Shit," Sam muttered. "Do you have the twenties? I can run them."

He handed her a plastic evidence bag with two twenties.

The information sank in. Maybe if she wasn't so tired she would have picked it up before. "It's one of us."

"I want to say that I trust everyone in here. I really do. I can't see any of them setting us up. But you and I both know it happens. The cartels have a shitload of money, and having an agent on their payroll is not unheard of. Between the two of us, we could name a half dozen corrupt agents in Texas alone who were caught in the last decade. Money or threats. It's not me or Clark—that I can promise you. But that's all I can promise. What we do know is that the traitor is someone who knew Lana was my CI, who gave her information to give to us. Once the person knew we'd taken the bait, he or she killed Lana so she couldn't identify them."

Sam's heart raced as she extrapolated. "And that person would have to be part of the team because we didn't set the day and time until *after* we raided Peña's house. But— there were cameras in the junkyard. They were watching."

"Yeah, but did you read the forensics report yet?"

"No."

"The cameras were duds. They didn't know Tom and I were in the junkyard—unless someone on our secure frequency told them."

The weight nearly suffocated Sam, but she shook it off. Traitor? On *her* watch? Hell, no. She would find the individual and cut off their balls. Put them in prison until they rotted.

"I have to call Houston. Don't say anything to anyone. *No one.*" She stood and walked to her temporary desk. She was about to pick up the landline when she realized that she didn't know what or who to trust. She pulled her cell phone from her pocket.

Tom said, "I'm going to shower and go back to the hospital. I left Clark's wife there. She's six months' pregnant, and she shouldn't be alone. But if you learn anything, let me know. I want to be there when you nail the bastard."

CHAPTER 32

Family was complicated, but when your brother was an ex-Marine turned mercenary who'd seen more violence, blood, and evil than 99.9 percent of the people on the planet, it became more complicated.

Temperatures dropped drastically at night in the desert. They had jackets, but Sean was grateful it wasn't raining. The air was colder and drier here than it had been in Texas, possibly because they were in the middle of nowhere, Mexico.

There was a time when Sean had seen Kane as a noble hero and wanted to join his brother in the battle against corruption, cartels, and criminals south of the border. He still viewed Kane as a hero—there were few people who would consistently risk their lives to save others in a violent world few Americans knew existed.

But Sean wasn't Kane, and he didn't want to be. He wanted a life. He didn't want to risk everything he was, everything he had, each and every day. Kane was hard—and there was no coming back from that hardness. That his brother had to be one of those people—one of the unsung heroes who cared about the money only because money funded their operations of saving people—both hurt and made him proud.

Kane would never have a woman like Lucy, and now that Sean *had* a Lucy, he was sad for his brother. Kane couldn't stay in one place long. The nightmares, both real and in dreams, ate him up. But that didn't matter: Kane had never been able to turn his back on violence and desperate poverty, nor could he walk away from punishing those who used the violence and poverty to further their own greedy agendas. But there had to be a line, a way to help the innocent and a way to live; a balance between evil and hope.

Lucy had been on the precipice when Sean first met her. She could have become like Kane, not a mercenary in the deserts and jungles of another country, but a mercenary within their own borders, fighting to save everyone but herself.

And that's what Sean feared now. That she would lose herself to the demons she still battled because she would do whatever it took to save the boys, to save Agent Donnelly, to save Bella, no matter what the cost. And the cost could be great—and not just her life.

Sean would do anything to spare Lucy from what lay ahead . . . but he knew that was impossible.

He could only be there for her when all this was over.

They were on the makeshift runway where he'd landed the plane, waiting for Kane's men to meet up with them. It was pitch-black, no moon, and the stars peeked out of high clouds. It could have been romantic, if he and Lucy were alone; instead, Sean was hyperalert for an attack.

Kane approached. "I can hear your tension."

Sean glanced around, made sure Lucy wasn't within earshot. Still, he whispered. "Lucy."

"She can't handle it?"

"She can." What did he want to say? What *could* he

say? He didn't want Kane's focus divided, but he also needed to protect Lucy. And not from the physical dangers they all faced. "I don't want her to lose herself."

At first Sean didn't think Kane understood what he meant, but he couldn't think of any other way to explain it. Of course Lucy was capable and trained—and even though the situation was dangerous and unpredictable, Sean trusted her instincts.

It was everything else. She'd already closed down her emotions, she'd already gotten that dark look in her eyes. He wanted her back, fully, not just part of her.

Then Kane said, "It's the hazard of our lives. We chose this path."

"Did we?" Kane did what he did because he was not only former military, but had lost his beloved sister to drugs and violence. Sean barely remembered Molly; Kane was only a year younger than her. Lucy did what she did because of the attack on her. She'd planned on being a linguist and traveling the world. Instead, she battled evil in her own backyard. Their fears, their anger, their need for justice—whether mercenary or legal—drove them. They couldn't change it. There was no real choice.

He heard a whistle, then Kane whistled back. A minute later a jeep approached, no lights.

Kane glanced at Sean. "We good?"

Sean nodded. What else could he do? Maybe Kane would never understand that for Lucy this was different; she had more of herself to lose.

Two men, dressed in black, jumped out of the jeep. Kane made introductions. Skipper and Blitz. Did anyone use their real names on Kane's squad?

"It's quiet, four guards ID'd. We have to bypass the town, it's controlled by Trejo."

"Can we drive in?"

"Partway. We have a hole for the jeep, need to walk half a kilometer."

Skipper walked over to Padre, and they hugged and smiled, but Sean couldn't hear what they were saying. Kane approached, gave Padre a gun and radio, then walked to the jeep. The six of them crammed into the vehicle with Blitz driving.

It didn't take long to reach the hole Skipper had mentioned. The hiding spot was a ravine between two small hills that overlooked the old prison. The town was to the north, about three hundred people living in ramshackle houses. According to Skipper, they were bought and paid for by Trejo, and they needed to avoid the place. Their goal was to take out the guards, rescue the boys and Agent Donnelly, and return to the plane without alerting anyone in the neighboring town—or alerting Trejo.

They were south-southwest of the dying town of Los Ramones, about thirty kilometers as the crow flies from the much larger city of Monterrey. But here, on the opposite side of the small Papagonos mountain range, they might as well be in the middle of nowhere. Good for stealth; bad because Sean didn't know the area.

He'd helped Kane on and off with missions—primarily as a pilot, and mostly with the sanction and backing of Rogan-Caruso-Kincaid Protective Services. Kane's specialty was hostage rescue, and Sean had aided as needed. But he wasn't generally on the ground; if he was, he guarded the plane, as Padre was doing now.

If the operation went south, they were dead. And Lucy's presence only complicated things. She was an agent of the U.S. government; if she were captured, she'd be tortured and killed. If she survived, she could lose her job. He knew none of that had registered with her, or if it had, she hadn't let it sink in. She'd *said* she didn't fear the Office of Professional

Responsibility, but Sean knew her career was important to her.

Just not as important as doing the right thing, no matter how dangerous.

He studied her as she listened to everything Kane said. She wasn't smiling. She was focused on the complex spread in front of them. Based on the information Michael and his team gave him, Kane drew a plan in the dirt.

Michael was Sean's responsibility. He'd gotten them this far, but Sean didn't trust the kid. Not completely. He was holding back something, and Sean couldn't figure out what. Kane sensed it, too. At the same time, the story was true—or close to true. Based on the information that Lucy had obtained, and Kane's knowledge of how the drug cartels operated, Michael was indeed a pawn, or a slave. But there was something more about why he escaped. Sean knew it. And so did Lucy and Kane. No one called the kid on it, and maybe that was the right call, but Sean didn't like the sense that they were all being manipulated.

Blitz whispered, "Two guards are sleeping, passed out by the looks of things, in the structure to the far north of the complex." He drew an X in the dirt with a stick. "Two are walking around, smoking and drinking. You'll be able to smell them a mile away. They seem to stay between here"—he pointed to the southernmost structure—"and here." He pointed to the central building, a crumbling two-story structure. "It's here that the boys are kept. There's a lock on the door, but it's crap. There's also something going on here." He pointed to a small shack to the west. "There's someone in there, better dressed, not a guard but consider him hostile."

"Did you count the hostages?"

"Negative. We had ears, no eyes."

"Michael," Kane said. He waited until the boy looked at him. "You were here one month ago. You said sixteen boys?"

He nodded and pointed to the two-story structure. "That's where we live. It's like a dorm. There are cells, but no doors. Most of the bars are missing. But they lock us in the building."

"What about this building?" Kane pointed on the dirt to the shack west of the prison.

Michael shrugged. "Just another place for the guards. There's a bathroom in there. A kitchen. They don't stay there. Jaime stays there when he comes, but he doesn't come much. Other men I don't know."

"Communications?" Kane asked his team.

"There's a generator," Blitz said. "We take that out, we take out their communications. Radios work, no cell coverage out here. Don't know what else they might have, we couldn't get that close."

"Blitz, you take the generator. Skipper, you take out the drunk guards. Sean, you stay with Michael here"—he pointed to a far-south structure—"until Lucy and I disable the patrol. On my signal, you and Michael breach the prison while Lucy and I secure the unknown subject in this small shack. If I were holding a fed, that's where I'd keep him." He pointed to what Sean thought of as Jaime's house. "Once we're clear, we'll back you up with the boys."

"If he's there," Sean said, "there'd be more guards."

Kane caught his eye, but Sean couldn't tell whether he agreed or not. Then Kane turned to Michael.

"You need to tell your brothers to be quiet and we'll get them out. Tell them whatever you need to—they have to be completely silent."

Michael nodded.

Blitz said, "The patrol has stopped outside the western barracks."

"What's there?" Kane asked.

"Best we could tell it was empty. Had some beds, chains,

a kitchen. An office, which is locked. New lock. Could be where they're holding the fed."

That meant there were two potential places for them to hold Donnelly.

"But no additional security," Kane said.

"I can get in," Sean said.

"Negative," Kane said. "First, get to the boys. Lucy and I will cover the shack and the empty barracks. Understood?"

"You're the boss," Sean said.

"Glad we're clear on that," Kane said, catching Sean's eye. "Let's do it."

They used the cover of night to come down from the hill, all six of them in black. Sean kept his senses focused on Michael, even though he could barely see the boy running low next to him.

Sean held Michael back at the southern structure while Lucy and Kane moved ahead. There were dim lights coming from makeshift light posts, bare bulbs hung on wires. The low grumble of an old generator to the west was the only sound. No television, no music, no traffic. The patrol weren't even talking to each other, just smoking their cigarettes, the tobacco mixed with sweat filling his nose.

He put his hand on Michael's shoulder to make him stop moving. The kid looked at Sean. Sean put his finger to his lips and Michael nodded.

They stayed against the wall of the decrepit building. Sean feared leaning on it would cause it to fall down, though the winds and storms that came through the desert told him the buildings would stand up. Appearances were deceiving, and not just in people.

And he waited, watching Kane and Lucy from his peripheral vision.

Kane and Lucy approached the guards from behind. Kane hit the larger guard between the shoulder blades and he went down to his knees. Immediately, Kane kicked his feet out from under him, grabbed the rifle, and hit the guard on the head.

Simultaneously Lucy did the same on the smaller guard. He dropped his weapon and Lucy kicked it away, then kicked him in the ass to keep him down. He wasn't unconscious, and cried out once in pain. Kane hit him with the butt of the other guard's gun and he went silent.

Sean listened for movement of other guards, an alarm of any kind, but heard nothing. They were on the far end of the complex and the one pained shout may not have been noticed, even in the still night. Or Skipper had already taken out both sleeping guards.

Lucy and Kane went directly to Jaime's shack, while Sean took Michael to the main two-story building, the prison. He picked the lock without trouble and they slipped inside.

The overwhelming scent of feces, urine, and blood hit Sean like a hammer. A lone, bare bulb in the small entry illuminated the packed-dirt floor and crumbling walls. The ceiling was low—Sean was only an inch over six feet but he had to duck his head to get through the archway that led to a narrow hall.

There were no sounds inside at first, nothing that told Sean that there was anyone in the building. He stopped, listened . . . heard breathing. A quiet murmuring, as if someone was trying not to cry.

Sean turned on his small flashlight and kept it dim in one hand, his gun in the other. If there were more than four guards, he didn't want to alert them, but he needed to see. Michael pointed to the right and Sean followed the boy's direction.

Then he smelled death.

He turned his light to the left and quickly turned it away. Little bodies, laid out on the filthy floor, flies buzzing. He'd seen the reflection of the dead eyes in the brief flash of light.

So had Michael.

"No," Michael said.

"Shh. Some are alive. We'll help them."

Michael groaned, a wholly unnatural sound, and pushed past Sean toward a rickety flight of stairs. Sean followed, the wood steps creaking under his weight.

"Kevin," Michael said in a loud whisper. "Paolo."

"Michael?" a small voice said.

"Yes, it's me. Shh."

"He said you were dead. It's been so long."

"Kevin, I brought help."

The cage Michael stood in front of was locked. Seven boys huddled in the corner with dirty blankets in a prison that reeked with more than the dead and dying. He held his flashlight between his teeth and picked this lock, though it took longer than it should. Rage filled him, so primal and violent that Sean's hands shook.

The boy called Kevin walked over and took Michael's hand through the bars. "You said you would come back and you did. They made us—they made us—" He started to cry, soundlessly.

"Don't," Michael said. "Don't think about it. We have a safe place." Michael looked at Sean. "A way out."

Sean told the boys, "You must be completely quiet."

They stared at him, all seven of the boys. Michael didn't. Michael was looking at the boys. "Where's Tommy?"

Kevin blinked back tears and shook his head.

A cry vibrated deep in Michael's throat.

"Michael," Sean said sternly. "I need your help."

The boy's fists clenched and unclenched. Sean popped the lock. "Kevin, get everyone in a line. Follow me out. Michael, take the rear, okay?"

Michael didn't move.

Sean grabbed his arm, hard enough to cause pain. "Michael. Focus."

Rage filled Michael's eyes as he glared at Sean. Sean felt the same way, but he controlled it because he had to, for all of them. But this boy wanted to hurt someone, and Sean was there. Michael punched him in the stomach, but Sean tightened his abs in time to take the impact. It still smarted.

"Save the living," Sean said. "If you don't do this, they will all die."

He grunted, in pain and anger and deep despair. Tears dampened his eyes, then were gone.

Michael motioned for the seven boys to exit. One was seriously limping, dragging his foot. Sean took a quick look: There was dried blood that had virtually glued his old jeans to his leg. The boy winced when Sean touched his ankle, but didn't cry out. A bandanna was tied around the injury.

A boy whispered, "They shot Tito last week."

Last week? And left him in here bleeding? The boy was hot to the touch: The wound was infected. He'd been shot and left without medical attention.

Sean felt the same rage he'd seen in Michael. And pride. The boy was brave beyond anyone Sean had met. Fourteen months he'd lived in hell and he hadn't broken. He'd been free, but had come back. For these kids. His brothers. Knowing he would most likely die, he came back anyway.

Sean picked up Tito; he weighed no more than sixty pounds and felt like bones and skin and not much else. They went down the stairs, slowly.

Gunfire erupted outside and the boys stopped, some crying out, some crouching. Sean stopped at the door but didn't dare go out. He said into the radio. "Status?"

More gunfire was the response.

CHAPTER 33

Lucy shot the guard three times center mass and he went down, but not before he got off a shot. It grazed her arm, burning her flesh. She grimaced and swallowed a cry of pain.

She and Kane took refuge in the small shack west of where Sean and Michael were with an unknown number of boys.

"How many?" Kane asked.

"I saw three. They came from the village."

He nodded at her arm. "How serious?"

"Not bad. Cover me." She put her gun down, pulled out her knife and sliced a strip off the hem of her shirt. She tied it around her upper arm, as a tourniquet, using her free hand and her teeth. "Flesh wound."

She picked her gun back up and slung the rifle she'd taken from the guard over her shoulder. Kane had watched her dress her wound without expression.

"What?" she asked.

"Competent first aid." That was the extent of his compliment. "There's going to be more. The village is seven minutes by car. We need to go."

They hadn't found Brad. There was no evidence that

he'd been here, but there was evidence that someone had been in the shack recently. A small ice chest still had melting ice. It couldn't have been there all day. A well-dressed man? Jaime Sanchez? Doubtful. Trejo himself? Would he come here? Michael said it was rare.

Kane was eyeing the status in the courtyard. "I see two. They have a radio. We need to take them simultaneously."

"Understood."

"Thirty yards. Can you do that?"

She took the gun off her back. "Yes.

They positioned themselves. Kane said, "They're at two o'clock. You take the one on the left, I'll take the one on the right. On three."

One. Two.

Three.

Kane opened the door and Lucy immediately took the shot. The gun jerked to the left, and she only winged the subject, but compensated for the recoil and fired two more rounds, both hitting the man's chest. Kane took out his target with a single shot to the head.

Her adrenaline was pumping, but she felt nothing. Maybe fear, but no remorse. And even the fear was buried. She was cold. How could she kill without feeling anything?

Kill or be killed.

They'd been confronted with a threat. They reacted. It was as simple as that.

Why did she think her life could be simple again?

Who are you fooling, Lucia? Your life hasn't been simple since the day your nephew was murdered when you were seven. And it got even more complicated after being raped and your vengeance against that bastard.

Kane was talking into his radio. She couldn't hear whoever responded, but Kane told her, "All buildings are empty. We need to go."

They ran out of the shack and toward the prison. Sean

wasn't standing outside. Kane said into his radio, "Sean, status?"

A moment later he said to Lucy, "He's just inside the door. One boy isn't mobile."

Out of the corner of her eye, Lucy saw a figure run along the perimeter. She raised her rifle, and Kane batted the barrel down. "That's Blitz. I'll cover. Get the boys."

Lucy hesitated only a second. Would she have shot him without knowing if he was a threat or a friend? She hoped not, but she didn't know. She was operating on instincts, and she wasn't certain hers were as finely tuned as they needed to be.

She knocked on the door. "It's me."

Sean opened it. The foul smells rolled out with the boys. He was carrying a child who couldn't have been more than ten.

"Move," Kane said.

Six boys, all barefoot, followed Sean out. Lucy looked. "Where's Michael?" she asked.

"Rear," Sean said.

He wasn't. The last boy exited and it wasn't Michael.

Lucy ran into the building.

"Get back here!" Kane ordered.

Lucy ignored him. She called out as loud as she dared, "Michael!"

No answer.

The smell hit her again. This time it wasn't just urine and feces; it was decomp. There was a dead body in here, and had been for days.

She rounded the corner and saw Michael standing in the middle of not one dead body, but many. She shined her flashlight over the carnage. Five bodies, all boys, all young and malnourished. From the stains in the dirt, and the wounds on their small bodies, they'd been shot multiple times, right here. Right where they fell.

"Michael, we have to go," Lucy said. "Now."

He didn't budge. He stared at them, frozen. Shock or fear, she didn't know. She squatted next to him and spun him around. He was so cold.

"Listen to me, Michael! We must leave or those seven boys you rescued will all die. Do you understand me?"

He stared at her, his eyes as cold as his skin. She shook him once, hard. "Michael!"

He nodded.

She still had to half drag him out of the building, as if his feet wouldn't obey his will. Or maybe he really didn't want to go. Survivor's guilt was powerful.

I should have been here. I should have died with them.

He would feel that, the pain and the guilt that he'd survived. There was no unseeing what they'd seen.

She stepped out and someone grabbed her. But she immediately knew it was Kane by the way he smelled, even though she couldn't see anything in the dark.

"I ordered everyone to leave. We can't go the same way."

"Why?"

"There're two trucks coming our way. We're going to create a distraction. I already set the charges; we need to run."

He turned to Michael. "Stay with me or they will kill you."

"Yes, sir," Michael whispered.

Kane looked over his head at Lucy. "Follow my lead."

Sean hadn't wanted to leave. Kane ordered him to, and Sean opened his mouth to tell him to fuck off. But Kane was right—if he and the boys stayed while Lucy searched for Michael, they would all die.

Still, leaving Lucy behind was the hardest thing Sean ever had to do. If it was anyone but Kane, he wouldn't have left.

He, Blitz, and Skipper took the seven boys back to the jeep. From their vantage point in the low hills where they'd hidden the vehicle, Sean saw a caravan of trucks moving in from the town to the prison. His stomach twisted in knots at the thought of Lucy being gunned down. Or captured. Tortured and raped and killed.

"I have to go back."

"No time," Skipper said. "Kane has already set the charges. You'll be killed or separated. Trust him."

He had to. He had to trust Kane to get Lucy out.

Blitz said, "Let's go, Rogan. Or they'll find the plane. We don't have time to dick around."

Sean sat precariously on the backside of the jeep, the boys all crowding into the backseat, sitting on one another except for the boy—Tito—with the injured leg. He sat on Skipper's lap while Blitz drove through the desert with no lights, the sound of the engine impossibly loud racing over the dark, empty sand.

Blitz got on the radio with Padre. "Start the plane, we need to bolt."

Sean said, "Padre's a pilot?"

"He doesn't have a license."

That wasn't a no. That meant he simply flew illegally.

Padre had the plane ready when they arrived. "We don't know how much time we have," Blitz began.

A rumbling explosion made the ground shake, and the boys all huddled together. A second explosion, even louder, rocked the plane.

Padre told the boys to get into the plane. Skipper carried Tito. Sean stood and stared at the glow in the east.

"Little Rogan, we need to leave," Padre said.

Trust Kane. He knows what he's doing. He'll protect Lucy with his life.

Sean turned to the plane, his stomach in knots.

CHAPTER 34

Michael hadn't said a word since they left his dead friends, but he followed Kane's orders to the letter.

Lucy pushed aside the vision of those dead boys, but they sat in the back of her mind. Kane's plan was smart, but the families of those five boys would never know what happened to them. They would be forgotten.

Not forgotten. You'll never forget them.

Michael knew them all. He would never forget, either. Neither would the seven they'd rescued, the seven boys Sean was flying back to Jack's safe house. The one needed a doctor.

Even though they hadn't found Brad, they'd saved seven children tonight. It was a victory, she had to remember that. Seven children were alive who would have been murdered if they'd done nothing.

Kane put his hand up to halt them. Lucy and Michael, a step behind, stopped.

Kane pointed to the last truck in the caravan. They'd thought there were only two trucks, but there were five, all filled with men from the town, all of whom had guns. They needed a vehicle, but they had to ensure no one could pursue them.

She nodded. They were going to take the last truck.

They hid behind one of the old shacks on the southern edge of the compound. This might have once been a guardhouse, but it was half gone; bullet holes had splintered most of the wood. Men passed them only feet away, the headlights of their trucks making them appear both ghostly and bigger than they were. There were shouts in Spanish, orders to secure, orders to shoot on sight. Lucy couldn't make out every word, but these were ordinary men who were tasked with murder. They were not trained soldiers, beyond whatever undisciplined training Vasco had implemented. How could anyone, no matter how bad their lives got, be party to the abuse and murder of twelve-year-old boys?

Kill or be killed.

She had to push reason aside. There was no rationale for this violence. There was corruption and manipulation and the targeted use of fear to control. She had to put herself in the head of men like Jaime Sanchez so she could figure out what they wanted, what their next move was. Trying to understand these men running by with guns, heading to the prison where five boys had already been slaughtered, would only distract her.

Kane held up three fingers. Then two. Then one. Then dropped his fist. The three of them ran low, along the edge of the unpaved road, past the trucks. Though the drivers had remained with the vehicles while their partners moved into the prison, they were standing by the driver's-side doors and not looking out the passenger windows. As long as they stayed low and close to the vehicles, out of the driver's peripheral vision, Lucy prayed they wouldn't be spotted.

They made it to the fourth truck in the line before they had trouble.

The driver was smoking a small cigar and pacing, rifle

slung over his shoulder. Kane put up his fist to halt Lucy behind him. She froze immediately.

The driver walked in front of the car. One more step and he'd see them.

He took that step.

The driver wasn't expecting to see anyone. He hesitated a fraction of a minute. He opened his mouth to shout, dropped his cigar to the dirt, but before he could lay hands on his rifle or utter a sound, Kane shot him between the eyes.

The sound echoed through the night. Lucy's heart skipped a beat.

Kane pulled a radio from his pocket, dialed in a frequency, then pressed a button.

The explosion knocked them to the dirt.

"Run," Kane ordered.

Lucy stumbled, got up, and grabbed Michael's hand to make sure he kept up with them. Kane started for the driver's side of the last truck, taking out the guard with a hard blow to the head with the butt of his rifle.

Another man stepped out of the passenger side, his gun aimed at Michael.

Lucy fired three rounds and the man dropped. She kicked the dead body aside so she could fully open the door. "Get in," she ordered Michael.

Kane was already in the driver's seat and had swept the back of the truck in case there were more shooters. There were none.

But there were a whole lot of guns.

Kane hesitated, just a moment, surprise crossing his face.

"Kane?" Lucy said. She looked back but didn't think she saw what he was seeing. All she saw were wooden crates of guns—mostly military-style assault rifles.

Kane didn't comment. He turned the ignition and made

a wide turn. He didn't head toward the village, but drove across the desert, looking at his compass to guide him. He tossed her a map. "I marked the route to Trejo's mansion."

She said, "You know something."

"Now's not the time."

"Tell me! What did you see back there?"

"American guns." He didn't say anything else, so Lucy pushed.

"Did our government send them down? Supporting one faction over another? Or are they stolen? Jack told me once about a group of soldiers who stole guns that were supposed to be destroyed. He'd tracked them down to Guatemala, retrieved the guns." She didn't know what happened to the thieves; she hadn't asked. "Is this something like that?" He still didn't answer her. "Kane, what the hell is going on?"

"I'm not sure yet."

"But you *think* you know."

"You need to stay out of this."

"I'm already in the middle of it!"

He didn't talk, and Lucy grew increasingly frustrated. She glanced back to where Michael sat staring at nothing, his face hard. His face blank.

The face of a victim.

"Sean and Kane's team will get your brothers back home," Lucy said. "I promise."

He turned his dark eyes to hers. They were empty. Then he turned away.

Her heart twisted at the pain the young man had buried inside. The grief that would consume him if he couldn't figure out how to let it out. Learn to live with it, learn to let it go.

Let it go? It would always be there. He has to learn to manage the pain, the cold, the unbearable drive to seek revenge.

Lucy faced forward and looked at the map under her pin light. "There's a wooden bridge about two kilometers away, then we'll be going into the mountains."

Kane kept driving. The silence of the desert was broken only by the rough transmission of the covered truck.

It was several minutes before he said, "A few months ago, a transport plane made an emergency stop in southern Mexico. Hostile territory. My team was called to assist in repairs and rescue. It was a potential diplomatic nightmare because the United States wasn't supposed to be flying across that part of airspace, but when they had a mechanical failure, they had no choice. By the time we arrived, the crew was dead and their cargo gone. The cargo was guns that had been stolen from a military base in the states, and the DEA tracked them to a cartel in Colombia. A small Special Forces team was sent, seized the weapons, and were returning when they went down."

"It wasn't a simple mechanical failure, was it?"

"I never saw the report; I don't know what happened. But those Marines were slaughtered. The weapons that disappeared are the same type we have now.

"If Trejo was behind it—he's planning something bigger than I suspect. Bigger than the DEA realizes. The DEA was the only nonmilitary group involved with the op— they provided the intelligence. They knew the flight information. Even if the cartel created the malfunction, someone had to give them the information in the first place. And someone who knew where the plane had gone down had only eight hours before I arrived to locate and kill the team and get away with several truckloads of guns. It would have taken time—which means they had hard intelligence."

"There's a mole in the DEA."

"There are many, but I usually figure out who they are real quick." He glanced at her. "To be honest, I give Sean information and suspicions, and he identifies the traitor.

He's better with computers and tracking money than I am." He paused. "Are you okay with that?"

"Does it matter?"

"Not to me. It would to Sean."

She didn't comment. Why would she have a problem with Sean helping root out corruption in law enforcement? She might have to turn a blind eye if he crossed lines, but she could live with it. She was well aware of what Jack had done in the past, what he likely still did now on a smaller scale. She would not hold Sean up to an arbitrary higher standard than she did her own brother.

"So why did they take Donnelly?" she asked. "He has information they need?"

"He pissed them off. When you get noble cops, they usually get themselves killed. Donnelly isn't bought and paid for. He's given a long leash because Sam Archer wants to do the job, but doesn't have the balls for it." He looked at her. "Not because she's a woman, so don't get your feminist sensibilities in a wad. You would have the balls for it."

"Another Kane Rogan compliment," she said dryly. "I might faint from the praise."

He almost smiled, then said, "If they took Donnelly for fun and games—he was in the Army, he was in Special Forces, he's not going to crack and give information—then he doesn't have much time."

"Don't you have anyone in the DEA or another agency you can call? Anyone you trust?"

"Don't be obtuse. This is a foreign country. Clandestine ops are the rule; the U.S. gets caught they need plausible deniability. Why do you think I do such a healthy business? How do you think RCK started in the first place? It sure wasn't protecting the rich and famous."

Kane was bitter about something, and Lucy couldn't put her finger on it. She didn't know him well, which made figuring out his angle that much more difficult. And he wasn't Jack—they were similar, but Kane was harder, angrier, edgier. That he'd told her so much surprised her. Maybe being shot at together had earned his trust.

But she knew her brother Jack, and the one thing that stood out as the same was a deep sense of honor and duty. They were both former military who still fought wars no one else wanted to fight. Except Jack had reconnected with his family, had fallen in love, had found a balance that kept him grounded.

Kane didn't have that. He rarely spoke to Sean or Duke. They rarely saw one another. Any conversations were work-related. There was no grounding in Kane's life, which meant, to Lucy, that his work was his only salvation. That made him both extremely good and extremely dangerous.

She filed away her assessment and focused on where they were. Kane was driving without lights, going too fast in her estimation, but she didn't comment. The truck bounced uncomfortably over the rough, open terrain, the engine labored.

Suddenly he made a sharp left turn and stopped the truck. He depressed a button on his radio a couple times. There was a rhythm, and Lucy wondered if it was code.

Half a minute later a brief flash of light reflected from a hundred yards away. Kane rolled the truck slowly in that direction, then grinned. When he smiled, he looked more like Sean. So much that it unnerved Lucy.

A man in black emerged and climbed into the back of the truck.

"Good to see you, buddy," he said. Not only was the man dressed in black, he *was* black, his skin as dark as his clothes.

"Ranger, Lucy. Lucy, Ranger."

"Jack's little sister." Ranger extended his fist. Lucy did the same, and he bumped hers. "Guess I'm on protection detail."

"She's fine. You'll stick to the boy."

"Hmm" was all Ranger said.

"You think I'd bring Jack's sister out here if she couldn't handle herself?"

"Why are you talking about me like I'm not here?" Lucy asked.

Ranger grinned, and all Lucy could see was his teeth and his eyes. "Kane has no manners." He looked at Michael and said, "Tough day."

"Tough fucking year," Michael responded, the first words he'd said since they'd fled the prison.

But his eyes were no longer empty. They were focused and intelligent.

The road changed, from rough desert to a narrow wooden bridge. The truck barely fit over it. Lucy couldn't see below, but she heard the water, and it sounded to be at least a thirty-foot drop.

As soon as they crossed, they were on a road—if the narrow, packed path could be called a road. It had been forged only because trucks had driven this way hundreds—thousands—of times.

Ranger said, "There's a hidey-hole around the next corner. Pull in to the left, go up the mountainside about twenty feet. It'll be tough. But there's a flat area there. I set up camp here during recon, and found a back way into the compound while waiting for your late ass to arrive."

Kane did as Ranger instructed, and Lucy thought for certain that they weren't going to make it—worse, that the truck was going to flip over, trapping them inside. The engine revved and groaned as Kane shifted to first gear. Then, miraculously, they reached the landing and were level again. Kane turned off the truck.

"Report," he said to Ranger.

"Main house, approximately twelve thousand square feet, three outbuildings. I counted eight guards on the perimeter. Minimum two more inside the main house. A foot patrol handles the mountain. They don't come this far down. Lazy bastards, but good for us. The guards outside aren't from around here—I suspect they're gangbangers from the States. The guards inside are former Mexican military."

"Did you see the fed?" Kane asked.

"Negative. A helicopter arrived on the opposite side of the house. There's a helipad. If they brought him in, that's how he came. I saw the little girl."

Lucy turned to face him. "Bella?"

"Only one girl, and she matches the photo Kane sent to me."

"Vasco Trejo is her biological father," Lucy said. "Jaime Sanchez kidnapped his niece for Trejo. She's an American citizen, and Trejo's name isn't on the birth certificate."

"We've dealt with foreign parental abductions many times," Kane said, irritated at something.

Lucy ignored his irritation. "If we don't bring her home, we'll never get her back."

"We'll bring her home," Kane said. "Change of plans."

"All ears," Ranger said.

"Lucy, you and Michael find Bella and bring her back here to the truck. Ranger and I will find Donnelly." He handed her a radio. "Do you know Morse code?"

She shook her head.

"Okay, new code. Ranger can fly anything. If we can't get back to the car, we're going to steal the chopper. You know Paul Revere?"

She tilted her head. "You mean, 'One if by land, two if by sea'?"

"Yes. Only it'll be one if by land—we'll meet you here at the truck—and two if by air."

"And I meet you at the chopper?"

"No. You use the truck. Can you drive it?"

She had no idea. "Yes," she said, but her hesitation worried Kane.

"If you can't get the truck down the mountain, go to the bridge and wait for extraction. I'll be there." He put the keys under the driver's seat. "Radio silence unless it's a damn emergency."

Michael said, "I want to go with you, Kane."

"No," Kane said.

"I need to do it!"

Kane turned around and looked Michael in the eye. "I know why you think you need to do it. You want revenge. Revenge will not take away the nightmares. Revenge will not make you better. Revenge will kill what's left of you. You will become one of them, not who you were meant to be."

Michael's bottom lip quivered. For the first time, Lucy saw the little boy. The scared child he was inside, the fear he kept buried. "They . . . They made my brothers kill each other. Because of me. Because Richie and I escaped. I'd promised to bring back help, but it was too late."

"It wasn't too late for seven of them. Don't make me cuff you to this truck, boy. Understood?"

Lucy said, "Michael, Bella knows and trusts you. She helped you escape. You need to help her now. You know this place. I don't. I need you to help me find her."

Michael didn't want to go with her. But the little boy was hiding again, and the hardened young man emerged. Lucy ached for him, that his childhood was over, that he would never reclaim the innocence of youth. It had been brutally stolen, beaten out of him. But had he had a childhood at all? His mother was murdered, he'd been abused, his father was in prison, he'd been moved from home to home. He'd already lived a tragic life; they could only go forward from today.

He had spent a year with the Popes. Could that year save him?

He finally said, "Only because she helped me."

Lucy tried not to let out a sigh of relief.

Kane said, "I'll notify you when I've disabled the security system."

Ranger leaned over and winked at Lucy. "You can trust him. Sean built the jammer. Little Rogan keeps us in some choice toys."

"She's a fucking fed, Ranger. She doesn't want to know." Kane assessed her.

"I'm here, aren't I?" Lucy said. "Let's get this done so we can all go back home."

They got out of the truck. Ranger led the way through the trees and underbrush.

The night continued to darken as the hour crept past four in the morning and the four of them disappeared into the mountain to find Brad and Bella.

Ryan called Lucy at four hoping to get company for breakfast and coffee. She didn't answer her cell phone.

He'd gone out on a limb when he talked to Juan last night. Juan was not at all happy that Lucy was interviewing Michael in an unknown location without Ryan or anyone else knowing where she was or assisting in the interview. Juan had a lot of questions that Ryan couldn't answer, and all Ryan said was, "I think we should trust her on this one, boss."

But she had never come to the hotel. Her overnight bag had been at the DEA office when he picked up his last night.

He tried Sean's number, and again it went straight to voice mail. If Lucy didn't show up to the debriefing in an hour, Juan would hear about it, and Ryan wouldn't be able to protect her.

He went to the twenty-four-hour diner next door to the hotel. The lot was filled with big rigs, but the diner itself was nearly empty. At dawn, the drivers would be coming in to eat and then get back on the road, but he had the place mostly to himself.

Then Sam Archer walked in, alone.

She hadn't slept. Dark circles made her look like she'd been hit in both eyes, and she wore the same clothes she'd had on yesterday. She looked around, jittery and suspicious, before sitting across from Ryan. "Where's your partner?"

"Sleeping," he lied. Well, it might not be a lie. She very well could be sleeping.

"I can't trust anyone except you and Kincaid. I need your help, but it has to be completely discreet."

"What do you need?"

"Someone on my payroll is working with Sanchez and Trejo. I need you to figure out who. But no one can know you're looking." She slid over a piece of paper. He unfolded it. There were three names. "One of these people set us up yesterday. They were the only three, other than you and Kincaid, who knew that Tom and Clark were in the junkyard and *when* they arrived. They would also know that we'd send in both teams to extract our agents, leaving one flank exposed. That enabled them to get Brad down the tunnel and into a waiting vehicle."

All three were DEA agents. Ryan knew each of them. He didn't want to believe Archer. He wanted to tell her she was a paranoid bitch who was destroying careers because of her guilt over Donnelly's kidnapping.

Except Lucy had already voiced her suspicions. Archer's theory clicked.

Archer leaned forward. "I'll tell the others that you and Lucy are on an FBI assignment related to the kidnapping of the girl. That'll give you time, and no one will think they're being scrutinized.

"One more thing—a prostitute was killed yesterday shortly before the sting. That's another reason these three are on the list. They don't have an alibi for the shooting."

"What does a dead prostitute have to do with all this?"

"We think she was paid a thousand dollars to give Tom and Clark information that ultimately led to the ambush. We couldn't find any of the money, except for the forty dollars she gave the clerk at the motel. I traced it. It was taken from the DEA evidence storage."

"I have to tell Juan. You know that."

She nodded. "He'll be discreet. Other than Tom Saldana, who brought me the evidence, the only person who knows is my boss in Houston. He's keeping it quiet until I give him a name. I need to give him the right name."

No cop ever wanted to turn against a fellow cop, but when the corruption was this big—when it resulted in the shooting of an agent and the likely murder of a kidnapped cop—there was no real choice.

"I'll do it."

CHAPTER 35

The residence at the top of the mountain was a virtual resort. The mansion was two stories of Spanish-style architecture with three towers and 360-degree views. There were few trees to speak of; mostly shorter shrubs with several scraggly Monterrey oaks. But the lawn was richly green and irrigated, and flowers bloomed freely between lush, thick-leaved bushes that Lucy thought were called Mexican fire brush. Large treelike shrubs with fans of palms were artfully arranged. There were two swimming pools—one a lap pool and one a decorative pool with a waterfall and hot tub. The landscaping alone must have cost a small fortune.

Paradise in the middle of the desert, a sanctuary only forty minutes from where five small boys had been murdered.

Any other night, Lucy suspected, it would be quiet. But tonight, after the explosion at the prison and the escape of the boys, the house was ablaze with light, and the guards were hyperalert.

She and Michael waited along the perimeter, at the edge of the cliff where the mountainside disappeared into the dark below.

She had to wait for Kane's signal. Otherwise their attempt to save Bella and Brad would become a suicide mission.

The patrol guards were gangbangers, as Ranger had surmised. Lucy suspected they were from San Antonio and surrounds, not Mexico. And they were young. Fourteen? Fifteen? If any of them were over eighteen she'd be surprised. She couldn't forget what Kane had told her about kidnapping boys to train them to be soldiers. Was this what Michael would have been had he been broken? The others? Was patrolling Trejo's complex a reward for compliance? How long had Trejo been operating down here? Since he left San Antonio after Bella had been conceived? If he was true to pattern, the boys he'd kidnapped seven years ago would be seventeen, eighteen, nineteen now. If they had survived.

"I killed someone," Michael whispered.

She wanted to tell him to be quiet, but he was talking so softly even she could barely hear him.

"I had to," he said.

She took his hand and squeezed it.

She turned her mouth to his ear and said, "I killed someone when I was eighteen. I had to do it, too."

He looked at her, eyes wide. Maybe she shouldn't have said anything. Maybe she should have just told him everything was going to be okay. But that would be a lie, and he would know it.

"Let's get Bella, then we can talk about it."

He just nodded.

A patrol of two was coming along the edge. Michael saw them at the same time as Lucy. The dark night and the slope of the mountainside hid them, but if the patrol shined a light toward their hiding spot, they'd be exposed.

Lucy didn't have to tell Michael to freeze; he went perfectly still. She had her handgun in front of her. She would shoot if she had to.

Don't think that they're young. They're trained killers. They won't hesitate to kill you; you can't hesitate to shoot.

They were young and had been scared, were still scared, but that wouldn't stop them from following orders from a man who scared them more than death itself.

Lucy wanted Trejo's head on a platter. Him and Jaime Sanchez. For horrific crimes against humanity.

The patrol passed. They didn't look down. They didn't even have a flashlight.

In her earpiece she heard Kane say, "It's down."

She acknowledged and nodded to Michael. They were headed for the main house, where Michael thought Bella would be, in the wing that Trejo kept for himself. It was the middle of the night; she should be sleeping. That was the only wing where the lights were out on the second floor.

It made sense to Lucy that Trejo would put his daughter in a luxurious room close to him. He wanted to win her over, shower her with gifts. The house. The pools. Dolls and toys and pretty dresses. A different form of bribery.

She hoped she was right about Bella, that she would come with her quietly.

They ran low to the ground, on the far perimeter, to the main house. There were lights in virtually every room downstairs. They couldn't go in through the main doors. There were several glass-paned doors off other rooms. Some had blinds closed, and she couldn't see if anyone was inside.

Lucy motioned for Michael to freeze. He did, lying flat on the ground behind a low stone wall that framed the back patio. She heard voices. Male voices, indistinct words. Someone was angry, but she didn't know who or why.

The why she could probably figure out.

The blinds were closed. She could make out shadows, the frames of two people. She glanced to the left. Double doors led into another room. The lights were off. This was her chance.

She whispered in Michael's ear, "Stay right behind me."

He nodded.

She crawled along the base of the wall for twenty-five feet, glanced up, and was directly in line with the dark double doors. She was about to hop the fence and run to the house when another set of doors twenty feet further down opened. A man stepped out to light a cigarette. A well-dressed man in a suit. But she'd never seen him before.

She looked at Michael, gestured, and mouthed, *Who is he?*

Michael shook his head.

Great. More people, more players. He wasn't a gang-banger, and he wasn't a guard. His suit was too expensive and he was too old. He didn't look Mexican, and had a manner that made Lucy think American. Another expatriate like Trejo? He was likely doing business with Trejo and could very well have his own security contingent.

Lucy itched to find another door to enter, but she feared any movement would alert the suit to their position. They were forced to wait him out.

The doors on the far right opened and another man stepped out. Lucy had never seen him before, either. Again, well dressed in a clean white shirt and pressed khaki slacks. He was in his thirties with slicked-back dark hair and dark eyes. Vasco Trejo? The American who betrayed his country and the boys?

She gestured to Michael. He cautiously looked. Then he whispered in her ear, "The general."

"Tobias, we have a situation," Trejo told the man in the expensive gray suit. "The plane didn't land where we expected."

Lucy was relieved. Sean had gotten the boys out. Michael relaxed next to her; he understood what that meant.

Tobias passed within feet of Lucy's hiding place as he walked over to the other man. "Consider it a loss," he said. "We'll rebuild."

"I don't want to fucking rebuild. I want what was stolen from me!"

Tobias spoke calmly. "There are always more." He had a slight accent. Neither Mexican nor American. A hybrid of something. Maybe a bit affected. Lucy was usually good with language, but she couldn't figure out where he was from.

"DeSantos is dead. His cover was blown. CPS is going to get a rectal exam by the feds. That source is burned."

"You need to choose your people more wisely. Relax, Vasco. The only problem you'll have is if all my guns aren't there. Once I get the report from my men, I'll leave and you live."

Trejo scowled. "Don't threaten me."

There must be a second way off the mountain, opposite the way they came in. They hadn't passed anyone leaving and heading for the prison complex.

"It's not a threat. You either give me the guns, or return my money with a loss fee of twenty percent, as you agreed to." Tobias paused. "What aren't you telling me, Vasco?"

"One of the trucks was stolen. It's only ten percent of the weapons, but—."

"Then you'll give me ten percent of the two million back."

"I have something better."

"There's nothing better than cash or guns."

"Yes, there is. Come inside."

They went back through the doors they'd come out of.

Lucy couldn't wait another minute. She didn't know when or if they'd leave the room. She crawled along the wall to the door that Tobias had originally vacated. There was a lone light on, no one inside. The door leading to what she presumed was the hall was closed. She and Michael slipped inside and closed the terrace door.

It was an office. Files from CPS were stacked on the desk. Dozens of files. That bastard—Lucy forced herself to remain calm. Getting angry now wasn't going to help her find Bella. And DeSantos was dead. The FBI knew he'd been working with Sanchez; they'd help CPS with their security.

She walked over to the door and listened. She heard nothing. Michael came close to her and whispered, "There's a back staircase, next to the kitchen. The big staircase is right outside this door, but the other staircase is better."

"When I say go, you lead."

Her heart raced and she willed it to slow down. It didn't obey. She closed her eyes and listened. No voices. She was two rooms away from Tobias and Trejo. There was a third man in that room. A guard? Sanchez?

She slowly cracked the door and peered out.

The lights were all on, but she saw no one. She opened the door wider, looked down the hall where the men were talking. That door was closed. She nodded to Michael.

He wasn't right there. He'd gone back into the room.

She didn't risk talking or closing the door. She crossed silently to where he stood next to the bookshelf. He was staring at a black box. The black box that had started this all. It was a perfect cube the width and height of a CD. It could hold maybe fifty CDs. And it was valuable to Trejo.

Which meant it was now valuable to the government. It could be anything, but if it helped them shut down drug pipelines or gunrunning or corrupt officials, they needed it.

He didn't look at her; he simply picked it up and tucked it under his arm. Then he followed Lucy to the door. She looked out again. Clear.

Michael led the way down the hall, their shoes making faint sounds on the tile floor. She winced and prayed no one could hear them. As if he sensed the same thing, Michael walked slower, with more purpose, and their footfalls became muted.

A shadow at the end of the hall had Lucy pushing Michael back. Then it disappeared. They moved again, past a dining room, past the kitchen where there were voices—young voices, talking about going to town to get laid when the job was over. Excited. Scared.

Just past the kitchen was a narrow staircase that led up. If anyone came up or down while they were on the staircase, they would be trapped—the bullets would have few places to go except to hit them.

They didn't have a choice.

There was no light on, and Lucy kept it that way. They took the stairs as fast as they dared and stopped just at the top of the landing. Standing flush against the wall, Lucy peered left and right. Michael motioned to the right: *That's Trejo's wing.*

Now or never.

The one positive was that they exited on the short side of the wing, so anyone coming up the main stairs couldn't see them. There were four doors on the right and three on the left. Double doors at the end of the hall. That, Lucy assumed, was Trejo's suite.

But where was Bella? Lucy doubted they had time to check each room, and she had no idea if there were others sleeping up here. If she were Trejo, how would she think?

He wanted Bella why? Because she'd been kept from him? Because his name wasn't on the birth certificate? Did he truly want a child, or did he take her as punishment for her mother who listed another man as her father?

It could go either way, Lucy realized, but would Jaime Sanchez turn his niece over to a man who would hurt her? Or did he truly believe that living here would be better for her?

For Jaime . . . it was punishing Mirabelle as much as it was keeping his employer happy. For Trejo . . . she leaned toward him wanting a prodigy. Wanting to keep her close.

Making sure no one had emerged from any of the rooms, she made her way immediately down the hall to the door closest to Trejo's suite.

It was locked from the outside.

This had to be it.

She motioned for Michael to be lookout while she picked the lock, wishing that Sean were here. He'd take half as long as she. The twenty seconds it took felt like twenty minutes.

She opened the door and they both slipped in. She had her gun ready in case she'd been wrong.

She hadn't been. There was a night-light next to the bed, bathing the room in a shiny pink glow. Everything was pink. Pink walls, pink comforter, pink rugs on the tile floor. And dark-haired Bella, curled into a fetal position, in a large pink bed, under a collection of letters that spelled ISABELLA in bright ballerinas.

Lucy motioned for Michael to stay by the door, to listen. She walked over to Bella and squatted next to the bed.

"Bella. Isabella," Lucy whispered.

She startled awake, a cry on her lips. Lucy put her hand over the girl's mouth.

"It's Lucy. Lucy Kincaid. Remember me?"

The girl nodded, her eyes brimming with tears. She pointed to her dresser.

Lucy looked. There was a voice monitor there, the light flickering from green to red.

Shit.

Lucy put her finger to her lips. She gestured to Michael and Bella smiled underneath Lucy's hand. Lucy leaned over and whispered directly into her ear and hoped the monitor didn't pick it up, "I'm going to take you home. But no one can know I'm here."

She nodded.

Lucy crept over to the door. If anyone came up, they'd know someone had picked the lock. She hoped and prayed no one did.

She didn't hear anyone outside the door. She went into the closet, wincing as the door creaked. She found shoes and a warm jacket. She handed them to Bella and again put her finger to her lips to remind her to be quiet.

Bella had just put on her shoes when gunfire sounded outside the house. She sucked in her breath, loudly. Lucy prayed Trejo and his people were too busy dealing with Kane to worry about Bella.

Lucy looked from Michael to Bella and for a split second was overwhelmed by the responsibility she had to protect these two young people. Michael put his arm around the girl and Lucy was relieved she didn't have to tell him to keep her close. She picked up a small bag with ballerinas on it and handed it to Michael. He put the black box in it, then put the bag on his back.

She held them back while she checked the hall. She heard voices at the top of the stairs, and closed the door again. Dammit, how could she get out of here?

She searched the room, looked out the windows, didn't see any other way out. She could jump two stories, she knew how to roll to prevent breaking her ankle or worse, but she couldn't expect Bella to do the same. There was nothing to climb down, either. No balcony off her bedroom, no trellis, no tree.

She pictured the layout of the outside. There *was* a balcony off Trejo's bedroom. Could they get out from there?

Michael tapped her and Lucy looked. Did he see that she had no idea how they were going to get out if they couldn't go the way they came?

He mouthed, *I know a way.*

She nodded.

He held his hand out. She knew what he wanted.

She removed the small 9mm Kahr that was in her pocket. She hoped she wasn't making a mistake.

In her pocket, her radio buzzed multiple times. Not one, two or three . . . but constant.

Something was wrong.

Really, Lucy, what's right?

More gunfire, on the southwest side of the property. She couldn't bring Michael and Bella to the firefight.

Michael listened, just as she had, then he went out. She and Bella followed. She heard voices on the main staircase, running downstairs through the hall, but no one was up here.

Yet.

Michael went directly to Trejo's suite.

The door was unlocked, and they all slipped inside. Michael whispered, "He has an escape tunnel, through the walls. Follow me."

Lucy said, "Michael, this is important. You need to take Bella to the truck and hide. Can you do that?"

He nodded.

"If anyone comes, you know what to do—only if you have to."

Again, he nodded and took Bella's hand.

He slid open what appeared to be a closet door. Instead it led down a dark, narrow passage, and then to stairs. "This goes under the complex, to the corner of the property," Michael said.

Lucy did not like closed, cramped places. Her fear was more than simple claustrophobia. It had to do with the time she'd been held captive for two days, trapped. Unable to move, unable to do anything but be hurt by the bastards who'd taken her.

She stumbled, grabbed the wall, and righted herself.

Michael glanced over his shoulder. She could barely see him; there were some dim lights, but they were few and far between. She focused on Michael, on Bella, and that Kane needed help.

The tunnel ended at a ladder. Lucy climbed up and checked the door. It was locked, but it was a simple mechanism. She focused her pin light on the hole and picked the lock, then slowly pushed the door open an inch and held it. She surveyed her surroundings.

They were in the far southwest corner, but there was a group of guards, at least six, surrounding the closest building only thirty yards away.

Just when she thought it couldn't get worse.

She released the door.

This constituted an emergency.

She said into her radio, "Status? I'm trapped on the southwest corner of the house, in a tunnel. Guards are thirty yards away."

Silence. Had they heard her? Couldn't Kane at least acknowledge her?

Or was he incapacitated? She couldn't think that he was dead.

No one was going to die tonight. There had already been too much death, too much suffering.

She heard in her radio, "Wait." And that was it. She didn't know if it was Ranger or Kane.

She waited what seemed like an unbearable eternity, but wasn't longer than a minute. Then the ground shook and she heard an explosion on the eastern side of the property. Lucy tumbled off the ladder, fell heavily on her butt.

A distraction.

Thank you, Kane.

She quickly climbed back up the ladder and checked the door.

All the guards were fleeing the area, heading east.

She pushed open the trapdoor and pulled Bella up and over the ledge. Michael scrambled up behind them.

"Do you know the way?" Lucy asked him.

"Yes. Are you sure?" He didn't want to leave, but she didn't know if it was his sense of protection for her and the team, or his desire for revenge.

She said quietly and firmly, "I'm trusting you with Bella. Go. Take cover."

She closed the trapdoor and didn't watch as Michael fled with little Bella. She ran over to the building that the guards had abandoned, plastering herself against the wall.

She took several deep breaths.

How had Kane created a diversion so far from his building? Why were the guards surrounding it in the first place? Is this where Brad was being held?

Keeping her back flush against the wall, she slithered over to the door. Gun in hand, she tried the knob. It turned.

She pushed the door in slowly.

Someone was watching her. They were close.

She turned, her finger on the trigger, ready to shoot.

She stared into blue eyes.

"Sean," she breathed, not even a voice, just a sigh.

He kissed her, hard and fast, then pulled her inside.

"How did you get back so fast?"

"I didn't board the plane. You think I was going to leave you?"

She hugged him, willed her heart to stop beating so loud she couldn't hear herself think. Then she pulled out her radio and said, "Sean's here." No response.

"Where's Kane?"

"I don't know. He must have set the explosion to distract the guards so I could get out. I don't know if he found Donnelly. I sent Michael back to the truck with Bella. We have to get to them."

Sean frowned. Lucy opened the door, looked around, and motioned for him to follow.

Her radio vibrated and she halted, then pulled it out and listened.

It was a code.

"Do you know Morse code?" she asked Sean.

He nodded and pulled them back into the shack.

He took her radio and listened to Kane's message.

A minute later he said, "They know where Donnelly is but they can't get to him. Kane wants us to meet up with him."

She nodded. What other choice did they have? They'd come here to get Brad; they couldn't leave him now. Trejo would certainly kill him.

Sean led the way out of the shack. One guard had returned. Before they were spotted, Sean knocked him out with a karate chop to his neck.

Sean led the way to a barn on the southern edge of the property. The guards were close, inspecting the corner of the mansion where Kane had lit the fuse.

Lucy saw Tobias and Trejo at the front door of the mansion. Trejo started running toward the barn. She hadn't seen Sanchez yet. Where was he?

They stayed in the shadows. The benefit of having young guards was that they were inexperienced. They looked for a leader, and whoever was supposed to be in charge wasn't giving the orders. Lucy and Sean ran to the back of the barn where Kane and Ranger had taken cover.

"What the hell happened?" Kane said.

Sean responded. "They spotted me on the mountain and tried to grab me. I knocked out one of the guards and hid in the shack where I found Lucy. If you hadn't set off the charge, they would have found me."

Kane turned to Lucy.

"I didn't know Sean was here," she said. "I needed the diversion to get Michael and Bella to safety."

"Where are they?"

"The truck." She hoped.

Kane nodded. "Donnelly is inside the barn. He's in a bad way. He knows we're here, but we couldn't get to him."

"Trejo is coming."

"They're going to kill him," Ranger said.

Kane concurred. "They know there's a breach; keeping him alive creates more problems."

"Plan?" Sean asked.

"We go in hot. That's the only way." Kane looked at Ranger. "You go with Kincaid. I'll go with my brother."

Sean tried to object. Kane was firm. "It's safer" was all he said.

Ranger had a knife in hand.

Lucy bit her lip, took a deep breath, and nodded that she was ready. She didn't want to do this. She had to.

Or Brad would be dead.

They left their post, walking around the exterior of the barn in opposite directions; Lucy with Ranger and Sean with his brother. Ranger took lead. First guard he saw he took down with a quick karate chop, not unlike the one Sean had used only moments ago. Lucy followed him around to the front of the barn. Sean and Kane rounded the opposite corner a half minute later. They made eye contact then rushed the doors together.

Lucy didn't know what to expect. What she saw was Jaime Sanchez and Vasco Trejo standing over a bloodied and beaten Brad Donnelly.

Sanchez immediately fired on them. Trejo took cover in one of the stalls. Sanchez followed, then fell to the ground as someone—Kane? Sean?—shot him. He wasn't moving.

Lucy dove for cover as well, her gun in hand, looking

for Sanchez or Trejo, but the stalls made it difficult to get
eyes on the suspects.

She saw Brad lying in the middle of the barn. She didn't
know if he was dead or alive.

Kane said, "Cover me, hard."

Lucy was stunned when he ran over to Brad. Ranger and
Sean immediately laid down a round of gunfire to cover
him, and Lucy followed, now that she understood what he
wanted. Kane dragged Brad into a stall to protect him from
the cross fire.

They crouched behind old equipment, uncertain if
Trejo and Sanchez were dead. Ranger motioned to Sean to
check the stall where Sanchez disappeared, and motioned
for Lucy to guard the door while he checked Trejo.

Sean called out, "Sanchez is dead."

A moment later Ranger said, "Trejo disappeared."

Kane said, "How the fuck did he get out?"

"This place is full of holes in the wall. He must have
slipped out. He'll be in hell soon." To Lucy he said, "You
sure the kids are clear?"

"Yes," she said. If Michael had obeyed her.

He cares for Bella. She saved him; he'll save her. Lucy
had to believe in him.

"Plan B," he said and pulled out a detonator.

As soon as he pressed the button a giant explosion rocked
the mountain. Lucy fell to the ground, her hands on her
head. She couldn't hear anything, but felt Ranger pulling
her up.

Go, go, go.

He was shouting at her, but she couldn't hear him.

She scrambled up and ran with him. She glanced back.
Sean was helping Kane drag Brad out of the barn.

When she emerged through the doors, her eyes widened
at the sight of the mansion engulfed in flames. "Chopper,"
Ranger said.

She shook her head. "Michael and Bella. They're at the truck."

"I'll get the fed out on the chopper," Ranger clarified. "You go to the truck."

The four of them, bringing Brad with them, ran toward the landing pad. Ranger jumped into the chopper. "I need to hot-wire this."

Sean leaned over and pressed some buttons, did something else that Lucy missed, and twisted a wire. The blades started turning.

"You rock, Little Rogan," Ranger said.

Kane strapped Brad into the copilot's seat. "Take him home, Ranger."

"Roger that."

They ran low, out of the way of the blades, toward the edge of the mountain as the chopper lifted into the sky. No guards were around to shoot them down. The entire complex was on fire.

"Let's get those kids home," Kane said and led the way.

Michael left Bella in the truck with the black box and told her to hide behind the seats. Then he crawled twenty feet up to get a better vantage point.

He knew that they'd been seen.

He'd tried to hide, to stay low, but the backpack Lucy had put the box in practically glowed in the dark. He didn't realize it until Bella said she heard something. He glanced back and saw that they stuck out like a big pink thumb.

He'd dumped the backpack in some bushes and ran with the box all the way to the truck. Hid inside. But they'd been followed.

So he lay there, gun out, watching. Listening.

He heard nothing.

Then an explosion—bigger than the one at the prison— made him slide down the mountainside several feet.

He lay there stunned, his arms over his head. When he could think, his first thought was that he didn't know how to drive the truck. If everyone was killed, how could he get off this mountain with Bella? He never wanted her to see what he'd seen.

He reluctantly took his hands off his head and crawled back up to the road. He peered carefully. From the location of the smoke and light, the mansion must have exploded. That had to be the work of Kane and the others. The general wouldn't blow up his own mansion.

Relief flooded through him. He would wait here, just like Lucy told him to do. He pulled the St. Jude medal from his shirt and kissed it, like he'd seen Father Flannigan do. Maybe there was a God after all.

He'd started crawling back down to the truck when he heard the chambering of a bullet.

He looked up. The general was standing on the path above him. His white clothes were dirty. Or was that blood? Definitely blood. His hair was as wild as his eyes. He had a gun only twenty feet from Michael's head. He wouldn't miss.

"You. I saw you. I didn't believe it."

Michael had Lucy's gun in his hand, but his hands were flat on the dirt. The early dawn was still hidden while they were among the trees, and the gun was black. The general must not have seen it.

"I will rebuild and I will dance on your grave," the general said. He spit on the ground, staggered a bit, then slipped. He clutched his stomach with his free hand. He'd certainly been shot. He was bleeding. But he still had a gun on Michael.

Suddenly the sound of a helicopter rose over the sound of the fire. The general half screamed in rage as he turned his face to the sky. "That bastard stole my chopper!"

Michael didn't know or care who he was talking about.

He aimed and fired the gun at the general. He pressed the trigger over and over, remembering Javier and Richie and Tommy and all the others this man killed. He was crying, no sound, just tears running down his face as the bullets stopped coming out of the gun. He still pressed the trigger, because evil always came back.

Then he heard crying. It wasn't him, it was a little girl.

Bella.

He looked in front of him. The general lay on the edge of the path, his chest a bloody mess, his eyes open and glazed.

He was dead.

He couldn't hurt anyone again.

Michael crawled back to the truck. He found Bella huddled on the floor, her arms over her head. He said, "Bella, it's okay. I killed the monster. He can never hurt us again."

CHAPTER 36

It was two in the afternoon by the time Lucy and Sean arrived in McAllen with Padre, the seven boys, Michael, and Bella. They had a story but weren't sure it would hold.

"It'll hold," Kane said. He had looked at Lucy. "Honesty is a good trait, but not this time."

Lucy had called Ryan the first time she had an opportunity, but he didn't answer. She left a voice mail saying that she was fine, she'd be at the McAllen hospital that afternoon and needed to talk to him.

Lucy wasn't surprised to see Sam Archer there—Ranger had delivered Brad hours before they arrived.

"How is he?" Lucy asked.

"He'll live." She closed her eyes, just a minute. "They tortured him. Bad." Then she breathed deeply and composed herself. "But he's alive." She looked at the boys, who all cowered around Padre and Michael. "What happened? Is that Bella Sanchez?"

"Yes. It's a long story." Three nurses spoke to Padre. One took Bella; the other two ushered the boys in another direction. Padre and Sean went with them. "Kane Rogan and his team found them. And Bella."

"Oh, dear God, I'm relieved. That many boys? What was he doing?"

"There were more. Dead." Lucy would never forget them. She caught Michael's eye as he rounded the corner. "That's what Kane said," she added quickly.

"Have you talked to your partner?"

It took her a moment to realize she was talking about Ryan. "Last night. I left a message earlier."

Sam looked around, then pulled Lucy to a quiet corner. "He's investigating something for me. There's a mole in my division. I narrowed it down to three names."

"Who?"

"Victor Gray and Chris Garber from the McAllen office. And Nicole Rollins from the San Antonio office. Brad's partner—I haven't told him yet. I won't—unless I get confirmation."

And then it clicked. The one thing that had been bugging her.

"It's Nicole."

"How can you be certain?"

"The ransom. Asking for Sanchez's two gangbangers to be released. Why not Mirabelle?"

"She was released."

"But no one outside knew that. Only us."

"She came late to the staging area with the maps of the warehouse," Lucy continued. "She stayed there when Tom and Clark were pinned down with fire." Lucy wondered about what Kane had told her earlier. "Was she involved in an operation several months ago related to guns stolen from a military base and found in Colombia? Six Marines were murdered when they were forced to land and the guns were stolen."

Sam dry-heaved. "Yes," she said, her voice clipped. "She developed the intel on that operation."

"She's been privy to everything in this case, from the planning of Operation Heatwave to the op at the warehouse," Lucy said. "Your agents in McAllen only got involved two days ago."

Nicole knew what car Lucy drove and could have rigged it; she knew where Bella and CeCe were staying in foster care. She was out of town when Lucy's house was broken into, but she could have hired the two thugs who'd attempted to intimidate Lucy.

"We need evidence," Sam said. "I can't go to my boss with an unproven theory. I hope your partner finds it."

Lucy wished she knew what was in the black box, but Kane told her it was now his.

"If it's important to law enforcement, I'll get it to the right people."

She didn't really have a choice. And Michael was okay with it. He'd handed it to Kane, not her.

Her phone vibrated. It was Ryan. "Hello? Ryan?"

"You're at the hospital? Are you okay?"

"I'm fine." She wasn't reporting the gunshot to her arm—it was minor. She'd have Sean re-dress it when they got home, and it was hidden under her jacket. "I came to check on Brad."

"Fucking amazing. Where have you been?"

She stuck to the story they'd all agreed to. "We interviewed Michael and he told us about the boys still locked up in Mexico. Sean called Kane. He and his team rescued them, brought them to Jack's house in Hidalgo."

"Why didn't you call? Send a team down?"

"Send an FBI team into Mexico?"

"I see your point. But—"

She hated lying. She felt physically ill. "It was hardly sanctioned, Ryan."

"And Isabella Sanchez?"

"Kane found her. I don't know the details. He's writing up a report—there's a process RCK uses for these sorts of things." She was deliberately vague. "I'm with Sam Archer. She told me about your assignment. It's Nicole."

"Well, fuck, Lucy. You took my thunder."

"How did you figure it out?"

"When this big black guy handed me a DVD. He said, 'Watch it.' Then he left."

Ranger. It had to be. Kane must have known exactly what was on those DVDs.

"And?"

"Sanchez or whoever had those disks must have been blackmailing her. She killed a drug dealer in San Antonio five years ago. Took his money and drugs. Don't know what happened to them, but the murder and theft is all on tape. She flashed her badge, he was unarmed, and she shot him."

Sam took the phone from Lucy and listened to Ryan repeat the information. Sam said, "She's at the DEA office right now. I have her doing a mountain of paperwork." She listened, then said, "Thank you, Ryan. I honestly couldn't have done this without you."

She handed the phone back to Lucy. Ryan said, "Lucy, I'm on my way to the office. I thought you might want to be part of the takedown."

"You earned it, Ryan. I did nothing."

"But you told me it was her. Just now."

"On a hunch. I didn't have the proof, you do. You have backup?"

"Juan sent Nate and Kenzie down; they're with me now. We'll get her. Let me know how Brad's doing."

"I will."

"Juan wants you back ASAP."

"I know. I'm in trouble."

"Maybe. I don't know. But Lucy? Don't lie to me again."
He hung up.

She stared at the phone. How had he known?

Lucy walked into Brad's room after Sam Archer left to
deal with the fallout of the Nicole Rollins situation. He
was sleeping. His head and chest were bandaged, and both
arms were in casts. His face was severely bruised.

He opened his eyes. One eye. The other was swollen
shut. "Hey," he said.

"Hey." She sat next to him. "I'm glad you're alive."

"Thank you." His voice was thick.

She bit her lip. "About that."

"Shh." He took a shallow breath. "I understand. Ranger
and Kane rescued me." He stared at her with his one good
eye. "But I will never forget it was you. I owe you my
life."

"No. We're on the same team."

"Not everyone."

"Sam told you."

He shut his eye. "I should have seen it."

"She was good."

"Good at being bad."

"We'll talk later." She started to walk away.

"Lucy?"

She looked over her shoulder.

"Don't say a word."

She frowned. "I don't understand."

"I see it in your eyes. Guilt. Because of the story. No
guilt. No regrets. Ranger told me about the boys. Remember, there are more people who need our help. And sometimes, rules get in the way."

She left, closing the door softly behind her. Rules. What
did she believe in anymore? She took the elevator to the
lobby, where she found Sean.

"Where's Padre?"

"He's staying with the boys," Sean said. "Bella's going to get a plane ride to San Antonio in a bit. The FBI is taking custody—two agents from the McAllen office will be with her at all times."

"They're going to interrogate her." Bella was seven. Convincing a child to lie—Lucy felt awful even asking her to do it. She didn't know if the girl would hold up.

"She says Michael saved her and a man called Kane. That's all she knows. They're not going to grill her. I think she might have already convinced herself you weren't even there."

Tears sprang to Lucy's eyes.

"Hey, princess." Sean pulled her into a tight embrace. "Don't cry. It's all going to be fine. Kane is a rock."

"Not that. I don't care about my job. I mean I do, but I wouldn't have done anything different. It's—everything. Michael. Bella. The boys. The dead."

"Padre is a good man. He's working on a plan. They'll be taken care of, given any help they need." Sean kissed her forehead. "And I'm going to take care of you."

"I want to see Michael before we go."

Several of the boys panicked when the hospital wanted to separate them, so Padre convinced the nurses to move patients around so that the eight boys—the seven they rescued and Michael—could be in the same pediatric room. The rooms fit only six so they moved in two extra beds.

They were all sleeping, given sedatives and IVs. They were malnourished, dehydrated, and Tito had a severe infection. He was the only boy not in the room, because he was in surgery. One of the young nurses was crying softly at the nurses' station.

Michael refused a sedative. Padre was sitting with him, and they both were keeping watch over the others.

Lucy approached and Padre stood up. "Lucy, would you mind sitting while I take a walk?"

She shook her head and sat in the chair he vacated. Padre left. She looked at the boys. So small, so defeated. It wasn't just a few people who were heartless and cruel; it was dozens. The people in the town that Trejo bought. The boys who'd grown up and punished the new boys. Nicole Rollins and Charlie DeSantos knowing what was happening and not caring. Not only not caring, but sending more boys down to suffer. To be broken.

Michael said, "Padre explained how much trouble you could be in if anyone knew you helped."

She nodded. "I'm sorry to ask you to lie."

"I think it's stupid. You saved everyone and they would fire you for it."

"It's complicated."

"It's dumb."

"That, too." She smiled, mostly so she didn't cry.

"I feel better," he said.

"Good."

"I killed him."

"I know."

She'd seen Trejo's bullet-ridden body. She'd taken her empty gun from Michael's grip and given it to Kane to destroy. If Trejo's body was found and the forensics analyzed, she couldn't have it traced back to her.

"Did you feel better when you killed that man?"

She didn't have to ask what he meant; she'd told him about Trask.

She wasn't going to lie to him.

"Yes. He hurt me in much the way the general hurt you." She squeezed her eyes shut. "I felt safer with Trask dead. But it also gave me pain, because I wanted to feel bad about taking a human life, and I didn't. Not him. It took me a long time not to see myself as a cold-hearted killer. I'm not the same girl. I don't want you to grow up thinking you'll be the same in ten years. You won't be. But I'm not worried."

"Why?" His voice cracked.

"Because you protected Bella over seeking revenge. And you can still cry."

She hugged him and they both cried.

CHAPTER 37

Lucy sat in Juan Casilla's office at seven o'clock Friday morning.

"I'm placing you on unpaid administrative leave," he said.

"I understand," she said. She forced herself to sit rigid in her chair, her hands clasped in her lap.

"Do you?"

"Yes, sir."

He closed his eyes and shook his head. "No one knew where you were on Thursday until you showed up at the hospital with eight kidnapped children. You didn't answer your phone. You didn't call in."

"I made a mistake."

"Don't lie to me, Lucy."

She didn't say anything.

"You don't think you did anything wrong, do you?"

"I'm sorry I disappointed you."

He didn't say anything for a long, long time. So long that Lucy started to fidget. She forced herself to freeze again.

"I read Brad Donnelly's report about what happened at Vasco Trejo's complex," Juan said. "Two mercenaries, with Michael Rodriguez, stormed the compound, rescued Bella

Borez, took out an unknown number of guards including Jaime Sanchez, then escaped. One mercenary flew out with Donnelly in a stolen helicopter, and then the other—someone you know very well—drove the two children back across the border, undetected, with a truckload of weapons that had been stolen from six murdered Marines five months ago."

He continued. "I also read an official RCK report about the operation, prepared by Kane Rogan, stating that he went down to Mexico with four other men—three employed by RCK and one a local priest—and the young Michael Rodriguez. They rescued seven minor American citizens and three of the men took them on a plane back across the border, to where you and Sean were waiting. Kane and the other mercenary, with Michael, went to Trejo's compound."

"Yes, sir."

"You let a minor child go with trained soldiers into a dangerous and hostile situation."

"Sir, he knew where the boys were and the location of Trejo's house."

"You should have given me the information. You violated the law, not to mention ethics. And truly, the only reason you're not being fired is because of those children. It would be hard to fire you when those boys see you as a hero."

"Sir, if I'd gone through proper channels instead of alerting Kane to the situation, Brad Donnelly would be dead."

"Maybe."

"He would be."

"How do you know? Were you there?" He stared at her. He knew. She saw it in his eyes. It took all her willpower not to tell him the entire truth.

She bit the inside of her cheek. "I saw the same report."

"Cut the bullshit, Lucy."

Her eyes widened. Juan Casilla didn't swear. Ever.

"I know damn well you went with them. And everyone is protecting you. I want to fire you because you scared me. But I had to step back and think why? Why was I scared when I send my team into dangerous situations all the time? I worry, but as a supervisor. This was different." He paused, the tendons in his neck vibrating. But he calmed his voice down. It obviously took him great effort to keep his emotions in check. "In three months, you've been to my house more than any other agent on my squad. My wife and children adore both you and Sean. You fit in with my family, maybe because you grew up in a big, happy Hispanic family. But I've read your files, Lucy. As your supervisor, I had to. I knew when you were assigned to me that it wasn't going to be easy. You don't think about yourself. That can be a great asset, but not if it gets you killed. And *that's* why I was scared."

She didn't know what to say. *I'm sorry* didn't seem appropriate. Because she wasn't.

Except she was sorry that she'd scared a man she respected and admired. He didn't deserve that.

"Juan," she said, her voice not sounding like her own, "if you want my resignation, I'll give it to you."

"I need you to take a break. Two weeks. Unpaid administrative leave. And I suggest you use that time to make it up to Ryan. He's hurt and angry and has every reason to be."

"Yes, sir."

"You can go."

She left, her chest tight, her stomach threatening to toss the single cup of coffee she'd forced down before she came.

She sat behind the wheel of her car for a long time. It physically hurt that she'd disappointed Juan. She liked and admired him so much. And she owed Ryan more than an apology.

She didn't regret anything she'd done, but she regretted not finding a way to alert her team that she was okay. Maybe there would have been a way . . . but admitting to the truth? That would put Brad, Kane, and the others in jeopardy. Juan *thought* they were lying to protect her, but he couldn't prove it. She couldn't risk Brad's career, Kane's status, or anyone, because they did it for her.

She hated that she'd put Juan in that position. She had mixed feelings about what she'd said and done—and about lying. She wasn't good at it. Obviously, because Juan read her like a book. All this could come back to haunt her.

But she wouldn't have changed anything.

With a sad heart, she drove home.

CHAPTER 38

When the front bell rang, Sean was surprised to see Kane on the security screen. He took the stairs down two at a time and opened the door to his brother.

"Kane. Come in."

Kane looked uncomfortable standing in Sean's large two-story entry. He looked up at the wide, curving staircase, then behind it to the deep, sunken living room. Sean hugged him. That seemed to make him even more uncomfortable.

"I can't stay."

"Okay. Let's go to the kitchen." Sean led the way. He grabbed two beers from the refrigerator and put them on the center island. He took a seat and motioned for his brother to do the same.

Kane took a long drink from the bottle. "I wanted to see how you were doing."

"We're good."

"I heard Lucy was put on administrative leave."

"Two weeks."

"She around?"

"Soon. She stopped by Saint Catherine's with Father Flannigan."

"Padre told me what you did."

"What did I do?"

"Bought that house, next to the church. For the boys."

Sean shrugged. "No big." He drank heavily. He'd been doing that a lot this week, since coming back from the prison. He'd never forget what happened there. He wanted to, and then felt guilty for wanting to forget. Those boys had suffered for months, two of them for over a year. Buying a damn house for eight broken boys was small beans compared with what they'd been through.

Kane drained his beer, helped himself to a second. This one he opened but didn't drink yet. "Is Lucy okay?"

"As you can expect."

"Does that mean she's cried, screamed, lashed out? Gotten angry?"

"Of course not." Sean tensed. "You don't think she's okay?"

"You said to me she would lose herself. I want to make sure she didn't. She handled herself much better than I expected. She did everything right, except going back for Michael and forcing us to split up."

"And that was wrong?" Sean was going to get angry if Kane pulled out the *There are always casualties* speech.

"No, not wrong. Human. I sometimes forget. What we did—I've done many times. I am who I am. But—" He stopped, obviously at a loss for words.

"She has me," Sean said. "She will survive and be stronger." He finished the beer, then went to get his second.

"She's damn special, Sean. You're extremely lucky."

Sean couldn't disagree. He'd thanked Kane for protecting her, back when they were still in Mexico, but he wouldn't forget any of this. Not his brother, not what happened, not the aftermath. For Kane this operation was almost typical, but at the same time he'd seen a subtle change in his brother. He wasn't sure what specifically had impacted him, but Sean would use it if it meant he could bring his family together again. The Rogans would never be the Kincaids, but they could be closer.

"You rarely come home," Sean said. But I want you to know, Kane—there's always a place for you here."

He looked around. "Big. Comfortable." He said it as if being content was a bad thing.

"I like comfort."

"I'd like to visit more often."

"More often?" Sean smirked. "You never visit. You didn't visit even once while I was in DC."

"You're my brother."

"So's Duke."

"Duke has his own life." He paused. "You understand this better than Duke."

"Maybe. Maybe not." Sean pulled out more beer. "Did you hear Nora had the baby last night?"

Kane's lips curved up just a fraction. "Duke and I don't talk much, outside of business. I heard you don't, either."

"Duke and I are fine." Sean didn't think Duke knew yet what had happened in Mexico. When he heard the truth—which he would—he might not be so fine with Sean. But Sean was no longer seeking his approval like he once did. The most important thing to Sean was that Lucy adjusted to her suspension and her new life here in San Antonio.

"What did they have? Boy? Girl? One of each?"

Sean laughed. "Girl."

Now Kane smiled. "Duke once told me he was afraid he'd have a boy like you."

"Yeah, well, Duke and I don't always see eye to eye, but he could do a lot worse than me."

"He was more afraid he'd have a boy who was smarter than him."

"Maybe this girl will be smarter than him." Sean paused, then added, "They named her Molly."

Kane looked away, rare emotion crossing his hard face. He stared out the window into the green backyard. "All this," he said quietly, "I started because of her."

"I know."

Molly, the oldest Rogan, who spiraled down into drug abuse until she died.

"Sometimes I wonder if it's worth the fight anymore. For every field I burn, ten more grow up. For every drug dealer I kill, ten more replace him."

"You told me once, if not us, who? If not now, when?"

"I stole that line."

"When you're ready to step away, there is plenty of work we can do here in the United States."

"We?"

"You're every bit as much a Rogan as I am."

"I'm not ready."

"I'm not going anywhere."

Lucy walked in through the garage door and saw Sean and Kane sitting across from each other at the kitchen island, smiling, drinking beer. For all Sean had said about what a jerk his brother could be, Sean obviously loved and admired him. And Kane, for all his hardness, loved and respected Sean.

"Hi, boys," she said. She walked over and hugged Kane, then sat on the stool next to Sean and took his hand.

Sean had said family was complicated, and had lamented that the Rogan family wasn't as close as the Kincaids. Maybe it was because they were mostly men, or because they'd lost their parents in a tragedy and didn't know how to bridge the grief and pain. But the mutual trust was evident from the minute she saw Kane and Sean sitting across the table in Jack's house in Hidalgo. And now, here, she was still stunned by the resemblance, Sean a younger, happier version of his brother.

She hadn't spoken to Kane since they'd parted at Jack's

house after bringing Bella and Michael home. Kane needed to deal with the guns in the truck and get cover from RCK for the operation.

She slid a picture over to Sean. "This is from Tito. The boy who'd been shot in the foot, the one you carried out of the prison."

It was a surprisingly good pencil sketch of Sean with a halo over his head and a group of boys sitting at his feet. It would have been sweet, except for the gun in Sean's hand.

"I'm no saint."

"To them, you are." She kissed him again. "And to me." She smiled at Kane. "I'm glad you came."

"Me, too."

"Stay for dinner. Stay the weekend."

"I don't think so."

"At least long enough to visit Michael. I think he could use you right now. This adjustment is hard, and Padre has to go back to Hidalgo."

"I'll see him on my way out of town."

"Dinner," Sean repeated. "I'm cooking."

"You can cook?"

Sean shook his head and sighed. "Damn straight. I can do anything, remember?"

Kane laughed. "Yes, yes, you can, Little Rogan."

Sean scowled. "Don't call me that."

Lucy took Sean's hand and said, "Since I have eight more days of forced, unpaid leave, I thought we should visit the *littlest* Rogan." She looked at Kane. Waited until he was looking at her. "You need to come, too."

"I have to get back."

"No, you don't. You *want* to get back," Lucy said. "You *need* to see your niece. To remember why we all do what we do."

Kane looked down at his beer.

"All right," he finally said. "I'll go."

Sean looked surprised, but Lucy wasn't. Kane wanted family, but he didn't know how family and what he did could work together. All family had ever been to him were people who helped him get his job done.

Now family meant more. It had to, to keep them hopeful for the future.

"I'll call the airport and have them fuel my plane," Sean said. "We'll leave first thing in the morning."

Don't miss the next two Lucy Kincaid books from
Allison Brennan!

Two great books.
One terrible villain.

 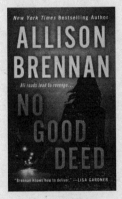

| Available in August 2015 | Available in November 2015 |

Read on for a sneak preview of BEST LAID PLANS....

CHAPTER ONE

Elise Hansen almost puked when she realized the guy was dead.

She bit her thumbnail, dreading what she had to do next.

"Why couldn't you have waited until *after* we screwed before you croaked?" she muttered.

But there was no turning back. She had the pictures she needed—he'd been out of it, but not so much that she couldn't get him into the right position—and now she had to finish it. In a manner of speaking.

Elise unbuckled his pants and pulled them down to his ankles. Then his boxers. He stunk, like he'd peed himself. She knew what she had to do, but it took her a minute to work up the courage.

"He's only going to get deader." She spit into her hand, then rubbed the guy's dick twice.

"Ugh." She ran to the bathroom to scour her hands. There was no soap, but the water got hot enough that she was satisfied there was no dead guy on her palm. She looked into the mirror—her makeup was still intact, but she reapplied the bright red lipstick because most of hers she'd smeared on the mark's neck and mouth.

No way in *hell* was she putting her mouth on his dick now that he was dead. Why couldn't he have just gone along for the ride from the beginning? She was young and cute and knew exactly what to do and say to get any guy off, even the most prudish prick. How could he say *no*? It made her job that much more difficult. And disgusting.

She'd damn well better get a bonus.

Elise left the bathroom and surveyed the room. Her prints and DNA were where they needed to be, her mark was half-naked, and she'd been in enough cheap motel rooms to know the scene looked exactly how she wanted it to.

She extracted his wallet from his pants and removed his cash—$120—then tossed the empty billfold on the nightstand. She grabbed his cell phone and pocketed it before walking out.

"*Señora!*"

Elise closed the door and froze.

"*Señora*, I'm here for *Señor* Worthington. He say to come back in one hour."

She turned and assessed the intruder. He was in his thirties, Mexican, with a moustache and rumpled clothes. A taxi was parked a few stalls down.

She showed her best seductive expression. "I wore him out." Then she winked. "I can wear you out, too, sugar."

He backed off. "Uh, I'm married." He held up his left hand to show her his ring.

"So was he. It'll be between you and me."

The taxi driver shook his head. "Can, um, you tell *Señor* that I'm here?"

She frowned. "He has the key." She knocked on the door, then shrugged. "Sorry. He sleeps like a rock, I guess." She hesitated, considering what this driver might do or say. Chances are he would leave but she couldn't count on it. She glanced around, saw no one, then bit her lip and said quietly, "You know, I really gotta go or my boss will take it out on my ass. I don't like being knocked around." She jogged away from the motel, keeping her head down.

The taxi driver didn't follow or comment.

At first, Elise thought getting caught outside the door would be trouble, but then she realized it could actually work to her benefit.

Once she was out of sight of the motel, she slowed to a walk and continued three blocks south. She opened the rear door of an idling black Mercedes, and settled back into the soft leather seat. The car pulled into traffic.

"Problems?"

"The guy didn't want to fuck. But I got the pictures, and everything else went as ordered." Sort of.

"Anyone see you?"

"Worthington's taxi driver returned. I hit on him and he scurried away."

Silence.

"What?" she said.

"You were supposed to be a scared whore, running because her john had a heart attack."

She rolled her eyes. "He barely spoke English."

"That doesn't matter! Dammit, Elise, can't you do one thing right?"

"I did it *all* right, and I'm not going to take shit from you. Told the driver that my boss would beat me if I didn't get back. Besides, he probably'll just disappear. He's a fucking taxi driver, not a rocket scientist."

"You're a fucking bitch."

"I learned from the best." She stuck her tongue out at the back of the driver's head. Mona Hill was an old whore; Elise was the next generation. But right now, they needed each other. "They'll find me and I'll play my part. I've already done my research. This is going to be a piece of cake."

"Don't get cocky. There's a lot at stake and we can't afford any screw-ups."

Elise scowled. Like Mona needed to tell *her* that?

Mona drove Elise ten minutes across town and pulled into a hotel roundabout. "Your john is waiting for you in room 606. Make sure you let the security cameras see you. And try to look at least a little scared."

"Nothing scares me." She took the card key from her driver.

"And that's what's going to get you killed, Elise. Fear can be healthy."

Fear? Not her. *Never.* Fear wasn't even in her vocabulary.

"This'll be a rough one," Mona continued, "but that'll play to our benefit."

"Maybe you should go fuck him then."

"Get out, and remember who owns you."

Elise got out of the car and slammed the door. *No one* owned her. She just let them think they did. She took a deep breath and tried to look scared.

It was hard to look scared when you'd been looking out for your own ass most of your life.

Because she had a hotel card key, she was able to access a side door and go up the stairs—not the elevator—to the sixth floor. She made a point to look down the hall both ways—let both security cameras see her, eyes downcast, looking skittish and guilty—then sought out room 606.

She let herself into the room. It was a whole world nicer than the motel she'd just left.

A man in his late forties lay partly clothed on the bed. She didn't know his name and he didn't know hers, but that didn't matter. Mona knew exactly who he was.

He was playing with himself while watching porn on the hotel's television. "You're late." He stood up. He was pudgy around the middle with a sharply receding hairline.

She pouted. "I'm sorry. I'll make it up to you." She looked at X-rated video he was watching. The girl was masturbating while sucking off the guy. "You want me to do that to you?"

"I want a lot of things." He licked his lips. "How old are you?"

"How old do you want me to be?"

"Legal."

She smiled. "I'm legal."

"You look younger."

Because she was, but she wasn't going to blow this job. Too much money at stake. Sure, she was a little nervous. Who wouldn't be? But it wasn't like she hadn't done it before.

Elise walked over to the hotel bar and took out a bottle of vodka. She took a long swig, then put the bottle down. She moved things around a bit, put her purse down. The other mark's phone slid partly out of her bag. She smiled, took another drink, and turned around.

He was right behind her.

"I picked this hotel because the walls are thick, and I want to hear you. Understand?" He grabbed her by the wrists. It hurt, but she didn't react.

"Yes. I need the money first."

He frowned, but gestured toward a white envelope on the desk. He dropped her wrists and went back to the bed, watching her closely. She picked up the envelope, glanced inside, quickly counted. Two hundred dollars.

That, on top of the thousand dollars she was being paid to set the jerk up. With the earlier job, she was pulling in over three thousand dollars tonight.

Not bad. But there was even more money for her down the road. Tonight was just icing on the cake.

She stuffed the envelope into her purse, adjusted the flap, then said, "What do you want me to call you?"

"Call me Daddy. And I'm going to spank you. Hard."

This was getting better by the minute.

"Spank me, Daddy," she said, and he did.

CHAPTER TWO

Sean woke up the moment Lucy climbed out of bed. He glanced at the bedside clock. It was 3:30 A.M.

Lucy slipped out of the room and Sean sat up. It had been months since Lucy had had a full night's sleep. This insomnia of hers was going to wear her out. And him. He'd found himself napping during the day for a couple hours after lunch, and he couldn't blame the heat.

It was more than insomnia. Lucy was physically and emotionally drained and wanted to hide it from everyone. Except, she couldn't hide it from him even if she wanted to.

He'd thought she was fine. After they'd rescued nine abused boys who'd been used as couriers for a drug cartel, Lucy had seemed to be unfazed by the whole operation. She'd saved lives. But to save lives, she'd had to take lives. She'd had to lie about defying orders even though her boss suspected what she'd done. She'd wanted to come clean but couldn't without damaging the careers and reputations of others.

She'd been put on administrative leave for two weeks and didn't blink. They'd spent part of her leave in Sacramento with his brother and newborn niece. While she'd been upset about disappointing her boss, she'd appeared content. She'd spent more time with her brother Jack and Sean's brother Kane than anyone else, but at the time Sean hadn't thought much about it.

That should have been his first clue. When he'd first met Lucy eighteen months ago, she had kept herself closed off from others, icy and distant. It had been a defense mechanism to manage the pain and rage from her past. Constantly training, running for miles, working long hours. She didn't let herself feel anything, and that meant the only time her emotions were free to escape was in sleep. And those emotions became nightmares, violent memories that Sean had helped Lucy overcome.

And for months, he'd thought they were over. After they'd moved to San Antonio in January, she rarely woke before dawn, her insomnia under control. But the nightmares had returned when they came home after her leave. He wanted to pull the details from her, because he didn't think she was being honest with him. She wasn't lying to him . . . just omitting details. She never wanted to worry him. But what she didn't understand, what Sean hadn't made clear enough, was that holding back made him worry more.

He thought time would fix the problem, as long as he was here for her, and some nights she did sleep soundly. But not tonight. The urge to hit something propelled him out of bed. He'd put in an aggressive workout later. Instead, he followed Lucy downstairs.

He thought she'd be in the kitchen brewing coffee—he smelled the rich coffee beans Lucy liked—but the pool lights were on. He walked outside and saw Lucy swimming laps, her long, curvy body as graceful as a mermaid's as she swam the breaststroke one way, flipped, and did the backstroke going back. He could watch her for hours. She'd swum in high school and college, but now she did it for fun. Or a workout. Or trying to out-swim her personal demons.

The late spring nights were cool, but not cold, and the

early morning air was refreshing. It would be another humid scorcher today, but right now the weather was perfect. Maybe there was a benefit to getting up at three thirty in the morning.

Sean liked everything about the Olmos Park house he'd picked out for them, but the pool had sold him. It wasn't as fancy as some of the others—no rock walls or elegant waterfalls or curving design. It was a large, black-bottomed rectangle and the only added touches were custom tiles along the edges and a raised infinity hot tub that dropped water into the pool below. When Lucy first saw the pool she grinned like a kid, then jumped in fully clothed. Such behavior was out of character, but also a testament to her complete and total joy, justifying Sean's decision to purchase the house and surprise her.

Sean wanted that Lucy back. The Lucy he knew was still in there, waiting for the nightmares to run their course.

After twenty laps, Lucy slowed down for a few more, then got out and spotted him. "I woke you up," she said. "I'm sorry."

He handed her a towel and kissed her lightly on the lips. "Do you want to talk about it?"

She shrugged and dried off. "I feel better." She drank from a water bottle. She was out of breath, but there was color in her cheeks.

He wrapped a hand around her neck and kissed her warmly. "I'm here."

"It helps."

"I want to do more."

"You do far more for me than you should. I need to stand on my own two feet. But having you here gives me peace. Know that. I'll get over this funk."

"It's more than a funk, Lucy. We've been back for two months and you've only slept through the night twice."

She frowned. "Are you keeping track?"

"No, not like that, but I love you and I know when you're not sleeping."

"The nightmares aren't so bad," she said. "They just seem real. They startle me, because I wake up at first not knowing that it was a dream. I think that's what's bothering me so much. There's like a minute or two when I don't know where I am, I don't know who I'm with, I think I'm still there."

"Where are you?"

She didn't answer the question, not directly. "It changes." But she didn't look him in the eye, and he feared she was retreating further into the past, beyond the imprisoned boys in Mexico, back to the darkest time of her life, when she'd been held captive by a psychopath and repeatedly raped.

Sean hugged her tightly, because he had to. For him as much as for her. She grabbed him just as tight. She whispered, "Let's go back to bed."

He kissed her. He would have made love to her in the pool, on the lounge chair, *anywhere*, but Lucy would be nervous having sex outside. And he wanted—needed—her to relax and feel how much he loved her. He picked her up and carried her inside.

As soon as he stepped through the door, the house phone rang. Lucy jumped out of his arms. "It's never good news before dawn," she said and answered the closest phone. "Hello?"

Sean watched her face. In two blinks she'd gone from romantic to panicked to professional.

"I'll be there in thirty minutes," she said a few minutes later then hung up. "That was Juan. A VIP is dead. Doesn't appear to be murder, but the circumstances are suspicious, and the dead guy is a government contractor with high-level security clearance. The powers that be want the FBI to take the lead."

The way she spoke surprised Sean. "Do you know him?"

"No, why?"

"Because you generally show more compassion for dead people."

She hesitated then said, "SAPD reports that the guy, fifty-four, was having sex with an underage prostitute when he died. They think heart attack, the girl got scared and ran. The police think the girl robbed him after he died. She was scared that her pimp would beat her senseless if she didn't bring back any money. And yet this pervert is the *victim*? If the police find her, they'll terrify her even more." She started up the stairs. Halfway up she turned around. "I'm sorry, Sean."

"No apologies. It's nice to see that fire back. But I will take a rain check on what you promised."

She smiled at him, warm and genuine with a hint of teasing. "I'm cashing in that rain check tonight." Then she ran up the stairs.

Maybe Lucy was okay. At least she sounded like she was back on track.

Sean went to the kitchen to make her breakfast. If he didn't feed her before she left, he knew she'd go without until lunch, and after that morning swim, she needed fuel.